The Wizard of Oz

The Wizard of Oz

L. FRANK BAUM

HarperFestival®
A Division of HarperCollinsPublishers

This book is dedicated by my
good friend & comrade.
My Wife
—L.F.B.

The Wizard of Oz was first published in 1899.

HarperCollins®, ☂®, and HarperFestival® are registered trademarks of
HarperCollins Publishers Inc.

The Wizard of Oz

Library of Congress Cataloging-in-Publication Data
Baum, L. Frank (Lyman Frank), 1856–1919.
  The Wizard of Oz / L. Frank Baum.
    p.   cm.
  Summary: After being transported by a cyclone to the land of Oz, Dorothy
and her dog are befriended by a scarecrow, a tin man, and a wizard who can
help Dorothy return home to Kansas.
  ISBN 0-694-01319-6
  [1. Fantasy.]   I. Title.
PZ7.B327Wi   1999   99-22562
[Fic]—dc21   CIP
                                                                     AC

Typography by Fritz Metsch

First HarperFestival edition, 1999

CONTENTS

INTRODUCTION

*F*OLKLORE, legends, myths and fairy tales have
followed childhood through the ages, for every
healthy youngster has a wholesome and instinctive love
for stories fantastic, marvelous and manifestly unreal.
The winged fairies of Grimm and Andersen have
brought more happiness to childish hearts than all
other human creations.

Yet the old time fairy tale, having served for generations, may now be classed as "historical" in the children's library; for the time has come for a series of newer
"wonder tales" in which the stereotyped genie, dwarf
and fairy are eliminated, together with all the horrible
and blood-curdling incidents devised by their authors
to point a fearsome moral to each tale. Modern education includes morality; therefore the modern child seeks
only entertainment in its wonder tales and gladly dis-
penses with all disagreeable incidents.

Having this thought in mind, the story of "The
Wizard of Oz" was written solely to please children of

today. It aspires to being a modernized fairy tale, in which the wonderment and joy are retained and the heartaches and nightmares are left out.

L. FRANK BAUM.
Chicago, April, 1900.

Chapter One

THE CYCLONE

———— ❧ ————

*D*OROTHY lived in the midst of the great Kansas prairies, with Uncle Henry, who was a farmer, and Aunt Em, who was the farmer's wife. Their house was small, for the lumber to build it had to be carried by wagon many miles. There were four walls, a floor and a roof, which made one room; and this room contained a rusty-looking cooking stove, a cupboard for the dishes, a table, three or four chairs, and the beds. Uncle Henry and Aunt Em had a big bed in one corner and Dorothy a little bed in another corner. There was no garret at all, and no cellar—except a small hole dug in the ground, called a cyclone cellar, where the family could go in case one of those great whirlwinds arose, mighty enough to crush any building in its path. It was reached by a trapdoor in the middle of the floor, from which a ladder led down into the small, dark hole.

When Dorothy stood in the doorway and looked around, she could see nothing but the great gray prairie on every side. Not a tree nor a house broke the broad sweep of flat country that reached to the edge of the sky in all directions. The sun had baked the plowed land into a gray mass, with little cracks running through it. Even the grass was not green, for the sun had burned the tops of the long blades until they were the same gray color to be seen everywhere. Once the house had been painted, but the sun blistered the paint and the rains washed it away, and now the house was as dull and gray as everything else.

When Aunt Em came there to live she was a young, pretty wife. The sun and wind had changed her, too. They had taken the sparkle from her eyes and left them a sober gray; they had taken the red from her cheeks and lips, and they were gray also. She was thin and gaunt, and never smiled now. When Dorothy, who was an orphan, first came to her, Aunt Em had been so startled by the child's laughter that she would scream and press her hand upon her heart whenever Dorothy's merry voice reached her ears; and she still looked at the little girl with wonder that she could find anything to laugh at.

Uncle Henry never laughed. He worked hard from morning till night and did not know what joy was. He was gray also, from his long beard to his rough boots, and he looked stern and solemn, and rarely spoke.

It was Toto that made Dorothy laugh, and saved her

from growing as gray as her other surroundings. Toto was not gray; he was a little black dog, with long silky hair and small black eyes that twinkled merrily on either side of his funny, wee nose. Toto played all day long, and Dorothy played with him, and loved him dearly.

Today, however, they were not playing. Uncle Henry sat upon the doorstep and looked anxiously at the sky, which was even grayer than usual. Dorothy stood in the door with Toto in her arms, and looked at the sky too. Aunt Em was washing the dishes.

From the far north they heard a low wail of the wind, and Uncle Henry and Dorothy could see where the long grass bowed in waves before the coming storm. There now came a sharp whistling in the air from the south, and as they turned their eyes that way they saw ripples in the grass coming from that direction also.

Suddenly Uncle Henry stood up.

"There's a cyclone coming, Em," he called to his wife. "I'll go look after the stock." Then he ran toward the sheds where the cows and horses were kept.

Aunt Em dropped her work and came to the door. One glance told her of the danger close at hand.

"Quick, Dorothy!" she screamed. "Run for the cellar!"

Toto jumped out of Dorothy's arms and hid under

the bed, and the girl started to get him. Aunt Em, badly frightened, threw open the trapdoor in the floor and climbed down the ladder into the small, dark hole. Dorothy caught Toto at last and started to follow her aunt. When she was halfway across the room there came a great shriek from the wind, and the house shook so hard that she lost her footing and sat down suddenly upon the floor.

Then a strange thing happened.

The house whirled around two or three times and rose slowly through the air. Dorothy felt as if she were going up in a balloon.

The north and south winds met where the house stood, and made it the exact center of the cyclone. In the middle of a cyclone the air is generally still, but the great pressure of the wind on every side of the house raised it up higher and higher, until it was at the very top of the cyclone; and there it remained and was carried miles and miles away as easily as you could carry a feather.

It was very dark, and the wind howled horribly around her, but Dorothy found she was riding quite easily. After the first few whirls around, and one other time when the house tipped badly, she felt as if she were being rocked gently, like a baby in a cradle.

Toto did not like it. He ran about the room, now here,

now there, barking loudly; but Dorothy sat quite still on the floor and waited to see what would happen.

Once Toto got too near the open trapdoor, and fell in; and at first the little girl thought she had lost him. But soon she saw one of his ears sticking up through the hole, for the strong pressure of the air was keeping him up so that he could not fall. She crept to the hole, caught Toto by the ear, and dragged him into the room again, afterward closing the trapdoor so that no more accidents could happen.

Hour after hour passed away, and slowly Dorothy got over her fright; but she felt quite lonely, and the wind shrieked so loudly all about her that she nearly became deaf. At first she had wondered if she would be dashed to pieces when the house fell again; but as the hours passed and nothing terrible happened, she stopped worrying and resolved to wait calmly and see what the future would bring. At last she crawled over the swaying floor to her bed, and lay down upon it; and Toto followed and lay down beside her.

In spite of the swaying of the house and the wailing of the wind, Dorothy soon closed her eyes and fell fast asleep.

Chapter Two

THE COUNCIL WITH THE MUNCHKINS

*S*HE was awakened by a shock, so sudden and severe that if Dorothy had not been lying on the soft bed she might have been hurt. As it was, the jar made her catch her breath and wonder what had happened; and Toto put his cold little nose into her face and whined dismally. Dorothy sat up and noticed that the house was not moving; nor was it dark, for the bright sunshine came in at the window, flooding the little room. She sprang from her bed and with Toto at her heels ran and opened the door.

The little girl gave a cry of amazement and looked about her, her eyes growing bigger and bigger at the wonderful sights she saw.

The cyclone had set the house down very gently—for a cyclone—in the midst of a country of marvelous beauty. There were lovely patches of greensward all about, with stately trees bearing rich and luscious fruits. Banks of gorgeous flowers were on every hand, and birds with rare and brilliant plumage sang and fluttered in the trees and bushes. A little way off was a small brook, rushing and sparkling along between green banks, and murmuring in a voice very grateful to a little girl who had lived so long on the dry, gray prairies.

While she stood looking eagerly at the strange and beautiful sights, she noticed coming toward her a group of the queerest people she had ever seen. They were not as big as the grown folk she had always been used to; but neither were they very small. In fact, they seemed about as tall as Dorothy, who was a well-grown child for her age, although they were, so far as looks go, many years older.

Three were men and one a woman, and all were oddly dressed. They wore round hats that rose to a small point a foot above their heads, with little bells around the brims that tinkled sweetly as they moved. The hats of the men were blue; the little woman's hat was white, and she wore a white gown that hung in pleats from her shoulders. Over it were sprinkled little stars that glistened in the sun like diamonds. The men were dressed in blue, of the same shade as their hats, and wore well-polished boots with a deep roll of blue at the tops. The men, Dorothy thought, were about as old as Uncle Henry, for two of them had beards. But the little woman was doubtless much older. Her face was covered with wrinkles, her hair was nearly white, and she walked rather stiffly.

When these people drew near the house where Dorothy was standing in the doorway, they paused and whispered among themselves, as if afraid to come farther. But the little old woman walked up to Dorothy, made a low bow and said, in a sweet voice:

"You are welcome, most noble Sorceress, to the land of the Munchkins. We are so grateful to you for having killed the Wicked Witch of the East, and for setting our people free from bondage."

Dorothy listened to this speech with wonder. What could the little woman possibly mean by calling her a sorceress, and saying she had killed the Wicked Witch of the East? Dorothy was an innocent, harmless little girl, who had been carried by a cyclone many miles from home; and she had never killed anything in all her life.

But the little woman evidently expected her to answer; so Dorothy said, with hesitation, "You are very kind, but there must be some mistake. I have not killed anything."

"Your house did, anyway," replied the little old woman, with a laugh, "and that is the same thing. See!" she continued, pointing to the corner of the house. "There are her two toes, still sticking out from under a block of wood."

Dorothy looked, and gave a little cry of fright. There, indeed, just under the corner of the great beam the house rested on, two feet were sticking out, shod in silver shoes with pointed toes.

"Oh dear! Oh dear!" cried Dorothy, clasping her hands together in dismay. "The house must have fallen on her. Whatever shall we do?"

"There is nothing to be done," said the little woman calmly.

"But who was she?" asked Dorothy.

"She was the Wicked Witch of the East, as I said," answered the little woman. "She has held all the Munchkins in bondage for many years, making them slave for her night and day. Now they are all set free, and are grateful to you for the favor."

"Who are the Munchkins?" inquired Dorothy.

"They are the people who live in this land of the East, where the Wicked Witch ruled."

"Are you a Munchkin?" asked Dorothy.

"No, but I am their friend, although I live in the land of the North. When they saw the Witch of the East was dead the Munchkins sent a swift messenger to me, and I came at once. I am the Witch of the North."

"Oh, gracious!" cried Dorothy. "Are you a real witch?"

"Yes, indeed," answered the little woman. "But I am

a good witch, and the people love me. I am not as powerful as the Wicked Witch was who ruled here, or I should have set the people free myself."

"But I thought all witches were wicked," said the girl, who was half frightened at facing a real witch.

"Oh, no, that is a great mistake. There were only four witches in all the Land of Oz, and two of them, those who live in the North and the South, are good witches. I know this is true, for I am one of them myself, and cannot be mistaken. Those who dwelt in the East and the West were, indeed, wicked witches; but now that you have killed one of them, there is but one Wicked Witch in all the Land of Oz—the one who lives in the West."

"But," said Dorothy, after a moment's thought, "Aunt Em has told me that the witches were all dead—years and years ago."

"Who is Aunt Em?" inquired the little old woman.

"She is my aunt who lives in Kansas, where I came from."

The Witch of the North seemed to think for a time, with her head bowed and her eyes upon the ground. Then she looked up and said, "I do not know where Kansas is, for I have never heard that country mentioned before. But tell me, is it a civilized country?"

"Oh, yes," replied Dorothy.

"Then that accounts for it. In the civilized countries I believe there are no witches left, nor wizards, nor sorceresses, nor magicians. But, you see, the Land of Oz has never been civilized, for we are cut off from all the rest of the world. Therefore we still have witches and wizards amongst us."

"Who are the wizards?" asked Dorothy.

"Oz himself is the Great Wizard," answered the Witch, sinking her voice to a whisper. "He is more powerful than all the rest of us together. He lives in the City of Emeralds."

Dorothy was going to ask another question, but just then the Munchkins, who had been standing silently by, gave a loud shout and pointed to the corner of the house where the Wicked Witch had been lying.

"What is it?" asked the little old woman, and looked, and began to laugh. The feet of the dead Witch had disappeared entirely, and nothing was left but the silver shoes.

"She was so old," explained the Witch of the North, "that she dried up quickly in the sun. That is the end of her. But the silver shoes are yours, and you shall have them to wear." She reached down and picked up the shoes, and after shaking the dust out of them handed them to Dorothy.

"The Witch of the East was proud of those silver

shoes," said one of the Munchkins, "and there is some charm connected with them; but what it is we never knew."

Dorothy carried the shoes into the house and placed them on the table. Then she came out again to the Munchkins and said:

"I am anxious to get back to my aunt and uncle, for I am sure they will worry about me. Can you help me find my way?"

The Munchkins and the Witch first looked at one another, and then at Dorothy, and then shook their heads.

"At the East, not far from here," said one, "there is a great desert, and none could live to cross it."

"It is the same at the South," said another, "for I have been there and seen it. The South is the country of the Quadlings."

"I am told," said the third man, "that it is the same at the West. And that country, where the Winkies live, is ruled by the Wicked Witch of the West, who would make you her slave if you passed her way."

"The North is my home," said the old lady, "and at its edge is the same great desert that surrounds this Land of Oz. I'm afraid, my dear, you will have to live with us."

Dorothy began to sob at this, for she felt lonely among all these strange people. Her tears seemed to grieve the kindhearted Munchkins, for they immediately took out their handkerchiefs and began to weep also. As for the little old woman, she took off her cap and balanced the point on the end of her nose, while she counted "One, two, three" in a solemn voice. At once the cap changed to a slate, on which was written in big, white chalk marks:

LET DOROTHY GO TO THE CITY OF EMERALDS

The little old woman took the slate from her nose, and having read the words on it, asked, "Is your name Dorothy, my dear?"

"Yes," answered the child, looking up and drying her tears.

"Then you must go to the City of Emeralds. Perhaps Oz will help you."

"Where is this city?" asked Dorothy.

"It is exactly in the center of the country, and is ruled by Oz, the Great Wizard I told you of."

"Is he a good man?" inquired the girl anxiously.

"He is a good Wizard. Whether he is a man or not I cannot tell, for I have never seen him."

"How can I get there?" asked Dorothy.

"You must walk. It is a long journey, through a country that is sometimes pleasant and sometimes dark and terrible. However, I will use all the magic arts I know of to keep you from harm."

"Won't you go with me?" pleaded the girl, who had begun to look upon the little old woman as her only friend.

"No, I cannot do that," she replied, "but I will give you my kiss, and no one will dare injure a person who has been kissed by the Witch of the North."

She came close to Dorothy and kissed her gently on the forehead. Where her lips touched the girl they left a round, shining mark, as Dorothy found out soon after.

"The road to the City of Emeralds is paved with yellow brick," said the Witch, "so you cannot miss it. When you get to Oz do not be afraid of him, but tell your story and ask him to help you. Good-bye, my dear."

The three Munchkins bowed low to her and wished her a pleasant journey, after which they walked away through the trees. The Witch gave Dorothy a friendly little nod, whirled around on her left heel three times, and straightway disappeared, much to the surprise of little Toto, who barked after her loudly enough when she had gone, because he had been afraid even to growl while she stood by.

But Dorothy, knowing her to be a witch, had expected her to disappear in just that way, and was not surprised in the least.

Chapter Three

HOW DOROTHY SAVED THE SCARECROW

<hr />

WHEN Dorothy was left alone she began to feel hungry. So she went to the cupboard and cut herself some bread, which she spread with butter. She gave some to Toto, and taking a pail from the shelf she carried it down to the little brook and filled it with clear, sparkling water. Toto ran over to the trees and began to bark at the birds sitting there. Dorothy went to get him, and saw such delicious fruit hanging from the branches that she gathered some of it, finding it just what she wanted to help out her breakfast.

Then she went back to the house, and having helped herself and Toto to a good drink of the cool, clear water, she set about making ready for the journey to the City of Emeralds.

Dorothy had only one other dress, but that happened to be clean and was hanging on a peg beside her bed. It was gingham, with checks of white and blue; and although the blue was somewhat faded with many washings, it was still a pretty frock. The girl washed herself carefully, dressed herself in the clean gingham, and tied her pink sunbonnet on her head. She took a little basket and filled it with bread from the cupboard, laying a white cloth over the top. Then she looked down at her feet and noticed how old and worn her shoes were.

"They surely will never do for a long journey, Toto," she said. And Toto looked up into her face with his little black eyes and wagged his tail to show he knew what she meant.

At that moment Dorothy saw lying on the table the silver shoes that had belonged to the Witch of the East.

"I wonder if they will fit me," she said to Toto. "They would be just the thing to take a long walk in, for they could not wear out."

She took off her old leather shoes and tried on the silver ones, which fitted her as well as if they had been made for her.

Finally she picked up her basket.

"Come along, Toto," she said. "We will go to the Emerald City and ask the Great Oz how to get back to Kansas again."

She closed the door, locked it, and put the key carefully in the pocket of her dress. And so, with Toto trotting along soberly behind her, she started on her journey.

There were several roads near by, but it did not take her long to find the one paved with yellow brick. Within a short time she was walking briskly toward the Emerald City, her silver shoes tinkling merrily on the hard, yellow roadbed. The sun shone bright and the birds sang sweetly, and Dorothy did not feel nearly so bad as you might think a little girl would who had been suddenly whisked away from her own country and set down in the midst of a strange land.

She was surprised, as she walked along, to see how pretty the country was about her. There were neat fences at the sides of the road, painted a dainty blue color, and beyond them were fields of grain and vegetables in abundance. Evidently the Munchkins were good farmers and able to raise large crops. Once in a while she would pass a house, and the people came out to look at her and bow low as she went by; for everyone knew she had been the means of destroying the Wicked Witch and setting them free from bondage. The houses of the Munchkins were odd-looking dwellings. Each was round, with a big dome for a roof. All were painted blue, for in this country of the East blue was the favorite color.

Toward evening, when Dorothy was tired with her long walk and began to wonder where she should pass the night, she came to a house rather larger than the rest. On the green lawn before it many men and women were dancing. Five little fiddlers played as loudly as possible, and the people were laughing and singing, while a big table near by was loaded with delicious fruits and nuts, pies and cakes, and many other good things to eat.

The people greeted Dorothy kindly, and invited her to supper and to pass the night with them; for this was the home of one of the richest Munchkins in the land, and his friends were gathered with him to celebrate their freedom from the bondage of the Wicked Witch.

Dorothy ate a hearty supper and was waited upon by the rich Munchkin himself, whose name was Boq. Then she sat upon a settee and watched the people dance.

When Boq saw her silver shoes he said, "You must be a great sorceress."

"Why?" asked the girl.

"Because you wear silver shoes and have killed the Wicked Witch. Besides, you have white in your frock, and only witches and sorceresses wear white."

"My dress is blue and white checked," said Dorothy, smoothing out the wrinkles in it.

"It is kind of you to wear that," said Boq. "Blue is the color of the Munchkins, and white is the witch color. So we know you are a friendly witch."

Dorothy did not know what to say to this, for all the people seemed to think her a witch, and she knew very well she was only an ordinary little girl who had come by the chance of a cyclone into a strange land.

When she had tired watching the dancing, Boq led her into the house, where he gave her a room with a pretty bed in it. The sheets were made of blue cloth, and Dorothy slept soundly in them till morning, with Toto curled up on the blue rug beside her.

She ate a hearty breakfast, and watched a wee Munchkin baby, who played with Toto and pulled his tail and crowed and laughed in a way that greatly amused Dorothy. Toto was a fine curiosity to all the people, for they had never seen a dog before.

"How far is it to the Emerald City?" the girl asked.

"I do not know," answered Boq gravely, "for I have never been there. It is better for people to keep away from Oz, unless they have business with him. But it is a long way to the Emerald City, and it will take you many days. The country here is rich and pleasant, but you must pass through rough and dangerous places before you reach the end of your journey."

This worried Dorothy a little, but she knew that only the Great Oz could help her get to Kansas again, so she bravely resolved not to turn back.

She bade her friends good-bye, and again started along

the road of yellow brick. When she had gone several miles she thought she would stop to rest, and so climbed to the top of the fence beside the road and sat down. There was a great cornfield beyond the fence, and not far away she saw a Scarecrow, placed high on a pole to keep the birds from the ripe corn.

Dorothy leaned her chin upon her hand and gazed thoughtfully at the Scarecrow. Its head was a small sack stuffed with straw, with eyes, nose, and mouth painted on it to represent a face. An old, pointed blue hat, that had belonged to some Munchkin, was perched on his head, and the rest of the figure was a blue suit of clothes, worn and faded, which had also been stuffed with straw. On the feet were some old boots with blue tops, such as every man wore in this country, and the figure was raised above the stalks of corn by means of the pole stuck up its back.

While Dorothy was looking earnestly into the queer, painted face of the Scarecrow, she was surprised to see one of the eyes slowly wink at her. She thought she must have been mistaken at first, for none of the scare-crows in Kansas ever wink; but presently the figure nodded its head to her in a friendly way. Then she climbed down from the fence and walked up to it, while Toto ran around the pole and barked.

"Good day," said the Scarecrow, in a rather husky voice.

"Did you speak?" asked the girl, in wonder.

"Certainly," answered the Scarecrow. "How do you do?"

"I'm pretty well, thank you," replied Dorothy politely. "How do you do?"

"I'm not feeling well," said the Scarecrow, with a smile, "for it is very tedious being perched up here night and day to scare away crows."

"Can't you get down?" asked Dorothy.

"No, for this pole is stuck up my back. If you will please take away the pole I shall be greatly obliged to you."

Dorothy reached up both arms and lifted the figure off the pole, for—being stuffed with straw—it was quite light.

"Thank you very much," said the Scarecrow, when he had been set down on the ground. "I feel like a new man."

Dorothy was puzzled at this, for it sounded queer to hear a stuffed man speak, and to see him bow and walk along beside her.

"Who are you?" asked the Scarecrow when he had stretched himself and yawned. "And where are you going?"

"My name is Dorothy," said the girl, "and I am going to the Emerald City, to ask the Great Oz to send me back to Kansas."

"Where is the Emerald City?" he inquired. "And who is Oz?"

"Why, don't you know?" she returned, in surprise.

"No, indeed. I don't know anything. You see, I am stuffed, so I have no brains at all," he answered sadly.

"Oh," said Dorothy, "I'm awfully sorry for you."

"Do you think," he asked, "if I go to the Emerald City with you, that Oz would give me some brains?"

"I cannot tell," she returned, "but you may come with me, if you like. If Oz will not give you any brains you will be no worse off than you are now."

"That is true," said the Scarecrow. "You see," he continued confidentially, "I don't mind my legs and arms and body being stuffed, because I cannot get hurt. If anyone treads on my toes or sticks a pin into me, it doesn't matter, for I can't feel it. But I do not want people to call me a fool, and if my head stays stuffed with straw instead of with brains, as yours is, how am I ever to know anything?"

"I understand how you feel," said the little girl, who was truly sorry for him. "If you will come with me I'll ask Oz to do all he can for you."

"Thank you," he answered gratefully.

They walked back to the road. Dorothy helped him over the fence, and they started along the path of yellow brick for the Emerald City.

Toto did not like this addition to the party at first. He smelled around the stuffed man as if he suspected there might be a nest of rats in the straw, and he often growled in an unfriendly way at the Scarecrow.

"Don't mind Toto," said Dorothy to her new friend. "He never bites."

"Oh, I'm not afraid," replied the Scarecrow. "He can't hurt the straw. Do let me carry that basket for you. I shall not mind it, for I can't get tired. I'll tell you a secret," he continued, as he walked along. "There is only one thing in the world I am afraid of."

"What is that?" asked Dorothy. "The Munchkin farmer who made you?"

"No," answered the Scarecrow. "It's a lighted match."

Chapter Four

THE ROAD THROUGH THE FOREST

———✦———

AFTER a few hours the road began to be rough, and the walking grew so difficult that the Scarecrow often stumbled over the yellow bricks, which were here very uneven. Sometimes, indeed, they were broken or missing altogether, leaving holes that Toto jumped across and Dorothy walked around. As for the Scarecrow, having no brains, he walked straight ahead, and so stepped into the holes and fell at full length on the hard bricks. It never hurt him, however, and Dorothy would pick him up and set him upon his feet again, while he joined her in laughing merrily at his own mishap.

The farms were not nearly so well cared for here as they were farther back. There were fewer houses and fewer fruit trees, and the farther they went the more dismal and lonesome the country became.

At noon they sat down by the roadside, near a little brook, and Dorothy opened her basket and got out some bread. She offered a piece to the Scarecrow, but he refused.

"I am never hungry," he said, "and it is a lucky thing I am not, for my mouth is only painted. If I should cut a hole in it so I could eat, the straw I am stuffed with would come out, and that would spoil the shape of my head."

Dorothy saw at once that this was true, so she only nodded and went on eating her bread.

"Tell me something about yourself and the country you came from," said the Scarecrow, when she had finished her dinner. So she told him all about Kansas, and how gray everything was there, and how the cyclone had carried her to this queer Land of Oz.

The Scarecrow listened carefully, and said, "I cannot understand why you should wish to leave this beautiful country and go back to the dry, gray place you call Kansas."

"That is because you have no brains," answered the girl. "No matter how dreary and gray our homes are, we people of flesh and blood would rather live there than in any other country, be it ever so beautiful. There is no place like home."

The Scarecrow sighed.

"Of course I cannot understand it," he said. "If your heads were stuffed with straw, like mine, you would probably all live in the beautiful places, and then Kansas would have no people at all. It is fortunate for Kansas that you have brains."

"Won't you tell me a story while we are resting?" asked the child.

The Scarecrow looked at her reproachfully, and answered:

"My life has been so short that I really know nothing whatever. I was only made day before yesterday. What happened in the world before that time is all unknown to me. Luckily, when the farmer made my head, one of the first things he did was to paint my ears, so that I heard what was going on. There was another Munchkin with him, and the first thing I heard was the farmer saying, 'How do you like those ears?'

"'They aren't straight,' answered the other.

"'Never mind,' said the farmer. 'They are ears just the same,' which was true enough.

"'Now I'll make the eyes,' said the farmer. So he painted my right eye, and as soon as it was finished I found myself looking at him and at everything around me with a great deal of curiosity, for this was my first glimpse of the world.

"'That's a rather pretty eye,' remarked the Munchkin who was watching the farmer. 'Blue paint is just the color for eyes.'

"'I think I'll make the other a little bigger,' said the farmer. And when the second eye was done I could see much better than before. Then he made my nose and my mouth. But I did not speak, because at that time I didn't know what a mouth was for. I had the fun of watching them make my body and my arms and legs. And when they fastened on my head, at last, I felt very proud, for I thought I was just as good a man as anyone.

"'This fellow will scare the crows fast enough,' said the farmer. 'He looks just like a man.'

"'Why, he is a man,' said the other, and I quite agreed with him. The farmer carried me under his arm to the cornfield, and set me up on a tall stick, where you found me. He and his friend soon after walked away and left me alone.

"I did not like to be deserted this way. So I tried to walk after them. But my feet would not touch the ground, and I was forced to stay on that pole. It was a lonely life to lead, for I had nothing to think of, having been made such a little while before. Many crows and other birds flew into the cornfield, but as soon as they saw me they flew away again, thinking I was a Munchkin; and this pleased me and made me feel that I was quite an important person. By and by an old crow flew near me, and after looking at me carefully he perched upon my shoulder and said:

"'I wonder if that farmer thought to fool me in this clumsy manner. Any crow of sense could see that you are only stuffed with straw.' Then he hopped down at my feet and ate all the corn he wanted. The other birds, seeing he was not harmed by me, came to eat the corn too, so in a short time there was a great flock of them about me.

"I felt sad at this, for it showed I was not such a good Scarecrow after all; but the old crow comforted me, saying, 'If you only had brains in your head you would be as good a man as any of them, and a better man than some of them. Brains are the only things worth having in this world, no matter whether one is a crow or a man.'

"After the crows had gone I thought this over, and decided I would try hard to get some brains. By good luck you came along and pulled me off the stake and from what you say I am sure the Great Oz will give me brains as soon as we get to the Emerald City."

"I hope so," said Dorothy earnestly, "since you seem anxious to have them."

"Oh, yes. I am anxious," returned the Scarecrow. "It is such an uncomfortable feeling to know one is a fool."

"Well," said the girl, "let us go." And she handed the basket to the Scarecrow.

There were no fences at all by the roadside now, and the land was rough and untilled. Toward evening they came to a great forest, where the trees grew so big and close together that their branches met over the road of yellow brick. It was almost dark under the trees, for the branches shut out the daylight; but the travelers did not stop, and went on into the forest.

"If this road goes in, it must come out," said the Scarecrow, "and as the Emerald City is at the other end of the road, we must go wherever it leads us."

"Anyone would know that," said Dorothy.

"Certainly; that is why I know it," returned the Scarecrow. "If it required brains to figure it out, I never should have said it."

After an hour or so the light faded away, and they found themselves stumbling along in the darkness. Dorothy could not see at all, but Toto could, for some dogs see very well in the dark; and the Scarecrow declared he could see as well as by day. So she took hold of his arm and managed to get along fairly well.

"If you see any house, or any place where we can pass the night," she said, "you must tell me; for it is very uncomfortable walking in the dark."

Soon after the Scarecrow stopped.

"I see a little cottage at the right of us," he said, "built of logs and branches. Shall we go there?"

"Yes, indeed," answered the child. "I am all tired out."

So the Scarecrow led her through the trees until they reached the cottage, and Dorothy entered and found a bed of dried leaves in one corner. She lay down at once, and with Toto beside her soon fell into a sound sleep. The Scarecrow, who was never tired, stood up in another corner and waited patiently until morning came.

Chapter Five

THE RESCUE OF THE TIN WOODMAN

––––→ ●◄––––

WHEN Dorothy awoke the sun was shining through the trees and Toto had long been out chasing birds around him. There was the Scarecrow, still standing patiently in his corner, waiting for her.

"We must go and search for water," she said to him.

"Why do you want water?" he asked.

"To wash my face clean after the dust of the road, and to drink, so the dry bread will not stick in my throat."

"It must be inconvenient to be made of flesh," said the Scarecrow thoughtfully, "for you must sleep and eat and drink. However, you have brains, and it is worth a lot of bother to be able to think properly."

They left the cottage and walked through the trees until they found a little spring of clear water, where Dorothy drank and bathed and ate her breakfast. She saw there was not much bread left in the basket, and the girl was thankful the Scarecrow did not have to eat anything, for there was scarcely enough for herself and Toto for the day.

When she had finished her meal, and was about to go back to the road of yellow brick, she was startled to hear a deep groan near by.

"What was that?" she asked timidly.

"I cannot imagine," replied the Scarecrow. "But we can go and see."

Just then another groan reached their ears, and the sound seemed to come from behind them. They turned and walked through the forest a few steps, when Dorothy discovered something shining in a ray of sunshine that fell between the trees. She ran to the place and then stopped short, with a little cry of surprise.

One of the big trees had been partly chopped through, and standing beside it, with an uplifted axe in his hands, was a man made entirely of tin. His head and arms and legs were jointed upon his body, but he stood perfectly motionless, as if he could not stir at all.

Dorothy looked at him in amazement, and so did the Scarecrow, while Toto barked sharply and made a snap at the tin legs, which hurt his teeth.

"Did you groan?" asked Dorothy.

"Yes," answered the tin man, "I did. I've been groaning for more than a year, and no one has ever heard me before or come to help me."

"What can I do for you?" she inquired softly, for she was moved by the sad voice in which the man spoke.

"Get an oilcan and oil my joints," he answered. "They are rusted so badly that I cannot move them at all. If I am well oiled I shall soon be all right again. You will find an oilcan on a shelf in my cottage."

Dorothy at once ran back to the cottage and found the oilcan, and then she returned and asked anxiously, "Where are your joints?"

"Oil my neck, first," replied the Tin Woodman. So she oiled it, and as it was quite badly rusted the Scarecrow took hold of the tin head and moved it gently from side to side until it worked freely, and then the man could turn it himself.

"Now oil the joints in my arms," he said. And Dorothy oiled them and the Scarecrow bent them carefully until they were quite free from rust and as good as new.

The Tin Woodman gave a sigh of satisfaction and lowered his axe, which he leaned against the tree.

"This is a great comfort," he said. "I have been holding that axe in the air ever since I rusted, and I'm glad to be able to put it down at last. Now, if you will oil the joints of my legs, I shall be all right once more."

So they oiled his legs until he could move them freely; and he thanked them again and again for his release, for he seemed a very polite creature, and very grateful.

"I might have stood there always if you had not come along," he said; "so you have certainly saved my life. How did you happen to be here?"

"We are on our way to the Emerald City to see the Great Oz," she answered, "and we stopped at your cottage to pass the night."

"Why do you wish to see Oz?" he asked.

"I want him to send me back to Kansas, and the Scarecrow wants him to put a few brains into his head," she replied.

The Tin Woodman appeared to think deeply for a moment. Then he said:

"Do you suppose Oz could give me a heart?"

"Why, I guess so," Dorothy answered. "It would be as easy as to give the Scarecrow brains."

"True," the Tin Woodman returned. "So, if you will allow me to join your party, I will also go to the Emerald City and ask Oz to help me."

"Come along," said the Scarecrow heartily, and Dorothy added that she would be pleased to have his company. So the Tin Woodman shouldered his axe and they all passed through the forest until they came to the road that was paved with yellow brick.

The Tin Woodman had asked Dorothy to put the

oilcan in her basket. "For," he said, "if I should get caught in the rain, and rust again, I would need the oilcan badly."

It was a bit of good luck to have their new comrade join the party, for soon after they had begun their journey again they came to a place where the trees and branches grew so thick over the road that the travelers could not pass. But the Tin Woodman set to work with his axe and chopped so well that soon he cleared a passage for the entire party.

Dorothy was thinking so earnestly as they walked along that she did not notice when the Scarecrow stumbled into a hole and rolled over to the side of the road. Indeed, he was obliged to call to her to help him up again.

"Why didn't you walk around the hole?" asked the Tin Woodman.

"I don't know enough," replied the Scarecrow cheerfully. "My head is stuffed with straw, you know, and that is why I am going to Oz to ask him for some brains."

"Oh, I see," said the Tin Woodman. "But, after all, brains are not the best things in the world."

"Have you any?" inquired the Scarecrow.

"No, my head is quite empty," answered the Woodman. "But once I had brains, and a heart also. So, having tried them both, I should much rather have a heart."

"And why is that?" asked the Scarecrow.

"I will tell you my story, and then you will know."

So, while they were walking through the forest, the Tin Woodman told the following story:

"I was born the son of a woodman who chopped down trees in the forest and sold the wood for a living. When I grew up I too became a woodchopper, and after my father died I took care of my old mother as long as she lived. Then I made up my mind that instead of living alone I would marry, so that I might not become lonely.

"There was one of the Munchkin girls who was so beautiful that I soon grew to love her with all my heart. She, on her part, promised to marry me as soon as I could earn enough money to build a better house for her. So I set to work harder than ever. But the girl lived with an old woman who did not want her to marry anyone, for she was so lazy she wished the girl to remain with her and do the cooking and the housework. So the old woman went to the Wicked Witch of the East, and promised her two sheep and a cow if she would prevent the marriage. Thereupon the Wicked Witch enchanted my axe, and when I was chopping away at my best one day, for I was anxious to get the new house and my wife as soon as possible, the axe slipped all at once and cut off my left leg.

"This at first seemed a great misfortune, for I knew a one-legged man could not do very well as a woodchopper. So I went to a tinsmith and had him make me a new leg out of tin. The leg worked very well, once I was used to it. But my action angered the Wicked Witch of the East, for she had promised the old woman I should not marry the pretty Munchkin girl. When I began chopping again, my axe slipped and cut off my right leg. Again I went to the tinner, and again he made me a leg out of tin. After this the enchanted axe cut off my arms, one after the other; but, nothing daunted, I had them replaced with tin ones. The Wicked Witch then made the axe slip and cut off my head, and at first I thought that was the end of me. But the tinner happened to come along, and he made me a new head out of tin.

"I thought I had beaten the Wicked Witch then, and I worked harder than ever; but I little knew how cruel my enemy could be. She thought of a new way to kill my love for the beautiful Munchkin maiden, and made my axe slip again, so that it cut right through my body, splitting me into two halves. Once more the tinner came to my help and made me a body of tin, fastening my tin arms and legs and head to it, by means of joints, so that I could move around as well as ever. But, alas! I had now no heart, so that I lost all my love for the Munchkin girl, and did not care whether I married her or not. I suppose she is still living with the old woman, waiting for me to come after her.

"My body shone so brightly in the sun that I felt very proud of it and it did not matter now if my axe slipped, for it could not cut me. There was only one danger— that my joints would rust. But I kept an oilcan in my cottage and took care to oil myself whenever I needed it. However, there came a day when I forgot to do this, and, being caught in a rainstorm, before I thought of the danger my joints had rusted, and I was left to stand in the woods until you came to help me. It was a terrible thing to undergo, but during the year I stood there I had time to think that the greatest loss I had known was the loss of my heart. While I was in love I was the happiest man on earth; but no one can love who has not a heart, and so I am resolved to ask Oz to give me one. If he does, I will go back to the Munchkin maiden and marry her."

Both Dorothy and the Scarecrow had been greatly interested in the story of the Tin Woodman, and now they knew why he was so anxious to get a new heart.

"All the same," said the Scarecrow, "I shall ask for brains instead of a heart; for a fool would not know what to do with a heart if he had one."

"I shall take the heart," returned the Tin Woodman; "for brains do not make one happy, and happiness is the best thing in the world."

Dorothy did not say anything, for she was puzzled to know which of her two friends was right, and she decided if she could only get back to Kansas and Aunt Em it did not matter so much whether the Woodman had no brains and the Scarecrow no heart, or each got what he wanted.

What worried her most was that the bread was nearly gone, and another meal for herself and Toto would empty the basket. To be sure neither the Woodman nor the Scarecrow ever ate anything, but she was not made of tin nor straw, and could not live unless she was fed.

Chapter Six

THE COWARDLY LION

ALL this time Dorothy and her companions had been walking through the thick woods. The road was still paved with yellow bricks, but these were much covered by dried branches and dead leaves from the trees, and the walking was not at all good.

There were few birds in this part of the forest, for birds love the open country where there is plenty of sunshine. But now and then there came a deep growl from some wild animal hidden among the trees. These sounds made the little girl's heart beat fast, for she did not know what made them; but Toto knew, and he walked close to Dorothy's side, and did not even bark in return.

"How long will it be," the child asked of the Tin Woodman, "before we are out of the forest?"

"I cannot tell," was the answer, "for I have never been to the Emerald City. But my father went there once, when I was a boy, and he said it was a long journey through a dangerous country, although nearer to the city where Oz dwells the country is beautiful. But I am not afraid so long as I have my oilcan, and nothing can hurt the Scarecrow, while you bear upon your forehead the mark of the Good Witch's kiss, and that will protect you from harm."

"But Toto!" said the girl anxiously. "What will protect him?"

"We must protect him ourselves if he is in danger," replied the Tin Woodman.

Just as he spoke there came from the forest a terrible roar, and the next moment a great Lion bounded into the road. With one blow of his paw he sent the Scarecrow spinning over and over to the edge of the road, and then he struck at the Tin Woodman with his sharp claws. But, to the Lion's surprise, he could make no impression on the tin, although the Woodman fell over in the road and lay still.

Little Toto, now that he had an enemy to face, ran barking toward the Lion, and the great beast had opened his mouth to bite the dog, when Dorothy, fearing Toto would be killed, and heedless of danger, rushed forward and slapped the Lion upon his nose as hard as she could, while she cried out:

"Don't you dare to bite Toto! You ought to be ashamed of yourself, a big beast like you, to bite a poor little dog!"

"I didn't bite him," said the Lion, as he rubbed his nose with his paw where Dorothy had hit it.

"No, but you tried to," she retorted. "You are nothing but a big coward."

"I know it," said the Lion, hanging his head in shame. "I've always known it. But how can I help it?"

"I don't know, I'm sure. To think of your striking a stuffed man, like the poor Scarecrow!"

"Is he stuffed?" asked the Lion in surprise, as he watched her pick up the Scarecrow and set him upon his feet, while she patted him into shape again.

"Of course he's stuffed," replied Dorothy, who was still angry.

"That's why he went over so easily," remarked the Lion. "It astonished me to see him whirl around so. Is the other one stuffed also?"

"No," said Dorothy, "he's made of tin." And she helped the Woodman up again.

"That's why he nearly blunted my claws," said the Lion. "When they scratched against the tin it made a cold shiver run down my back. What is that little animal you are so tender of?"

"He is my dog, Toto," answered Dorothy.

"Is he made of tin, or stuffed?" asked the Lion.

"Neither. He's a—a—a meat dog," said the girl.

"Oh! He's a curious animal and seems remarkably

small, now that I look at him. No one would think of biting such a little thing except a coward like me," continued the Lion sadly.

"What makes you a coward?" asked Dorothy, looking at the great beast in wonder, for he was as big as a small horse.

"It's a mystery," replied the Lion. "I suppose I was born that way. All the other animals in the forest naturally expect me to be brave, for the Lion is everywhere thought to be the King of Beasts. I learned that if I roared very loudly every living thing was frightened and got out of my way. Whenever I've met a man I've been awfully scared. But I just roared at him, and he has always run away as fast as he could go. If the elephants and the tigers and the bears had ever tried to fight me, I should have run myself—I'm such a coward; but just as soon as they hear me roar they all try to get away from me, and of course I let them go."

"But that isn't right. The King of Beasts shouldn't be a coward," said the Scarecrow.

"I know it," returned the Lion, wiping a tear from his eye with the tip of his paw. "It is my great sorrow, and makes my life very unhappy. But whenever there is danger, my heart begins to beat fast."

"Perhaps you have heart disease," said the Tin Woodman.

"It may be," said the Lion.

"If you have," continued the Tin Woodman, "you ought to be glad, for it proves you have a heart. For my part, I have no heart, so I cannot have heart disease."

"Perhaps," said the Lion thoughtfully, "if I had no heart I should not be a coward."

"Have you brains?" asked the Scarecrow.

"I suppose so. I've never looked to see," replied the Lion.

"I am going to the Great Oz to ask him to give me some," remarked the Scarecrow, "for my head is stuffed with straw."

"And I am going to ask him to give me a heart," said the Woodman.

"And I am going to ask him to send Toto and me back to Kansas," added Dorothy.

"Do you think Oz could give me courage?" asked the Cowardly Lion.

"Just as easily as he could give me brains," said the Scarecrow.

"Or give me a heart," said the Tin Woodman.

"Or send me back to Kansas," said Dorothy.

"Then, if you don't mind, I'll go with you," said the Lion, "for my life is simply unbearable without a bit of courage."

"You will be very welcome," answered Dorothy, "for

you will help to keep away the other wild beasts. It seems to me they must be more cowardly than you are if they allow you to scare them so easily."

"They really are," said the Lion, "but that doesn't make me any braver, and as long as I know myself to be a coward I shall be unhappy."

So once more the little company set off upon the journey, the Lion walking with stately strides at Dorothy's side. Toto did not approve this new comrade at first, for he could not forget how nearly he had been crushed between the Lion's great jaws. But after a time he became more at ease, and presently Toto and the Cowardly Lion had grown to be good friends.

During the rest of that day there was no other adventure to mar the peace of their journey. Once, indeed, the Tin Woodman stepped upon a beetle that was crawling along the road, and killed the poor little thing. This made the Tin Woodman very unhappy, for he was always careful not to hurt any living creature; and as he walked along he wept several tears of sorrow and regret. These tears ran slowly down his face and over the hinges of his jaw, and there they rusted. When Dorothy presently asked him a question the Tin Woodman could not open his mouth, for his jaws were tightly rusted together. He became greatly frightened at this and made many motions to Dorothy to relieve him, but she could not understand. The Lion was also puzzled to know what was wrong. But the Scarecrow seized the oilcan from Dorothy's basket and oiled the Woodman's jaws, so that after a few moments he could talk as well as before.

"This will serve me a lesson," said he, "to look where I step. For if I should kill another bug or beetle I should surely cry again, and crying rusts my jaws so that I cannot speak."

Thereafter he walked very carefully, with his eyes on the road, and when he saw a tiny ant toiling by he would step over it, so as not to harm it. The Tin Woodman knew very well he had no heart, and therefore he took great care never to be cruel or unkind to anything.

"You people with hearts," he said, "have something to guide you, and need never do wrong; but I have no heart, and so I must be very careful. When Oz gives me a heart, of course I needn't mind so much."

Chapter Seven

THE JOURNEY TO
THE GREAT OZ

*T*HEY were obliged to camp out that night under a large tree in the forest, for there were no houses near. The tree made a good, thick covering to protect them from the dew, and the Tin Woodman chopped a great pile of wood with his axe, and Dorothy built a splendid fire that warmed her and made her feel less lonely. She and Toto ate the last of their bread, and now she did not know what they would do for breakfast.

"If you wish," said the Lion, "I will go into the forest and kill a deer for you. You can roast it by the fire, since your tastes are so peculiar that you prefer cooked food, and then you will have a very good breakfast."

"Don't! Please don't," begged the Tin Woodman. "I should certainly weep if you killed a poor deer, and then my jaws would rust again."

But the Lion went away into the forest and found his own supper, and no one ever knew what it was, for he didn't mention it. And the Scarecrow found a tree full of nuts and filled Dorothy's basket with them, so that she would not be hungry for a long time. She thought this was very kind and thoughtful of the Scarecrow, but she laughed heartily at the awkward way in which the poor creature picked up the nuts. His padded hands were so clumsy and the nuts were so small that he dropped almost as many as he put in the basket. But the Scarecrow did not mind how long it took him to fill the basket, for it enabled him to keep away from the fire, as he feared a spark might get into his straw and burn him up. So he kept a good distance away from the flames, and only came near to cover Dorothy with dry leaves when she lay down to sleep. These kept her very snug and warm, and she slept soundly until morning.

When it was daylight, the girl bathed her face in a little rippling brook, and soon after they all started toward the Emerald City.

This was to be an eventful day for the travelers. They had hardly been walking an hour when they saw before them a great ditch that crossed the road and divided the forest as far as they could see on either side. It was a very wide ditch, and when they crept up to the edge and looked into it they could see it was also very deep, and there were many big, jagged rocks at the bottom. The sides were so steep that none of them could climb down, and for a moment it seemed that their journey must end.

"What shall we do?" asked Dorothy despairingly.

"I haven't the faintest idea," said the Tin Woodman, and the Lion shook his shaggy mane and looked thoughtful.

But the Scarecrow said, "We cannot fly, that is certain. Neither can we climb down into this great ditch. Therefore, if we cannot jump over it, we must stop where we are."

"I think I could jump over it," said the Cowardly Lion, after measuring the distance carefully in his mind.

"Then we are all right," answered the Scarecrow, "for you can carry us all over on your back, one at a time."

"Well, I'll try it," said the Lion. "Who will go first?"

"I will," declared the Scarecrow, "for, if you found that you could not jump over the gulf, Dorothy would be killed, or the Tin Woodman badly dented on the rocks below. But if I am on your back it will not matter so much, for the fall would not hurt me at all."

"I am terribly afraid of falling, myself," said the Cowardly Lion, "but I suppose there is nothing to do but try it. So get on my back and we will make the attempt."

The Scarecrow sat upon the Lion's back, and the big

beast walked to the edge of the gulf and crouched down.

"Why don't you run and jump?" asked the Scarecrow.

"Because that isn't the way we Lions do these things," he replied. Then giving a great spring, he shot through the air and landed safely on the other side. They were all greatly pleased to see how easily he did it, and after the Scarecrow had got down from his back the Lion sprang across the ditch again.

Dorothy thought she would go next. So she took Toto in her arms and climbed on the Lion's back, holding tightly to his mane with one hand. The next moment it seemed as if she were flying through the air; and then, before she had time to think about it, she was safe on the other side. The Lion went back a third time and got the Tin Woodman, and then they all sat down for a few moments to give the beast a chance to rest, for his great leaps had made his breath short, and he panted like a big dog that has been running too long.

They found the forest very thick on this side, and it looked dark and gloomy. After the Lion had rested they started along the road of yellow brick, silently wondering, each in his own mind, if ever they would come to the end of the woods and reach the bright sunshine again. To add to their discomfort, they soon heard strange noises in the depths of the forest, and the Lion whispered to them that it was in this part of the country that the Kalidahs lived.

"What are the Kalidahs?" asked the girl.

"They are monstrous beasts with bodies like bears and heads like tigers," replied the Lion, "and with claws so long and sharp that they could tear me in two as easily as I could kill Toto. I'm terribly afraid of the Kalidahs."

"I'm not surprised that you are," returned Dorothy. "They must be dreadful beasts."

The Lion was about to reply when suddenly they came to another gulf across the road. But this one was so broad and deep that the Lion knew at once he could not leap across it.

So they sat down to consider what they should do, and after serious thought the Scarecrow said, "Here is a great tree, standing close to the ditch. If the Tin Woodman can chop it down, so that it will fall to the other side, we can walk across it easily."

"That is a first-rate idea," said the Lion. "One would almost suspect you had brains in your head, instead of straw."

The Woodman set to work at once, and so sharp was his axe that the tree was soon chopped nearly through. Then the Lion put his strong front legs against the tree and pushed with all his might, and slowly the big tree tipped and fell with a crash across the ditch, with its top branches on the other side.

They had just started to cross this queer bridge when a sharp growl made them all look up, and to their horror they saw running toward them two great beasts with bodies like bears and heads like tigers.

"They are the Kalidahs!" said the Cowardly Lion, beginning to tremble.

"Quick!" cried the Scarecrow. "Let us cross over."

So Dorothy went first, holding Toto in her arms, the Tin Woodman followed, and the Scarecrow came next. The Lion, although he was certainly afraid, turned to face the Kalidahs, and then he gave so loud and terrible a roar that Dorothy screamed and the Scarecrow fell over backward, while even the fierce beasts stopped short and looked at him in surprise.

But, seeing they were bigger than the Lion, and remembering that there were two of them and only one of him, the Kalidahs again rushed forward, and the Lion crossed over the tree and turned to see what they would do next. Without stopping an instant the fierce beasts also began to cross the tree. And the Lion said to Dorothy, "We are lost, for they will surely tear us to pieces with their sharp claws. But stand close behind me, and I will fight them as long as I am alive."

"Wait a minute!" called the Scarecrow. He had been thinking what was best to be done, and now he asked the Woodman to chop away the end of the tree that rested on their side of the ditch. The Tin Woodman began to use his axe at once, and, just as the two Kalidahs were nearly across, the tree fell with a crash into the gulf, carrying the ugly, snarling brutes with it, and both were dashed to pieces on the sharp rocks at the bottom.

"Well," said the Cowardly Lion, drawing a long breath of relief, "I see we are going to live a little while longer, and I am glad of it, for it must be a very uncomfortable thing not to be alive. Those creatures frightened me so badly that my heart is beating yet."

"Ah," said the Tin Woodman sadly, "I wish I had a heart to beat."

This adventure made the travelers more anxious than ever to get out of the forest, and they walked so fast that Dorothy became tired, and had to ride on the Lion's back. To their great joy the trees became thinner the farther they advanced, and in the afternoon they suddenly came upon a broad river, flowing swiftly just before them. On the other side of the water they could see the road of yellow brick running through a beautiful country, with green meadows dotted with bright flowers and all the road bordered with trees hanging full of delicious fruits. They were greatly pleased to see this delightful country before them.

"How shall we cross the river?" asked Dorothy.

"That is easily done," replied the Scarecrow. "The Tin Woodman must build us a raft, so we can float to the other side."

So the Woodman took his axe and began to chop down small trees to make a raft, and while he was busy at this the Scarecrow found on the riverbank a tree full of fine fruit. This pleased Dorothy, who had eaten nothing but nuts all day, and she made a hearty meal of the ripe fruit.

But it takes time to make a raft, even when one is as industrious and untiring as the Tin Woodman, and when night came the work was not done. So they found a cozy place under the trees where they slept well until the morning. And Dorothy dreamed of the Emerald City, and of the good Wizard Oz, who would soon send her back to her own home again.

Chapter Eight

THE DEADLY POPPY FIELD

———————⇒ ⊶ ⇐————————

*O*UR little party of travelers awakened the next morning refreshed and full of hope, and Dorothy breakfasted like a princess off peaches and plums from the trees beside the river. Behind them was the dark forest they had passed safely through, although they had suffered many discouragements. But before them was a lovely, sunny country that seemed to beckon them on to the Emerald City.

To be sure, the broad river now cut them off from this beautiful land. But the raft was nearly done, and after the Tin Woodman had cut a few more logs and fastened them together with wooden pins, they were ready to start. Dorothy sat down in the middle of the raft and held Toto in her arms. When the Cowardly Lion stepped upon the raft it tipped badly, for he was big and heavy; but the Scarecrow and the Tin Woodman stood upon the other end to steady it, and they had long poles in their hands to push the raft through the water.

They got along quite well at first, but when they

reached the middle of the river the swift current swept the raft downstream, farther and farther away from the road of yellow brick. And the water grew so deep that the long poles would not touch the bottom.

"This is bad," said the Tin Woodman, "for if we cannot get to the land we shall be carried into the country of the Wicked Witch of the West, and she will enchant us and make us her slaves."

"And then I should get no brains," said the Scarecrow.

"And I should get no courage," said the Cowardly Lion.

"And I should get no heart," said the Tin Woodman.

"And I should never get back to Kansas," said Dorothy.

"We must certainly get to the Emerald City if we can," the Scarecrow continued, and he pushed so hard on his long pole that it stuck fast in the mud at the bottom of the river. Then, before he could pull it out again—or let go—the raft was swept away, and the poor Scarecrow left clinging to the pole in the middle of the river.

"Good-bye!" he called after them, and they were very sorry to leave him. Indeed, the Tin Woodman began to cry, but fortunately remembered that he might rust, and so dried his tears on Dorothy's apron.

Of course this was a bad thing for the Scarecrow.

"I am now worse off than when I first met Dorothy,"

he thought. "Then, I was stuck on a pole in a cornfield, where I could make-believe scare the crows, at any rate. But surely there is no use for a Scarecrow stuck on a pole in the middle of a river. I am afraid I shall never have any brains, after all!"

Down the stream the raft floated, and the poor Scarecrow was left far behind. Then the Lion said, "Something must be done to save us. I think I can swim to the shore and pull the raft after me, if you will only hold fast to the tip of my tail."

So he sprang into the water, and the Tin Woodman caught fast hold of his tail. Then the Lion began to swim with all his might toward the shore. It was hard work, although he was so big. But by and by they were drawn out of the current, and then Dorothy took the Tin Woodman's long pole and helped push the raft to the land.

They were all tired out when they reached the shore at last and stepped off upon the pretty green grass, and they also knew that the stream had carried them a long way past the road of yellow brick that led to the Emerald City.

"What shall we do now?" asked the Tin Woodman, as the Lion lay down on the grass to let the sun dry him.

"We must get back to the road, in some way," said Dorothy.

"The best plan will be to walk along the riverbank until we come to the road again," remarked the Lion.

So, when they were rested, Dorothy picked up her basket and they started along the grassy bank, back to the road from which the river had carried them. It was a lovely country, with plenty of flowers and fruit trees and sunshine to cheer them; and had they not felt so sorry for the poor Scarecrow, they could have been very happy.

They walked along as fast as they could, Dorothy only stopping once to pick a beautiful flower; and after a time the Tin Woodman cried out, "Look!"

Then they all looked at the river and saw the Scarecrow perched upon his pole in the middle of the water, looking very lonely and sad.

"What can we do to save him?" asked Dorothy.

The Lion and the Woodman both shook their heads, for they did not know. So they sat down upon the bank and gazed wistfully at the Scarecrow until a Stork flew by, who, upon seeing them, stopped to rest at the water's edge.

"Who are you and where are you going?" asked the Stork.

"I am Dorothy," answered the girl, "and these are my friends, the Tin Woodman and the Cowardly Lion. We are going to the Emerald City."

"This isn't the road," said the Stork, as she twisted her long neck and looked sharply at the queer party.

"I know it," returned Dorothy, "but we have lost the Scarecrow, and are wondering how we shall get him again."

"Where is he?" asked the Stork.

"Over there in the river," answered the little girl.

"If he weren't so big and heavy I would get him for you," remarked the Stork.

"He isn't heavy a bit," said Dorothy eagerly, "for he is stuffed with straw. If you will bring him back to us, we shall thank you ever and ever so much."

"Well, I'll try," said the Stork. "But if I find he is too heavy to carry I shall have to drop him in the river again."

So the big bird flew into the air and over the water till she came to where the Scarecrow was perched upon his pole. Then the Stork with her great claws grabbed the Scarecrow by the arm and carried him up into the air and back to the bank, where Dorothy and the Lion and the Tin Woodman and Toto were sitting.

When the Scarecrow found himself among his friends again, he was so happy that he hugged them all, even the Lion and Toto. And as they walked along he sang "Tol-de-ri-de-oh!" at every step, he felt so gay.

"I was afraid I should have to stay in the river

forever," he said, "but the kind Stork saved me. If I ever get any brains I shall find the Stork again and do her some kindness in return."

"That's all right," said the Stork, who was flying along beside them. "I always like to help anyone in trouble. But I must go now, for my babies are waiting in the nest for me. I hope you will find the Emerald City and that Oz will help you."

"Thank you," replied Dorothy. Then the kind Stork flew into the air and was soon out of sight.

They walked along listening to the singing of the brightly colored birds and looking at the lovely flowers which now became so thick that the ground was carpeted with them. There were big yellow and white and blue and purple blossoms, besides great clusters of scarlet poppies, which were so brilliant in color they almost dazzled Dorothy's eyes.

"Aren't they beautiful?" the girl asked, as she breathed in the spicy scent of the bright flowers.

"I suppose so," answered the Scarecrow. "When I have brains, I shall probably like them better."

"If I only had a heart, I should love them," added the Tin Woodman.

"I always did like flowers," said the Lion. "They seem so helpless and frail. But there are none in the forest so bright as these."

They now came upon more and more of the big scarlet poppies, and fewer and fewer of the other flowers. And soon they found themselves in the midst of a great meadow of poppies. Now it is well known that when there are many of these flowers together, their odor is so powerful that anyone who breathes it falls asleep. And if the sleeper is not carried away from the scent of the flowers, he sleeps on and on forever. But Dorothy did not know this, nor could she get away from the bright red flowers that were everywhere about. So presently her eyes grew heavy and she felt she must sit down to rest and to sleep.

But the Tin Woodman would not let her do this.

"We must hurry and get back to the road of yellow brick before dark," he said, and the Scarecrow agreed with him. So they kept walking until Dorothy could stand no longer. Her eyes closed in spite of herself. Then she forgot where she was and fell among the poppies, fast asleep.

"What shall we do?" asked the Tin Woodman.

"If we leave her here she will die," said the Lion. "The smell of the flowers is killing us all. I myself can scarcely keep my eyes open, and the dog is asleep already."

It was true. Toto had fallen down beside his little mistress. But the Scarecrow and the Tin Woodman, not being made of flesh, were not troubled by the scent of the flowers.

"Run fast," said the Scarecrow to the Lion. "Get out of this deadly flower bed as soon as you can. We will bring the little girl with us, but if you should fall asleep you are too big to be carried."

So the Lion aroused himself and bounded forward as fast as he could go. In a moment he was out of sight.

"Let us make a chair with our hands and carry her," said the Scarecrow. So they picked up Toto and put the dog in Dorothy's lap. Then they made a chair with their hands for the seat and their arms for the arms and carried the sleeping girl between them through the flowers.

On and on they walked, and it seemed that the great carpet of deadly flowers that surrounded them would never end. They followed the bend of the river, and at last came upon their friend the Lion, lying fast asleep among the poppies. The flowers had been too strong for the huge beast and he had given up at last, falling only a short distance from the end of the poppy bed, where the sweet grass spread in beautiful green fields before them.

"We can do nothing for him," said the Tin Woodman sadly. "He is much too heavy to lift. We must leave him here to sleep on forever, and perhaps he will dream that he has found courage at last."

"I'm sorry," said the Scarecrow. "The Lion was a very good comrade for one so cowardly. But let us go on."

They carried the sleeping Dorothy to a pretty spot beside the river, far enough from the poppy field to prevent her breathing any more of the poison of the flowers. Here they laid her gently on the soft grass and waited for the fresh breeze to waken her.

Chapter Nine

THE QUEEN OF THE
FIELD MICE

*W*E cannot be far from the road of yellow brick now," remarked the Scarecrow, as he stood beside the girl, "for we have come nearly as far as the river carried us away."

The Tin Woodman was about to reply when he heard a low growl, and turning his head (which worked beautifully on hinges) he saw a strange beast come bounding over the grass toward them. It was, indeed, a great, yellow wildcat, and the Woodman thought it must be chasing something, for its ears were lying close to its head and its mouth was wide open, showing two rows of ugly teeth, while its red eyes glowed like balls of fire. As it came nearer the Tin Woodman saw that running before the beast was a little gray Field Mouse, and although he had no heart he knew it was wrong for the wildcat to try to kill such a pretty, harmless creature.

So the Woodman raised his axe, and as the wildcat ran by he gave it a quick blow that cut the beast's head clean off from its body, and it rolled over at his feet in two pieces.

The Field Mouse, now that it was freed from its enemy, stopped short. Then coming slowly up to the Woodman it said, in a squeaky little voice, "Oh, thank you! Thank you ever so much for saving my life."

"Don't speak of it, I beg of you," replied the Woodman. "I have no heart, you know, so I am careful to help all those who may need a friend, even if it happens to be only a mouse."

"Only a mouse!" cried the little animal indignantly. "Why, I am a Queen—the Queen of all the Field Mice!"

"Oh, indeed," said the Woodman, making a bow.

"Therefore you have done a great deed, as well as a brave one, in saving my life," added the Queen.

At that moment several mice were seen running up as fast as their little legs could carry them, and when they saw their Queen they exclaimed:

"Oh, your Majesty, we thought you would be killed! How did you manage to escape the great wildcat?" They all bowed so low to the little Queen that they almost stood upon their heads.

"This funny tin man," she answered, "killed the wildcat and saved my life. So hereafter you must all serve him and obey his slightest wish."

"We will!" cried all the mice, in a shrill chorus. And

then they scampered in all directions, for Toto had awakened from his sleep, and seeing all these mice around him he gave one bark of delight and jumped right into the middle of the group. Toto had always loved to chase mice when he lived in Kansas, and he saw no harm in it.

But the Tin Woodman caught the dog in his arms and held him tight, while he called to the mice, "Come back! Come back! Toto shall not hurt you."

At this the Queen of the Mice stuck her head out from underneath a clump of grass and asked, in a timid voice, "Are you sure he will not bite us?"

"I will not let him," said the Woodman. "So do not be afraid."

One by one the mice came creeping back, and Toto did not bark again, although he tried to get out of the Woodman's arms, and would have bitten him had he not known very well he was made of tin. Finally one of the biggest mice spoke.

"Is there anything we can do," it asked, "to repay you for saving the life of our Queen?"

"Nothing that I know of," answered the Woodman. However, the Scarecrow, who had been trying to think, but could not because his head was stuffed with straw, said quickly, "Oh, yes! You can save our friend, the Cowardly Lion, who is asleep in the poppy bed."

"A Lion!" cried the little Queen. "Why, he would eat us all up."

"Oh, no," declared the Scarecrow. "This Lion is a coward."

"Really?" asked the Mouse.

"He says so himself," answered the Scarecrow, "and he would never hurt anyone who is our friend. If you will help us to save him I promise that he shall treat you all with kindness."

"Very well," said the Queen, "we will trust you. But what shall we do?"

"Are there many of these mice which call you Queen and are willing to obey you?"

"Oh, yes. There are thousands," she replied.

"Then send for them all to come here as soon as possible, and let each one bring a long piece of string."

The Queen turned to the mice that attended her and told them to go at once and get all her people. As soon as they heard her orders they ran away in every direction as fast as possible.

"Now," said the Scarecrow to the Tin Woodman, "you must go to those trees by the riverside and make a truck that will carry the Lion."

So the Woodman went at once to the trees and began to work. And he soon made a truck out of the limbs of trees, from which he chopped away all the leaves and branches. He fastened it together with wooden pegs and made the four wheels out of short pieces of a big tree trunk. So fast and so well did he work that by the time the mice began to arrive the truck was all ready for them.

They came from all directions, and there were thousands of them—big mice and little mice and middle-sized mice—and each one brought a piece of string in his mouth. It was about this time that Dorothy woke from her long sleep and opened her eyes. She was greatly astonished to find herself lying upon the grass, with thousands of mice standing around and looking at her timidly. But the Scarecrow told her about everything.

Turning to the dignified little Mouse, he said, "Permit me to introduce to you her Majesty, the Queen."

Dorothy nodded gravely and the Queen made a curtsy, after which she became quite friendly with the little girl.

The Scarecrow and the Woodman now began to fasten the mice to the truck, using the strings they had brought. One end of a string was tied around the neck of each mouse and the other end to the truck. Of course the truck was a thousand times bigger than any of the mice who were to draw it. But when all the mice had been harnessed, they were able to pull it quite easily. Even the Scarecrow and the Tin Woodman could sit on it, and were drawn swiftly by their queer little horses to the place where the Lion lay asleep.

After a great deal of hard work—for the Lion was heavy—they managed to get him up on the truck. Then the Queen hurriedly gave her people the order to start, for she feared if the mice stayed among the poppies too long they also would fall asleep.

At first the little creatures, many though they were, could hardly stir the heavily loaded truck; but the Woodman and the Scarecrow both pushed from behind, and they got along better. Soon they rolled the Lion out of the poppy bed to the green fields, where he could breathe the sweet, fresh air again, instead of the poisonous scent of the flowers.

Dorothy came to meet them and thanked the little mice warmly for saving her companion from death. She had grown so fond of the big Lion she was glad he had been rescued.

Then the mice were unharnessed from the truck and scampered away through the grass to their homes. The Queen of the Mice was the last to leave.

"If ever you need us again," she said, "come out into the field and call, and we shall hear you and come to your assistance. Good-bye!"

"Good-bye!" they all answered, and away the Queen ran, while Dorothy held Toto tightly lest he should run after her and frighten her.

After this they sat down beside the Lion until he should awaken. And the Scarecrow brought Dorothy some fruit from a tree near by, which she ate for her dinner.

Chapter Ten

THE GUARDIAN OF THE GATES

*I*T was some time before the Cowardly Lion awakened, for he had lain among the poppies a long while, breathing in their deadly fragrance. When he did open his eyes and roll off the truck, he was very glad to find himself still alive.

"I ran as fast as I could," he said, sitting down and yawning, "but the flowers were too strong for me. How did you get me out?"

Then they told him of the field mice, and how they had generously saved him from death; and the Cowardly Lion laughed.

"I have always thought myself very big and terrible. Yet such little things as flowers came near to killing me, and such small animals as mice have saved my life. How strange it all is! But, comrades, what shall we do now?"

"We must journey on until we find the road of yellow brick again," said Dorothy. "Then we can keep on to the Emerald City."

So, the Lion being fully refreshed and feeling quite himself again, they all started upon the journey. They so greatly enjoyed the walk through the soft, fresh grass that it was not long before they reached the road of yellow brick and turned again toward the Emerald City where the Great Oz dwelt.

The road was smooth and well paved now, and the country about was beautiful, so that the travelers rejoiced in leaving the forest far behind, and with it the many dangers they had met in its gloomy shades. Once more they could see fences built beside the road, but these were painted green. When they came to a small house, in which a farmer evidently lived, that also was painted green. They passed by several of these houses during the afternoon. Sometimes people came to the doors and looked at them as if they would like to ask questions, but no one came near them nor spoke to them because they were very much afraid of the great Lion. The people were all dressed in clothing of a lovely emerald-green color and wore peaked hats like those of the Munchkins.

"This must be the Land of Oz," said Dorothy, "and we are surely getting near the Emerald City."

"Yes," answered the Scarecrow. "Everything is green here, while in the country of the Munchkins blue was the favorite color. But the people do not seem to be as friendly as the Munchkins, and I'm afraid we shall be unable to find a place to pass the night."

"I should like something to eat besides fruit," said the girl, "and I'm sure Toto is nearly starved. Let us stop at the next house and talk to the people."

So, when they came to a good-sized farmhouse, Dorothy walked boldly up to the door and knocked.

A woman opened it just far enough to look out, and said, "What do you want, child, and why is that great Lion with you?"

"We wish to pass the night with you, if you will allow us," answered Dorothy. "The Lion is my friend and comrade, and would not hurt you for the world."

"Is he tame?" asked the woman, opening the door a little wider.

"Oh, yes," said the girl, "and he is a great coward, too. He will be more afraid of you than you are of him."

"Well," said the woman, after thinking it over and taking another peep at the Lion, "if that is the case you may come in, and I will give you some supper and a place to sleep."

So they all entered the house, where there were, besides the woman, two children and a man. The man had hurt his leg, and was lying on the couch in a corner. They seemed greatly surprised to see so strange a company.

While the woman was busy laying the table the man asked, "Where are you all going?"

"To the Emerald City," said Dorothy, "to see the Great Oz."

"Oh, indeed!" exclaimed the man. "Are you sure that Oz will see you?"

"Why not?" she replied.

"Why, it is said that he never lets anyone come into his presence. I have been to the Emerald City many times, and it is a beautiful and wonderful place; but I have never been permitted to see the Great Oz, nor do I know of any living person who has seen him."

"Does he never go out?" asked the Scarecrow.

"Never. He sits day after day in the great Throne Room of his palace, and even those who wait upon him do not see him face to face."

"What is he like?" asked the girl.

"That is hard to tell," said the man thoughtfully. "You see, Oz is a Great Wizard, and can take on any form he wishes. So that some say he looks like a bird; and some say he looks like an elephant; and some say he looks like a cat. To others he appears as a beautiful fairy, or a brownie, or in any other form that pleases him. But who the real Oz is, when he is in his own form, no living person can tell."

"That is very strange," said Dorothy, "but we must

try, in some way, to see him, or we shall have made our journey for nothing."

"Why do you wish to see Oz?" asked the man.

"I want him to give me some brains," said the Scarecrow eagerly.

"Oh, Oz could do that easily enough," declared the man. "He has more brains than he needs."

"And I want him to give me a heart," said the Tin Woodman.

"That will not trouble him," continued the man. "Oz has a large collection of hearts, of all sizes and shapes."

"And I want him to give me courage," said the Cowardly Lion.

"Oz keeps a great pot of courage in his Throne Room," said the man, "which he has covered with a golden plate, to keep it from running over. He will be glad to give you some."

"And I want him to send me back to Kansas," said Dorothy.

"Where is Kansas?" asked the man, with surprise.

"I don't know," replied Dorothy sorrowfully, "but it is my home, and I'm sure it's somewhere."

"Very likely. Well, Oz can do anything; so I suppose he will find Kansas for you. But first you must get to see him, and that will be a hard task; for the Great Wizard does not like to see anyone, and he usually has his own way. But what do YOU want?" he continued, speaking to Toto. Toto only wagged his tail, for, strange to say, he could not speak.

The woman now called to them that supper was ready, so they gathered around the table and Dorothy ate some delicious porridge and a dish of scrambled eggs and a plate of nice white bread, and enjoyed her meal. The Lion ate some of the porridge, but did not care for it, saying it was made from oats and oats were food for horses—not for lions. The Scarecrow and the Tin Woodman ate nothing at all. Toto ate a little of everything, and was glad to get a good supper again.

The woman now gave Dorothy a bed to sleep in, and Toto lay down beside her, while the Lion guarded the door of her room so she might not be disturbed. The Scarecrow and the Tin Woodman stood up in a corner and kept quiet all night, although of course they could not sleep.

The next morning, as soon as the sun was up, they started on their way, and soon saw a beautiful green glow in the sky just before them.

"That must be the Emerald City," said Dorothy.

As they walked on, the green glow became brighter and brighter, and it seemed that at last they were nearing the end of their travels. Yet it was afternoon before they came to the great wall that surrounded the City. It was high and thick and of a bright green color.

In front of them, and at the end of the road of yellow brick, was a big gate, all studded with emeralds that glittered so in the sun that even the painted eyes of the Scarecrow were dazzled by their brilliancy.

There was a bell beside the gate, and Dorothy pushed the button and heard a silvery tinkle sound within. Then the big gate swung slowly open, and they all passed through and found themselves in a high arched room, the walls of which glistened with countless emeralds.

Before them stood a little man about the same size as the Munchkins. He was clothed all in green, from his head to his feet, and even his skin was of a greenish tint. At his side was a large green box.

When he saw Dorothy and her companions the man asked, "What do you wish in the Emerald City?"

"We came here to see the Great Oz," said Dorothy.

The man was so surprised at this answer that he sat down to think it over.

"It has been many years since anyone asked me to see Oz," he said, shaking his head in perplexity. "He is powerful and terrible, and if you come on an idle or foolish errand to bother the wise reflections of the Great Wizard, he might be angry and destroy you all in an instant."

"But it is not a foolish errand, nor an idle one,"

replied the Scarecrow. "It is important. And we have been told that Oz is a good Wizard."

"So he is," said the green man, "and he rules the Emerald City wisely and well. But to those who are not honest, or who approach him from curiosity, he is most terrible, and few have ever dared ask to see his face. I am the Guardian of the Gates, and since you demand to see the Great Oz I must take you to his palace. But first you must put on the spectacles."

"Why?" asked Dorothy.

"Because if you did not wear spectacles the brightness and glory of the Emerald City would blind you. Even those who live in the City must wear spectacles night and day. They are all locked on, for Oz so ordered it when the City was first built, and I have the only key that will unlock them."

He opened the big box, and Dorothy saw that it was filled with spectacles of every size and shape. All of them had green glasses in them. The Guardian of the Gates found a pair that would just fit Dorothy and put them over her eyes. There were two golden bands fastened to them that passed around the back of her head, where they were locked together by a little key that was at the end of a chain the Guardian of the Gates wore around his neck. When they were on, Dorothy could not take them off had she wished, but of course she did not wish to be blinded by the glare of the Emerald City. So she said nothing.

Then the green man fitted spectacles for the Scarecrow and the Tin Woodman and the Lion, and even on little Toto. And all were locked fast with the key.

Then the Guardian of the Gates put on his own glasses and told them he was ready to show them to the palace. Taking a big golden key from a peg on the wall, he opened another gate, and they all followed him through the portal into the streets of the Emerald City.

Chapter Eleven

THE EMERALD CITY OF OZ

———◆———

*E*VEN with eyes protected by the green spectacles, Dorothy and her friends were at first dazzled by the brilliancy of the wonderful City. The streets were lined with beautiful houses all built of green marble and studded everywhere with sparkling emeralds. They walked over a pavement of the same green marble, and where the blocks were joined together were rows of emeralds, set closely, and glittering in the brightness of the sun. The windowpanes were of green glass. Even the sky above the City had a green tint, and the rays of the sun were green.

There were many people—men, women, and children—walking about, and these were all dressed in green clothes and had greenish skins. They looked at Dorothy and her strangely assorted company with wondering eyes, and the children all ran away and hid behind their mothers when they saw the Lion. But no one spoke to them. Many shops stood in the street, and Dorothy saw that everything in them was green. Green candy and green popcorn were offered for sale, as well as green shoes, green hats, and green clothes of all sorts. At one place a man was selling green lemonade, and when the children bought it Dorothy could see that they paid for it with green pennies.

There seemed to be no horses nor animals of any kind. Instead, the men carried things around in little green carts, which they pushed before them. Everyone seemed happy and contented and prosperous.

The Guardian of the Gates led them through the streets until they came to a big building, exactly in the middle of the City, which was the Palace of Oz, the Great Wizard. There was a soldier before the door, dressed in a green uniform and wearing a long green beard.

"Here are strangers," said the Guardian of the Gates to him, "and they demand to see the Great Oz."

"Step inside," answered the soldier, "and I will carry your message to him."

So they passed through the Palace gates and were led into a big room with a green carpet and lovely green furniture set with emeralds. The soldier made them all wipe their feet upon a green mat before entering this room. When they were seated he said politely, "Please make yourselves comfortable while I go to the door of the Throne Room and tell Oz you are here."

They had to wait a long time before the soldier returned. When, at last, he came back, Dorothy asked:

"Have you seen Oz?"

"Oh, no," returned the soldier. "I have never seen him. But I spoke to him as he sat behind his screen, and gave him your message. He said he will grant you an audience, if you so desire. But each one of you must enter his presence alone, and he will admit but one each day. Therefore, as you must remain in the Palace for several days, I will have you shown to rooms where you may rest in comfort after your journey."

"Thank you," replied the girl. "That is very kind of Oz."

The soldier now blew upon a green whistle, and at once a young girl, dressed in a pretty green silk gown, entered the room. She had lovely green hair and green eyes, and she bowed low before Dorothy as she said, "Follow me and I will show you your room."

So Dorothy said good-bye to all her friends except Toto, and taking the dog in her arms followed the green girl through seven passages and up three flights of stairs until they came to a room at the front of the Palace. It was the sweetest little room in the world, with a soft comfortable bed that had sheets of green silk and a green velvet counterpane. There was a tiny fountain in the middle of the room, that shot a spray of green perfume into the air, to fall back into a beauti-fully carved green marble basin. Beautiful green flow-ers stood in the windows, and there was a shelf with a row of little green books. When Dorothy had time to open these books she found them full of queer green pictures that made her laugh, they were so funny.

In a wardrobe were many green dresses, made of silk and satin and velvet. And all of them fitted Dorothy exactly.

"Make yourself perfectly at home," said the green girl, "and if you wish for anything ring the bell. Oz will send for you tomorrow morning."

She left Dorothy alone and went back to the others. These she also led to rooms, and each one of them found himself lodged in a very pleasant part of the Palace. Of course this politeness was wasted on the Scarecrow; for when he found himself alone in his room he stood stu-pidly in one spot, just within the doorway, to wait till morning. It would not rest him to lie down, and he could not close his eyes. So he remained all night star-ing at a little spider which was weaving its web in a cor-ner of the room, just as if it were not one of the most wonderful rooms in the world. The Tin Woodman lay down on his bed from force of habit, for he remembered when he was made of flesh. Not being able to sleep, he passed the night moving his joints up and down to make sure they kept in good working order. The Lion would have preferred a bed of dried leaves in the forest, and did not like being shut up in a room. But he had too much sense to let this worry him. He sprang upon the bed and rolled himself up like a cat and purred himself asleep in a minute.

The next morning, after breakfast, the green maiden came to fetch Dorothy, and she dressed her in one of the prettiest gowns—made of green brocaded satin. Dorothy put on a green silk apron and tied a green ribbon around Toto's neck, and they started for the Throne Room of the Great Oz.

First they came to a great hall in which were many ladies and gentlemen of the court, all dressed in rich costumes. These people had nothing to do but talk to each other, but they always came to wait outside the Throne Room every morning, although they were never permitted to see Oz.

As Dorothy entered they looked at her curiously, and one of them whispered, "Are you really going to look upon the face of Oz the Terrible?"

"Of course," answered the girl, "if he will see me."

"Oh, he will see you," said the soldier who had taken her message to the Wizard, "although he does not like to have people ask to see him. Indeed, at first he was angry and said I should send you back where you came from. Then he asked me what you looked like, and when I mentioned your silver shoes he was very much interested. At last I told him about the mark upon your forehead, and he decided he would admit you to his presence."

Just then a bell rang, and the green girl said to Dorothy, "That is the signal. You must go into the Throne Room alone."

She opened a little door and Dorothy walked boldly through and found herself in a wonderful place. It was a big, round room with a high arched roof, and the walls and ceiling and floor were covered with large emeralds set closely together. In the center of the roof was a great light, as bright as the sun, which made the emeralds sparkle in a wonderful manner.

But what interested Dorothy most was the big throne of green marble that stood in the middle of the room. It was shaped like a chair and sparkled with gems, as did everything else. In the center of the chair was an enormous Head, without a body to support it or any arms or legs whatever. There was no hair upon this head, but it had eyes and nose and mouth, and was much bigger than the head of the biggest giant.

As Dorothy gazed upon this in wonder and fear, the eyes turned slowly and looked at her sharply and steadily. Then the mouth moved, and Dorothy heard a voice.

"I am Oz, the Great and Terrible. Who are you, and why do you seek me?"

It was not such an awful voice as she had expected to come from the big Head. So she took courage and answered, "I am Dorothy, the Small and Meek. I have come to you for help."

The eyes looked at her thoughtfully for a full minute. Then said the voice, "Where did you get the silver shoes?"

"I got them from the Wicked Witch of the East, when my house fell on her and killed her," she replied.

"Where did you get the mark upon your forehead?" continued the voice.

"That is where the Good Witch of the North kissed me when she bade me good-bye and sent me to you," said the girl.

Again the eyes looked at her sharply, and they saw she was telling the truth. Then Oz asked, "What do you wish me to do?"

"Send me back to Kansas, where my Aunt Em and Uncle Henry are," she answered earnestly. "I don't like your country, although it is so beautiful. And I am sure Aunt Em will be dreadfully worried over my being away so long."

The eyes winked three times, and then they turned up to the ceiling and down to the floor and rolled around so queerly that they seemed to see every part of the room. And at last they looked at Dorothy again.

"Why should I do this for you?" asked Oz.

"Because you are strong and I am weak. Because you are a Great Wizard and I am only a little girl."

"But you were strong enough to kill the Wicked Witch of the East," said Oz.

"That just happened," returned Dorothy simply. "I could not help it."

"Well," said the Head, "I will give you my answer. You have no right to expect me to send you back to Kansas unless you do something for me in return. In this country everyone must pay for everything he gets. If you wish me to use my magic power to send you home again you must do something for me first. Help me and I will help you."

"What must I do?" asked the girl.

"Kill the Wicked Witch of the West," answered Oz.

"But I cannot!" exclaimed Dorothy, greatly surprised.

"You killed the Witch of the East and you wear the silver shoes, which bear a powerful charm. There is now but one Wicked Witch left in all this land, and when you can tell me she is dead I will send you back to Kansas—but not before."

The little girl began to weep, she was so much disappointed. And the eyes winked again and looked upon her anxiously, as if the Great Oz felt that she could help him if she would.

"I never killed anything, willingly," she sobbed. "Even if I wanted to, how could I kill the Wicked Witch? If you, who are Great and Terrible, cannot kill her yourself, how do you expect me to do it?"

"I do not know," said the Head. "However, that is my answer, and until the Wicked Witch dies you will not see your uncle and aunt again. Remember that the Witch is Wicked—tremendously Wicked—and ought to be killed. Now go, and do not ask to see me again until you have done your task."

Sorrowfully Dorothy left the Throne Room and went back where the Lion and the Scarecrow and the Tin Woodman were waiting to hear what Oz had said to her.

"There is no hope for me," she said sadly, "for Oz will not send me home until I have killed the Wicked Witch of the West—and that I can never do."

Her friends were sorry, but could do nothing to help her. So Dorothy went to her own room and lay down on the bed and cried herself to sleep.

The next morning the soldier with the green whiskers came to the Scarecrow and said, "Come with me, for Oz has sent for you."

So the Scarecrow followed him and was admitted into

the great Throne Room, where he saw, sitting in the emerald throne, a most lovely Lady. She was dressed in green silk gauze and wore upon her flowing green locks a crown of jewels. Growing from her shoulders were wings, gorgeous in color and so light that they fluttered if the slightest breath of air reached them.

When the Scarecrow had bowed, as prettily as his straw stuffing would let him, before this beautiful creature, she looked upon him sweetly.

"I am Oz, the Great and Terrible. Who are you, and why do you seek me?"

Now the Scarecrow, who had expected to see the great Head Dorothy had told him of, was much astonished; but he answered her bravely.

"I am only a Scarecrow, stuffed with straw. Therefore I have no brains, and I come to you praying that you will put brains in my head instead of straw, so that I may become as much a man as any other in your dominions."

"Why should I do this for you?" asked the Lady.

"Because you are wise and powerful, and no one else can help me," answered the Scarecrow.

"I never grant favors without some return," said Oz, "but this much I will promise. If you will kill for me the Wicked Witch of the West, I will bestow upon you a great many brains, and such good brains that you will be the wisest man in all the Land of Oz."

"I thought you asked Dorothy to kill the Witch," said the Scarecrow, in surprise.

"So I did. I don't care who kills her. But until she is dead I will not grant your wish. Now go, and do not seek me again until you have earned the brains you so greatly desire."

The Scarecrow went sorrowfully back to his friends and told them what Oz had said; and Dorothy was surprised to find that the Great Wizard was not a Head, as she had seen him, but a lovely Lady.

"All the same," said the Scarecrow, "she needs a heart as much as the Tin Woodman."

On the next morning the soldier with the green whiskers came to the Tin Woodman and said, "Oz has sent for you. Follow me."

So the Tin Woodman followed him and came to the great Throne Room. He did not know whether he would find Oz a lovely Lady or a Head, but he hoped it would be the lovely Lady. "For," he said to himself, "if it is the Head, I am sure I shall not be given a heart, since a head has no heart of its own and therefore cannot feel for me. But if it is the lovely Lady I shall beg hard for a heart, for all ladies are themselves said to be kindly hearted."

But when the Woodman entered the great Throne

Room he saw neither the Head nor the Lady, for Oz had taken the shape of a most terrible Beast. It was nearly as big as an elephant, and the green throne seemed hardly strong enough to hold its weight. The Beast had a head like that of a rhinoceros, only there were five eyes in its face. There were five long arms growing out of its body, and it also had five long, slim legs. Thick, woolly hair covered every part of it, and a more dreadful-looking monster could not be imagined. It was fortunate the Tin Woodman had no heart at that moment, for it would have beat loud and fast from terror. But being only tin, the Woodman was not at all afraid.

"I am Oz, the Great and Terrible," spoke the Beast, in a voice that was one great roar. "Who are you, and why do you seek me?"

"I am a Woodman, and made of tin. Therefore I have no heart, and cannot love. I pray you to give me a heart that I may be as other men are."

"Why should I do this?" demanded the Beast.

"Because I ask it, and you alone can grant my request," answered the Woodman.

Oz gave a low growl at this, but said gruffly, "If you indeed desire a heart, you must earn it."

"How?" asked the Woodman.

"Help Dorothy to kill the Wicked Witch of the

West," replied the Beast. "When the Witch is dead, come to me, and I will then give you the biggest and kindest and most loving heart in all the Land of Oz."

So the Tin Woodman was forced to return sorrowfully to his friends and tell them of the terrible Beast he had seen. They all wondered greatly at the many forms the Great Wizard could take upon himself.

"If he is a Beast when I go to see him," said the Lion, "I shall roar my loudest, and so frighten him that he will grant all I ask. And if he is the lovely Lady, I shall pretend to spring upon her, and so compel her to do my bidding. And if he is the great Head, he will be at my mercy; for I will roll this head all about the room until he promises to give us what we desire. So be of good cheer, my friends, for all will yet be well."

The next morning the soldier with the green whiskers led the Lion to the great Throne Room and bade him enter the presence of Oz.

The Lion at once passed through the door, and glancing around saw, to his surprise, that before the throne was a Ball of Fire, so fierce and glowing he could scarcely bear to gaze upon it. His first thought was that Oz had by accident caught on fire and was burning up. Yet, when he tried to go nearer, the heat was so intense that it singed his whiskers, and he crept back tremblingly to a spot nearer the door.

Then a low, quiet voice came from the Ball of Fire, and these were the words it spoke:

"I am Oz, the Great and Terrible. Who are you, and why do you seek me?"

And the Lion answered, "I am a Cowardly Lion, afraid of everything. I came to you to beg that you give me courage, so that in reality I may become the King of Beasts, as men call me."

"Why should I give you courage?" demanded Oz.

"Because of all Wizards you are the greatest, and alone have power to grant my request," answered the Lion.

The Ball of Fire burned fiercely for a time, and the voice said, "Bring me proof that the Wicked Witch is dead, and that moment I will give you courage. But as long as the Witch lives, you must remain a coward."

The Lion was angry at this speech, but could say nothing in reply, and while he stood silently gazing at the Ball of Fire it became so furiously hot that he turned tail and rushed from the room. He was glad to find his friends waiting for him, and told them of his terrible interview with the Wizard.

"What shall we do now?" asked Dorothy sadly.

"There is only one thing we can do," returned the Lion, "and that is to go to the land of the Winkies, seek out the Wicked Witch, and destroy her."

"But suppose we cannot?" said the girl.

"Then I shall never have courage," declared the Lion.

"And I shall never have brains," added the Scarecrow.

"And I shall never have a heart," spoke the Tin of Woodman.

"And I shall never see Aunt Em and Uncle Henry," said Dorothy, beginning to cry.

"Be careful!" cried the green girl. "The tears will fall on your green silk gown and spot it."

So Dorothy dried her eyes and said, "I suppose we must try it; but I am sure I do not want to kill anybody, even to see Aunt Em again."

"I will go with you; but I'm too much of a coward to kill the Witch," said the Lion.

"I will go too," declared the Scarecrow; "but I shall not be of much help to you, I am such a fool."

"I haven't the heart to harm even a Witch," remarked the Tin Woodman; "but if you go I certainly shall go with you."

Therefore it was decided to start upon their journey the next morning, and the Woodman sharpened his axe on a green grindstone and had all his joints properly oiled. The Scarecrow stuffed himself with fresh straw and Dorothy put new paint on his eyes that he might see better. The green girl, who was very kind to them, filled Dorothy's basket with good things to eat, and fastened a little bell around Toto's neck with a green ribbon.

They went to bed quite early and slept soundly until daylight, when they were awakened by the crowing of a green cock that lived in the yard of the Palace, and the cackling of a hen that had laid a green egg.

Chapter Twelve

THE SEARCH FOR THE
WICKED WITCH

---➤➤◄---

*T*HE soldier with the green whiskers led them
through the streets of the Emerald City until
they reached the room where the Guardian of the Gates
lived. This officer unlocked their spectacles to put them
back in his great box, and then he politely opened the
gate for our friends.

"Which road leads to the Wicked Witch of the
West?" asked Dorothy.

"There is no road," answered the Guardian of the
Gates. "No one ever wishes to go that way."

"How, then, are we to find her?" inquired the girl.

"That will be easy," replied the man, "for when she
knows you are in the country of the Winkies she will
find you, and make you all her slaves."

"Perhaps not," said the Scarecrow, "for we mean to
destroy her."

"Oh, that is different," said the Guardian of the Gates.
"No one has ever destroyed her before, so I naturally

thought she would make slaves of you, as she has of the rest. But take care. She is wicked and fierce, and may not allow you to destroy her. Keep to the West, where the sun sets, and you cannot fail to find her."

They thanked him and bade him good-bye, and turned toward the West, walking over fields of soft grass dotted here and there with daisies and butter-cups. Dorothy still wore the pretty silk dress she had put on in the Palace, but now, to her surprise, she found it was no longer green, but pure white. The ribbon around Toto's neck had also lost its green color and was as white as Dorothy's dress.

The Emerald City was soon left far behind. As they advanced the ground became rougher and hillier, for there were no farms nor houses in this country of the West, and the ground was untilled.

In the afternoon the sun shone hot in their faces, for there were no trees to offer them shade; so that before night Dorothy and Toto and the Lion were tired, and lay down upon the grass and fell asleep, with the Woodman and the Scarecrow keeping watch.

Now the Wicked Witch of the West had but one eye, yet that was as powerful as a telescope, and could see everywhere. So, as she sat in the door of her castle, she happened to look around and saw Dorothy lying asleep, with her friends all about her. They were a long distance off, but the Wicked Witch was angry to find them in her country. So she blew upon a silver whistle that hung around her neck.

At once there came running to her from all directions a pack of great wolves. They had long legs and fierce eyes and sharp teeth.

"Go to those people," said the Witch, "and tear them to pieces."

"Are you not going to make them your slaves?" asked the leader of the wolves.

"No," she answered. "One is of tin, and one of straw; one is a girl and another a Lion. None of them is fit to work, so you may tear them into small pieces."

"Very well," said the wolf, and he dashed away at full speed, followed by the others.

It was lucky the Scarecrow and the Woodman were wide awake and heard the wolves coming.

"This is my fight," said the Woodman, "so get behind me and I will meet them as they come."

He seized his axe, which he had made very sharp, and as the leader of the wolves came on the Tin Woodman swung his arm and chopped the wolf's head from its body, so that it immediately died. As soon as he could raise his axe another wolf came up, and he also fell under the sharp edge of the Tin Woodman's weapon. There were forty wolves, and forty times a wolf was

killed, so that at last they all lay dead in a heap before
the Woodman.

Then he put down his axe and sat beside the
Scarecrow, who said, "It was a good fight, friend."

They waited until Dorothy awoke the next morning.
The little girl was quite frightened when she saw the
great pile of shaggy wolves, but the Tin Woodman told
her all. She thanked him for saving them and sat down
to breakfast, after which they started again upon their
journey.

Now this same morning the Wicked Witch came to
the door of her castle and looked out with her one eye
that could see far off. She saw all her wolves lying dead,
and the strangers still traveling through her country.
This made her angrier than before, and she blew her silver whistle twice.

Straightway a great flock of wild crows came flying
toward her, enough to darken the sky.

And the Wicked Witch said to the King Crow, "Fly
at once to the strangers. Peck out their eyes and tear
them to pieces."

The wild crows flew in one great flock toward
Dorothy and her companions. When the little girl saw
them coming she was afraid.

But the Scarecrow said, "This is my battle. Lie down
beside me and you will not be harmed."

So they all lay upon the ground except the Scarecrow, and he stood up and stretched out his arms. And when the crows saw him they were frightened—as these birds always are by scarecrows—and did not dare to come any nearer.

But the King Crow said, "It is only a stuffed man. I will peck his eyes out."

The King Crow flew at the Scarecrow, who caught it by the head and twisted its neck until it died. And then another crow flew at him, and the Scarecrow twisted its neck also. There were forty crows, and forty times the Scarecrow twisted a neck, until at last all were lying dead beside him. Then he called to his companions to rise, and again they went upon their journey.

When the Wicked Witch looked out again and saw all her crows lying in a heap, she got into a terrible rage, and blew three times upon her silver whistle.

Forthwith there was heard a great buzzing in the air, and a swarm of black bees came flying toward her.

"Go to the strangers and sting them to death!" commanded the Witch, and the bees turned and flew rapidly until they came to where Dorothy and her friends were walking. But the Woodman had seen them coming, and the Scarecrow had decided what to do.

"Take out my straw and scatter it over the little girl and the dog and the Lion," he said to the Woodman, "and the bees cannot sting them." This the Woodman did, and as Dorothy lay close beside the Lion and held Toto in her arms, the straw covered them entirely.

The bees came and found no one but the Woodman to sting, so they flew at him and broke off all their stings against the tin, without hurting the Woodman at all. And as bees cannot live when their stings are broken that was the end of the black bees, and they lay scattered thick about the Woodman, like little heaps of fine coal.

Then Dorothy and the Lion got up, and the girl helped the Tin Woodman put the straw back into the Scarecrow again, until he was as good as ever. So they started upon their journey once more.

The Wicked Witch was so angry when she saw her black bees in little heaps like fine coal that she stamped her foot and tore her hair and gnashed her teeth. And then she called a dozen of her slaves, who were the Winkies, and gave them sharp spears, telling them to go to the strangers and destroy them.

The Winkies were not a brave people, but they had to do as they were told. So they marched away until they came near to Dorothy. Then the Lion gave a great roar and sprang toward them, and the poor Winkies were so frightened that they ran back as fast as they could.

When they returned to the castle the Wicked Witch

beat them well with a strap, and sent them back to their work, after which she sat down to think what she should do next. She could not understand how all her plans to destroy these strangers had failed. However, she was a powerful Witch, as well as a wicked one, and she soon made up her mind how to act.

There was, in her cupboard, a Golden Cap, with a circle of diamonds and rubies running round it. This Golden Cap had a charm. Whoever owned it could call three times upon the Winged Monkeys, who would obey any order they were given. But no person could command these strange creatures more than three times. Twice already the Wicked Witch had used the charm of the Cap. Once was when she had made the Winkies her slaves, and set herself to rule over their country. The Winged Monkeys had helped her do this. The second time was when she had fought against the Great Oz himself, and driven him out of the land of the West. The Winged Monkeys had also helped her in doing this. Only once more could she use this Golden Cap, for which reason she did not like to do so until all her other powers were exhausted. But now that her fierce wolves and her wild crows and her stinging bees were gone, and her slaves had been scared away by the Cowardly Lion, she saw there was only one way left to destroy Dorothy and her friends.

So the Wicked Witch took the Golden Cap from her cupboard and placed it upon her head. Then she stood upon her left foot and said slowly:

"Ep-pe, pep-pe, kak-ke!"

Next she stood upon her right foot and said:

"Hil-lo, hol-lo, hel-lo!"

After this she stood upon both feet and cried in a loud voice:

"Ziz-zy, zuz-zy, zik!"

Now the charm began to work. The sky was darkened, and a low rumbling sound was heard in the air. There was a rushing of many wings, a great chattering and laughing, and the sun came out of the dark sky to show the Wicked Witch surrounded by a crowd of monkeys, each with a pair of immense and powerful wings on his shoulders.

One, much bigger than the others, seemed to be their leader. He flew close to the Witch and said, "You have called us for the third and last time. What do you command?"

"Go to the strangers who are within my land and destroy them all except the Lion," said the Wicked Witch. "Bring that beast to me, for I have a mind to harness him like a horse and make him work."

"Your commands shall be obeyed," said the leader. Then, with a great deal of chattering and noise, the

Winged Monkeys flew away to the place where Dorothy and her friends were walking.

Some of the Monkeys seized the Tin Woodman and carried him through the air until they were over a country thickly covered with sharp rocks. Here they dropped the poor Woodman, who fell a great distance to the rocks, where he lay so battered and dented that he could neither move nor groan.

Others of the Monkeys caught the Scarecrow, and with their long fingers pulled all of the straw out of his clothes and head. They made his hat and boots and clothes into a small bundle and threw it into the top branches of a tall tree.

The remaining Monkeys threw pieces of stout rope around the Lion and wound many coils about his body and head and legs, until he was unable to bite or scratch or struggle in any way. Then they lifted him up and flew away with him to the Witch's castle, where he was placed in a small yard with a high iron fence around it so that he could not escape.

But Dorothy they did not harm at all. She stood, with Toto in her arms, watching the sad fate of her comrades and thinking it would soon be her turn. The leader of the Winged Monkeys flew up to her, his long, hairy arms stretched out and his ugly face grinning terribly; but he saw the mark of the Good Witch's kiss upon her forehead and stopped short, motioning the others not to touch her.

"We dare not harm this little girl," he said to them, "for she is protected by the Power of Good, and that is greater than the Power of Evil. All we can do is to carry her to the castle of the Wicked Witch and leave her there."

So, carefully and gently, they lifted Dorothy in their arms and carried her swiftly through the air until they came to the castle, where they set her down upon the front doorstep.

Then the leader said to the Witch, "We have obeyed you as far as we were able. The Tin Woodman and the Scarecrow are destroyed, and the Lion is tied up in your yard. The little girl we dare not harm, nor the dog she carries in her arms. Your power over our band is now ended, and you will never see us again."

Then all the Winged Monkeys, with much laughing and chattering and noise, flew into the air and were soon out of sight.

The Wicked Witch was both surprised and worried when she saw the mark on Dorothy's forehead, for she knew well that neither the Winged Monkeys nor she, herself, dare hurt the girl in any way. She looked down at Dorothy's feet, and seeing the Silver Shoes, began to tremble with fear, for she knew what a powerful charm belonged to them. At first the Witch was tempted to run away from Dorothy. But she happened to look into the child's eyes and saw how simple the soul behind them was, and that the little girl did not know of the wonderful power the Silver Shoes gave her. So the Wicked Witch laughed to herself, and thought, "I can still make her my slave, for she does not know how to use her power."

Then she said to Dorothy, harshly and severely, "Come with me, and see that you mind everything I tell you. If you do not I will make an end of you, as I did of the Tin Woodman and the Scarecrow."

Dorothy followed her through many of the beautiful rooms in her castle until they came to the kitchen, where the Witch bade her clean the pots and kettles and sweep the floor and keep the fire fed with wood.

Dorothy went to work meekly, with her mind made up to work as hard as she could; for she was glad the Wicked Witch had decided not to kill her.

With Dorothy hard at work, the Witch thought she would go into the courtyard and harness the Cowardly Lion like a horse. It would amuse her, she was sure, to make him draw her chariot whenever she wished to go to drive. But as she opened the gate the Lion gave a loud roar and bounded at her so fiercely that the Witch was afraid, and ran out and shut the gate again.

"If I cannot harness you," said the Witch to the Lion, speaking through the bars of the gate, "I can starve you. You shall have nothing to eat until you do as I wish."

So after that she took no food to the imprisoned Lion. But every day she came to the gate at noon and asked, "Are you ready to be harnessed like a horse?"

And the Lion would answer, "No. If you come in this yard, I will bite you."

The reason the Lion did not have to do as the Witch wished was that every night, while the woman was asleep, Dorothy carried him food from the cupboard. After he had eaten he would lie down on his bed of straw, and Dorothy would lie beside him and put her head on his soft, shaggy mane, while they talked of their troubles and tried to plan some way to escape. But they could find no way to get out of the castle, for it was constantly guarded by the yellow Winkies, who were the slaves of the Wicked Witch and too afraid of her not to do as she told them.

The girl had to work hard during the day, and often the Witch threatened to beat her with the same old umbrella she always carried in her hand. But, in truth, she did not dare to strike Dorothy, because of the mark upon her forehead. The child did not know this, and was full of fear for herself and Toto. Once the Witch struck

Toto a blow with her umbrella and the brave little dog flew at her and bit her leg in return. The Witch did not bleed where she was bitten, for she was so wicked that the blood in her had dried up many years before.

Dorothy's life became very sad as she grew to understand that it would be harder than ever to get back to Kansas and Aunt Em again. Sometimes she would cry bitterly for hours, with Toto sitting at her feet and looking into her face, whining dismally to show how sorry he was for his little mistress. Toto did not really care whether he was in Kansas or the Land of Oz so long as Dorothy was with him; but he knew the little girl was unhappy, and that made him unhappy too.

Now the Wicked Witch had a great longing to have for her own the Silver Shoes which the girl always wore. Her bees and her crows and her wolves were lying in heaps and drying up, and she had used up all the power of the Golden Cap. But if she could only get hold of the Silver Shoes, they would give her more power than all the other things she had lost. She watched Dorothy carefully, to see if she ever took off her shoes, thinking she might steal them. But the child was so proud of her pretty shoes that she never took them off except at night and when she took her bath. The Witch was too much afraid of the dark to dare go in Dorothy's room at night to take the shoes, and her dread of water was greater than her fear of the dark, so she never came near when Dorothy was bathing. Indeed, the old Witch never touched water, nor ever let water touch her in any way.

But the wicked creature was very cunning, and she finally thought of a trick that would give her what she wanted. She placed a bar of iron in the middle of the kitchen floor, and then by her magic arts made the iron invisible to human eyes. So that when Dorothy walked across the floor she stumbled over the bar, not being able to see it, and fell at full length. She was not much hurt, but in her fall one of the Silver Shoes came off. Then before she could reach it, the Witch had snatched it away and put it on her own skinny foot.

The wicked woman was greatly pleased with the success of her trick, for as long as she had one of the shoes she owned half the power of their charm, and Dorothy could not use it against her, even had she known how to do so.

The little girl, seeing she had lost one of her pretty shoes, grew angry, and said to the Witch, "Give me back my shoe!"

"I will not," retorted the Witch, "for it is now my shoe, and not yours."

"You are a wicked creature!" cried Dorothy. "You have no right to take my shoe from me."

"I shall keep it, just the same," said the Witch, laughing at her, "and someday I shall get the other one from you, too."

This made Dorothy so very angry that she picked up the bucket of water that stood near and dashed it over the Witch, wetting her from head to foot.

Instantly the wicked woman gave a loud cry of fear, and then, as Dorothy looked at her in wonder, the Witch began to shrink and fall away.

"See what you have done!" she screamed. "In a minute I shall melt away."

"I'm very sorry, indeed," said Dorothy, who was truly frightened to see the Witch actually melting away like brown sugar before her very eyes.

"Didn't you know water would be the end of me?" asked the Witch, in a wailing, despairing voice.

"Of course not," answered Dorothy. "How should I?"

"Well, in a few minutes I shall be all melted, and you will have the castle to yourself. I have been wicked in my day, but I never thought a little girl like you would ever be able to melt me and end my wicked deeds. Look out—here I go!"

With these words the Witch fell down in a brown, melted, shapeless mass and began to spread over the clean boards of the kitchen floor. Seeing that she had really melted away to nothing, Dorothy drew another bucket of water and threw it over the mess. She then swept it all out the door. After picking out the silver shoe, which was all that was left of the old woman, she cleaned and dried it with a cloth, and put it on her foot again. Then, being at last free to do as she chose, she ran out to the courtyard to tell the Lion that the Wicked Witch of the West had come to an end, and that they were no longer prisoners in a strange land.

Chapter Thirteen

THE RESCUE

◆───

*T*HE Cowardly Lion was much pleased to hear that the Wicked Witch had been melted by a bucket of water, and Dorothy at once unlocked the gate of his prison and set him free. They went in together to the castle, where Dorothy's first act was to call all the Winkies together and tell them that they were no longer slaves.

There was great rejoicing among the yellow Winkies, for they had been made to work hard during many years for the Wicked Witch, who had always treated them with great cruelty. They kept this day as a holiday, then and ever after, and spent the time in feasting and dancing.

"If our friends, the Scarecrow and the Tin Woodman, were only with us," said the Lion, "I should be quite happy."

"Don't you suppose we could rescue them?" asked the girl anxiously.

"We can try," answered the Lion.

So they called the yellow Winkies and asked them if they would help to rescue their friends, and the Winkies said that they would be delighted to do all in their power for Dorothy, who had set them free from bondage. So she chose a number of the Winkies who looked as if they knew the most, and they all started away. They traveled that day and part of the next until they came to the rocky plain where the Tin Woodman lay, all battered and bent. His axe was near him, but the blade was rusted and the handle broken off short.

The Winkies lifted him tenderly in their arms, and carried him back to the Yellow Castle again, Dorothy shedding a few tears by the way at the sad plight of her old friend, and the Lion looking sober and sorry.

When they reached the castle Dorothy said to the Winkies, "Are any of your people tinsmiths?"

"Oh, yes. Some of us are very good tinsmiths," they told her.

"Then bring them to me," she said. And when the tinsmiths came, bringing with them all their tools in baskets, she inquired, "Can you straighten out those dents in the Tin Woodman, and bend him back into shape again, and solder him together where he is broken?"

The tinsmiths looked the Woodman over carefully and then answered that they thought they could mend him so he would be as good as ever. So they set to work in one of the big yellow rooms of the castle and worked for three days and four nights, hammering and twisting and bending and soldering and polishing and pounding at the legs and body and head of the Tin Woodman, until at last he was straightened out into his old form, and his joints worked as well as ever. To be sure, there were several patches on him, but the tinsmiths did a good job, and as the Woodman was not a vain man he did not mind the patches at all.

When at last he walked into Dorothy's room and thanked her for rescuing him, he was so pleased that he wept tears of joy, and Dorothy had to wipe every tear carefully from his face with her apron, so his joints would not be rusted. At the same time her own tears fell thick and fast at the joy of meeting her old friend again, and these tears did not need to be wiped away. As for the Lion, he wiped his eyes so often with the tip of his tail that it became quite wet, and he was obliged to go out into the courtyard and hold it in the sun till it dried.

"If we only had the Scarecrow with us again," said the Tin Woodman, when Dorothy had finished telling him everything that had happened, "I should be quite happy."

"We must try to find him," said the girl.

So she called the Winkies to help her, and they

walked all that day and part of the next until they came to the tall tree in the branches of which the Winged Monkeys had tossed the Scarecrow's clothes.

It was a very tall tree, and the trunk was so smooth that no one could climb it; but the Woodman said at once, "I'll chop it down, and then we can get the Scarecrow's clothes."

Now while the tinsmiths had been at work mending the Woodman himself, another of the Winkies, who was a goldsmith, had made an axe-handle of solid gold and fitted it to the Woodman's axe, instead of the old broken handle. Others polished the blade until all the rust was removed and it glistened like burnished silver.

As soon as he had spoken, the Tin Woodman began to chop, and in a short time the tree fell over with a crash, whereupon the Scarecrow's clothes fell out of the branches and rolled off on the ground.

Dorothy picked them up and had the Winkies carry them back to the castle, where they were stuffed with nice, clean straw—and behold! here was the Scarecrow, as good as ever, thanking them over and over again for saving him.

Now that they were reunited, Dorothy and her friends spent a few happy days at the Yellow Castle, where they found everything they needed to make them comfortable.

But one day the girl thought of Aunt Em, and said, "We must go back to Oz, and claim his promise."

"Yes," said the Woodman, "at last I shall get my heart."

"And I shall get my brains," added the Scarecrow joyfully.

"And I shall get my courage," said the Lion thoughtfully.

"And I shall get back to Kansas," cried Dorothy, clapping her hands. "Oh, let us start for the Emerald City tomorrow!"

This they decided to do. The next day they called the Winkies together and bade them good-bye. The Winkies were sorry to have them go, and they had grown so fond of the Tin Woodman that they begged him to stay and rule over them and the Yellow Land of the West. Finding they were determined to go, the Winkies gave Toto and the Lion each a golden collar. To Dorothy they presented a beautiful bracelet studded with diamonds. To the Scarecrow they gave a gold-headed walking stick, to keep him from stumbling. And to the Tin Woodman they offered a silver oilcan, inlaid with gold and set with precious jewels.

Every one of the travelers made the Winkies a pretty speech in return, and all shook hands with them until their arms ached.

Dorothy went to the Witch's cupboard to fill her basket with food for the journey, and there she saw the Golden Cap. She tried it on her own head and found that it fitted her exactly. She did not know anything about the charm of the Golden Cap, but she saw that it was pretty. So she made up her mind to wear it and carry her sunbonnet in the basket.

Then, being prepared for the journey, they all started for the Emerald City. And the Winkies gave them three cheers and many good wishes to carry with them.

Chapter Fourteen

THE WINGED MONKEYS

*Y*OU will remember there was no road—not even a pathway—between the castle of the Wicked Witch and the Emerald City. When the four travelers went in search of the Witch she had seen them coming, and so sent the Winged Monkeys to bring them to her. It was much harder to find their way back through the big fields of buttercups and bright daisies than it was being carried. They knew, of course, they must go straight east, toward the rising sun, and they started off in the right way. But at noon, when the sun was over their heads, they did not know which was east and which was west, and that was the reason they were lost in the great fields. They kept on walking, however, and at night the moon came out and shone brightly. So they lay down among the sweet-smelling yellow flowers and slept soundly until morning—all but the Scarecrow and the Tin Woodman.

The next morning the sun was behind a cloud, but

they started on, as if they were quite sure which way they were going.

"If we walk far enough," said Dorothy, "I am sure we shall sometime come to someplace."

But day by day passed away, and they still saw nothing before them but the scarlet fields. The Scarecrow began to grumble a bit.

"We have surely lost our way," he said, "and unless we find it again in time to reach the Emerald City, I shall never get my brains."

"Nor I my heart," declared the Tin Woodman. "It seems to me I can scarcely wait till I get to Oz, and you must admit this is a very long journey."

"You see," said the Cowardly Lion, with a whimper, "I haven't the courage to keep tramping forever, without getting anywhere at all."

Then Dorothy lost heart. She sat down on the grass and looked at her companions, and they sat down and looked at her, and Toto found that for the first time in his life he was too tired to chase a butterfly that flew past his head. So he put out his tongue and panted and looked at Dorothy as if to ask what they should do next.

"Suppose we call the field mice," she suggested. "They could probably tell us the way to the Emerald City."

"To be sure they could," cried the Scarecrow. "Why didn't we think of that before?"

Dorothy blew the little whistle she had always carried about her neck since the Queen of the Mice had given it to her. In a few minutes they heard the pattering of tiny feet, and many of the small gray mice came running up to her.

Among them was the Queen herself, who asked, in her squeaky little voice, "What can I do for my friends?"

"We have lost our way," said Dorothy. "Can you tell us where the Emerald City is?"

"Certainly," answered the Queen; "but it is a great way off, for you have had it at your backs all this time." Then she noticed Dorothy's Golden Cap, and said, "Why don't you use the charm of the Cap, and call the Winged Monkeys to you? They will carry you to the City of Oz in less than an hour."

"I didn't know there was a charm," answered Dorothy, in surprise. "What is it?"

"It is written inside the Golden Cap," replied the Queen of the Mice. "But if you are going to call the Winged Monkeys we must run away, for they are full of mischief and think it great fun to plague us."

"Won't they hurt me?" asked the girl anxiously.

"Oh, no. They must obey the wearer of the Cap.

Good-bye!" And she scampered out of sight, with all the mice hurrying after her.

Dorothy looked inside the Golden Cap and saw some words written upon the lining. These, she thought, must be the charm, so she read the directions carefully and put the Cap upon her head.

"Ep-pe, pep-pe, kak-ke!" she said, standing on her left foot.

"What did you say?" asked the Scarecrow, who did not know what she was doing.

"Hil-lo, hol-lo, hel-lo!" Dorothy went on, standing this time on her right foot.

"Hello!" replied the Tin Woodman calmly.

"Ziz-zy, zuz-zy, zik!" said Dorothy, who was now standing on both feet. This ended the saying of the charm, and they heard a great chattering and flapping of wings, as the band of Winged Monkeys flew up to them.

The King bowed low before Dorothy, and asked, "What is your command?"

"We wish to go to the Emerald City," said the child, "and we have lost our way."

"We will carry you," replied the King, and no sooner had he spoken than two of the Monkeys caught Dorothy in their arms and flew away with her. Others took the Scarecrow and the Woodman and the Lion, and one little Monkey seized Toto and flew after them, although the dog tried hard to bite him.

The Scarecrow and the Tin Woodman were rather frightened at first, for they remembered how badly the Winged Monkeys had treated them before. But they saw that no harm was intended, so they rode through the air quite cheerfully, and had a fine time looking at the pretty gardens and woods far below them.

Dorothy found herself riding easily between two of the biggest Monkeys, one of them the King himself. They had made a chair of their hands and were careful not to hurt her.

"Why do you have to obey the charm of the Golden Cap?" she asked.

"That is a long story," answered the King, with a Winged laugh. "But as we have a long journey before us, I will pass the time by telling you about it, if you wish."

"I shall be glad to hear it," she replied.

"Once," began the leader, "we were a free people, living happily in the great forest, flying from tree to tree, eating nuts and fruit, and doing just as we pleased without calling anybody master. Perhaps some of us were rather too full of mischief at times, flying down to pull the tails of the animals that had no wings, chasing birds, and throwing nuts at the people who walked in the forest. But we were careless and happy and full of fun, and enjoyed every minute of the day. This was many years ago, long before Oz came out of the clouds to rule over this land.

"There lived here then, away at the North, a beautiful princess, who was also a powerful sorceress. All her magic was used to help the people, and she was never known to hurt anyone who was good. Her name was Gayelette, and she lived in a handsome palace built from great blocks of ruby. Everyone loved her, but her greatest sorrow was that she could find no one to love in return, since all the men were much too stupid and ugly to marry one so beautiful and wise. At last, however, she found a boy who was handsome and manly and wise beyond his years. Gayelette made up her mind that when he grew to be a man she would make him her husband. So she took him to her ruby palace and used all her magic powers to make him as strong and good and lovely as any woman could wish. When he grew to manhood, Quelala, as he was called, was said to be the best and wisest man in all the land, while his manly beauty was so great that Gayelette loved him dearly, and hastened to make everything ready for the wedding.

"My grandfather was at that time the King of the Winged Monkeys which lived in the forest near Gayelette's palace, and the old fellow loved a joke better than a good dinner. One day, just before the wedding, my grandfather was flying out with his band when he saw Quelala walking beside the river. He was dressed in a rich costume of pink silk and purple velvet, and my grandfather thought he would see what he could do. At his word the band flew down and seized Quelala, carried him in their arms until they were over the middle of the river, and then dropped him into the water.

"'Swim out, my fine fellow,' cried my grandfather, 'and see if the water has spotted your clothes.' Quelala was much too wise not to swim, and he was not in the least spoiled by all his good fortune. He laughed, when he came to the top of the water, and swam in to shore. But when Gayelette came running out to him she found his silks and velvet all ruined by the river.

"The princess was angry, and she knew, of course, who did it. She had all the Winged Monkeys brought before her, and she said at first that their wings should be tied and they should be treated as they had treated Quelala, and dropped in the river. But my grandfather pleaded hard, for he knew the Monkeys would drown in the river with their wings tied, and Quelala said a kind word for them also. So Gayelette finally spared them, on condition that the Winged Monkeys should ever after do three times the bidding of the owner of the

Golden Cap. This Cap had been made for a wedding present to Quelala, and it is said to have cost the princess
half her kingdom. Of course my grandfather and all the
other Monkeys at once agreed to the condition, and
that is how it happens that we are three times the slaves
of the owner of the Golden Cap, whosoever he may be."

"And what became of them?" asked Dorothy, who
had been greatly interested in the story.

"Quelala being the first owner of the Golden Cap,"
replied the Monkey, "he was the first to lay his wishes
upon us. As his bride could not bear the sight of us, he
called us all to him in the forest after he had married her
and ordered us always to keep where she could never
again set eyes on a Winged Monkey, which we were glad
to do, for we were all afraid of her.

"This was all we ever had to do until the Golden Cap
fell into the hands of the Wicked Witch of the West,
who made us enslave the Winkies, and afterward drive
Oz himself out of the Land of the West. Now the
Golden Cap is yours, and three times you have the right
to lay your wishes upon us."

As the Monkey King finished his story Dorothy
looked down and saw the green, shining walls of the
Emerald City before them. She wondered at the rapid
flight of the Monkeys, but was glad the journey was
over. The strange creatures set the travelers down care-

fully before the gate of the City, the King bowed low to Dorothy, and then flew swiftly away, followed by all his band.

"That was a good ride," said the little girl.

"Yes, and a quick way out of our troubles," replied the Lion. "How lucky it was you brought away that wonderful Cap!"

Chapter Fifteen

THE DISCOVERY OF OZ THE TERRIBLE

———❦———

THE four travelers walked up to the great gate of Emerald City and rang the bell. After ringing several times, it was opened by the same Guardian of the Gates they had met before.

"What! Are you back again?" he asked, in surprise.

"Do you not see us?" answered the Scarecrow.

"But I thought you had gone to visit the Wicked Witch of the West."

"We did visit her," said the Scarecrow.

"And she let you go again?" asked the man, in wonder.

"She could not help it, for she is melted," explained the Scarecrow.

"Melted! Well, that is good news, indeed," said the man. "Who melted her?"

"It was Dorothy," said the Lion gravely.

"Good gracious!" exclaimed the man, and he bowed very low indeed before her.

Then he led them into his little room and locked the spectacles from the great box on all their eyes, just as he had done before. Afterward they passed on through the gate into the Emerald City. When the people heard from the Guardian of the Gates that Dorothy had melted the Wicked Witch of the West, they all gathered around the travelers and followed them in a great crowd to the Palace of Oz.

The soldier with the green whiskers was still on guard before the door, but he let them in at once. There they were again met by the beautiful green girl, who showed each of them to their old rooms at once, so they might rest until the Great Oz was ready to receive them.

The soldier had the news carried straight to Oz that Dorothy and the other travelers had come back again, after destroying the Wicked Witch. But Oz made no reply. They thought the Great Wizard would send for them at once, but he did not. They had no word from him the next day, nor the next, nor the next. The waiting was tiresome and wearing, and at last they grew vexed that Oz should treat them in so poor a fashion, after sending them to undergo hardships and slavery. So the Scarecrow at last asked the green girl to take another message to Oz, saying if he did not let them in to see him at once they would call the Winged Monkeys to help them, and find out whether he kept his promises or not. When the

Wizard was given this message he was so frightened that he sent word for them to come to the Throne Room at four minutes after nine o'clock the next morning. He had once met the Winged Monkeys in the Land of the West, and he did not wish to meet them again.

The four travelers passed a sleepless night, each thinking of the gift Oz had promised to bestow on him. Dorothy fell asleep only once, and then she dreamed she was in Kansas, where Aunt Em was telling her how glad she was to have her little girl at home again.

Promptly at nine o'clock the next morning the green-whiskered soldier came to them, and four minutes later they all went into the Throne Room of the Great Oz.

Of course, each one of them expected to see the Wizard in the shape he had taken before, and all were greatly surprised when they looked about and saw no one at all in the room. They kept close to the door and closer to one another, for the stillness of the empty room was more dreadful than any of the forms they had seen Oz take.

Presently they heard a solemn Voice, that seemed to come from somewhere near the top of the great dome.

"I am Oz, the Great and Terrible. Why do you seek me?"

They looked again in every part of the room, and then, seeing no one, Dorothy asked, "Where are you?"

"I am everywhere," answered the Voice, "but to the eyes of common mortals I am invisible. I will now seat myself upon my throne, that you may converse with me." Indeed, the Voice seemed just then to come straight from the throne itself. So they walked toward it and stood in a row.

"We have come to claim our promise, O Oz," Dorothy said.

"What promise?" asked Oz.

"You promised to send me back to Kansas when the Wicked Witch was destroyed," said the girl.

"And you promised to give me brains," said the Scarecrow.

"And you promised to give me a heart," said the Tin Woodman.

"And you promised to give me courage," said the Cowardly Lion.

"Is the Wicked Witch really destroyed?" asked the Voice, and Dorothy thought it trembled a little.

"Yes," she answered, "I melted her with a bucket of water."

"Dear me," said the Voice, "how sudden! Well, come to me tomorrow, for I must have time to think it over."

"You've had plenty of time already," said the Tin Woodman angrily.

"We shan't wait a day longer," said the Scarecrow.

"You must keep your promises to us!" exclaimed Dorothy.

The Lion thought it might be as well to frighten the Wizard, so he gave a large, loud roar, which was so fierce and dreadful that Toto jumped away from him in alarm and tipped over the screen that stood in a corner. As it fell with a crash they looked that way, and the next moment all of them were filled with wonder. For they saw, standing in just the spot the screen had hidden, a little old man, with a bald head and a wrinkled face, who seemed to be as much surprised as they were. The Tin Woodman, raising his axe, rushed toward the little man and cried out, "Who are you?"

"I am Oz, the Great and Terrible," said the little man, in a trembling voice. "But don't strike me—please don't—and I'll do anything you want me to."

Our friends looked at him in surprise and dismay.

"I thought Oz was a great Head," said Dorothy.

"And I thought Oz was a lovely Lady," said the Scarecrow.

"And I thought Oz was a terrible Beast," said the Tin Woodman.

"And I thought Oz was a Ball of Fire," exclaimed the Lion.

"No, you are all wrong," said the little man meekly. "I have been making believe."

"Making believe!" cried Dorothy. "Are you not a Great Wizard?"

"Hush, my dear," he said. "Don't speak so loud, or you will be overheard—and I should be ruined. I'm supposed to be a Great Wizard."

"And aren't you?" she asked.

"Not a bit of it, my dear. I'm just a common man."

"You're more than that," said the Scarecrow, in a grieved tone. "You're a humbug."

"Exactly so!" declared the little man, rubbing his hands together as if it pleased him. "I am a humbug."

"But this is terrible," said the Tin Woodman. "How shall I ever get my heart?"

"Or I my courage?" asked the Lion.

"Or I my brains?" wailed the Scarecrow, wiping the tears from his eyes with his coat sleeve.

"My dear friends," said Oz, "I pray you not to speak of these little things. Think of me, and the terrible trouble I'm in at being found out."

"Doesn't anyone else know you're a humbug?" asked Dorothy.

"No one knows it but you four—and myself," replied Oz. "I have fooled everyone so long that I thought I should never be found out. It was a great mistake my ever letting you into the Throne Room. Usually I will not see even my subjects, and so they believe I am something terrible."

"But I don't understand," said Dorothy, in bewilderment. "How was it that you appeared to me as a great Head?"

"That was one of my tricks," answered Oz. "Step this way, please, and I will tell you all about it."

He led the way to a small chamber in the rear of the Throne Room, and they all followed him. He pointed to one corner, in which lay the great Head, made out of many thicknesses of paper, and with a carefully painted face.

"This I hung from the ceiling by a wire," said Oz. "I stood behind the screen and pulled a thread, to make the eyes move and the mouth open."

"But how about the voice?" she inquired.

"Oh, I am a ventriloquist," said the little man. "I can throw the sound of my voice wherever I wish, so that you thought it was coming out of the Head. Here are the other things I used to deceive you." He showed the Scarecrow the dress and the mask he had worn when he seemed to be the lovely Lady. And the Tin Woodman saw that his terrible Beast was nothing but a lot of skins, sewn together, with slats to keep their sides out. As for the Ball of Fire, the false Wizard had hung that also from the ceiling. It was really a ball of cotton, but when oil was poured upon it the ball burned fiercely.

"Really," said the Scarecrow, "you ought to be ashamed of yourself for being such a humbug."

"I am—I certainly am," answered the little man sorrowfully. "But it was the only thing I could do. Sit down, please, there are plenty of chairs. I will tell you my story."

So they sat down and listened while he told the following tale.

"I was born in Omaha—"

"Why, that isn't very far from Kansas!" cried Dorothy.

"No, but it's farther from here," he said, shaking his head at her sadly. "When I grew up I became a ventriloquist, and at that I was very well trained by a great master. I can imitate any kind of a bird or beast." Here he mewed so like a kitten that Toto pricked up his ears and looked everywhere to see where she was. "After a time," continued Oz, "I tired of that, and became a balloonist."

"What is that?" asked Dorothy.

"A man who goes up in a balloon on circus day, so as to draw a crowd of people together and get them to pay to see the circus," he explained.

"Oh," she said, "I know."

"Well, one day I went up in a balloon and the ropes got twisted, so that I couldn't come down again. It went way up above the clouds, so far that a current of air struck it and carried it many, many miles away. For a day and a night I traveled through the air, and on the morning of the second day I awoke and found the balloon floating over a strange and beautiful country.

"It came down gradually, and I was not hurt a bit. But I found myself in the midst of a strange people, who, seeing me come from the clouds, thought I was a Great Wizard. Of course I let them think so, because they were afraid of me, and promised to do anything I wished them to.

"Just to amuse myself, and keep the good people busy, I ordered them to build this City, and my Palace; and they did it all willingly and well. Then I thought, as the country was so green and beautiful, I would call it the Emerald City. And to make the name fit better I put green spectacles on all the people, so that everything they saw was green."

"But isn't everything here green?" asked Dorothy.

"No more than in any other city," replied Oz. "But when you wear green spectacles, why of course everything you see looks green to you. The Emerald City was built a great many years ago, for I was a young man when the balloon brought me here, and I am a very old man now. But my people have worn green glasses on their eyes so long that most of them think it really is an Emerald City, and it certainly is a beautiful place, abounding in jewels and precious metals, and every good thing that is needed to make one happy. I have been good to the people, and they like me. But ever since this Palace was built, I have shut myself up and would not see any of them.

"One of my greatest fears was the Witches, for while I had no magical powers at all I soon found out that the Witches were really able to do wonderful things. There were four of them in this country, and they ruled the people who live in the North and South and East and West. Fortunately, the Witches of the North and South were good, and I knew they would do me no harm. But the Witches of the East and West were terribly wicked, and had they not thought I was more powerful than they themselves, they would surely have destroyed me. As it was, I lived in deadly fear of them for many years. So you can imagine how pleased I was when I heard your house had fallen on the Wicked Witch of the East. When you came to me, I was willing to promise anything if you would only do away with the other Witch. Now that you have melted her, I am ashamed to say that I cannot keep my promises."

"I think you are a very bad man," said Dorothy.

"Oh, no, my dear! I'm really a very good man, but I'm a very bad Wizard, I must admit."

"Can't you give me brains?" asked the Scarecrow.

"You don't need them. You are learning something every day. A baby has brains, but it doesn't know much. Experience is the only thing that brings knowledge, and the longer you are on earth the more experience you are sure to get."

"That may all be true," said the Scarecrow, "but I shall be very unhappy unless you give me brains."

The false Wizard looked at him carefully.

"Well," he said with a sigh, "I'm not much of a magician, as I said. But if you will come to me tomorrow morning, I will stuff your head with brains. I cannot tell you how to use them, however. You must find that out for yourself."

"Oh, thank you—thank you!" cried the Scarecrow. "I'll find a way to use them, never fear!"

"But how about my courage?" asked the Lion anxiously.

"You have plenty of courage, I am sure," answered Oz. "All you need is confidence in yourself. There is no living thing that is not afraid when it faces danger. True courage is in facing danger when you are afraid, and that kind of courage you have in plenty."

"Perhaps I have, but I'm scared just the same," said

the Lion. "I shall really be very unhappy unless you give me the sort of courage that makes one forget he is afraid."

"Very well, I will give you that sort of courage to-morrow," replied Oz.

"How about my heart?" asked the Tin Woodman.

"Why, as for that," answered Oz, "I think you are wrong to want a heart. It makes most people unhappy. If you only knew it, you are in luck not to have a heart."

"That must be a matter of opinion," said the Tin Woodman. "For my part, I will bear all the unhappiness without a murmur, if you will give me the heart."

"Very well," answered Oz meekly. "Come to me to-morrow and you shall have a heart. I have played Wizard for so many years that I may as well continue the part a little longer."

"And now," said Dorothy, "how am I to get back to Kansas?"

"We shall have to think about that," replied the little man. "Give me two or three days to consider the matter and I'll try to find a way to carry you over the desert. In the meantime you shall all be treated as my guests, and while you live in the Palace my people will wait upon you and obey your slightest wish. There is only one thing I ask in return for my help—such as it is. You must keep my secret and tell no one I am a humbug."

They agreed to say nothing of what they had learned, and went back to their rooms in high spirits. Even Dorothy had hope that "The Great and Terrible Humbug," as she called him, would find a way to send her back to Kansas, and if he did she was willing to forgive him everything.

Chapter Sixteen

THE MAGIC ART OF THE
GREAT HUMBUG

*N*EXT morning the Scarecrow said to his friends:
"Congratulate me. I am going to Oz to get
my brains at last. When I return I shall be as other
men are."

"I have always liked you as you were," said Dorothy
simply.

"It is kind of you to like a Scarecrow," he replied.
"But surely you will think more of me when you hear
the splendid thoughts my new brain is going to turn
out." Then he said good-bye to them all in a cheerful
voice and went to the Throne Room, where he rapped
upon the door.

"Come in," said Oz.

The Scarecrow went in and found the little man sitting down by the window, engaged in deep thought. "I
have come for my brains," remarked the Scarecrow, a
little uneasily.

"Oh, yes. Sit down in that chair, please," replied Oz. "You must excuse me for taking your head off, but I shall have to do it in order to put your brains in their proper place."

"That's all right," said the Scarecrow. "You are quite welcome to take my head off, as long as it will be a better one when you put it on again."

So the Wizard unfastened his head and emptied out the straw. Then he entered the back room and took up a measure of bran, which he mixed with a great many pins and needles. Having shaken them together thoroughly, he filled the top of the Scarecrow's head with the mixture and stuffed the rest of the space with straw, to hold it in place.

When he had fastened the Scarecrow's head on his body again he said to him, "Hereafter you will be a great man, for I have given you a lot of bran-new brains."

The Scarecrow was both pleased and proud at the fulfillment of his greatest wish, and having thanked Oz warmly he went back to his friends.

Dorothy looked at him curiously. His head was quite bulged out at the top with brains.

"How do you feel?" she asked.

"I feel wise indeed," he answered earnestly. "When I get used to my brains I shall know everything."

"Why are those needles and pins sticking out of your head?" asked the Tin Woodman.

"That is proof that he is sharp," remarked the Lion.

"Well, I must go to Oz and get my heart," said the Woodman. So he walked to the Throne Room and knocked at the door.

"Come in," called Oz, and the Woodman entered and said, "I have come for my heart."

"Very well," answered the little man. "But I shall have to cut a hole in your breast, so I can put your heart in the right place. I hope it won't hurt you."

"Oh, no," answered the Woodman. "I shall not feel it at all."

So Oz brought a pair of tinner's shears and cut a small, square hole in the left side of the Tin Woodman's breast. Then, going to a chest of drawers, he took out a pretty heart, made entirely of silk and stuffed with sawdust.

"Isn't it a beauty?" he asked.

"It is, indeed!" replied the Woodman, who was greatly pleased. "But is it a kind heart?"

"Oh, very!" answered Oz. He put the heart in the Woodman's breast and then replaced the square of tin, soldering it neatly together where it had been cut.

"There," said he. "Now you have a heart that any man might be proud of. I'm sorry I had to put a patch on your breast, but it really couldn't be helped."

"Never mind the patch," exclaimed the happy Woodman. "I am very grateful to you, and shall never forget your kindness."

"Don't speak of it," replied Oz.

Then the Tin Woodman went back to his friends, who wished him every joy on account of his good fortune.

The Lion now walked to the Throne Room and knocked at the door.

"Come in," said Oz.

"I have come for my courage," announced the Lion, entering the room.

"Very well," answered the little man. "I will get it for you."

He went to a cupboard and reaching up to a high shelf took down a square green bottle, the contents of which he poured into a green-gold dish, beautifully carved. Placing this before the Cowardly Lion, who sniffed at it as if he did not like it, the Wizard said:

"Drink."

"What is it?" asked the Lion.

"Well," answered Oz, "if it were inside of you, it would be courage. You know, of course, that courage is always inside one; so that this really cannot be called courage until you have swallowed it. Therefore I advise you to drink it as soon as possible."

The Lion hesitated no longer, but drank till the dish was empty.

"How do you feel now?" asked Oz.

"Full of courage," replied the Lion, who went joyfully back to his friends to tell them of his good fortune.

Oz, left to himself, smiled to think of his success in giving the Scarecrow and the Tin Woodman and the Lion exactly what they thought they wanted. "How can I help being a humbug," he said, "when all these people make me do things that everybody knows can't be done? It was easy to make the Scarecrow and the Lion and the Woodman happy, because they imagined I could do anything. But it will take more than imagination to carry Dorothy back to Kansas, and I'm sure I don't know how it can be done."

Chapter Seventeen

HOW THE BALLOON WAS LAUNCHED

F OR three days Dorothy heard nothing from Oz. These were sad days for the little girl, although her friends were all quite happy and contented. The Scarecrow told them there were wonderful thoughts in his head, but he would not say what they were because he knew no one could understand them but himself. When the Tin Woodman walked about he felt his heart rattling around in his breast, and he told Dorothy he had discovered it to be a kinder and more tender heart than the one he had owned when he was made of flesh. The Lion declared he was afraid of nothing on earth, and would gladly face an army of men or a dozen of the fierce Kalidahs.

Thus each of the little party was satisfied except Dorothy, who longed more than ever to get back to Kansas.

On the fourth day, to her great joy, Oz sent for her,

and when she entered the Throne Room he greeted her pleasantly.

"Sit down, my dear. I think I have found the way to get you out of this country."

"And back to Kansas?" she asked eagerly.

"Well, I'm not sure about Kansas," said Oz, "for I haven't the faintest notion which way it lies. But the first thing to do is to cross the desert, and then it should be easy to find your way home."

"How can I cross the desert?" she inquired.

"Well, I'll tell you what I think," said the little man. "You see, when I came to this country it was in a balloon. You also came through the air, being carried by a cyclone. So I believe the best way to get across the desert will be through the air. Now, it is quite beyond my powers to make a cyclone. But I've been thinking the matter over, and I believe I can make a balloon."

"How?" asked Dorothy.

"A balloon," said Oz, "is made of silk, which is coated with glue to keep the gas in it. I have plenty of silk in the Palace, so it will be no trouble to make the balloon. But in all this country there is no gas to fill the balloon with, to make it float."

"If it won't float," remarked Dorothy, "it will be of no use to us."

"True," answered Oz. "But there is another way to

make it float, which is to fill it with hot air. Hot air isn't as good as gas, for if the air should get cold the balloon would come down in the desert, and we should be lost."

"We!" exclaimed the girl. "Are you going with me?"

"Yes, of course," replied Oz. "I am tired of being such a humbug. If I should go out of this Palace my people would soon discover I am not a Wizard, and then they would be vexed with me for having deceived them. So I have to stay shut up in these rooms all day, and it gets tiresome. I'd much rather go back to Kansas with you and be in a circus again."

"I shall be glad to have your company," said Dorothy.

"Thank you," he answered. "Now, if you will help me sew the silk together, we will begin to work on our balloon."

So Dorothy took a needle and thread, and as fast as Oz cut the strips of silk into proper shape the girl sewed them neatly together. First there was a strip of light green silk, then a strip of dark green and then a strip of emerald green; for Oz had a fancy to make the balloon in different shades of the color about them. It took three days to sew all the strips together, but when it was finished they had a big bag of green silk more than twenty feet long.

Then Oz painted it on the inside with a coat of thin

glue, to make it airtight, after which he announced that the balloon was ready.

"But we must have a basket to ride in," he said. So he sent the soldier with the green whiskers for a big clothes basket, which he fastened with many ropes to the bottom of the balloon.

When it was all ready, Oz sent word to his people that he was going to make a visit to a great brother Wizard who lived in the clouds. The news spread rapidly throughout the city and everyone came to see the wonderful sight.

Oz ordered the balloon carried out in front of the Palace, and the people gazed upon it with much curiosity. The Tin Woodman had chopped a big pile of wood, and now he made a fire of it, and Oz held the bottom of the balloon over the fire so that the hot air that arose from it would be caught in the silken bag. Gradually the balloon swelled out and rose into the air, until finally the basket just touched the ground.

Then Oz got into the basket and said to all the people in a loud voice, "I am now going away to make a visit. While I am gone the Scarecrow will rule over you. I command you to obey him as you would me."

The balloon was by this time tugging hard at the rope that held it to the ground, for the air within it was hot, and this made it so much lighter in weight than the air without that it pulled hard to rise into the sky.

"Come, Dorothy!" cried the Wizard. "Hurry up, or the balloon will fly away."

"I can't find Toto anywhere," replied Dorothy, who did not wish to leave her little dog behind. Toto had run into the crowd to bark at a kitten, and Dorothy at last found him. She picked him up and ran toward the balloon.

She was within a few steps of it, and Oz was holding out his hands to help her into the basket, when, crack! went the ropes, and the balloon rose into the air without her.

"Come back!" she screamed. "I want to go, too!"

"I can't come back, my dear," called Oz from the basket. "Good-bye!"

"Good-bye!" shouted everyone, and all eyes were turned upward to where the Wizard was riding in the basket, rising every moment farther and farther into the sky.

And that was the last any of them ever saw of Oz, the Wonderful Wizard, though he may have reached Omaha safely, and be there now, for all we know. But the people remembered him lovingly.

"Oz was always our friend," they said to one another.

"When he was here he built for us this beautiful Emerald City, and now he is gone he has left the Wise Scarecrow to rule over us."

Still, for many days they grieved over the loss of the Wonderful Wizard, and would not be comforted.

Chapter Eighteen

AWAY TO THE SOUTH

*D*OROTHY wept bitterly at the passing of her hope to get home to Kansas again; but when she thought it all over she was glad she had not gone up in a balloon. And she also felt sorry at losing Oz, and so did her companions.

The Tin Woodman came to her and said:

"Truly I should be ungrateful if I failed to mourn for the man who gave me my lovely heart. I should like to cry a little because Oz is gone, if you will kindly wipe away my tears, so that I shall not rust."

"With pleasure," she answered, and brought a towel at once. Then the Tin Woodman wept for several minutes, and she watched the tears carefully and wiped them away with the towel. When he had finished, he thanked her kindly and oiled himself thoroughly with his jeweled oilcan, to guard against mishap.

The Scarecrow was now the ruler of the Emerald City, and although he was not a Wizard the people were proud of him. "For," they said, "there is not another city in all the world that is ruled by a stuffed man." And, so far as they knew, they were quite right.

The morning after the balloon had gone up with Oz, the four travelers met in the Throne Room and talked matters over. The Scarecrow sat in the big throne and the others stood respectfully before him.

"We are not so unlucky," said the new ruler, "for this Palace and the Emerald City belong to us, and we can do just as we please. When I remember that a short time ago I was up on a pole in a farmer's cornfield, and that now I am the ruler of this beautiful City, I am quite satisfied with my lot."

"I also," said the Tin Woodman, "am well-pleased with my new heart; and, really, that was the only thing I wished in all the world."

"For my part, I am content in knowing I am as brave as any beast that ever lived, if not braver," said the Lion modestly.

"If Dorothy would only be content to live in the Emerald City," continued the Scarecrow, "we might all be happy together."

"But I don't want to live here," cried Dorothy. "I want to go to Kansas, and live with Aunt Em and Uncle Henry."

"Well, then, what can be done?" inquired the Woodman.

The Scarecrow decided to think, and he thought so hard that the pins and needles began to stick out of his brains.

Finally he said, "Why not call the Winged Monkeys, and ask them to carry you over the desert?"

"I never thought of that!" said Dorothy joyfully. "It's just the thing. I'll go at once for the Golden Cap."

When she brought it into the Throne Room she spoke the magic words, and soon the band of Winged Monkeys flew in through the open window and stood beside her.

"This is the second time you have called us," said the Monkey King, bowing before the little girl. "What do you wish?"

"I want you to fly with me to Kansas," said Dorothy. But the Monkey King shook his head.

"That cannot be done," he said. "We belong to this country alone, and cannot leave it. There has never been a Winged Monkey in Kansas yet, and I suppose there never will be, for they don't belong there. We shall be glad to serve you in any way in our power, but we cannot cross the desert. Good-bye."

And with another bow, the Monkey King spread his wings and flew away through the window, followed by all his band.

Dorothy was ready to cry with disappointment. "I

have wasted the charm of the Golden Cap to no purpose," she said, "for the Winged Monkeys cannot help me."

"It is certainly too bad!" said the tenderhearted Woodman.

The Scarecrow was thinking again, and his head bulged out so horribly that Dorothy feared it would burst.

"Let us call in the soldier with the green whiskers," he said, "and ask his advice."

So the soldier was summoned and entered the Throne Room timidly, for while Oz was alive he never was allowed to come farther than the door.

"This little girl," said the Scarecrow to the soldier, "wishes to cross the desert. How can she do so?"

"I cannot tell," answered the soldier, "for nobody has ever crossed the desert, unless it is Oz himself."

"Is there no one who can help me?" asked Dorothy earnestly.

"Glinda might," he suggested.

"Who is Glinda?" inquired the Scarecrow.

"The Witch of the South. She is the most powerful of all the Witches, and rules over the Quadlings. Besides, her castle stands on the edge of the desert, so she may know a way to cross it."

"Glinda is a Good Witch, isn't she?" asked the child.

"The Quadlings think she is good," said the soldier, "and she is kind to everyone. I have heard that Glinda is a beautiful woman, who knows how to keep young in spite of the many years she has lived."

"How can I get to her castle?" asked Dorothy.

"The road is straight to the South," he answered, "but it is said to be full of dangers to travelers. There are wild beasts in the woods, and a race of queer men who do not like strangers to cross their country. For this reason none of the Quadlings ever come to the Emerald City."

The soldier then left them and the Scarecrow said:

"It seems, in spite of dangers, that the best thing Dorothy can do is to travel to the Land of the South and ask Glinda to help her. For, of course, if Dorothy stays here she will never get back to Kansas."

"You must have been thinking again," remarked the Tin Woodman.

"I have," said the Scarecrow.

"I shall go with Dorothy," declared the Lion, "for I am tired of your city and long for the woods and the country again. I am really a wild beast, you know. Besides, Dorothy will need someone to protect her."

"That is true," agreed the Woodman. "My axe may be of service to her; so I also will go with her to the Land of the South."

"When shall we start?" asked the Scarecrow.

"Are you going?" they asked, in surprise.

"Certainly. If it wasn't for Dorothy I should never have had brains. She lifted me from the pole in the cornfield and brought me to the Emerald City. So my good luck is all due to her, and I shall never leave her until she starts back to Kansas for good and all."

"Thank you," said Dorothy gratefully. "You are all very kind to me. But I should like to start as soon as possible."

"We shall go tomorrow morning," returned the Scarecrow. "So now let us all get ready, for it will be a long journey."

Chapter Nineteen

ATTACKED BY THE FIGHTING TREES

———◄►►◄►———

*T*HE next morning Dorothy kissed the pretty green girl good-bye, and they all shook hands with the soldier with the green whiskers, who had walked with them as far as the gate. When the Guardian of the Gates saw them again, he wondered greatly that they could leave the beautiful City to get into new trouble. But he at once unlocked their spectacles, which he put back into the green box, and gave them many good wishes to carry with them.

"You are now our ruler," he said to the Scarecrow. "So you must come back to us as soon as possible."

"I certainly shall if I am able," the Scarecrow replied. "But I must help Dorothy to get home, first."

As Dorothy bade the good-natured Guardian a last farewell she said:

"I have been very kindly treated in your lovely City, and everyone has been good to me. I cannot tell you how grateful I am."

"Don't try, my dear," he answered. "We should like to keep you with us, but if it is your wish to return to Kansas, I hope you will find a way." He then opened the gate of the outer wall, and they walked forth and started upon their journey.

The sun shone brightly as our friends turned their faces toward the Land of the South. They were all in the best of spirits, and laughed and chatted together. Dorothy was once more filled with the hope of getting home, and the Scarecrow and the Tin Woodman were glad to be of use to her. As for the Lion, he sniffed the fresh air with delight and whisked his tail from side to side in pure joy at being in the country again, while Toto ran around them and chased the moths and butterflies, barking merrily all the time.

"City life does not agree with me at all," remarked the Lion, as they walked along at a brisk pace. "I have lost much flesh since I lived there, and now I am anxious for a chance to show the other beasts how courageous I have grown."

They now turned and took a last look at the Emerald City. All they could see was a mass of towers and steeples behind the green walls, and high up above everything the spires and dome of the Palace of Oz.

"Oz was not such a bad Wizard, after all," said the Tin

Woodman, as he felt his heart rattling around in his breast.

"He knew how to give me brains, and very good brains, too," said the Scarecrow.

"If Oz had taken a dose of the same courage he gave me," added the Lion, "he would have been a brave man."

Dorothy said nothing. Oz had not kept the promise he made her, but he had done his best. So she forgave him. As he said, he was a good man, even if he was a bad Wizard.

The first day's journey was through the green fields and bright flowers that stretched about the Emerald City on every side. They slept that night on the grass, with nothing but the stars over them; and they rested very well indeed.

In the morning they traveled on until they came to a thick wood. There was no way of going around it, for it seemed to extend to the right and left as far as they could see. Besides, they did not dare change the direction of their journey for fear of getting lost. So they looked for the place where it would be easiest to get into the forest.

The Scarecrow, who was in the lead, finally discovered a big tree with such wide-spreading branches that there was room for the party to pass underneath. So he walked forward to the tree, but just as he came under the first branches they bent down and twined around him, and the next minute he was raised from the ground and flung headlong among his fellow travelers.

This did not hurt the Scarecrow, but it surprised him, and he looked rather dizzy when Dorothy picked him up.

"Here is another space between the trees," called the Lion.

"Let me try it first," said the Scarecrow, "for it doesn't hurt me to get thrown about." He walked up to another tree, as he spoke, but its branches immediately seized him and tossed him back again.

"This is strange," exclaimed Dorothy. "What shall we do?"

"The trees seem to have made up their minds to fight us, and stop our journey," remarked the Lion.

"I believe I will try it myself," said the Woodman, and shouldering his axe, he marched up to the first tree that had handled the Scarecrow so roughly. When a big branch bent down to seize him the Woodman chopped at it so fiercely that he cut it in two. At once the tree began shaking all its branches as if in pain, and the Tin Woodman passed safely under it.

"Come on!" he shouted to the others. "Be quick!"

They all ran forward and passed under the tree without injury, except Toto, who was caught by a small branch and shaken until he howled. But the Woodman promptly chopped off the branch and set the little dog free.

The other trees of the forest did nothing to keep them back, so they made up their minds that only the first row of trees could bend down their branches, and that probably these were the policemen of the forest, and given this wonderful power in order to keep strangers out of it.

The four travelers walked with ease through the trees until they came to the farther edge of the wood. Then, to their surprise, they found before them a high wall which seemed to be made of white china. It was smooth, like the surface of a dish, and higher than their heads.

"What shall we do now?" asked Dorothy.

"I will make a ladder," said the Tin Woodman, "for we certainly must climb over the wall."

Chapter Twenty

THE DAINTY CHINA COUNTRY

———⟫●⟪———

WHILE the Woodman was making a ladder from wood which he found in the forest Dorothy lay down and slept, for she was tired by the long walk. The Lion also curled himself up to sleep, and Toto lay beside him.

The Scarecrow watched the Woodman while he worked, and said to him, "I cannot think why this wall is here, nor what it is made of."

"Rest your brains and do not worry about the wall," replied the Woodman. "When we have climbed over it, we shall know what is on the other side."

After a time the ladder was finished. It looked clumsy, but the Tin Woodman was sure it was strong and would answer their purpose. The Scarecrow waked Dorothy and the Lion and Toto, and told them that the ladder was ready. The Scarecrow climbed up the ladder first, but he was so awkward that Dorothy had to follow close behind and keep him from falling off. When he got his head over the top of the wall the Scarecrow said, "Oh, my!"

"Go on," exclaimed Dorothy.

So the Scarecrow climbed farther up and sat down on the top of the wall, and Dorothy put her head over and cried, "Oh, my!" just as the Scarecrow had done.

Then Toto came up, and immediately began to bark, but Dorothy made him be still.

The Lion climbed the ladder next, and the Tin Woodman came last; but both of them cried, "Oh, my!" as soon as they looked over the wall. When they were all sitting in a row on the top of the wall, they looked down and saw a strange sight.

Before them was a great stretch of country having a floor as smooth and shining and white as the bottom of a big platter. Scattered around were many houses made entirely of china and painted in the brightest colors. These houses were quite small, the biggest of them reaching only as high as Dorothy's waist. There were also pretty little barns, with china fences around them. Many cows and sheep and horses and pigs and chickens, all made of china, were standing about in groups.

But the strangest of all were the people who lived in this queer country. There were milkmaids and shepherdesses, with brightly colored bodices and golden spots all over their gowns; and princesses with most gorgeous frocks of silver and gold and purple; and shepherds dressed in knee breeches with pink and yellow and blue stripes down them, and golden buckles on their shoes; and princes with jeweled crowns upon their heads, wearing ermine robes and satin doublets; and funny clowns in ruffled gowns, with round red spots upon their cheeks and tall, pointed caps. And, strangest of all, these people were all made of china, even to their clothes, and were so small that the tallest of them was no higher than Dorothy's knee.

No one did so much as look at the travelers at first, except one little purple china dog with an extra-large head, which came to the wall and barked at them in a tiny voice, afterward running away again.

"How shall we get down?" asked Dorothy.

They found the ladder so heavy they could not pull it up, so the Scarecrow fell off the wall and the others jumped down upon him so that the hard floor would not hurt their feet. Of course they took pains not to light on his head and get the pins in their feet. When all were safely down they picked up the Scarecrow, whose body was quite flattened out, and patted his straw into shape again.

"We must cross this strange place in order to get to the other side," said Dorothy, "for it would be unwise for us to go any other way except due South."

They began walking through the country of the china people, and the first thing they came to was a china milkmaid milking a china cow. As they drew near, the cow suddenly gave a kick and kicked over the stool, the pail, and even the milkmaid herself, and all fell on the china ground with a great clatter.

Dorothy was shocked to see that the cow had broken her short leg off, and that the pail was lying in several small pieces, while the poor milkmaid had a nick in her left elbow.

"There!" cried the milkmaid angrily. "See what you have done! My cow has broken her leg, and I must take her to the mender's shop and have it glued on again. What do you mean by coming here and frightening my cow?"

"I'm very sorry," returned Dorothy. "Please forgive us."

But the pretty milkmaid was much too vexed to make any answer. She picked up the leg sulkily and led her cow away, the poor animal limping on three legs. As she left them the milkmaid cast many reproachful glances over her shoulder at the clumsy strangers, holding her nicked elbow close to her side.

Dorothy was quite grieved at this mishap.

"We must be very careful here," said the kind-hearted Woodman, "or we may hurt these pretty little people so they will never get over it."

A little farther on Dorothy met a most beautifully

dressed young Princess, who stopped short as she saw the strangers and started to run away.

Dorothy wanted to see more of the Princess, so she ran after her. But the china girl cried out, "Don't chase me! Don't chase me!"

She had such a frightened little voice that Dorothy stopped and said, "Why not?"

"Because," answered the Princess, also stopping, a safe distance away, "if I run I may fall down and break myself."

"But could you not be mended?" asked the girl.

"Oh, yes; but one is never so pretty after being mended, you know," replied the Princess.

"I suppose not," said Dorothy.

"Now there is Mr. Joker, one of our clowns," continued the china lady, "who is always trying to stand upon his head. He has broken himself so often that he is mended in a hundred places, and doesn't look at all pretty. Here he comes now, so you can see for yourself."

Indeed, a jolly little clown came walking toward them, and Dorothy could see that in spite of his pretty clothes of red and yellow and green he was completely covered with cracks, running every which way and showing plainly that he had been mended in many places.

The Clown put his hands in his pockets, and after

puffing out his cheeks and nodding his head at them saucily, he said:

> "My lady fair,
> Why do you stare
> At poor old Mr. Joker?
> You're quite as stiff
> And prim as if
> You'd eaten up a poker!"

"Be quiet, sir!" said the Princess. "Can't you see these are strangers, and should be treated with respect?"

"Well, that's respect, I expect," declared the Clown, and immediately stood upon his head.

"Don't mind Mr. Joker," said the Princess to Dorothy. "He is considerably cracked in his head, and that makes him foolish."

"Oh, I don't mind him a bit," said Dorothy. "But you are so beautiful," she continued, "that I am sure I could love you dearly. Won't you let me carry you back to Kansas, and stand you on Aunt Em's mantel? I could carry you in my basket."

"That would make me very unhappy," answered the china Princess. "You see, here in our country we live contentedly, and can talk and move around as we please. But whenever any of us are taken away our joints at once stiffen, and we can only stand straight and look pretty. Of course that is all that is expected of us when we are on mantels and cabinets and drawing-room tables, but our lives are much pleasanter here in our own country."

"I would not make you unhappy for all the world!" exclaimed Dorothy. "So I'll just say good-bye."

"Good-bye," replied the Princess.

They walked carefully through the china country. The little animals and all the people scampered out of their way, fearing the strangers would break them, and after an hour or so the travelers reached the other side of the country and came to another china wall.

It was not so high as the first, however, and by standing upon the Lion's back they all managed to scramble to the top. Then the Lion gathered his legs under him and jumped on the wall. But just as he jumped, he upset a china church with his tail and smashed it all to pieces.

"That was too bad," said Dorothy, "but really I think we were lucky in not doing these little people more harm than breaking a cow's leg and a church. They are all so brittle!"

"They are, indeed," said the Scarecrow, "and I am thankful I am made of straw and cannot be easily damaged. There are worse things in the world than being a Scarecrow."

Chapter Twenty-One

THE LION BECOMES THE KING OF BEASTS

AFTER climbing down from the china wall the travelers found themselves in a disagreeable country, full of bogs and marshes and covered with tall, rank grass. It was difficult to walk without falling into muddy holes, for the grass was so thick that it hid them from sight. However, by carefully picking their way, they got safely along until they reached solid ground. Here the country seemed wilder than ever, and after a long and tiresome walk through the underbrush they entered another forest, where the trees were bigger and older than any they had ever seen.

"This forest is perfectly delightful," declared the Lion, looking around him with joy. "Never have I seen a more beautiful place."

"It seems gloomy," said the Scarecrow.

"Not a bit of it," answered the Lion. "I should like to live here all my life. See how soft the dried leaves are under your feet and how rich and green the moss is that clings to these old trees. Surely no wild beast could wish a pleasanter home."

"Perhaps there are wild beasts in the forest now," said Dorothy.

"I suppose there are," returned the Lion, "but I do not see any of them about."

They walked through the forest until it became too dark to go any farther. Dorothy and Toto and the Lion lay down to sleep, while the Woodman and the Scarecrow kept watch over them as usual.

When morning came, they started again. Before they had gone far they heard a low rumble, as of the growling of many wild animals. Toto whimpered a little, but none of the others was frightened, and they kept along the well-trodden path until they came to an opening in the wood, in which were gathered hundreds of beasts of every variety. There were tigers and elephants and bears and wolves and foxes and all the others in the natural history, and for a moment Dorothy was afraid. But the Lion explained that the animals were holding a meeting, and he judged by their snarling and growling that they were in great trouble.

As he spoke several of the beasts caught sight of him, and at once the great assemblage hushed as if by magic.

The biggest of the tigers came up to the Lion and bowed, saying, "Welcome, O King of Beasts! You have come in good time to fight our enemy and bring peace to all the animals of the forest once more."

"What is your trouble?" asked the Lion quietly.

"We are all threatened," answered the tiger, "by a fierce enemy which has lately come into this forest. It is a most tremendous monster, like a great spider, with a body as big as an elephant and legs as long as a tree trunk. It has eight of these long legs, and as the monster crawls through the forest he seizes an animal with a leg and drags it to his mouth, where he eats it as a spider does a fly. Not one of us is safe while this fierce creature is alive, and we had called a meeting to decide how to take care of ourselves when you came among us."

The Lion thought for a moment.

"Are there any other lions in this forest?" he asked.

"No; there were some, but the monster has eaten them all. And, besides, they were none of them nearly so large and brave as you."

"If I put an end to your enemy, will you bow down to me and obey me as King of the Forest?" inquired the Lion.

"We will do that gladly," returned the tiger.

And all the other beasts roared with a mighty roar, "We will!"

"Where is this great spider of yours now?" asked the Lion.

"Yonder, among the oak trees," said the tiger, pointing with his forefoot.

"Take good care of these friends of mine," said the Lion, "and I will go at once to fight the monster."

He bade his comrades good-bye and marched proudly away to do battle with the enemy.

The great spider was lying asleep when the Lion found him, and it looked so ugly that its foe turned up his nose in disgust. Its legs were quite as long as the tiger had said, and its body covered with coarse black hair. It had a great mouth, with a row of sharp teeth a foot long; but its head was joined to the pudgy body by a neck as slender as a wasp's waist. This gave the Lion a hint of the best way to attack the creature. As he knew it was easier to fight it asleep than awake, he gave a great spring and landed directly upon the monster's back. Then, with one blow of his heavy paw, all armed with sharp claws, he knocked the spider's head from its body. Jumping down, he watched it until the long legs stopped wiggling, when he knew it was quite dead.

The Lion went back to the opening where the beasts of the forest were waiting for him and said proudly, "You need fear your enemy no longer."

Then the beasts bowed down to the Lion as their King, and he promised to come back and rule over them as soon as Dorothy was safely on her way to Kansas.

Chapter Twenty-Two

THE COUNTRY OF THE
QUADLINGS

T HE four travelers passed through the rest of the forest in safety, and when they came out from its gloom saw before them a steep hill, covered from top to bottom with great pieces of rock.

"That will be a hard climb," said the Scarecrow, "but we must get over the hill, nevertheless."

So he led the way and the others followed. They had nearly reached the first rock when they heard a rough voice cry out, "Keep back!"

"Who are you?" asked the Scarecrow.

Then a head showed itself over the rock and the same voice said, "This hill belongs to us, and we don't allow anyone to cross it."

"But we must cross it," said the Scarecrow. "We're going to the country of the Quadlings."

"But you shall not!" replied the voice, and there stepped from behind the rock the strangest man the travelers had ever seen.

He was quite short and stout and had a big head, which was flat at the top and supported by a thick neck full of wrinkles. But he had no arms at all, and, seeing this, the Scarecrow did not fear that so helpless a creature could prevent them from climbing the hill. So he said, "I'm sorry not to do as you wish, but we must pass over your hill whether you like it or not," and he walked boldly forward.

As quick as lightning the man's head shot forward and his neck stretched out until the top of the head, where it was flat, struck the Scarecrow in the middle and sent him tumbling, over and over, down the hill. Almost as quickly as it came the head went back to the body, and the man laughed harshly as he said, "It isn't as easy as you think!"

A chorus of boisterous laughter came from the other rocks, and Dorothy saw hundreds of the armless Hammer-Heads upon the hillside, one behind every rock.

The Lion became quite angry at the laughter caused by the Scarecrow's mishap, and giving a loud roar that echoed like thunder, he dashed up the hill.

Again a head shot swiftly out, and the great Lion went rolling down the hill as if he had been struck by a cannon ball.

Dorothy ran down and helped the Scarecrow to his

feet, and the Lion came up to her, feeling rather bruised and sore, and said, "It is useless to fight people with shooting heads. No one can withstand them."

"What can we do, then?" she asked.

"Call the Winged Monkeys," suggested the Tin Woodman. "You have still the right to command them once more."

"Very well," she answered, and putting on the Golden Cap she uttered the magic words. The Monkeys were as prompt as ever, and in a few moments the entire band stood before her.

"What are your commands?" inquired the King of the Monkeys, bowing low.

"Carry us over the hill to the country of the Quadlings," answered the girl.

"It shall be done," said the King, and at once the Winged Monkeys caught the four travelers and Toto up in their arms and flew away with them. As they passed over the hill the Hammer-Heads yelled with vexation, and shot their heads high in the air, but they could not reach the Winged Monkeys, which carried Dorothy and her comrades safely over the hill and set them down in the beautiful country of the Quadlings.

"This is the last time you can summon us," said the leader to Dorothy. "So good-bye and good luck to you."

"Good-bye, and thank you very much," returned the

girl. And the Monkeys rose into the air and were out of sight in a twinkling.

The country of the Quadlings seemed rich and happy. There was field upon field of ripening grain, with well-paved roads running between, and pretty rippling brooks with strong bridges across them. The fences and houses and bridges were all painted bright red, just as they had been painted yellow in the country of the Winkies and blue in the country of the Munchkins. The Quadlings themselves, who were short and fat and looked chubby and good-natured, were dressed all in red, which showed bright against the green grass and the yellowing grain.

The Monkeys had set them down near a farmhouse, and the four travelers walked up to it and knocked at the door. It was opened by the farmer's wife, and when Dorothy asked for something to eat the woman gave them all a good dinner, with three kinds of cake and four kinds of cookies, and a bowl of milk for Toto.

"How far is it to the Castle of Glinda?" asked the child.

"It is not a great way," answered the farmer's wife. "Take the road to the South and you will soon reach it."

Thanking the good woman, they started afresh and walked by the fields and across the pretty bridges until they saw before them a very beautiful Castle. Before the gates were three young girls, dressed in handsome red uniforms trimmed with gold braid.

As Dorothy approached, one of them said to her, "Why have you come to the South Country?"

"To see the Good Witch who rules here," she answered. "Will you take me to her?"

"Let me have your name, and I will ask Glinda if she will receive you." They told who they were, and the girl soldier went into the Castle. After a few moments she came back to say that Dorothy and the others were to be admitted at once.

this queer country. There were milkmaids and shep
herdesses, with brightly colored bodices and golden
spots all over their gowns; and princesses with most
gorgeous frocks of silver and gold and purple; and shep
herds dressed in knee-breeches with pink and yellow

Chapter Twenty-Three

GLINDA GRANTS DOROTHY'S WISH

———◦◦◦———

*B*EFORE they went to see Glinda, however, they were taken to a room of the Castle, where Dorothy washed her face and combed her hair, and the Lion shook the dust out of his mane, and the Scarecrow patted himself into his best shape, and the Woodman polished his tin and oiled his joints.

When they were all quite presentable they followed the soldier girl into a big room where the Witch Glinda sat upon a throne of rubies.

She was both beautiful and young to their eyes. Her hair was a rich red in color and fell in flowing ringlets over her shoulders. Her dress was pure white but her eyes were blue, and they looked kindly upon the little girl.

"What can I do for you, my child?" she asked.

Dorothy told the Witch all her story: how the cyclone had brought her to the Land of Oz, how she had found her companions, and of the wonderful adventures they had met with.

"My greatest wish now," she added, "is to get back to Kansas, for Aunt Em will surely think something dreadful has happened to me, and that will make her put on mourning. And unless the crops are better this year than they were last, I am sure Uncle Henry cannot afford it."

Glinda leaned forward and kissed the sweet, up-turned face of the loving little girl.

"Bless your dear heart," she said, "I am sure I can tell you of a way to get back to Kansas." Then she added, "But if I do, you must give me the Golden Cap."

"Willingly!" exclaimed Dorothy. "Indeed, it is of no use to me now, and when you have it you can command the Winged Monkeys three times."

"And I think I shall need their service just those three times," answered Glinda, smiling.

Dorothy then gave her the Golden Cap, and the Witch said to the Scarecrow, "What will you do when Dorothy has left us?"

"I will return to the Emerald City," he replied, "for Oz has made me its ruler and the people like me. The only thing that worries me is how to cross the hill of the Hammer-Heads."

"By means of the Golden Cap I shall command the Winged Monkeys to carry you to the gates of the

Emerald City," said Glinda, "for it would be a shame to deprive the people of so wonderful a ruler."

"Am I really wonderful?" asked the Scarecrow.

"You are unusual," replied Glinda.

Turning to the Tin Woodman, she asked, "What will become of you when Dorothy leaves this country?"

He leaned on his axe and thought a moment. Then he said, "The Winkies were very kind to me, and wanted me to rule over them after the Wicked Witch died. I am fond of the Winkies. If I could get back again to the Country of the West, I should like nothing better than to rule over them forever."

"My second command to the Winged Monkeys," said Glinda "will be that they carry you safely to the land of the Winkies. Your brain may not be so large to look at as those of the Scarecrow, but you are really brighter than he is—when you are well polished—and I am sure you will rule the Winkies wisely and well."

Then the Witch looked at the big, shaggy Lion and asked, "When Dorothy has returned to her own home, what will become of you?"

"Over the hill of the Hammer-Heads," he answered, "lies a grand old forest, and all the beasts that live there have made me their King. If I could only get back to this forest, I would pass my life very happily there."

"My third command to the Winged Monkeys," said Glinda, "shall be to carry you to your forest. Then, having used up the powers of the Golden Cap, I shall give it to the King of the Monkeys, that he and his band may thereafter be free for evermore."

The Scarecrow and the Tin Woodman and the Lion now thanked the Good Witch earnestly for her kindness.

Then Dorothy exclaimed, "You are certainly as good as you are beautiful! But you have not yet told me how to get back to Kansas."

"Your Silver Shoes will carry you over the desert," replied Glinda. "If you had known their power you could have gone back to your Aunt Em the very first day you came to this country."

"But then I should not have had my wonderful brains!" cried the Scarecrow. "I might have passed my whole life in the farmer's cornfield."

"And I should not have had my lovely heart," said the Tin Woodman. "I might have stood and rusted in the forest till the end of the world."

"And I should have lived a coward forever," declared the Lion, "and no beast in all the forest would have had a good word to say to me."

"This is all true," said Dorothy, "and I am glad I was of use to these good friends. But now that each of them has had what he most desired, and each is happy in having a kingdom to rule beside, I think I should like to go back to Kansas."

"The Silver Shoes," said the Good Witch, "have wonderful powers. And one of the most curious things about them is that they can carry you to any place in the world in three steps, and each step will be made in the wink of an eye. All you have to do is to knock the heels together three times and command the shoes to carry you wherever you wish to go."

"If that is so," said the child joyfully, "I will ask them to carry me back to Kansas at once."

She threw her arms around the Lion's neck and kissed him, patting his big head tenderly. Then she kissed the Tin Woodman, who was weeping in a way most dangerous to his joints. But she hugged the soft, stuffed body of the Scarecrow in her arms instead of kissing his painted face, and found she was crying herself at this sorrowful parting from her loving comrades.

Glinda the Good stepped down from her ruby throne to give the little girl a good-bye kiss, and Dorothy thanked her for all the kindness she had shown to her friends and herself.

Dorothy now took Toto up solemnly in her arms, and having said one last good-bye she clapped the heels of her shoes together three times.

"Take me home to Aunt Em!"

Instantly she was whirling through the air, so swiftly that all she could see or feel was the wind whistling past her ears.

The Silver Shoes took but three steps, and then she stopped so suddenly that she rolled over upon the grass several times before she knew where she was.

At length, however, she sat up and looked about her.

"Good gracious!" she cried.

For she was sitting on the broad Kansas prairie, and just before her was the new farmhouse Uncle Henry built after the cyclone had carried away the old one. Uncle Henry was milking the cows in the barnyard, and Toto had jumped out of her arms and was running toward the barn, barking joyously.

Dorothy stood up and found she was in her stocking-feet. For the Silver Shoes had fallen off in her flight through the air, and were lost forever in the desert.

Chapter Twenty-Four

HOME AGAIN

AUNT Em had just come out of the house to water the cabbages when she looked up and saw Dorothy running toward her.

"My darling child!" she cried, folding the little girl in her arms and covering her face with kisses. "Where in the world did you come from?"

"From the Land of Oz," said Dorothy gravely. "And here is Toto, too. And oh, Aunt Em! I'm so glad to be at home again!"

that they were in great trouble.

As he spoke several of the beasts caught sight of him

at once the great assemblage rushed as if by magic

The biggest of the tigers came up to the Lion and

Praise for the Historical Novels
of Robin Maxwell

"Utterly engrossing and glittering with color. Lorenzo the Magnificent, Botticelli, Leonardo da Vinci, and his courageous, passionate mother, Caterina, move through the pages of this book, radiating life and touching the heart."
—Sandra Worth, author of *The King's Daughter*

"Focuses on the unsùng genius who was Leonardo da Vinci's mother, a woman of intellectual curiosity and maternal instincts toward the son who was torn from her. She moved in a world that included the glittering Medicis and the villainous Savonarola, all of whom are well limnèd in this sparkling epic. Set in the sunshine of fifteenth-century Tuscany, the novel continually delights with intriguing details, from the bottega workshops of the great Italian masters to the minutiae of an alchemist's laboratory."
—Vicki León, author of the Uppity Women series

"From the dusty streets of Vinci to the glories of Lorenzo Il Magnifico's Florence and the conspiratorial halls of Rome and Milan, *Signora da Vinci* is a tour de force celebration of one woman's unquenchable ardor for knowledge and of a secret world that historical fiction readers rarely see."
—C. W. Gortner, author of *The Last Queen*

"*Signora da Vinci* is without a doubt the best historical fiction I have read all year. In her most remarkable novel yet, Robin Maxwell takes us back to the turbulent times of the Italian Renaissance.... A masterful blend of fact and fiction, *Signora da Vinci* mesmerizes."
—Michelle Moran, author of *The Heretic Queen*

Mademoiselle Boleyn

"Robin Maxwell offers a fascinating glimpse at the ambitious girl who will grow into the infamous queen."
—Susan Holloway Scott, author of *The King's Favorite*

"[A] historically plausible account of Anne Boleyn's adolescence in France as a courtier of King Francois ... lavishly imagined ... [an] accomplished rehabilitation of much-maligned Anne as an empowered woman."
—*Kirkus Reviews*

BOOKS BY ROBIN MAXWELL

The Secret Diary of Anne Boleyn

The Queen's Bastard: A Novel

Virgin: Prelude to the Throne

The Wild Irish: A Novel of Elizabeth I and the Pirate O'Malley

To the Tower Born: A Novel of the Lost Princes

Mademoiselle Boleyn: A Novel

Signora da Vinci

ROBIN MAXWELL

NAL NEW AMERICAN LIBRARY

New American Library
Published by New American Library, a division of
Penguin Group (USA) Inc., 375 Hudson Street,
New York, New York 10014, USA
Penguin Group (Canada), 90 Eglinton Avenue East, Suite 700, Toronto,
Ontario M4P 2Y3, Canada (a division of Pearson Penguin Canada Inc.)
Penguin Books Ltd., 80 Strand, London WC2R 0RL, England
Penguin Ireland, 25 St. Stephen's Green, Dublin 2,
Ireland (a division of Penguin Books Ltd.)
Penguin Group (Australia), 250 Camberwell Road, Camberwell, Victoria 3124,
Australia (a division of Pearson Australia Group Pty. Ltd.)
Penguin Books India Pvt. Ltd., 11 Community Centre, Panchsheel Park,
New Delhi - 110 017, India
Penguin Group (NZ), 67 Apollo Drive, Rosedale, North Shore 0632,
New Zealand (a division of Pearson New Zealand Ltd.)
Penguin Books (South Africa) (Pty.) Ltd., 24 Sturdee Avenue,
Rosebank, Johannesburg 2196, South Africa

Penguin Books Ltd., Registered Offices: 80 Strand, London WC2R 0RL, England

First published by New American Library, a division of Penguin Group (USA) Inc.

First Printing, January 2009
3 5 7 9 10 8 6 4 2

Copyright © Robin Maxwell, 2009
Readers Guide copyright © Penguin Group (USA) Inc., 2009
All rights reserved

⬛ REGISTERED TRADEMARK—MARCA REGISTRADA

LIBRARY OF CONGRESS CATALOGING-IN-PUBLICATION DATA
Maxwell, Robin, 1948–
Signora da Vinci / Robin Maxwell.
p. cm.
ISBN 978-0-451-22580-1
1. Caterina, 15th cent.—Fiction.   2. Leonardo, da Vinci, 1452–1519—Fiction.
3. Artists—Italy—Fiction.   4. Mothers and sons—Italy—Fiction.   I. Title.
PS3563.A9254S54 2009
813'.54—dc22   2008030630

Set in Bembo
Designed by Alissa Amell

Printed in the United States of America

PUBLISHER'S NOTE
This is a work of fiction. Names, characters, places, and incidents either are the product of the author's imagination or are used fictitiously, and any resemblance to actual persons, living or dead, business establishments, events, or locales is entirely coincidental.

The recipe contained in this book is to be followed exactly as written. The publisher is not responsible for your specific health or allergy needs that may require medical supervision. The publisher is not responsible for any adverse reactions to the recipes contained in this book.

The publisher does not have any control over and does not assume any responsibility for author or third-party Web sites or their content.

The Alchemist's Daughter

CHAPTER 1

A lie.

I needed a fresh lie to help me escape the house this day. Call it "deceit," I corrected myself as I threw another log in the furnace, enduring its searing blast on my face before shutting the iron door with a clank. I had chosen the fattest log in the woodpile. The bigger it was the longer the fire would burn without needing tending—all part of my deceit. *Use the word, Caterina,* I scolded myself. *You will be telling Papa a lie so you can run barefoot in the hills today instead of doing your chores.*

I grabbed the handle of the bellows and gave them several mighty squeezes, imagining the fierce heat its wind would create inside my father's alchemical furnace, then threw off my leather apron and face mask and turned to go.

I could see he was making a batch of alcohol on his worktable, the still with its two-headed spouts and receiving flasks all rigged together in a confusing array. It should not have been confusing, I knew. He had been trying to teach me for weeks—a simple process to create a substance especially useful in the apothecary. But my mind, of late, had been elsewhere. *Anywhere* else but in Papa's alchemical laboratory, his medicinal garden, or his apothecary shop, where I normally helped him.

A plan was forming in my head. I went back to the furnace and threw in one more log for good measure, praying I would not burn down the house with my inferno of deceit. *Had that been one of Dante's*

Seven Deadly Sins? I tried to remember as I started down the stairs from the top floor to the second.

Here I stopped in my bedchamber, a small room with enough space for my covered bed, a chair, a desk, and several wooden chests that held my belongings. I avoided looking at my prettily painted "marriage chest," the one Aunt Magdalena had insisted on giving me a year ago when I'd turned thirteen, the one she'd begun to fill with linens, fine smocks, and baby things—all that a girl would need as a young bride.

But the sight of it seemed to mock me. *Who would marry me?* I had never learned the "womanly skills." And Papa, despite his sister's nagging, had more excuses than hairs on his head. I was too young, he told her, though of course girls my age were marrying all the time. There was no one suitable in Vinci, he'd insisted, but of course there were other towns nearby, larger places like Empoli and Pistoia, and of course Florence just a day's ride away.

But the truth of my unsuitability for marriage, I realized as I knelt before the plain wooden chest at the foot of my bed, I was now holding in my hands. It was my much-worn copy of Plato's *Timaeus* . . . in Greek. No one would want so freakishly educated a girl as I was.

A girl with secrets even worse than that.

I carefully wrapped the book in a scarlet and gold silk scarf Papa had given my mother before she died—it was now one of my prized possessions—and carefully placed the package in my sturdy cloth herb sack. I took the stairs down another flight, knowing I would find there in the kitchen or sitting room the first obstruction to my hoped-for day of freedom.

"Eat something, Caterina!" I heard, before I saw, Aunt Magdalena calling out as she bent over, retrieving our morning bread from the oven. Her substantial buttocks pointing in my direction blocked sight of all the rest of her, but her position made my "Not hungry!" and my flight down the final set of stairs all the easier. This last would be the difficult part.

All along this lower staircase bunches of drying greenery hung, flower side down, wafting lovely fragrances all round my head, announcing my descent into the world of the apothecary. The entire ground floor, inside and out, was dedicated to the herbal arts. The storeroom and drying room into which the staircase emerged was piled bottom to top with barrels and crates, giant jars and boxes that, through their pungent odors as much as their lettering, sang of exotic lands and mysterious spices.

But I could not linger here. My devious plan took me outside to the garden, Papa's apothecary garden. I suppose it was mine as well. I was more than useful amidst vegetation. Owned great knowledge of it. Took much pleasure in it. This morning, however, I would shamelessly exploit it. Even destroy a part of it . . . for my selfish purposes.

But it was spring. A fresh, glorious, sun-spangled morning. And it was *not* my scheduled day for gathering plants in the wild—ones that either refused to grow in our garden or ones that needed restocking, either by seed or seedling.

I had to be outdoors this day. I'd woken with my blood racing and my lungs aching for the crisp moist air that could only be found near running water.

I knew Papa needed me at the shop. There were countless poultices to be pounded this day, seeds to be ground into fine powder. Decoctions to be mixed for our neighbors, who so depended on Ernesto, the well-loved apothecary of Vinci. There being no physicians or surgeons in our tiny village, he had treated the wealthiest landowners and the poorest farmworkers alike. He was even distinguished as a worker of the occasional miracle. I walked in his golden shadow—beloved child in the image of her sorely missed mother. Good-natured young neighbor who was always willing to run an errand or lend an ear to a bit of complaining, and not much of a gossip.

I hurried to a corner of the garden where I knew the verbena to grow. There it was, a fine healthy clump growing in the loamy earth near the garden wall. Before I allowed myself to ponder my wickedness

I gave a final surreptitious glance around me, grasped the base of the greenery and ripped out the clump, roots and all. Stowing it in a waxed cloth bag, I stuffed it in my herb sack and stood.

I straightened my skirts and brushed off some small clods of earth that had fallen on my bodice. As I cleaned myself I could not help but notice the size of my breasts—an altogether new development—one that I suspected had more than a little to do with my recent untoward wildness.

Herb sack over my shoulder, I came back through the storeroom, and doing my best to calm myself, envision myself as the dutiful, *truthful* daughter I had always been, I let myself in through the back door of Papa's apothecary shop. With its shelves of herbs and jars of potions—bottles of leaves and barks and spices—it was a simple and humble workplace. It was small—for the house itself was small, as most of the four-story homes in Vinci were—and twice as long as it was wide. If a family had a business, it would be found, like Papa's shop, on the ground floor in the front, facing the street.

An easy and graceful exit was not to be mine this day. Signora Grasso was sliding a basket of ripe tomatoes across the counter at Papa with a grateful smile. Grateful, I wondered, for the cure he had provided for her daughter's liver flux or for accepting his payment in vegetables?

"Caterina, beautiful child!" she called out at the sight of me. "I tell you, Ernesto, she is growing more lovely every day. The image of her mother." She looked me up and down so carefully one would have thought she was buying a horse. "But I must say she has your height. Though there are some men who might not mind a tall girl."

"Is there anything else I can help you with today, signora?" Papa said in that soothing, unrushed fashion the townspeople loved so much. He was, indeed, a long, lanky man with the air of good health about him and a splendid headful of silver hair. He dressed simply and unassumingly, a style that so matched his nature.

"Well, I do have a rash, Ernesto, in a place I will tell you about, but not show you," she said confidentially.

Just then the bell over the front door jangled and my heart soared. Now there were *two* patients to distract him.

"Papa," I said, "I find we are out of verbena."

His eyebrows furrowed. "Did we not have a good patch of it near the south wall?"

"We did," I said, grateful for the small honesty before the larger lie. "But we used it up."

"Used it up?"

"Remember? Signora D'Aretino for her jaundice and Signor Martoni and his son for their eyes . . . ?" I paused, as though I had a dozen more who had used up our supply, though I really did not. But I knew very well how long my father allowed himself to ponder trivialities, and was not surprised when a moment later he said, "Yes, Caterina, would you go and get us some? And it would be the time, would it not, to find us some woad along the river?"

"Woad," I repeated, thrilled that my plan had succeeded. I'd forgotten we had nearly spent our supply of the plant that, made into an ointment, was used in the treatment of ulcers. We both knew it would just be coming into flower.

"I'll go immediately," I called, already half out the door. I did not wish to hear any last-minute requests, or reminders to finish my chores before leaving. And I knew the alchemical fire would burn quite happily with no further attention till I returned in the afternoon.

As I walked the cobbled streets of Vinci—a hilltop village of perhaps fifty households—with its church and the old castle the only buildings of any size, I pondered my newfound rebellion and felt a touch of shame.

Papa had given me so much . . . and this was how I repaid him. Ernesto was the only parent I had ever known, my mother having died of a fever within weeks of giving birth to me, all of her desperate husband's potions unable to save her. Throughout my young childhood I had been cherished and doted upon. All the love my widowed father owned he lavished on me. There were no beatings. No abuses.

I was made to do the lightest of chores, as everything else was seen to by Magdalena.

Most days I had sat on the apothecary counter and entertained Papa's customers. I was a natural mimic and could replicate birdsong, a braying mule, or a neighbor's laugh. Several days a week Papa would take me up into the hills while he picked the herbs that did not grow in his garden. I loved to hide from him in the tall grasses, chase butterflies, or throw my arms wide and race the wind.

He showed me the springs where birds gathered to drink and bathe. They always seemed ecstatic, taking their turns in the shallows. Papa and I would laugh as the sleek feathered creatures turned into shaggy, bedraggled monsters. All in all very little had been expected of me. It gave Papa joy just to know I was such a carefree little girl.

On my eighth birthday everything changed.

He had taken me to a cave that, until then, he'd kept secret from me. It was dark except for a single shaft of light that shone in from its rocky roof. We'd stood silently in that beam of sunlight, altogether illuminated yet surrounded by utter blackness.

"Eight," he said, his portentous voice echoing in the cavern. "Eight is the greatest of all numbers."

"Why, Papa?"

"It is the number of Infinity." At our feet in the sand he drew the number and the symbol, and taking my finger traced it round and round, showing me how it had no beginning and no end. "Eight is the number of endless possibility. Worlds untold. You are eight years old, Caterina. Now begins your true life. Now begins your education."

And so it had.

That evening after Magdalena had gone home, Papa, carrying a torch, took me up the stairs past our bedrooms to the third-floor landing. Here were two rooms, his *sanctum sanctorum*, that until then had been locked and I'd been forbidden to enter. Obedient child that I was I had obeyed his prohibitions.

First he had unlocked the street-side door. When we entered I found myself in a bright, airy, but unadorned room. It was filled with tables, and the surface of every one of them was covered in books.

Certainly I had seen books before. Papa would always have one near his bed at night. Sometimes if I couldn't sleep and wandered into his room for comfort I would find him, by the light of a candle, leaning on one elbow over the open pages. He would always close the book and welcome me into his bed to warm me and rock me, and tell me a story. He kept a book of medicines in his apothecary—a list of the curative properties of plants. I thought nothing of these books, no more than I did of the Bible from which the Vinci friars read every Sunday at mass.

But here were dozens of hand-copied books lying on the tables, some of them very large, their pages spread open. Papa held his torch over one of these and I saw not just written words but beautiful golden leaves and vines intertwined with giant letters, and tiny pictures on the pages in every color and hue.

"This manuscript," he told me, his voice suffused with awe, "is one thousand years old."

One *thousand*? "Where did you get such a book, Papa?" I asked as I moved slowly round the tables looking at the volumes, which he allowed me, very carefully, to open. I saw many in Latin, which, though I had not learned to read or write, I recognized as such. But there were others with letters that appeared in strange jagged shapes, and others in graceful curves.

"Tell me, you must tell me how you came to have so many books."

As I was doing, he now began to move about his library, stopping to gaze at a text, holding his torch above his eyes, squinting down and reading a bit, nodding now and again. After a while he began to talk, weaving a story in the same way he had done on those sleepless nights of mine. But these were no stories of dragons and their mountain lairs, or spirits that inhabited the heads of waterlillies.

This was the story of his adventurous youth and his apprenticeship to the notorious Florentine historian and scholar Poggio Bracciolini, himself in the employ of the greatest man in Florence, Cosimo de' Medici.

"He is still today much loved for his modesty and humble leadership despite his astonishing wealth," Papa told me, "but in the old days Cosimo took up the notion that the learned men of his beloved city must begin reading the ancient Greek and Roman writers, scrolls and codices that had been scattered all around the world after the destruction of the great library in Alexandria—that is, Egypt. Many of them were hidden from the Christian church fathers, who thought them heretical."

"What is 'heretical,' Papa?"

"Heretical is believing any notion that the priests cannot find in the Holy Scripture. Heretical is a dangerous thing to be. Heretical is what I am, sweet girl."

I must have looked terrified, for he picked me up and smothered me in a warm embrace. Then, clearing a place on one of the library tables, he sat me down on it.

"Dangerous or not, Caterina, what lies within the pages of these books are truths that we must never allow to be lost to the world. Truths that must be learned by you."

"Me?" My voice was very small and filled with dread. Hadn't Papa just told me that the books were heretical and that this was dangerous?

"Listen to me." He knelt before me so his face was close to mine and he spoke with a passion I had never before heard in his always kindly voice. "You are a female child. In this society of ours you might as well be a clod of cow manure."

I stared at him without understanding. I was loved, even coddled in my home. If other girls my age were treated differently, I was yet unaware.

"Soon your 'only worth' will become apparent—your 'marriageability.' If you should marry higher than your station, you will be thought to be increasing your family's wealth, its standing and connections."

I really did not comprehend his meaning. *Wealth. Standing. Connections.*

These were words never spoken in our household. I guessed they were in short supply here. Surely I had heard the older girls and women speak of marriage as they sat in their basket-weaving circles by the Vincio River, and until then I had always expected to marry.

"But in other places, other times, Caterina—ancient times, pagan times," he went on, "females were revered. They were high priestesses. Rulers of great lands. They were even supreme goddesses, worshipped by all."

"Goddesses?" I said uncomprehendingly. "Like the Virgin Mary?"

"No." He shook his head and laughed a small laugh, then picked up a book with the strange angular letters, and placed it in my lap. "This is the Greek language," he told me. "In this book the author speaks of Isis, Egyptian goddess of life and love and all of Nature."

"Does she know Jesus?" I asked.

"No, Caterina, Isis had been a goddess for thousands of years before Jesus was born. But you," my father told me as he lifted me down off the table, "you will learn to read Greek and Latin and Hebrew—the language of the Jews. I believe that if a female is good enough to become a goddess, then a little girl is good enough to become a scholar."

"You will teach me, Papa?"

"Yes, I will teach you."

"But you never told me how you came to have all these books. Or about Poggio."

"Quite right. I'm afraid I went off on a tangent."

"What is a 'tangent'?" I said. "And what is a 'pagan'?"

He laughed again. "I can see that I have the makings of a true scholar before me, for a true scholar has a mind full of endless questions. Now come along. There's much more to see."

Much more! I thought, my brain suddenly afire. *What wonders could he possibly have left to show me?*

I watched breathlessly as he put the key in the door to the third-floor room overlooking the apothecary garden and unlocked it. Neatly organized as this top-floor chamber was, a darkness pervaded it, so unlike the cheerful apothecary on the ground floor, or the many-windowed library. A sharp biting smell assaulted my nostrils, so different from the shop's vegetal fragrance.

Immediately apparent were the tables upon which stood connected arrays of vials, funnels, and oddly shaped vessels. Along one wall was a large furnace with bellows attached, and a store of various fuels for it—from coal and wood to rushes and pitch.

Near the garden window a large manuscript lay open on a pedestal. One wall of shelves held trays, scales, strainers, basins, and ladles. There were flasks of myriad shapes, some with long necks, some with two spouts, and one that coiled like a serpent.

What arrested my attention most, however, were two beakers—one that appeared stained with soot and was like a great egg that, with a hinge, opened and closed at the top, sitting perched on a three-legged cradle. Another of clear glass stood on the floor, two whole feet wide at its bottom, and as high as Papa's chest. *Where had such amazing artifacts come from?*

Now my nostrils were assailed by a familiar smell, but one that occurring inside our house mystified me.

"Papa," I said, "I smell horse droppings."

"You've a good nose, Caterina. It is as you say, but the dung is 'fermenting.'" He showed me an earthen vessel that, when I moved closer, emitted a stronger smell of the stuff. "In a closed vessel it will work upon itself and create a gentle source of heat. Most all of my work here, my 'experiments,' require some form of heat. Come closer, let me show you the furnace. It is called an athenor. Don't be afraid," he said gently. "You and this furnace will soon be very well acquainted." He took my hand and led me close. Even with its door closed the thing gave off a withering heat.

"Child, I am what is called an alchemist, and this furnace is the heart and soul of this chamber, this alchemical laboratory, for it is through fire that nature itself can be changed. Alchemists, they say, are the Masters of Fire."

From the hook he removed a leather apron and, slipping it over his head, pulled the garment over his body, crossing its long thick straps behind his back and knotting them in front. Then to my amazement and delight he took a second leather apron from the hook—one much smaller, just my size—and slipped it over my head.

"We speak in a secret language—though the church abhors and forbids it—seeking truth through *knowledge*, rather than through faith."

I was very still and silent as he fitted the apron around me. It was reminiscent of a religious ceremony before this fiery altar, Papa's movements no less reverent than the local priest's as he placed the wafers on our tongues and the wine chalice to our lips during communion.

"You should never approach the open furnace without protection," he said, now placing a small leather mask over my face, doing the same with one of his own.

As he opened the furnace door I had gone beyond awe—this magical chamber, its sights and smells, we two like mystical creatures in our animal-skin costumes approaching the profane and sacred alchemical fire.

"The flames can never be allowed to burn out. Everything is done to maintain a steady temperature." He pulled from the woodpile a fat log and set it on the stone floor in front of the athenor. Then with a brush he'd removed from a bucket of thick black pitch, he slathered the log with a coating of the stuff. Now donning heavy gloves and with almost tender care he placed the pitch-covered wood into the fire. "I will set it at night before bedtime, and see to it in the morning, first thing waking." As the heat flared he closed the furnace door. "Sometimes in the middle of the night I wake, worried that the fire has gone out. I come upstairs . . . move back, Caterina. . . ." Now he pressed the arms of the bellows several times together. ". . . and I feed the dragon."

I wondered then why I had never noticed his comings and goings.

"But since I first lit it all those years ago, I have never once let it die. Your mother helped me before she passed away"—he pulled off his mask and gently removed mine—"and now *you* will become the keeper of the alchemical fire."

And so I had.

I'd learned the secret language of the alchemist and assumed, even in my youth, the healthy, patient, and humble attributes of the profession that my father instilled in me. He taught me the modes of fermentation, distillation, putrefaction, and extraction. Reduction, coagulation, tinction, and crystallization. My small fingers were thrust into coal, dirt, and sand baths. I became adept at handling pelican beakers, earthenware crucibles, and calcinating dishes. I became proficient in measuring substances on a scale, and the correct use of a dissolving furnace.

There were different classes of alchemists, Papa told me. Ones who sought spiritual transformation from the philosophic teachings. Ones who put great stock in the mineral sphere, and others—like himself—who were more attuned to the "vegetable world," seeking applications for use in the apothecary. But most alchemists were amateurs—"puffers," he called them—who sought the "philosopher's stone" or "elixir" that would transmute base metal into gold. These men were not simply greedy, he'd told me, but caused men like himself serious trouble with the church. Anyone known as an alchemist, no matter his motives, was branded as a heretic, an evil sorcerer. But in the end, if caught, even a man like himself—who used the results of his experiments to heal the sick—would suffer on a pyre in as much agony as a man seeking fame and the glitter of gold.

Too, I began in earnest my education in the apothecary arts—how and when to cut the leaves of a plant just at the moment its flowers came fully into bloom, when the active principle of the herb was at its strongest. How seeds needed to be harvested when most mature, and that roots were best lifted in autumn, once the top growth of the plant had begun to die back.

I became expert at drying and preserving leaves for winter use. That muslin bags placed over the hanging flower heads would catch escaping seeds. How one should gather certain plants early in the day and gently shake the dew from them, and to be sure that everything used in our medicines was free from insects and disease. Papa taught me very carefully that in certain plants one part—say the flower—might contain a medicine, but the root of the same might be poisonous.

I most enjoyed tending our apothecary garden, watching the seeds we buried in the moist earth sprout, grow to seedlings, and bush into fine plants. We grew agrimony for tonic, and chamomile for soothing tea. Clary seeds steeped in water formed a paste that was used to bathe the eyes or draw thorns from the hands. Dandelion helped kidneys, and water made from soaking dill helped farting babies.

Leaves from our elderberry hedge we took up to the alchemical laboratory. Heated together with lard and suet, then strained through a fine sieve, this was a wonderful treatment for burns, chilblains, and the bite of certain insects. An infusion of feverfew, also concocted on the third floor, was invaluable for bringing down a person's temperature. I learned to grind marigold into ointments for ulcers and wounds, and decoct the syrup of mallow for stubborn coughs deep in the lungs.

But just as important, Papa taught me that in speaking with those in need of care, we should always make little show of ourselves and refrain from praising our remedies. Gossip was forbidden, as idle chatter was never a help for the sick. An apothecary was best when in full harmony with his work. "Scholarly and intelligent," my father would remind me to be. The famous Greek physician Galen had always said that a doctor was, by nature, a philosopher.

But that was not all I learned. Not the least of it! Having been allowed admittance into my father's library, I became its most frequent visitor. Early morning and every evening after the shop was closed the contents of those books and manuscripts was shunted into my head. Papa was a stern tutor, though always kind, for he found me a perfect student—diligent, quick to learn, and "once taught, never forgotten."

But how could I forget that which was written on those pages? The wisdom of the ages. Fantastical stories of gods and men. The way to know right from wrong. The magic in numbers. The evil in men's hearts. Heroic adventures and the throes of romantic passion.

I came to understand that two thousand years had passed since some of the books I was reading had been written. And by whom. The Greeks—Plato, Euripides, Homer, Xenophon—and the ancient Romans—Ovid, Virgil, Livius, Cato.

And I heard, too, the story—this was Papa's favorite—of how an apothecary from the tiny Tuscan village of Vinci had come to acquire such a remarkable library. Poggio Bracciolini became a legend in our house. In the pay of Cosimo de' Medici, Poggio's many missions to the farthest reaches of Europe, Persia, and Africa had delivered untold treasures into the hands of the richest man in the world. Not gold. Not jewels . . . but books.

Those that were lost after the barbarian invasion of the Roman Empire.

Some were originals, the ones that could be pried or bribed away from their owners. Others could only be copied in the hand of Poggio himself. He had found in Ernesto a willing assistant, fearless no matter where their travels took them—into the frozen wastes of the Swiss Alps or the burning deserts of the Holy Land. Sometimes they were confined to a dark, moldering basement cell with only the light of a single candle to work by. Sometimes they were chased from mosques by irate Mohammedans with flashing scimitars who saw the pair as thieves and invaders.

My father had been tireless and, more, appreciated fully the gift of this unique profession. Day after month after year he copied, then *learned*, the sacred languages of Latin, Greek, and Hebrew. He was so quick and adept he found he had time to spare, and Poggio, endlessly grateful for this enthusiastic protégé, allowed Ernesto in the times he was meant to be eating, sleeping, or resting to make copies of the books for himself.

With all these manuscripts delivered into the Medici's hands, the adventurer Poggio grew rich beyond his wildest dreams. In Florence he retired to a life of writing and dissolution. His own father had been a poor village apothecary, and the son had bought the man a shop and the house above it in the great city. It was into a second apprenticeship with the elder Poggio that my father learned his present trade. Living and working there Ernesto, like a sponge, had soaked up the knowledge of herbs and the compounding of medicine, and the other "secret endeavors" old Signor Bracciolini had shared with him.

Florence, however, held no magic for my father. With his priceless books and his new profession, he moved from the big city to the small mountain village of Vinci, a day's ride due west of Florence, along the Arno River. There he had found love with my mother, after whom I was named, and the respect of his neighbors for his careful ministrations. Of the secret heresies he practiced in the third-floor laboratory of his house, none of them were aware.

So from the age of eight I had developed an understanding of, and strict adherence to, the principle of *secrecy*. Perhaps the greatest of my father's secrets was that he was, in his deepest heart and soul, a pagan. I had learned the meaning of that word as well. He worshipped the natural world, the Elements and the Cosmos, all of which he believed were more potent forces than the Judean teacher and healer called Jesus, and the dangerously corrupt church that had grown up around him. He never forced me to share in his beliefs, but in time I found them very comfortable to my nature.

That said, my father and I appeared to all in Vinci as the best of Christians. We attended mass, made our communion, swore our allegiance to the pope and Rome. Papa donated the money to have a fresco painted at the altar of the local church, and took tender care of the friars at no charge. Regarding this deception, my father told me it was better to be a living hypocrite than a dead truth teller. Our beliefs, he insisted, were no one's business but our own.

As I grew older I became well known for my forays into the countryside collecting herbs and medicines for my father's shop. No other girl had the freedom to roam alone as I did. As far as I knew, no other girl desired such solitary wanderings.

The others of my age and sex were kept at the hearths with their mothers, learning those womanly skills my aunt Magdalena wished me to know, going out only to church or in groups with the village women to weave reed baskets by the river. They ended their childhoods by leaving their fathers' houses and moving into their husbands' houses, or in many instances the houses of their husbands' fathers.

All of them expected to marry.

All of them were virgins.

My father and I had, without speaking of it, delayed talk of my marriage. The only thing that Magdalena's nagging at her brother-in-law yielded were his claims that I was different from the other girls, better and brighter than them. My father and I were both content with our private life of scholarship and service to the village through the apothecary shop.

It therefore came to me as something of a shock in my fourteenth spring when a strange upwelling of "womanly humors" took hold of me. I had, of course, been expecting my menses. And I had endured Magdalena clucking over the buds that had grown into prettily rounded breasts, the dark silken hair sprouting under my arms and between my legs. But the unbidden urges, moods, and black melancholies that assailed me, and the pleasant but unnerving sensations that tingled in the place I made water, these were things my aunt had never spoken of. And of them my father was entirely unaware.

Whereas I had always happily and unfailingly stoked the alchemist furnace, tended our apothecary garden, and made thoughtful and appropriate conversation with Papa's clients, suddenly I had become a wild thing. I felt trapped in the too-dark house, bored with every task my father assigned me, unable to concentrate on Pythagorean geometry, and loathing the smell of his sulfurous laboratory.

All of what seethed inside me I hid from him, afraid that the raw animal I had become would be unlovable to him. At home I remained his adored Caterina, his precious little scholar and helpmate. I was the picture of perfection.

Out in the fields I would hoist up my skirts and run like a boy in a solo footrace, just run and shout into the wind. It was the only way I knew to release the demon between my legs.

"Caterina, come sit with us!"

I was jolted from my reverie by the voice and startled to see how far I had come from the village, out past the olive groves on the hillside, through the pastures where sheep grazed, and all the way down to the riverbank. There I saw before me the girls and women of the town, wickerwork in their laps and strewn about them on red wool rugs.

I was sorry they had seen me, for I had no wish to insult them but no use for idle chatter this day. I had no use for *anything* save an indolent walk down the reedy banks of the Vincio, filling my sack with fragrant herbs and flowers.

"I'm on an errand for my father!" I called back with my most friendly smile.

"Forget your father! Come sit with us!" they called. Signora Palma was the most insistent.

"If I don't go pick some valerian, Signora Segretti will not get her nerve tonic and will make all your lives miserable when you go to her shop to buy bread!"

When I heard a chorus of shouts and good-natured curses I knew I was safe to go. I set my eyes on the path going downriver, closing out the sound of chattering women, attuned myself to birdsong, rushing water, and the rustling whisper of reeds along the bank.

I delighted in nature. Except for Papa, nothing was so dear to me in life but what lived and breathed, grew and died in the hills and meadows and caves around Vinci. For a moment I considered visiting a certain cavern where grew a special mold that kept a wound from suppurating. But no. Today I envisioned a sun-dappled meadow along the river path far enough upstream that no one from town would bother me.

I could already see up ahead that the meadow next to the path was a riot of lungwort flowers, their deep rose heads on tall stalks so delicate that the whole field of them was tossed by the softest of breezes. I decided to walk to a place in the river that elbowed around a tiny eruption of boulders and trees, making for a small waterfall, thick with greenery on either side. Moss covered the ground in a thick mattress. It was pure heaven.

Once at my destination I sat down, and opening my herb sack, I heaved into the river the incriminating verbena. Then I dug deeper till I found my red and gold wrapped book. I had marked the place where I had left off Plato's most fabulous of all tales, that of the lost continent of Atlantis. More interesting to me these days were not his ruminations on the perfection of the Atlantean society, nor its tragic war with Athens, but the great love affair of the god-king Poseidon and his Earth mistress Clieto. How he had ascended from the stars, married her, and sired on her five sets of twin sons.

My imagination had carried me back, as the Greek sage had written, nine thousand years before even *he* had ever been born! Just the antiquity of it filled me with wonder. But nothing was as enthralling as the romance of a god with a human. This day I read and reread those passages of *Timaeus* that evoked such a love. It aroused me, disturbed my passions. I closed my eyes and imagined what it would feel like to have the hands of a man from the heavens on my body. They would be strong, yet tender. As he was a god, he would know my mind, know my nature, know what would pleasure me. . . .

Caterina! I scolded myself. *You must stop indulging in these sensual fantasies. You will drive yourself mad!* I felt my armpits soaked with perspiration. My skirts were suddenly too heavy, my bodice strings too tightly drawn.

I stripped down to my shift and, closing my eyes again, lay on my back in the shallow water, letting it ripple over my belly and breasts, hoping to cool them.

"*Scuse.*"

The single word, spoken in a near whisper, but so unexpectedly, had me suddenly thrashing in the shallows, trying to cover my near nakedness. I grabbed for my skirt and bodice, holding them over my breasts, which, through the wet shift, were not only visible but spiking two hard nipples.

I turned to the male voice, but with me on the ground and him standing, my first sight revealed only a torso—a tall, well-dressed one at that, in a fine doublet of rust and gray. The stockings encapsulated shapely calves and muscular thighs.

That was all I saw before I scrambled to my feet and turned away from him, pulling my clothing back on.

"I saw you lying there," the man said. "I wondered if you were hurt."

"Not hurt. No." I was finally covered enough to face him. When I did I received another shock: the man's face was achingly handsome. Amidst a lion's mane of pale wavy hair were broad cheekbones tapering into a proud, chiseled jaw. The eyes were set far apart, their color light hazel. The nose was straight and long, though not unpleasantly so, ending in a fine tip rather than the hooked beak with which so many Italian men were endowed. His lips were thin but carefully shaped, and he was smiling at me with a lopsided grin that all of a sudden caused my mouth to go dry, and my groin to grow damp.

"I am Piero, son of Antonio," he said.

The name was familiar to me. "The big house just inside the old castle wall?" I asked, finally finding a less-than-stupid voice.

"That's the one. With the waterwheel on the side, and the grain mill. . . ." His voice was strong and melodious. Though he had been speaking of a mill in his house, his eyes seemed to be saying something different. Something like, "You are beautiful. A goddess. I cannot stop staring at you."

But I was *not* imagining it. His eyes had never left my face. He stared so deeply at me I grew even more uncomfortable.

"I should go," I said and looked for my sack, which was lying on the ground just behind him. Awkward and trying desperately not to touch him, I snatched it up, stuffing my copy of the *Timaeus* inside.

"What are you doing out here by yourself in the first place?" he asked.

"Gathering herbs. I help my father in the apothecary."

"Ah."

"Last year he treated your mother for her bowel affliction," I said. I remembered the incident because of the extreme pain the woman had suffered, the great relief my father's potion had given her, and how payment from one of the wealthiest families in town had been made more than six months later, and with no thanks at all.

"How is it that your father allows a young girl to be wandering around in the hills on her own?"

"I am not a young girl," I said. "I am a young woman." I wondered if my tone was unpleasantly defiant, but his smile told me he had not been offended in the least.

"What have you gathered so far?" he asked me. It seemed as though he was struggling as hard as I was to make conversation.

"Nothing so far."

"Nothing?!" He laughed, and immediately I loved the sound of it. "I don't think you're out here picking herbs for your apothecary father at all," he said. "I think you're a gypsy escaped from your band."

"I'm not, really!" I cried. I knew the man was flirting with me, a game I had never engaged in but knew something about, having listened to girls gossip. *What should I do?* I wondered. I did not wish him to think me a woman of no virtue. I lowered my eyes demurely and stared at the ground.

"What's your name?" His voice was low and somehow demanding, and again I was aware that the triangle between my thighs was alive with sensation.

"Caterina," I answered, then, forgetting restraint, looked him directly in the eye. "My father sometimes calls me Cato."

"Cato? That's a man's name!"

I enjoyed surprising him. "Not just any man," I continued. "Cato was a great Roman who—"

"I know who Cato was." He looked at me oddly. "I just wondered why a girl should know such things."

Oh no! I had erred. In my desire to flirt and appear worldly, I had divulged the most important of family secrets—my education. So I shrugged like a silly girl.

"That's all I know of him," I said, my second lie of the day. My father had called me Cato because, even as a child, I had been bold and stubborn, demanding the toys or food or hugs I wanted. The great Roman had been described by Plutarch as a man who would strike boldly without flinching. Standing his ground.

This young man was amused. He knew I was lying.

"By your own description you also seem to know what herbals to pick for your father's apothecary," he said. "You're a bit precocious for a beautiful young girl. Forgive me," he added quickly. "Young woman."

There, he'd said it! He did think I was beautiful.

"Why are you out here?" I asked him, groping for a way to continue this exchange.

"Just out for a walk. I'm home for a time from Florence, where I've begun to practice law. I'm a notary."

I attempted to suppress my admiration. The Notaries Guild was the foremost of all the guilds, the profession a noble one. Piero da Vinci, I quickly decided, was a man of substance.

And very handsome.

"I think I should start home," I said.

"Won't you disappoint your father?" I must have looked confused. "You've gathered no herbs."

I flustered and flushed red. "I'll pick them on the way back."

"Will you allow me to accompany you?"

"I don't see why not."

I led him to a field where angelica grew and stopped to pick some. I could feel Piero was watching me, and all at once, as if it were the most natural thing in the world, I allowed myself to bask in his warm gaze. I *felt* beautiful. Knew the sun was casting a shine on the black silk of my hair, the breeze pushing the skirts against my legs to show their shapeliness.

"You've very long legs for a girl," he said, as though reading my mind.

As a god would do, I thought. I was happy to be facing away so he couldn't see me blush.

"Like a young colt," he went on.

"You should not be talking about my legs," I told him in a tone that was unconvincingly stern, "or any other part of my body."

"Why is that?"

"It is improper."

"Might I comment on your pretty dark hair?"

"I suppose."

"Or your lovely hands?"

"My hands are not lovely." I looked down at them. There was soot under my fingernails from pulling a double pelican out from an ash bath that morning, and green stains from the elder ointment I'd made yesterday.

"Why don't you let me decide that?" Piero said, coming around in front of me. He'd picked up both my hands in his before I could stop him.

I wanted to die with shame.

"Well, they are a bit grimy."

I tried to pull them away, but he held them firmly. "But the fingers are long and shapely . . . like your legs."

"Let go!" I cried, but I was very much enjoying being teased.

"And the skin, where it's not green or black"—he laughed at his own joke—"is soft and creamy white. Kissable." Before I knew what had happened he had leaned down and placed his warm lips on the back of my hand, lingering there for what seemed like forever.

Feeling a sudden twitch of pleasure between my thighs, I jerked my hand away.

"I'm going home now," I announced, starting back toward the river path.

"I'll walk back with you," he said, following me.

"No!" I shouted.

He stopped short.

"Have I offended you, Caterina? It was not my intention."

"You haven't offended me. It's just . . ." I lowered my voice, as if anyone could hear. "There are women at the river, weaving baskets."

He was amused. "And you would not want them to see us walking together."

"Alone and unchaperoned? No, I would not. There's already enough gossip in this village."

"You're quite right about that. What do you suggest?"

"About what?"

"How should we make our way home without inflaming the gossip-weavers?"

I liked this young man. He was not simply handsome and charming. He was intelligent. He had just made up an excellent new word.

"I know another way home," I said. "But it takes us through a marsh and over some jagged rocks. If I show it to you, you will keep your hands to yourself."

"Must I?"

"Yes. And no more . . ." I suddenly became shy.

"Comments on your body parts?"

"Exactly."

"Then lead the way."

He kept his word that day. A perfect gentleman. We spoke little as he followed close behind me. Only when I sank suddenly into a too-soft spot in the marsh did he reach out and catch my arm, quickly releasing it once I was upright. When the village was in sight we stopped and stood side by side.

"I have to see you again," he said. His voice was husky and urgent.

"You will," I replied, then teased him, "at church."

"Caterina!"

"I'll be gathering herbs again."

"When?"

"I have chores, Piero."

"When?"

"Tomorrow." I looked down at my feet. "Early in the morning. I can tell Papa I need to gather the mallow before the dew dries."

"What place?"

"The meadow where you told me I had the legs of a colt."

"The meadow where I kissed your hand."

He grasped my hand again, but this time opened my fingers and placed it over his chest. "You must bring me a remedy for my aching heart," he said.

Then he let me go on ahead so we would not be seen together. By the time I returned to the apothecary I was dazed. I had no answer for Papa as to why my shoes were muddy or why I had not collected any verbena or woad.

I went up to my room and flopped on my bed. *What had happened?* I wondered. I had spoken to a young man. Been teased by him. Had had my hand kissed. Promised to meet him again . . . secretly.

I would not think of it till tomorrow, I decided. I stood up and climbed to the third floor to check the furnace, which indeed needed another log. I swept the laboratory floor with tremendous industry, then went across to the library and opened the *Cabala* to a page of text I'd lately had difficulty translating. I set my mind to the task and was soon immersed in it.

But that night when I fell asleep I dreamed of a handsome horseman who'd arrived on a road through the clouds—a god with light hazel eyes.

*A*fter that, almost every day I found excuses to leave my father's house and meet Piero. We'd seek the privacy of the woods, a cave, the edge of a field. He would bring a blanket. I would take him to the small secret waterfall where grew myrtle and sweet cicely. We'd take off our slippers and dangle our feet in the cool rushing water. We talked easily, laughed at almost anything. My shyness evaporated as quickly as the dew on a hot summer morning, and soon I had blossomed from the studious young hermaphrodite Caterina/Cato into the woman I had, on that first afternoon, insisted I was.

Somehow I'd known how to kiss him, let my whole body melt effortlessly into his in a standing embrace. Later we'd lay back on the blanket in each other's arms, me with my head in the sweet, musky nest of his shoulder.

He talked of his family. I would admire his father, he insisted, a man who had refused to follow his family tradition of the notary's profession. Instead, Antonio da Vinci had wisely invested his money in property—groves and vineyards and farms. Piero's mother was rather stern and prudish, he told me, but would take to me, given time. He was sure of it.

Of his younger brother, Francesco, he had few kind words.

"He is a feckless boy, no ambition whatsoever. He's content to stroll from farm to field to orchard."

"He takes more after your father then, as you take after your grand-father," I observed.

"No," Piero insisted, flushing with irritation. "My father may not have chosen the law as a profession, but he is a clever businessman. Francesco wanders around talking to his goats!"

Despite the harsh words, Piero introduced me to Francesco one afternoon, bringing him to our assignation, a gesture that delighted me. It was clear Piero wished to "show me off" to his feckless brother, thinking we would like each other.

We did.

I saw much of myself in the gentle young man, his extreme love of the natural world, and his ease moving through it. Whereas Piero pined for the rich, exciting life in the city, Francesco stopped to gaze at every flowering bush and stuck his nose into the fragrant blossoms. Animals of all kinds loved him—the horse he rode, the birds he fed from his hands. Even sheep followed him around.

"The sheep especially," Piero had once blithely commented one day as Francesco rode off after a picnic we had shared at the river.

"What do you mean?" I asked, confused.

"I mean that he sodomizes sheep, among others. My dear brother is a *Florenzer*."

"I'm sorry, I don't understand."

"Caterina, Francesco does not love women. He loves men."

I was growing very confused. I knew nothing of such things.

"Why do you call a man who loves other men a *Florenzer*?" I asked.

"Because Florence is teeming with them. They're so common there that the Germans have taken to calling their deviants after our city. Now all of Europe is doing the same." Piero softened, brushing a strand of hair off my forehead. "Francesco likes you, though. If he weren't a *Florenzer* he would probably be in love with you"—he pulled me to him—"like I am."

I smiled inwardly. Piero had never said those words before. I could not ignore them, but I did not wish to speak of such things so forthrightly. "What about your sister?" I asked. "She's married to a much older man, is she not?"

He nodded, tracing the line of my chin with his finger. "They've moved to Pistoia. He has designed a new gun. One so small it can be held in one hand. I think one day he'll grow very rich . . ." Piero smiled. "Like me."

"Is she in love with him?" I asked almost shyly.

"My sister with her husband?"

I nodded.

"No."

"Do you think people who love each other should marry?" I said.

"No," he answered matter-of-factly, "unless those people are you and me." He turned to me and kissed me very sweetly.

The words and the kiss were like a pitch-covered log thrown on a fire. I pulled him to me and soon we lay perspiring, disheveled and panting as if we had both run a distance.

Piero sat up suddenly. "I will talk to your father tomorrow morning."

The breath went out of me. Any normal girl would have insisted on such assurances from the first moment a man began courting her. For that matter, any normal girl would not have made her own choice of a husband, nor spent every afternoon lying alone in a field with him, kissing and touching and longing to give away her virginity.

Piero had always been the one to rein in our passions, stifle our urges. He was a man of the law, he had stated with pride. He wished for a proper wife and legitimate children, most especially sons who would carry on not only his bloodline but his honorable profession. His father and Francesco, despite their many declarations of enjoying the livings they had chosen, he believed, had made a terrible error. His own son would never make that same mistake.

Now Piero was determined to ask for my hand.

I had been, in a part of me, dreading this moment. Of course I wished for marriage with Piero, was longing for my new life as a respectable wife. But I knew, in some part of me, that my father would disapprove of the match.

He did not think well of Piero's family. The incident of his parents' late payment and less thanks for the apothecary bill was but a fraction of it. Piero's father had a reputation in the village for cheating his workers, cutting wages in a bad season rather than taking the loss himself, and showing no concern whatsoever if his employees were injured or became ill. He was even stingy with the widows of tenants whose families had worked his land for generations.

It was all this that had kept me from mentioning even once to my father that I had fallen in love and was planning to leave his home for the home of this wealthy—but in his mind, undistinguished—family. This, as well as the thought that Piero was an unsuitable husband for a girl with a mind so filled with education, philosophy, and heresy as I was.

I loved Piero so that I had, of late, found myself cursing Papa for having made me into the freakish woman I was. All I wanted was a normal life with my husband. Where we lived—Vinci or Pistoia or Florence or the ends of the earth—didn't matter. Nor did how many children, girls or boys, as long as we had them.

Sometimes I cursed myself. I was the most ungrateful daughter who had ever lived. Dear Papa, who had been both loving father and mother to me, was suddenly the enemy, he who had opened my eyes to worlds most men and virtually all women had no privilege to know. I was content to open my legs, and like any ordinary woman, let that be enough to take me through the rest of an ordinary life.

But of course Piero was right. He must speak to my father. We stood and he helped me arrange my clothes and hair, and blotted my cheeks with cool water from his flask, so I didn't appear to be a girl who had wrestled all afternoon with a man ten years her elder.

His eyes had gone suddenly liquid. Smiling with a quiet happiness he took my face into his cupped hands. "My little wife," he said. "Mother of my children."

That was all I needed to hear. What was left of my restraint fell away and my womanly humors took hold. I kissed him in a way I had not, in all those afternoons, kissed him before. In a way that, having heard his intentions, left no doubt as to my own.

We made love that day, on a rug under the broad branches of a fruited walnut. Gentle as Piero was—constantly kissing my face and whispering in hoarse gasps how beautiful I was, how long and graceful were my legs, how like honeyed hills were my breasts—I found the act more painful than pleasurable. I secretly prayed there was more to lovemaking than this and afterward, when I saw the spot of virgin's blood on the rug, I began to weep.

My lover comforted me very sweetly, and we made plans for his visit to my father's house the next morning. He would go home now and tell his family of our plans.

I could hardly breathe on the walk home, quivering with mixed delight and fear. What would my father say? Would he be angry that I had kept so important a secret from him? Would he, despite his low regard for Piero's family, accept him as my husband? And most terrifying, would Father be able to tell from looking at me that I had lost my virginity?

When I reached our house I noticed on the cobbled street in front of the apothecary a clutch of gossiping villagers to whom I managed a *"Bon giorno."* They all returned it with friendly smiles, and I realized how easy it was for me to smile back. I was going to be the wife of Piero, the up-and-coming notary!

Inside I found my father just wrapping a package for a woman who, by her reedy thin body, could only be Signora Malatesta. In the package was surely the poultice for her husband, who was suffering from arthritis. Her back was to me as I entered but I heard her say, "I cannot see the door, Ernesto, but by the look on your face there is only one person who could be walking through it."

It was true. My father's delight in his only child was known by all of his clients, patients, patrons, and customers, and that constituted nearly every villager in Vinci. I could see his handsome face now, the reserved closemouthed smile and the crinkling at the corners of his eyes.

"*Bon giorno*, Signora Malatesta," I said and, after giving my father a quick peck, added, "I'm going upstairs." That was our code for "I'm going to tend the alchemical furnace."

As I passed through the storeroom I heard him call after me, "Did you bring the hyssop?" I pretended I was out of hearing and clomped extra noisily up the stairs. In fact I had entirely forgotten to pick any. In the last weeks, every day I'd gone in the hills to meet Piero, I had been careful whether before or after seeing him to do whatever I had told my father was my purpose—to pick an herb, gather moss or a fungus.

This day all of it had gone out of my head. Today I would either confess that I had forgotten to pick the hyssop or explain to him the real reason I had been staying away so often from the shop and our own apothecary garden.

I was racked by a chaos of emotion, wishing desperately on one hand for Papa's workday to be finished so I could tell him my glorious news, scheming on the other to keep the announcement secret till Piero arrived in the morning. I was tending toward the latter, for I was worried. I believed there was less chance of my father saying no to a grown man, a respectable Florentine notary, than to his fourteen-year-old love-struck daughter.

Piero was charming. He would make it clear that he was better than his family and that, in any event, nothing would satisfy him except Ernesto's blessings on the marriage. The religious and philosophical differences between Piero and me, I decided, could be overlooked if there were love and children and a full family life.

The more I considered it, the surer I was that surprise was to be my greatest help with Papa. I did not know how I would conceal my excitement till the next morning, and go about my chores, and sit across from him at the table as we ate our evening meal. Or for that matter, how I would get a wink of sleep that night.

In the end it had been torture, sweet as it was, torture all the same. For so many years my father and I had shared the same secrets, held ourselves apart from the world. Though I tried to push such thoughts from my mind I knew that I had betrayed his trust, stolen away from our "camp" to Piero's, and nothing I had known would ever be the same again.

The moment the sun rose I was up. I bathed carefully, even washing my hair and brushing it till it fell in dark silken curls around my shoulders. I could hear Magdalena at her housework on the second floor, and my father's footsteps on the stairs going down to the apothecary.

In my daze I remembered only belatedly about the alchemical fire and raced upstairs to the laboratory to pile hardwood into the furnace, hurriedly stoking it with the bellows.

Down again, a kiss on Magdalena's forehead, ignoring her admonition to eat something, and quickly down to the shop.

Piero had promised to arrive just after opening, and I wanted to be there for every moment of the revelation, the argument—if there was to be one—and the inevitable grant of Papa's blessings.

There were two customers waiting when father opened the door. Signora Malatesta, looking ashamed, needed a new poultice, as she had allowed the dog to run away with the one she'd been given for her husband yesterday. A young man came in and showed my father some ugly boils on his back.

I became impatient almost immediately, trying not to grimace when Father instructed me to get on the ladder in the storeroom and fetch down the most aged nettle.

I thought I would scream as I mashed the unpleasant leaves for Signora Malatesta's poultice, and I actually did let out a yelp when, in my nervousness, I knocked a bottle of horsetail tincture all over my chest.

I raced back up to my room, terrified I would miss Piero's entrance, but by the time I had changed into a fresh bodice and reentered the shop, my love had still not arrived.

More customers came and more time passed. I was annoyed that Piero had not come at the time he said he would. As morning became afternoon I became angry, and when Magdalena called us up for our midday meal I barked at my father that I had no appetite. He looked baffled at my outburst and said that if I was not eating I could watch the shop while he did.

My whole body was trembling with anticipation. *Where was Piero?* Something must have happened to him! Perhaps he was hurt, ill. That must be the case, for he was never ever late for our meetings. *I should go to him.* He needed me. Might need the services of my father.

I was half out the door when I realized I could not just leave without my father's permission. And what reason would I give? I had not today—as on all the other days of the secret trysts—given him fair warning of my journeying out to the hills, necessitated by a lack of mullein, or our only jarful of woad salve turning rancid and needing replacement.

It would seem odd for me to suddenly rush out. And what if I did, and missed Piero's visit altogether? There were several ways through the streets of Vinci from his house to ours. He might be stopping along the way to bring us a small gift. What if he was even now in a field picking some pretty flowers? *Oh, why could he have not come when he said he would?*

My father had returned from his dinner, his usual good-natured self, though eyeing me suspiciously, for I was not prone to such outbursts as I'd made that morning.

I silently decided that my only course was to wait for Piero's arrival, whatever time that was, at least until closing.

The rest of the afternoon moved with the speed of a lethargic snail, my nerves fraying with every passing minute. When Father had closed the door on the last customer I could bear it no longer.

"I'm going out!" I fairly shouted.

"Out?" he said mildly. "Out where? To do what?"

I had not prepared an answer and instead stood spluttering helplessly in the doorway. "I'm just going, Papa!"

"Caterina . . ."

I slammed out and began a fast walk toward the old castle and the mill house that stood in its shadows.

It was a fine house that Piero's family had built five generations before. Three stories high, a large portion of it was devoted to a grain mill inside, driven by a cleverly designed waterwheel on the outside. On one side stretching far down the hill was a long, narrow olive orchard whose trees now, in high summer, were bursting with plump green fruit. The back wall of the main enclosure was, indeed, the ancient Vinci Castle bulwark, but the whole of its large gardens and its several outbuildings were enclosed by shorter but still-sturdy masonry walls.

The front gate was imposing, two high wooden doors, crossed and studded with iron fittings, proclaiming that the family inside was important and prosperous.

The gate was firmly shut.

I wished to pound on it and cry out Piero's name, but even in my desperate state I knew that to be a fatal mistake. A future wife of this house must be dignified, not some mad shrieking creature.

I stood there pretending serenity, praying that a family member or servant would exit or enter. I would calmly ask them of Piero's whereabouts. But with no one coming or going I found myself pacing, blowing up little clouds of dust around my feet.

The sun was beginning to set. I could not stand here in the dark. *I must act!*

I picked my way around the perimeter of the wall till I reached the olive orchard. I chose my target. There was a huge ancient tree so close to the compound wall that it overhung the garden.

I hiked up my skirts and climbed it.

Protected from sight by the gray-green leaves of the olive tree, I peered down into the yard. Little was happening. Just a few chickens scratching in the dirt, a stable boy carrying tack into the barn. No one I recognized as family was anywhere to be seen.

I pounded the tree trunk with frustration, crying out at the pain.

"Caterina?" I heard a man say from below.

My heart leapt. I looked down, only to sink with the gravest disappointment at seeing not the da Vinci heir, but Francesco.

"What are you doing up there?" he asked. "Come down. You'll hurt yourself."

I allowed myself to be helped from the tree, trying to regain something of my dignity. Finally we were face-to-face. The brothers resembled each other, I thought, though Piero was taller, and Francesco's features were softer, sweeter.

"Do you know where Piero is?" I finally managed to utter with something resembling calm.

"I do, Caterina. He is in Florence."

"Florence!" My calm shattered instantly. "How can he be in Florence? He was meant to come to my father's house this morning to ask him for my hand."

"I know," Francesco said.

He knew! It was no secret then. All the family must have known of our plans.

"Why did he go without coming to tell me?" I demanded. "When is he coming back?"

Francesco looked stricken. "He will not be coming back for some time." Francesco paused to collect his words. "My father . . . our father . . . is very angry at him. They quarreled."

"They quarreled over me," I said, feeling the skin on my arms rise in gooseflesh.

He nodded.

"Last night, Piero announced his intention to marry you."

I smiled, heartened at that, even though I knew it would be the only good news I would hear from Francesco.

"Father told Piero he was dreaming if he thought he would be allowed to marry . . ." He grimaced as he said, ". . . the likes of you."

"The likes of me," I repeated.

"They are not my words, Caterina, and if you do not wish me to go on . . ."

"No! I want you to tell me everything." I clutched at his arm. "Everything."

This he did, with as much gentleness as he possessed in his gentle soul. But nothing could soften the knife edge as it sliced through me with every callous, offensive sentiment. What could Piero have been thinking? My family was nothing, my father a minor tradesman who took his payment in duck eggs. Piero was meant for much better than a poor village girl. When he married—to a girl his father and grand-father would choose for him—it would be into a family of wealth and high position. The girl's substantial dowry would serve to enrich her husband's family's coffers.

Then Antonio da Vinci asked his son if he had deflowered the apothecary's daughter. Piero had not attempted to deny it. His mother and grandmother had sniffed in disgust. The acknowledgment of my lost virginity had finalized the conversation.

Suddenly Francesco looked down at his feet, loath to continue.

"What did your father say?" I insisted.

"That you were no better than a common prostitute. When Grand-father asked what Piero would do if he'd made you pregnant, Mother and Grandmother stood and left the room."

With those words my knees jellied. The thought of pregnancy had never entered my head. We were to be married. If there had been a child it was meant to be born legitimate. *We were to be married!*

"Did he not fight for me?" I cried. "Even a little?"

Francesco regarded me with pity. "I told you what they said, Ca-terina. How could my brother have fought for you?" Francesco shook his head. "He is heir to this greedy, self-serving family. He should have known better!"

I remember little after that. There must have been moonlight, for even in the night I was able to make my way into the hills, stumbling as I went, caring nothing for my scraped knees and torn skirts. I wan-dered like a wraith up the river shore, collapsing in the shallows to weep, loudly cursing Piero and his miserable family, and finally and most viciously, cursing myself.

How could I have been so stupid? I was a fourteen-year-old girl. No one in the village knew of my father's honorable profession in the service of Poggio, who, in turn, had served Cosimo de' Medici himself. No one knew Ernesto was anything more than a poor country herbalist. And even if Piero's family had known of the vast treasure of books and manuscripts kept in my father's study, it would have meant nothing. All that mattered to them was a fat dowry and a step up into Florentine society. None of that could I offer their son.

And I was a whore at that.

I lay on my back staring up at the stars. They seemed to mock me with their cold, distant sparkle, as if to say, "We haven't a care for you, you poor worthless creature. Rule your own fate? See where it's gotten you."

I cried for so long and so hard that I was altogether emptied, and fell into a dreamless sleep. I woke after dawn, damp all over, the shape of grass spikes gouged into the flesh of my cheek.

I found my way back to the village, ignoring my neighbors, refusing to answer their cheerful hellos. At home I found my father frantic with worry, and Magdalena, relief having turned to annoyance, clucked disapprovingly at my disheveled appearance. Tongues would already be wagging, she scolded.

I could not look my father in the eye. I pulled out of the fierce embrace in which I allowed him to hold me for only a moment before climbing the stairs to my room.

Only later did I learn, or even care, that the fire in his sacred furnace had, for the first time since it had been lit, been allowed to burn down and die.

CHAPTER 3

The day after I returned from Piero's betrayal I drank great quantities of willow leaf tincture to prevent the joining of Piero's seed with my own. I believed in its efficacy and that the vitriol coursing through my veins and surely engorging my organs would kill anything trying to live there and grow.

In the following weeks I was silent in my rage, telling no one—not even my father—the source of it. Fury grew and festered into something sick and pustulent in the deepest part of me.

I became openly irritable, ignored washing or brushing my hair, ate portions that would better suit a large man than a slender girl, and I grew fat and slovenly, my face crisscrossed with white-headed pimples. I lay abed every night obsessed with thoughts of Piero and his family, revenge I would take, even magic potions I would compound to recapture his love if he should ever return from Florence. I refused to go to the hills to collect the herbs for my father's apothecary, and snapped rudely at his patrons. No one understood the change that had come over Caterina—sweet, affable daughter of Ernesto.

In my confused and anguished state I had overlooked the first missed menses, but by the second I had recovered enough of my good sense to realize that the white willow tincture had failed as a contraceptive.

I was pregnant.

I was carrying in my belly the spawn of weak-livered Piero da Vinci. This made me livid. I would not have it, I decided. If I believed

Aristotle, the fetus at this stage was still an animal and not a person. I would kill the thing, I decided. Flush it out of my body. Then, perhaps, I could put Piero out of my thoughts forever. Find the joy I had known in my girl's life. Return to my father's good graces and redeem myself with the villagers I had repeatedly insulted.

When Papa was asleep I crept up the stairs to his study. I found the texts from Galen, Avicenna, Dioscorides, and Rhazes. I frantically perused the sections on contraception and abortifacants. Many named the same herbs "to provoke the menses," while only a few claimed to "kill embryos and cause them to fall from the womb." But some of these substances were extinct in the world, the best of all abortificants—silphium—gone for a thousand years. Others were not to be found in Italy—squirting cucumber made into a juice, or elephant dung to be used in a suppository. Some, like myrrh and savin, were presently missing from my father's apothecary shelves, he awaiting shipments from distant lands at the port in Pisa. The alchemical texts, with mention of special stones, herbs, and stars that could cause an abortion, were obtuse and the least helpful of all.

The truth was there had been no cause, in all the time I had been helping my father, to end a pregnancy in Vinci. Many women came to him for help in *preventing* conception, realizing the old wives' tales, like burning a mule's hoof over hot coals, were harebrained. But pregnancy was, except in plague years, always a blessing, and my only knowledge of ending life in the womb was that which I had read in a book. The subject was not one I had even discussed with my father.

I was left to pore over the ancient medical manuscripts myself in the flickering light of a candle, wondering if the decoctions and suppositories suggested would kill the thing inside . . . without killing me as well. Then, consumed by melancholy, I considered that death was no worse a fate than giving birth to a bastard child in a small town.

It was therefore with more than a small draught of fear that I mixed a foul-smelling brew of those ingredients at hand in the apothecary named as abortificants—rue, betony, pennyroyal, and juniper sap—and desperate girl that I was, swallowed it just before the sun rose, climbing back up to my room and into my bed.

Almost at once I became sick to my stomach, and by the time Aunt Magdalena had arrived and my father was opening the apothecary door, I was retching violently and screeching in high-pitched cries that echoed down the stairs, all the way into the shop.

Papa and Magdalena were suddenly at my bedside, weeping as they ministered to me, begging me to tell them what was wrong. By then I was so terrified of dying—something I suddenly knew with great clarity I did not wish for myself—that I blurted out the ingredients I had ingested, and for what purpose.

The pain and delirium were so great I cannot say how they saved my life that day. But they did. I was weak as a kitten for a week after that, and could not swallow anything but the thinnest broth of salted vegetables.

The fetus, despite its host's attempt to poison it, had refused to be expelled. And after that attempt, as I regained the health of my body and my mind, I changed in my feelings for that which grew inside me.

It had earned my respect. It was strong and stubborn, and soon I could feel its life pulsing inside me, bubbles and butterfly wings that long before the turns and kicks and thumps began spoke to me . . . as if "speaking" could describe the communication.

I believed it to be a female and began to call the child Leonora, the name of my father's mother. My loathing turned to love, and the scandalous swelling under my skirts, now known to the villagers, delighted me, despite their shock. Some had rightly guessed at my attempted abortion, and to the wicked gossip was added outrage. I had blasphemed against God. Attempted murder. My father and I were visited by the church elders, who chastised me and forbade us coming back into church.

Papa was secretly delighted at the prohibition, tired of pretending his Christianity. The thought of losing me to death that terrible day had also cleared his mind of all anger toward me for the pregnancy.

He shared my fury at the spineless Piero and his disgraceful family, and swore he was joyful at the prospect of a grandchild. He would happily raise it with me, giving the boy or girl all the love that a father would.

The months would have passed joyfully enough had the villagers left me alone. But once my condition became impossible to conceal it was, to them, as if the doorway to Hell had opened and I—one of Satan's minions—had been sent through the portal to our town.

Mine was to be the first illegitimate child born in Vinci for several generations. All the unmarried girls had managed to stay within the strict bounds of piety and chastity, or else had been blessed with great good fortune.

I refused to name the father, not wishing to bring Piero's family into it. What was the point? Even if it had been rape, it would have made no difference. All believed that any girl who'd been so used was in large part responsible for her own ravishment. That she had, in fact, done harm to the soul of the man who had raped her.

Of course, this was not the case. I had *encouraged* Piero's advances, and could only condemn him for his weakness, never violence.

In any event, the townspeople were enraged by my scandalous condition. Gossip festered about the identity of the father and how Ernesto had failed so miserably in the upbringing of his daughter. I, according to my once-friendly neighbors and local churchmen, was a wicked whore, and what was worse, had fooled them all into thinking I was a sweet, virtuous girl.

None would allow me to help my father in the preparation of their remedies. My very presence in the apothecary shop was intolerable to the customers. And once I had begun my treks into the hills to pick herbs again, Papa received complaints that such wanderings were dangerous for the boys and men in the village, as I might lure them into sin. Mothers would hurry their daughters away from the window when I passed, as even the sight of me might corrupt them.

Therefore, no one but my father and Magdalena spoke to me for nearly five months. Strange as it seems, I minded my ostracism very little. When Papa called the villagers small-minded and cruel, I believed him. And as my time drew near, the spirit of my child resounded in every part of my being. I could hardly bear the wait for her birth.

Leonora. My sweet girl.

I faltered only once—upon hearing that Piero had taken a wife, the daughter of a rich notary from Pistoia. Her generous dowry was the talk of Vinci. The wedding had taken place in Florence, but Piero's fortunes were not yet high enough for them to immediately take up residence in the city. They came to live, instead, in the da Vinci house near the old castle wall, his bride, Albiera, doing as all good wives did, staying at home sewing and busying herself with other small domestic chores.

As before, Piero came and went from and into Florence for his business, which was, everyone said, bringing him some small fame, with the promise of wealth in the future. It was my good fortune never to run across either of them in all the time of my pregnancy, though I was sure news of my profligacy must have reached the da Vinci household. There never was, nor did I expect, any acknowledgment that my child was also a child of that family.

Of course I grieved at the blow of Piero's marriage, one that quashed any fantasies I still quietly harbored that one day he would grow a backbone, stand up to his parents and marry me. When we heard the news Papa held me in his arms and let me cry a few bitter tears before admonishing me to see the thing for what it was—a worthless family and pathetic son, neither one we would desire to be part of our lives, or the life of my child.

But finally the blessed day was upon us. Healthy and ripe as a summer peach, I was brought to bed. My father paced nervously in his room as Magdalena worked between my outstretched thighs to bring forth the squalling infant—not Leonora, but a boy, *Leonardo*. My aunt reported that in all her years of midwifery, she had never seen a babe spring more enthusiastically from the womb than my son. He seemed to dive into her arms, she said, as though he had had quite enough of the darkness and silence, and craved the outer world.

Even in my haze of pain and fatigue I was aware that his cries were immediate and lusty. And when Magdalena had bathed Leonardo, he had flailed his chubby little limbs around so zealously, she defied the common practice of swaddling him, instead placing him loosely in a blanket and into my waiting arms.

Magic happened then. I fell in love with my son. Wholly and ir-retrievably.

All those months of our souls' voices joined had not been imag-ined. We *knew* each other. He was blind still, as all newborns are, but he ceased crying the moment he was laid upon my chest and snuggled deep into me, a safe nest. There was no hesitation at taking the nipple, and I overflowed with mother's milk. He suckled so enthusiastically that the sweet white liquid pooled around his mouth and dripped down my breast.

By the time Magdalena allowed Papa in to see us, I was laughing aloud at the sight of my ravenous son and weeping all at once. For joy. For relief. And for the preciousness of the gift that had come from so much pain—the life I had tried in my fury at Piero to snuff out like a candle.

Leonardo was beautiful from the very first. Within the hour of his birth, his color was fair with a pinkish tint, his features were dis-tinct, the cheeks chubby, the chin pointed, the nose delicate. I longed to see his eyes, sure that when they opened they would be large and bright.

Papa confirmed Leonardo's unusual prettiness for a newborn and held him in his arms with such trembling pride I wept again, this time for sheer happiness. The mistake I believed I had made in giving my-self to Piero was nothing of the sort. This child was meant to be born, his absent father be damned.

I slept that April night, the eve of the church's celebration of Christ's resurrection, with my child slung in a hammock near my bed. Many times I awoke to his cries for a feeding, and Magdalena, dear and bleary-eyed woman, was there to place him at my breast.

Come morning I was exhausted. I was sleeping so deeply I never heard the pounding at the shop door, or my father's angry shouts. Not until the commotion reached the hall outside my bedroom was I alarmed. Magdalena was nowhere in sight, though now I heard her voice raised with those of several men, my father one of them.

I sat up quickly and pulled Leonardo, stirring from his own sleep, into my protective clutches.

The door to my room flew open.

Papa, red-faced with a look that could only be described as murderous, was trying to block the entrance of a company of angry men, with Magdalena behind, helplessly flapping her hands like the wings of a panicked chicken, her face wet with tears.

This was dire, whatever it was, though I did not understand its meaning until I recognized amidst the party Piero and his brother, Francesco. Then I heard what my father was shouting. "He is not yours to take!" and the blood froze in my veins.

But my father and I knew very well the conventions of fatherless children. So many illegitimate ones were unloved, abandoned or even murdered without a trace of guilt or punishment. Even married widows, if they took new husbands, were forced most times to give up their babies to their late husbands' families. Their sons especially.

"Our family's lineage is at stake here!" I heard the oldest da Vinci man shout indignantly. "Unity of our line and our honor *always* prevails over the feelings of the mother!"

This terrifying confraternity was making headway into my room despite Papa's bodily efforts to impede them. I hugged my child hard to my chest and he began to wail.

In that moment Piero, hearing the cry, stepped forward, his face a confused mask of shame and paternal pride. This was his firstborn son, bastard or not, and it was his right, by all the unnatural laws of the land, to possess him.

"No, don't take him!" I shrieked. "Please, please! Piero, no!"

As he strode to the bedside he steadfastly averted his eyes from me, as if our gazes meeting would thwart his ability to act. But when he reached out to our son, who was screaming with the terror I could not but convey to him, Piero hesitated. He did look stricken, as though he knew what he meant to do was devilish, and would crush the girl he had once loved so sincerely.

Then his father cried out, "Take the child, Piero! Now!"

I clutched his arm with clawed fingers.

"You cannot do this," I whispered with a fierceness I did not know I possessed.

But he did do it, never looking at me.

Once he placed his hands on Leonardo I ceased to struggle, incapable of any act that might hurt my child.

It was as if, in that instant when the men left the room, the sun was extinguished. I vaguely remember Papa shouting threats after them, and Magdalena wailing. Then there was silence, and a gaping emptiness in my arms.

I was beyond tears, and I knew that no consolation would be offered by my father, for there was no consolation to be had.

We had failed to prepare for the worst, and the worst had happened.

It was the end of joy, and in the blaze of suffering I felt nothing worse in all the world could ever happen—to me, to have my son ripped from my arms, and to Leonardo, who would know the barest affection from a family that regarded him as a worthless bastard son.

It was Easter Sunday and everyone in Vinci had gone to church. News of Leonardo's paternity spread like a house fire. The villagers fell on the news like a pack of starving dogs on a lame hare. Piero da Vinci was an up-and-coming young man who brought nothing but honor on our town. His poor new wife—"very wealthy and virtuous"— would be made to suffer the indignity of an illegitimate child being brought into a fresh new marriage. I, of course, was a low seductress, a villainous prostitute whose vices threatened one of Vinci's finest and most upstanding of families.

All this gossip had been dragged out of Magdalena when she returned from mass, despite my father's protests that I not be subjected to more pain. I was determined to hear it, every word of it, perhaps as a way of punishing myself, for of course there was no one to blame for this catastrophe except me.

Later that day my son was baptized in a private ceremony at the church—one to which I was not invited. There was one saving grace, he had been named Leonardo—Leonardo de Piero da Vinci. When I learned this I was again brought to tears, as I knew this had to have been Piero's doing. It was the single noble act he had successfully accomplished, for no one in his lineage had ever been named Leonardo. Standing at the font, his father and grandfather would have been fuming under their hats. I wondered what had possessed Piero. Guilt? Honor? What was left of the love he had once felt for me?

But it was cold comfort all the same.

The next days were again spent in that black well of gloom. Mostly I slept. Whatever I ate I vomited back up. My breasts ached horribly, and the milk seeped from them like tears, wetting my nightgowns and bedclothes. Magdalena worried and clucked over me, urging me to leave my bed and begin to live again. Papa, when he came frequently to my room, looked beaten and helpless, and ten years older than he had been three days before. There were times that I lay there and willed my heart to stop beating. Times that I imagined, in great detail, dressing, walking into the hills at the place by the river that Leonardo had been conceived, wading in and drowning myself.

There was no end to my self-pity.

Then one morning I heard Magdalena's urgent voice as she tried to rouse me from one of those stuporous slumbers.

"Caterina! Wake up! You've got a visitor."

A visitor? Who would visit me?

"Sit up! Wash your face! Quickly!"

She brought the bowl of water to my bed, and a brush that she used to untangle my hair.

"You smell terrible. This will never do."

"Who is here, Aunt?" I said, still groggy.

"The brother, the brother!"

"The brother?" I repeated stupidly.

But before I could make sense of any of it, there was Francesco da Vinci, cap in hand, standing in my bedroom doorway, Papa behind him with a look so perplexed it did nothing to help me understand what was happening.

Francesco himself was nervous as a horse with a snake at its feet. Nevertheless, he took a few steps into my room and gave me a small bow.

I pulled myself up in bed. Picking up the water bowl, Magdalena withdrew, and gently grasping my father's arm, led him away. Not till I heard their feet on the stairs did Francesco speak.

"Caterina . . . ," he said, but quickly fell silent.

I just stared at him, like a poor mute.

"Caterina, I am sorry for what has happened."

"What have *you* got to be sorry for?" It surprised me, finding my voice. Its bitterness surprised me even more.

"It's a terrible thing, taking the boy like they did. But even more terrible . . ." He stopped again, now having uttered those frightening words.

"What is more terrible, Francesco? Tell me!"

"The child won't suckle. He refuses the teat."

"Who is the wetnurse?" I demanded, throwing off the covers and swinging my legs out of bed.

"Angelina Lucchasi. She's a good woman, and trying very hard, but the boy . . ."

"*Leonardo,*" I whispered fiercely. "Call him by his name."

Francesco looked as though he would himself cry. He put his hand to his forehead and squeezed his temples. "Leonardo is suffering. He is starving. If he does not eat . . ."

"What is his father doing about this?!" I shouted. I stood, but my weak legs would not hold. Francesco lurched toward me and helped me back onto the bed. I was gripping his hands with fingers like vises.

Now tears were coming down Francesco's face. "Piero does nothing. He says that soon Leonardo will become so hungry he will take the nipple. Grow fat as a piglet. But what if he doesn't? Caterina, you must do something!"

I think my mouth was agape—with horror, with loathing, with utter confusion. "What can *I* do?" I cried, pounding Francesco's chest. He was stoic, as though believing he deserved even more punishment.

"You must come home with me. Now. Come to our house and offer yourself as Leonardo's wetnurse."

The words were so unexpected, so unimaginable and yet so perfectly sensible. For a moment I envisioned the scene as I stood before the family, felt the heat of my humiliation, and desperation for their acceptance.

Then the image vanished. There was not a moment to spare. "Go," I said to Francesco. "I need to get dressed. You wait downstairs. Send up my father and my aunt."

Finally he smiled, and for the first time I remember thinking that there was one good man in an otherwise despicable family.

So I went with Francesco, he quaking in his heart as much as I was. They could easily turn me away, call my suggestion the ravings of a madwoman. But this young man had to live on with them and their scorn. Would he be thought a traitor? Some low coward siding with the enemy?

He unlatched the back gate and we passed through the yard I'd seen for the first time from over the wall in the branches of an olive tree. There was even less happening than on that summer day the year before. Above the unnaturally loud buzz of a hundred flies at a pile of dung, I could hear from inside the house the sound of Leonardo's wailing. But now, to my dismay, I realized his voice was weaker, almost gasping. Suddenly my bodice was wet, and I had to bite my lip to keep from crying.

"Hurry!" I said to Francesco, who took my arm and picked up his pace.

I knew I could not afford to weep before the da Vinci men. Neither could I appear too strong, for that would certainly offend them. *Oh, how would I know what to do, what to say?* I was fifteen years old and had nothing to guide me but the love of my son.

When Francesco stood aside, leaving me framed in the archway of the da Vincis' dining room, my arms crossed protectively across my chest, I think that despite my previous imaginings of this very moment, I was as stunned at the sight of them as they were of me.

Piero and his wife, Albiera, were there, side by side. She was a girl no older than me with a long, narrow face and little flesh on her bones. Piero's father, Antonio, sat at one end of the long polished table, his wife, Lucia, at the other. Piero's elderly grandfather, who stared at me with loathing, was seated at an empty place that was certainly Francesco's.

Momentous as this scene was, something greater had gripped my attention. Leonardo's cries were closer now, in a room just above us. I knew I should address Piero and his father, but each time I opened my mouth to speak, another mournful howl or hiccupping whimper closed it again. Antonio raised his chin to his wife and stepdaughter, and without another word they stood obediently and pushed back their chairs.

But I wanted them to see this, hear this. They were women as I was, and should understand the need that had brought me, like an invader, into their home. Antonio was waving them out of the room, but I determined that they would not leave until I had said my piece.

"Look at me!" I shouted and flung my arms wide. My bodice was soaking wet with milk. I glared at Piero. "Listen to our son!"

Standing beside him, Albiera winced, but I had more to say.

"Leonardo is crying out for *me*. I am here. He needs to be fed. You must let me feed him!"

Antonio sat rigid, his jaws grinding. He refused to meet Piero's pleading stare.

"Take this whore out of here, Francesco," the older man growled.

"Just let her speak, Grandfather," the boy begged, his voice trembling.

"Give us a room in the attic," I said. "Anywhere. We'll be no bother to anyone." Still no one spoke. "Please, may I see him now?"

"How do you dare come into our home in such a rude manner?" Antonio snarled at me. I could see in that moment how the man would frighten even his sons. "You deeply offend my father, me, and my wife, and you disrespect my son's new bride."

"I will stop him crying," I said directly to Piero, dangerously ignoring the senior men of this family. "Isn't that what you want?"

Piero was trembling with an answer that he, in his cowardice, could not speak.

Finally I addressed Antonio and his father, conquering my fear of them with simple truth.

"Leonardo is Piero's blood. Your blood. Do you want your first grandson to die? For he will die without me." The words were tumbling from me effortlessly now. They were appropriately accompanied by a fresh round of Leonardo's wailing. "I am his mother. Those cries . . . they are his call to me." I pressed my palm to my milk-wet bodice. "These are my cries for *him*!"

The two wives, far from understanding my womanly pleas, looked wholly scandalized. But Antonio's overblown hubris had finally been pricked by my words.

"You will live as the other servants," he commanded me, not daring to meet his father's eyes. "You will speak to no one in the family unless you are spoken to first."

I could see the older man spluttering, speechless with rage at his son's decision.

I swallowed hard. This was to be more demeaning than I had imagined.

"You will—"

"What if I need something for Leonardo, or if he is—"

"Are you deaf, young woman!" Antonio thundered, clearly unused to a woman's defiance. "I have told you never to speak first!"

I remember feeling the stone floor under my slippers, and a kind of earthly strength that rose through my feet and legs and straightened my spine. I knew I was about to suffer a long and terrible indignity, but I would first have my say.

"If all is well with my son," I pressed on, "I will have nothing to say to you, signors." I looked at Piero. "Or you." I briefly lowered my eyes, acknowledging the women of the house, then went on. "But if he should take ill, or have need of this family in any way, I will speak to anyone I please about it." I looked at Antonio again. "I am your grandson's wetnurse now, a servant in your house. But I am not your slave."

Antonio looked indignant, ready to lash out at the impudent girl standing in his dining room.

Before he could speak again, I added, "I want to see my boy. Please."

That was how it was decided.

I was taken upstairs to a fine bedchamber, where Signora Lucchasi was rocking my red-faced, squalling infant in a wooden cradle. He looked drawn and miserable, so unlike the peaceful, beautiful newborn I'd held just a few days before.

The woman, shocked as she was by my appearance, gratefully stood back and allowed me to lift Leonardo from the crib.

It took only a moment for him to recognize my touch, my smell, the sound of my voice crooning his name. As I laid him on the great bed and loosened the tight swaddling blanket that imprisoned his tiny body, the choked sobs ceased. I touched his face, all of his limbs, and stroked his heaving chest with two fingers, making a tiny circle around his heart.

I lifted him into my arms again and, finding a high-backed chair, sat down and opened my dress. He needed no help finding my breast, and weak as he was, began to suckle noisily and ferociously as he had done before. He blew a sigh of contentment through his nostrils and fed that way for some minutes. Finally I felt his tiny muscles relax into me, and he rolled away from the feeding. Then, like a miracle, he turned his head and opened his eyes. He saw me. Saw his mother for the first time. He never blinked, just took in the sight.

I smiled quickly, determined that the first human expression he would ever know would be one of happiness. Then his hunger forced him back to the teat. I sighed, heavy with relief and joy, cradled down to kiss the top of his head and closed my eyes. It was only then that I felt his tiny, warm hand on my cheek, resting there light and comfortable and infinitely possessive.

I thought my heart would burst with the grace and beauty of the gesture. *Leonardo. He was mine again, and I was his.* And I swore in that moment to every god that would listen and all the Fates I could defy, that nothing would ever hurt my child, and that we would never be parted again.

The time I spent as my son's wetnurse in the home of Piero's father and grandfather, with the man I had loved, and his wife, who treated me like the lowest of servants, was difficult in the extreme. Leonardo and I lived in a portion of the barn made into a crude residence, with the smell of cattle dung infusing everything around us every hour of the day and night. We were ignored, by and large, by the da Vincis, except for disdainful glances or, if I insisted on something for Leonardo's well-being, the briefest of conversations.

They pretended generosity by allowing me every Sunday off, but would not permit me to take Leonardo when I went to see Papa. My visits were therefore cut cruelly short, as I missed him painfully, but how could I deprive my son of his feedings?

Thankfully my milk seemed to satisfy him, and kept him healthy. He fell victim to none of the illnesses of childhood, and developed the sweetest and happiest temperament. Truly, we needed this rude family not at all. My son and I were inseparable and full of joy in each other's company.

He never failed to delight and surprise me with his cleverness. He took his first steps—though no one ever believed me—at six months. It took longer than usual for him to speak, but when he did—he was almost two—there was no silencing him. He learned how to question first. And question he did

"What is this?" "What is that?" "Why?" Endlessly. He needed only to be answered once. Then the name of the flower or bird or insect or object was permanently sealed in his head.

I would see him sitting in the yard staring for the longest time at a grasshopper climbing a stalk of grass. I could swear he was *studying* it, as my father would study the sediment left in the bottom of one of his beakers. Then would come the two-year-old's questions and observations. A barrage of them. "Why he green?" "He eats leaf." Then a squeal of delight. "He cleans leg!" "Why so long leg?"

It surprised me at first that although he loved living creatures, Leonardo was not unduly disturbed if they died. He was simply fascinated with them in their dead state and took great pleasure in touching and examining them, in endless sessions in his tiny dexterous fingers, simply happy they were not squirming away or biting him.

It seemed that this time was more difficult for Piero than it was for me, as I had Leonardo. For Leonardo's part, he hardly realized that the man was his father, or that he needed anything more than an adoring mother.

The only light in the family was Francesco. He was the kindest young man I had ever known. I sometimes thought he could not possibly share the same blood with the others, so different was he. Francesco would visit with us in the barn, sneaking us treats from the kitchen, or fashioning small toys for Leonardo out of wood, some of them that moved. These, in particular, were engrossing for Leonardo, who fixed on them as if they were one of his insects, lacking the living spark but nevertheless something to observe and manipulate.

Francesco would, on a pleasant morning on his way to the fields and herds he oversaw, come and ask me if he might bring my boy with him for the day, promising to take good care of all his needs. I'd watch them as they disappeared out the back gate into the olive orchard, Leonardo riding on "Unca Cecco's" shoulders or slung like a small sack of grain under one arm, Leonardo always giggling or squealing with delight in his uncle's company. It was clear as a winter night that Piero's brother wished Leonardo had been *his* son, and was repenting of his horrid family's sins by his loving ways.

To me, Francesco was a sweet brother, a blessing I had never known growing up. It rarely occurred to me that, close as we had become, the handsome young man never made a romantic advance on a pretty young woman. Occasionally I remembered what Piero had said about Francesco being a "Florenzer," a man who loved other men, but it seemed irrelevant. A friend, a brother, a kind uncle. That was what mattered.

One cold winter evening as Leonardo slept in his hammock, Francesco had sneaked into the barn with an extra armful of wood for our fire. He looked troubled as he coaxed a bit more heat into our little room, so I gently coaxed the truth from him.

"My brother's become unbearable to live with," he said. "He still longs for you so desperately. You know that, don't you?" When I did not answer he went on. "Everyone in the house can see it."

"Why did he do it?" I said. "Why did he promise to marry me when he knew it was impossible?"

"Our father is a cold, unfeeling man. A man who beats his wife. Frequently. On a whim. He rules all his children with his fists as well . . . even his favorite, Piero." The admission seemed to surprise Francesco as the words fell from his lips. "Piero believed that when he broke away to make a name for himself as a notary he would be free from our father's law. He had dreams of his own family—one he could raise away from here, in Florence, with dignity and honor. A family so unlike our own."

Francesco grew embarrassed, his eyes dropping to where his booted toe pushed straw aimlessly around the earthen floor.

"But Piero miscalculated his own strength, his own backbone . . . and our father's outrage. 'I always thought you had at least half a brain!' he'd shouted that night Piero came home and announced he was marrying you. 'You and your ridiculous dreams!'" Francesco had begun to enjoy playacting his angry father. "'How could you be so *stupid* to think you could raise yourself in society by marrying a worthless village girl with no dowry! What could you have been thinking? You must believe that I would never disinherit you.'"

"What *was* he thinking?" I asked quietly.

"Piero did love you, Caterina. And he wished so heartily to be different from his father. Now . . ." Francesco was unable to go on. But I demanded with my eyes that he finish what he had started. "Now the love he had for you has turned to bitterness. Hatred, even. Having to see you at a distance every day eats at him. And his wife is furious that the woman Piero really desires, but is forbidden to touch, is living in the family barn with his beautiful son—his only child. And nothing Piero does causes her own belly to quicken."

I knew what Francesco said was true. Sometimes I would hear Piero and Albiera from their bedroom window. His joyless grunts, her pained whimpers. As every month went by with the laundress bringing out Albiera's bloody rags to wash, it was clear even to me that the mood in the house was growing darker.

Francesco shook his head morosely.

I put my sisterly arms around him, feeling strangely light and happy for having heard such uncheerful news. "Then I suppose Leonardo and I are better off in this stinking barn than in your grim household," I said.

Francesco managed a smile. "We three have each other."

"Unca Cecco!"

We turned to see my sparkling-eyed boy peeking his head over the edge of his hammock and grinning with delight. He threw his blanket onto the floor.

"Play!" he demanded and began to giggle.

*T*hose two bittersweet years ended suddenly one afternoon when I was summoned to the villa. The da Vincis were at their dinner, much as they had been when, after Leonardo's birth, I'd barged in demanding to have my son back. This time they were expecting me, prepared with their rod-straight spines and expressions that looked as though the lot of them had swallowed sour dishrags. Only Piero's grandfather seemed diminished. He was very thin and frail, and his eyes glittered brightly with the dementia that Francesco told me had overtaken him in the past years.

Once again Piero was like a small boy cowering in the shadow of his father, saying nothing at all but leveling me with a look of furious impotence. With his eyes, poor Francesco implored my forgiveness for what was to come.

"My wife informs me," Antonio da Vinci began, "that in the case of Piero's son, the time for a wetnurse is long past."

"I still have milk in my breasts," I answered him quickly, "and Leonardo—you persist in refusing to call him by name—is thriving on it. Many children are nursed till they are—"

"There is more," Antonio snapped, cutting me off. "And you will obey the rules I set down when you came to live under our roof and eat our food, burn our wood. Speak *only* when spoken to. Keep silent and respectful." He fixed his jaw with so tight a clenching I thought I would soon hear the bones of his face cracking. "It has come to my attention that my daughter-in-law's infertility may have causes other than natural ones."

I was stunned, silenced, expecting as always the worst from this family, but never so sordid an accusation as this.

"You are, after all, an apothecary's daughter, with knowledge of—"

"Say not another word, Signor da Vinci," I said, finally finding my voice. "This is a serious crime of which you are accusing me. Have you any proof?"

"Of course we have proof, you little whore!" his old father cried in a shrill, almost hysterical tone.

"Albiera's maid found pennyroyal leaves in the bottom of her wineglass," Antonio said. "Pennyroyal, I am told, brings on an abortion."

"And how do you suppose I slipped these leaves into Albiera's wineglass? I'm not allowed anywhere near this house."

"A girl as devious and sinful as yourself could always—"

"Devious and sinful as I may be," I interrupted him with chilly indignation, "I am not stupid. Anyone who knows a thing about pennyroyal realizes that its effects are neutralized by the alcohol in wine. It would best have been ground up and put in her soup."

"You think evil thoughts about me all the time!" Albiera cried. "Who needs herbs when you and your father can lay curses on me?"

"The only curse on you," I said quietly, "is a womb laid bare by your own frigid nature. You poison yourself with hatred and jealousy and then blame me."

Albiera turned to Piero. "Tell her to shut her mouth," she spat. "Tell her. Right now!"

Piero's lip trembled violently. His face turned ashen.

"Piero . . . ," his grandfather threatened.

"You will not address my wife like that," he finally said to me in a voice that was pitifully weak. So weak, in fact, that it embarrassed his father.

"There will be no need for apologies or confessions," Antonio said, turning to me, "as you will be leaving this house immediately. Vacate your rooms."

"My rooms?" I cried. "Do you mean the stench-ridden, rodent-infested corner of your barn to which you banished your grandson?"

Antonio became very still and very cold. I think if I had been nearer him he would have struck me. "As for my only grandson," he began again, "do not think for a moment he will be going with you when you leave."

Now it was I who grew cold. In the surprise of the accusation and heated defense of myself I had failed to anticipate that this was the very reason I had been summoned here.

They were taking Leonardo from me a second time!

"If you are not gone within the hour, I shall call the church authorities. You will be accused of the crime of witchcraft, and laying curses on this family!"

Now I saw the old man grinning horribly.

"Father," Francesco interjected in a strong, calm voice. "You know very well this is a false accusation."

Antonio glared at his younger son, the boy who had brought no glory to this family—only whispers that he was a sodomite and heretic.

"Leonardo does indeed thrive in Caterina's care," Francesco went on with more courage than I ever imagined he had. "Who will look after the boy if she goes?"

"Cook," Antonio answered flatly.

"Cook!" Francesco argued. "Cook barely has time for her own chores. She—"

"Silence!" Antonio smashed his closed fist on the table so hard the plates and goblets rattled.

"Get out," he said without bothering to look at me again. "Never show your face in this house again." Then he turned to his wife. "Tell them to bring on the main course."

*M*y reputation when I left the da Vinci household was in tatters. I had borne an illegitimate child and lived as a servant in his father's family barn. I wanted to push from my memory the moment I left Leonardo in Francesco's arms and took my leave of the da Vinci villa. But I could never forget the woeful expression on his cherubic face and how, even protected by the warm embrace of his uncle, my son knew this was a terrible and unnatural parting from me. He set up a heartbreaking wail that followed me out the front gate and far down the cobbled street of Vinci.

I took up my old room over the apothecary and helped my father quietly in the back garden and storeroom, mixing potions and poultices, leaving the shop and its customers, all of whom still held a grudge against the "low woman" I was, to him. Though I had a place of warmth and love under my father's roof, and loyal Aunt Magdalena, life felt a hollow thing. My boy was just across the small village, yet he might have been a thousand miles away.

Of course, there was not a man or woman in the village who wanted me as a daughter-in-law. This concerned me not at all, but as soon as I had come back to my father's house it began to cause the da Vincis some concern.

They started trying to marry me off.

Notes and letters appeared at our door with what they considered a very wise plan. An unmarried man named Tonio Buti de Vaca was a lime burner who lived just outside Vinci with his parents, elder brother, sister-in-law, and their children, crowded into a tiny clutch of run-down houses, barns, and sheds.

Papa and I knew of the Buti family, and the reputation of Tonio. In his youth he had been known as "Accattabriga"—a troublemaker, a quarrel picker, the reason he was unmarriageable. This man was the best they could do, Piero's father wrote, for "a girl such as Caterina."

Papa was, in fact, more angry than I at the da Vincis' audacity. We ignored their first letter, their second and third. Suddenly all correspondence stopped, and we learned the reason. Tonio "the quarreler" Buti had married another girl by the name of Caterina, and she began to have his children immediately. Finally I was left in peace.

But never was Leonardo far from my mind.

It was agony being separated from him. Many times I contemplated marching into the da Vinci house demanding to see him, but I knew it would have amounted to nothing, or worse, created more gossip in the village.

Then one day as I was leaving the apothecary in the spring of 1456, a strange figure appeared at the end of our street. At a distance he seemed unnaturally tall. It took me a moment to realize it was a man with a small child riding on his shoulders.

I let out a shout and went running for them. It was Francesco, lovely Francesco, and my Leonardo, no longer an infant but a little boy.

When I reached them Leonardo, with no hesitation, flew off his uncle's shoulders into my arms. I wept and clutched him tightly, kissing his curls and cheeks and eyes and he, though dry-eyed, kept whispering, "Mama, Mama," and making soft sounds like tiny gasps of laughter.

Francesco, bless his loving heart, began bringing Leonardo as often as he could to my father's house. He reported that his brother and still-childless wife had moved to Florence. Piero was climbing the social ladder and making a real name for himself as a Florentine Notary of the Republic. At the da Vinci villa their age-addled grandfather had died, altogether convinced that I had been the Catarina who'd married Tonio Buti. Their father and mother were getting old and were crankier than ever, and with Piero away they cared even less than they had about the daily routine of their only grandchild. They never even missed him when he was gone from the house.

Francesco had kept a close watch over his nephew, keeping the memory of me alive in his mind. Leonardo had cried bitterly for months after my banishment, but Francesco always promised him that when he was old enough, he would bring him to me.

That spring day was the fulfillment of the promise. Though years in the keeping, it set firmly in my son's head a kind of trust in his uncle and in myself, a trust that endured and made him strong, and a believer that all things, no matter how difficult, were possible.

Suddenly my life became a happy one.

Leonardo was a little clown who entertained Papa and me with his acrobatics and practical jokes and with the small creatures he would bring us, pointing out their features—things that no one had ever thought to observe. How the knee joint of a baby hare moved in ropy sinews under the fur; how the orange pollen of an asphodel stuck to the feet of a honeybee; how a certain kind of rock from the river shone with glittering crystals in the sunlight. His powers of observation were, from the earliest age, nearly obsessive, but his flawless character, kindness, and good humor prevailed over all.

At first my son's visits to Papa's house caused a small scandal, but as the da Vincis didn't seem to care, talk soon died away. My darling Leonardo came nearly every day.

There were countless times that he, his uncle Francesco, and I would traipse up into the hills on herb-picking adventures. I had made those sojourns alone as a girl, perfectly content with my solitude. But now in the company of two of the brightest, sweetest souls in the universe, my pleasure was multiplied into boundless joy. We laughed and sang and waded in the river. We threw out rugs and lolled in the shade of trees, stuffing ourselves with cheese and bread, heaping them with Magdalena's wonderful grape and olive compote.

But the greatest of delights were our explorations. I had always believed myself wise in the ways of plant and animal life, and Francesco had worked among his vines and fields, orchards and herds for many years, and was expert in their ways. It was therefore shocking to discover that an eight-year-old boy might teach us something new about the natural world on almost every walk we took.

Leonardo's was a brilliance made entirely from his acute powers of observation. He did not see a thing as others did. He would perceive a hundred points of interest in an object where Francesco and I might see one.

A flower, for instance. He would see not simply its color—yellow— but variance of the yellow in its petal from lighter to darker and how, if you looked closely—he was always exhorting Francesco and me to "look closely"—one could see an area that bled from yellow to pink and wondered what took place on that boundary. Was it a "war" between the pink and yellow, or a friendly line between them?

He might hold a petal up to the sunlight and study the pattern of veins, Some that he likened to rivers, and others to trees, how the petals glowed if they were alive, but lost the glow once they were dry and dead. And of course he wished to know the purpose of every part of the flower, and questioned us unmercifully.

The curves of a flower's stamen fascinated him, and it was this that became the subject of his very first drawing. I had been unaware he had brought paper and a sliver of black charcoal from Papa's house. I came up behind him and saw him lying on his belly on the rug, as he often did, the object of his passionate observation laid out in a patch of sunlight under his nose. But this day his shoulders were hunched, and his posture revealed an even fiercer intensity than usual.

When I came around I saw him staring at a single pale stamen on the end of a stem that he'd placed against a patch of dark red in the rug. The rest of the lily from which it had been taken lay in pieces nearby. The paper I recognized as a blank page from his grandfather's apothecary diary. I wondered if Leonardo had asked for it, or appropriated it without Papa knowing.

The stamen almost completely filled the page, which in itself was a revelation to me. I had never seen this portion of a flower in such dimensions. But the simplicity of the subject in the drawing, and the perfection with which it was rendered by my son's hand, took my breath away. The curve of the almost ethereal stem, the plumpness of its dark head, and the detail of a thousand minuscule dots of pollen covering it so astonished me I was struck speechless.

I sat down just next to him, but he was too intent to acknowledge me. He was making an attempt at shading the stem, giving it depth and a sense of roundness. *How does he know how to do that?* I thought. *No one has ever put a piece of charcoal in his hand and shown him how to draw!*

"It's very good, Leonardo," I finally said, wishing to give praise and encouragement, but not so much as I really felt, which, I feared, might scare him or turn him away from his efforts. "Is that difficult for you?" I asked.

"No," he answered, somewhat absently. "Not difficult. Interesting." He never looked up from the drawing.

I smiled to myself. "Interesting" had become Leonardo's favorite word of late. There were very few things under heaven he did not describe as such.

All at once a thick cloud blocked the sunlight over our rug, and his drawing was thrown into shade. It did not seem to perturb Leonardo, who continued, with great precision, to add more tiny dots of pollen to the head of the stamen.

"Do you think Papa would like it?" he asked suddenly but in the most matter-of-fact tone possible.

The question took me by storm. I stalled for time, even as I answered his question with another question—one whose answer I already knew. "Do you mean your grandpapa Ernesto?"

"No," he said quietly. My *father*."

There was no way to answer this truthfully without being hurtful. Piero had shown not the slightest interest in his bastard son since the day he'd been born. It amazed me that Leonardo even considered him. Now it was all too apparent that my boy had never forgotten his blood father and wished, as all children did, for his approval.

"Your father is very busy in Florence," I said, trying for evenness in my voice.

"Is that why he never sees me?"

"It is," I whispered.

Why is this happening now? I thought. Leonardo had never raised such questions before. It always seemed that he was content with his lot in life. There were so many besides myself—Francesco and now Magdalena and his grandfather Ernesto—who loved him.

"Mama, look!"

Lost as I was in worry, Leonardo's exclamation surprised me. He pointed to a spot just in front of our faces. A thin shaft of sunlight had pierced the cloud above and now illuminated the patch of meadow before us with an unearthly brilliance.

The purple lavender and orange mallow were overlit, and shone with incredible hues. The air itself, where before it had simply seemed transparent, was suddenly vibrating with sparkling motes of dust, its center a swarm of minuscule gnats that hovered in a frenzied airborne dance.

"How beautiful!" I cried and grabbed Leonardo's hand. Silently and together we shared the miraculous, barely daring to breathe. A few moments later the shaft broadened and dispersed into normal light, and as quickly as the natural spectacle had appeared, it vanished.

My son turned to me with a look of transported joy, and smiled broadly. There were no words that attended the smile. None were needed. Then he turned back to his drawing with sheer contentment and said nothing more of his father.

Coming into his grandfather's home became the crowning glory of Leonardo's childhood. When he reached the age of reasoning, Papa took him into the apothecary to gain knowledge of plant medicine. When I'd left home at fifteen I had not finished my own studies, so I began learning again along with my son.

Together, joyfully, we dove into my father's collection of books and manuscripts, and though none of the da Vincis knew it, Leonardo came to be well taught in Latin, and even a smattering of the Greek language. It used to make me smile to watch my father teaching my son the same lessons in philosophy and geography and geometry that he had taught me at the same age.

Leonardo showed himself to be left-handed, a tendency that—had he been more public a child—would have earned him the reputation of a heretic or a Satanist. The da Vincis provided only the most rudimentary tutors for him, and for only a few hours a week. For the benefits of these men Leonardo learned to write with his right hand, and so became ambidextrous.

Papa, Leonardo, and I would sit together for hours over a story from the *Odyssey*, Leonardo on his feet the whole time, acting out all the parts himself. He liked the monsters best, and using an imagination that was preternatural added and embellished Homer's descriptions of places and creatures and fantastical phenomena so that I could never, thereafter, feel satisfied with the great Greek's much paler and more restrained version of the tales.

Leonardo was a marvel in Papa's apothecary garden. He never tired of tending the plants and watching how the changing of the seasons changed what grew there. His favorite thing was planting a seed and watching it spring to life. He would run inside to make glowing reports on the progress of growth. "Mama, Grandfather, come see!" he would cry. "The foxglove seedlings grew an inch overnight! If only I could stay here tonight I could take a candle and lay on my belly and watch it grow!"

But of course we all knew he would never be allowed to stay the night. Disinterested as his da Vinci grandparents were, they would certainly be furious to learn how great was our influence on Leonardo.

It was a magical day when my father opened to his grandson his clandestine third-story alchemical laboratory. Leonardo was fascinated that when I was hardly older than he, I had tended the furnace every day. The idea of secrecy appealed to his nature, and thus he acquired the habit in his own affairs. He found secret hiding places on every floor of my father's house and, I suspected, one in the apothecary garden. He took great pleasure in them, squirreling away little treasures he had found on our outdoor adventures—a rodent skull or the skin of a snake—or odd gifts from the laboratory—nuggets of cinnabar or silver.

For all his extraordinary brilliance my son was also a silly prankster. The more he could terrify Papa and me the better. Once when the three of us were together in the laboratory Leonardo called out sharply so that we turned in time to see him standing over an open beaker of boiling oil with a cup of red wine in his hand. Before we could shout "No!" he'd heaved the wine into the beaker. Spectacular multicolored flames shot up to the ceiling, nearly setting the house on fire.

For that he was punished, being barred from Papa's laboratory for a month. It had been worth it, he'd told me, repressing a grin, just to see the looks of horror on our faces.

Another time as I readied myself for sleep I pulled down the covers on my bed and shrieked, finding on my pillow a hideous moving monster with flashing red eyes. I jumped back so violently I crashed to the floor. Once I'd caught my breath I crawled on my hands and knees back to the bed with sure knowledge this "thing" had been created by my darling and utterly perverse child. On closer examination I saw he had fabricated most of it out of dissected and recombined bats, lizards, snakes, and geckos. These parts of the miniature "dragon" were stationary, but its midsection was very much alive—a clear glass jar containing a variety of crickets, beetles, and locusts—all jumping about with abandon. The beast's two large "eyes" held similarly enclosed squirming centipedes, chosen, I deduced, for their bright scarlet color.

Papa came rushing in in his nightshirt, alarmed by my screeching. Despite my initial terror I found myself laughing, and he with me. Part devil, part angel—surely there was no one in the world like our Leonardo.

No punishment was levied for the monster in my bed, though this time we did elicit a promise that there would be no further pranks that could kill either his mother or grandfather by heart-stopping fright.

Meanwhile, Leonardo's drawing, which had begun simply enough, became expert and even awe-inspiring. He was better able, and more likely, to draw things that were alive than inanimate objects, like houses or bridges. He drew insects with great precision, compelled by the strangeness and symmetry of their anatomy. The dogs and cats and horses he rendered were stunningly alive, and projected the love he had of all living things.

It was when Leonardo began studies of the human face, though, using his grandfather and me and his uncle Francesco as his subjects, that we fully realized the boy's unlimited talent. The question, of course, was what should be done about it.

Francesco told us that whenever his brother deigned to come back to Vinci for a visit, he bragged about his new friends in Florence, some in the Notaries Guild, many merchants, and one artisan with a bottega that was getting more and more commissions from the new head of the Medici clan—a maestro called Andrea Verrocchio.

I had had little or nothing to do with Piero in the past ten years, and all that I knew of his paternal efforts with Leonardo made me despise him. It was true and customary that an illegitimate son was prohibited from attending university or taking up an apprenticeship in any legal field. Our son was therefore ineligible to become a Notary of the Republic. But in addition to ignoring the child almost entirely, Piero was making no effort whatsoever to find a trade of any kind for Leonardo. He was far too busy with his social climbing in Florence and in trying, still unsuccessfully, to impregnate—after Albiera had died—his new young bride.

This infuriated me. I knew the da Vincis would never allow Leonardo to train as an apothecary with his grandfather. It was barely acceptable that Leonardo spent time at the shop. I had dreams of running Piero through with a sword, that still-handsome face spurting blood from mouth and nostrils. I woke with my cheeks wet with tears, and my jaw sore from grinding.

One afternoon when Leonardo had taken his leave, my father came to sit with me.

"Caterina. I see how troubled you are, and I know the cause."

"Then you know the solution is impossible," I said, growing emotional.

"There is a solution. But it will mean going and speaking to Piero."

I burst into tears of frustration. But Papa did not move to hold or comfort me. He just waited for me to calm.

"In order to face him you must harden yourself. This is a formidable task. You know very clearly the suggestion you will make on Leonardo's behalf. Prepare a good case for it. But restrain every impulse you have to argue with the man—it will only anger him. Yet you cannot allow him to make you feel small. And you must succeed, Caterina. Your son's future depends upon it."

It was nearly six months later when Francesco alerted me to Piero's upcoming visit to his family. By then I was prepared, but I had endured too much humiliation in the da Vinci villa to have such a confrontation there.

I showed up instead in front of the Vinci church the first Sunday Piero was home from Florence. As they filed out, the villagers stared at me as though being forced to clean scum from the bottom of a cattle trough. I stood tall, though, and I must say I drew pleasure from the shock on Piero's face when he exited the double doors with his pretty new wife on his arm and found me blocking his way.

Before he had time to bluster I said very loudly, so the priest and all the nosy parishioners could hear, "I must speak to you about our son." His wife went pale, but in order to prevent a scene he whispered something to her, and she grimly scurried down the steps.

Piero took my elbow and guided me away from the church and into an alley, looking every which way to be sure no one could overhear us.

"What do you think you're doing?" he demanded, his voice arching in anger.

I wasted no time and drew out from under my arm a folio of Leonardo's drawings. I opened it in front of Piero and silently showed him one splendid example after another of our child's brilliant artwork.

To his credit, Piero's indignation at my audacity faded quickly. It would have been impossible, even for this ass of a man, to be unmoved by his own son's talent. Still, he was determined to make things as difficult for me as possible.

"It's very good," he said. "But what do you expect me to do about it?"

I held my temper admirably and spoke in a soft, friendly tone.

"Francesco mentioned that you have been befriended by a well-known artisan in Florence." Really, Francesco had told me that Piero was licking the heels of this man, whose fame was growing with every new Medici commission. "I think he called him Verrocchio."

Piero straightened. "That is true, Maestro Verrocchio thinks very highly of me."

I managed a smile. "Do you think it is possible to have him consider Leonardo for an apprenticeship?"

There was silence from Piero as he considered this. I could see that lawyerly mind clicking away, tallying up the benefits to himself, and any possible unpleasant consequences. My patience was running thin.

"I cannot see the harm in showing him the drawings," I said. "You yourself thought they were good."

Finally Piero looked me squarely in the eye.

"You're ready to send your son away? You've fought like a baited bear since his birth to keep him close to you."

This was the hardest part. With these words Piero had skewered me as if on a sword, as I had done to him in my dream.

"Yes. I think he should go." The words sounded so hard to my ears. "If he doesn't learn a trade, he'll be nothing but a worthless vagabond, and it will reflect badly on you and your family's good name."

He considered this in another lengthy silence. Then without a word, he took the folio from my hands.

"I'll see what my friend can do."

Now it was I quaking with emotion.

"Thank you, Piero," I said, and turning, walked quickly away so he would not see me weeping.

It took more than a year for arrangements to be made, but in the end the apprenticeship was set and Leonardo's excitement at the thought of beginning his career grew to a fevered pitch.

The only agony, I feared, would be in our parting.

Cato

J had refused to shed tears that day when my boy of thirteen, fresh-faced and gangly limbed, had climbed on the back of Piero's horse and disappeared from my sight. I believed that my other separations from Leonardo would prepare me for this one. I had initiated it. It was clearly in my son's best interests. He would be surrounded by a community of artists and be taught by one of Italy's greatest masters. It would put an end to his lowly status as the village bastard, and provide a chance for him to grow into manhood and rise to a well-deserved glory. We had both promised, of course, to write to each other. These were all indisputable blessings.

Yet it felt as though my heart had been wrenched forcibly from my chest. In the days and weeks after he left my breath came in short gasps. I slept poorly, and when I did sleep my dreams were somber at best, nightmares at worst. I lost my appetite for food, and nothing Magdalena prepared had the slightest flavor in my mouth. I lost weight and developed an alarming pallor.

My work for Papa in the apothecary was lifeless and slipshod. He was forced to remind me several times of potions I was meant to prepare, and the keeping of the alchemical fire, once a mystical ritual, became nothing more than a tiresome chore.

Oh Mama!
I hardly have words to tell you about my new life. Except for missing you and Grandfather and Uncle Francesco and the countryside, I

feel that, like some sailor from the Odyssey, I have washed up on the shores of Paradise. Not Florence itself. I hardly have time to go outside the bottega's front door. We work all the time. But I have made friends with all my fellow pupils, and I _love_ Maestro Verrocchio. He is, I think you would agree if you met him, a very fine man and a teacher of much excellence and well-deserved respect.

The workshop is as busy as a beehive in spring, all of us apprentices and journeymen rushing around, or heads bent over in deep concentration. There is always something that needs doing. Until recently I was still a "dogsbody" who swept floors and made paintbrushes or ground colors. But I am a full apprentice now, and the maestro gives me great responsibilities, even though I am very young. He says I learn quickly (and he whispers that he sees greatness in me). Already I understand the principle of how to put figures on a plane, how to represent a man's head and the technique of perspective. And I have graduated into figure drawing—of the naked body!

At first, so I did not waste expensive paper, I was made to work in metalpoint on a coated wood panel. But now my draughtsman's studies are on paper and soon I hope to be allowed to use colors. Of course I am learning to sculpt in clay, and my favorite subject is horses. I have made dozens of little figures of them, which the maestro says are quite impressive.

Today I helped with my first cartoon. That is where the maestro's outline for a painting is drawn on paper. Then a student—me!—pricks holes with a pin all along the lines. The pricked paper is laid up against a prepared wood panel and dusted with charcoal. The dark dust filters through the pinholes and when the paper is removed, there is the outline of the drawing on the wood panel.

We apprentices are expected to give total obedience to our master, but this is no problem for me, as I adore my maestro. He has such a big, warm heart, and he is so hardworking himself. He is never, ever idle. He always has something in his hands and expects us all to do the same.

He still supports his family, so I suppose he _must_ be industrious, but I think work gives him great joy, and therefore the bottega is a joyful

place to be. It is no secret, even among the youngest boys, that the mae-
stro was a bastard son and that he had the misfortune in his youth to
kill a boy by accident. He was tried and imprisoned for a while and fi-
nally let go, but then the next year his father died. So he has had a hard
beginning. Perhaps that is why he is so kind to me.

Father never comes to see me. He is very busy with the many con-
vents he works for. But no matter. I am happy here with my new fam-
ily, though of course I will always love you best.

Your son,
Leonardo

I'm ashamed to say I wept reading this letter and the others he
wrote about his wonderful new life. I wasted many precious sheets of
paper rewriting letters back to him, as I did not wish him to see my
tearstains giving lie to the cheerful words I had written. I believed
time would heal the gaping wound his departure had left in my soul,
but I was wrong. Months growing into years only caused the chasm to
fill with bitterness and, worse, self-pity.

On a spring day in the third year of Leonardo's absence, I mistak-
enly ground the poisonous leaves of belladonna, and not the healing
leaves of marigold, into a salve for Signora Carlotti's skin rash. Had it
not been for Papa's keen eye as he pushed it across the counter to her,
then retracted it, saying the salve must be remade with fresher ingredients, the poor woman would have died a horrible death.

When he later confronted me with my mistake I began to tremble
violently, as though I'd been caught naked in an Alpine snowstorm.
The strength left my legs and I dropped to the floor in a heap. But I
was dry-eyed, my tears all spent.

Papa helped me stand, but I refused his arm as I climbed the stairs
to my room. There I lay, still as a corpse for the rest of the day and
night, wide-eyed and awake, though paralyzed with loathing for myself and the life I was leading.

The idea came with the first rays of dawn. It was an image of the

Egyptian goddess Isis, whose beloved husband, Osiris, had been killed in battle, his body broken into pieces by his evil brother and scattered all over the world. In her great love for Osiris, and with the greatest courage, Isis found every piece and, putting them back together, breathed life into his resurrected body. *What had become of my courage?* I wondered. I had once possessed a great measure of it. *Could I not resurrect it myself?*

I dressed and walked up into the hills along the river path. At the waterfall I removed every stitch of clothing and stepped beneath the torrent of icy meltwater come recently from the snow-covered mountains. The freezing shock on my skin forced a shout from my lungs, but the sound, when it came, was a passing from the deepest part of me of all of my pain and my fury. I stood there bellowing my rage, daring Isis to come to this sad, wasted woman and infuse her with strength to do what must be done.

She came to me that day—Queen of the World, bringer of life and love. She came and brought me all I asked for, and more than I ever in my wildest imaginings could have dreamed.

I went to Papa in his laboratory that night and told him my plan.

Leonardo was in Florence, a young apprentice at Maestro Verrocchio's bottega, but his only family in the city was his father, an ice-hearted man who loved his son not at all. I believed, in fact, that Piero despised the boy, regarded him as an advertisement for his greatest failure. He had been unable to sire a single legitimate male heir on either of his young wives. His only son was a bastard, birthed by a girl not fit for marriage into his proud and ambitious family. Leonardo might as well be an orphan in the city, as much attention as his father was paying him. He needed family there.

He needed me.

I would move to Florence and set up shop as an apothecary. If I sold Mama's rings I would surely have enough to rent a small place until I began earning a living.

Papa sat himself down on the stool near his athenor and closed his eyes. He rested his chin on his chest, remaining silent for a space of time that felt endless to me, for I was waiting word from my most honored advisor, tutor, and sage. His hands, fingertips stained with the essence of herbs and burnt minerals, lightly clutched his knees. Finally he spoke.

"Surely you have the skills for an apothecary, but I do not like to think of you alone in that city. I have always believed that Florence is the worst of all places to be born a woman."

"I'll just have to manage," I snapped, unhappy at Papa's response. But I could see him wearing a certain expression of intense concentration he used when pondering the deepest mysteries or the most difficult of mathematical calculations.

"What if you went to Florence . . ." His pause was long and very grave. ". . . disguised as a man?"

"A man?"

"A *young* man." He was thinking as he spoke. "You are thirty-one. As a male you would look twenty, perhaps. Luckily, men are clean-shaven these days." He was regarding me intensely as he spoke. "And you are tall, so your height alone will not give you away. Of course you would practice lowering your voice."

I was staring at him gape-mouthed, but my excitement was rising as the possibilities became clear to me. "Twenty is young for a fully trained apothecary," I reasoned, "but I might say I was setting up shop for my uncle and master . . . who is soon to follow." The rest seemed suddenly logical. "My uncle could grow ill and die . . . but by then my customers would trust me."

I saw him begin to waver, as though he suddenly realized how insane was his idea. I sat down next to him on the bench and took one of his hands in mine.

"How can I approve of this?" he said solemnly.

"Do you approve of me being separated from my only child?" I asked. "Do you approve of my wasting away before your eyes? Do you approve of my endless grief?"

"Caterina . . ."

"It is the only way. I cannot ask you to leave Vinci. And you're right, it is madness trying to live a free life in Florence as a woman alone."

He closed his eyes, comprehending the enormity of it all. Then he said quietly, "I own a house in Florence."

"What?"

His brows furrowed. "Poggio's bequest. It's been so many years, I'd almost forgotten. When my master died, he left me his already deceased father's apothecary in Florence, and the residence above it. It never passed through my mind either to inhabit or sell it. The place has been sitting idle for years. If it is still there, it will be a rattrap."

"Will you write and discover its condition?" I said, hardly believing this stroke of luck.

He did not answer immediately. But now my determination had taken hold.

"Papa, *please*. You love me as I love Leonardo," I said. "How can you say no?"

Of course he had not said no, and our mad plan began immediately to take shape.

The guise we had chosen for me was that of a young city scholar. This meant a round-necked robe, pleated at the shoulders, hanging straight and untied at the waist to below the knee. Beneath were a shirt and hose. On my feet would be round-toed felt slippers with a strap across the instep. My breasts would have to be bound.

With the suffering of three years past having rent from me all appetite for food, the female curves had melted from my body. My cheeks were gaunt, and only the muscles in my limbs, worked hard in everyday labor, remained firm and healthy.

The small risings that had once been breasts the size of large Spanish oranges needed little in the way of hiding. Aunt Magdalena had wanted to help me, but I'd refused, saying that I would have to learn to do the binding and unbinding of them with a broad strip of cotton myself, for it was alone that I meant to live.

Of my womanly functions I was, ironically, free. My menses had stopped, as if to say, "What use do you have of me anymore?"

It was strange and rather awful having to cut my hair. My father did it for me, shaping it into the pageboy's length and style just touching my shoulders. This was how scholarly boys wore it, having borrowed it from the courtly lads of fashion. But the high, rounded, flat-topped cap required to finish the costume of a scholar ruined the stylishness of the haircut. It was a small price to pay to carry off my ruse.

In the end I made more than a passable young man. If you had put me in a brown robe and tonsured my head I would have been taken as a proper religious ascetic.

Perfect. Except that I was a heretic.

It was my day of leavetaking.

By candlelight, as I was making my final preparations to leave, Papa placed before the front door a good-sized casket. It had, in fact, been my mother's wedding chest, beautifully painted, as the custom was, with birds and flowers.

I looked at him questioningly and he lifted his chin to say I should open it. Inside were the most precious of his hand-copied manuscripts. Books that had educated him. The same books that had educated me, and Leonardo as well.

"You cannot mean to do this, Papa," I said, my eyes filling with tears I had so far refused to let fall.

"I've read them all. A hundred times. I can recite them in my sleep. And I've kept enough for myself. But you will need the books, Caterina. To continue your studies. And when you are in the company of the great men of Florence . . ."

"I, in the company of great . . . ?"

"When that happens," he insisted, "these manuscripts will be your currency, more valuable than a pile of gold florins."

That he believed in me so profoundly—his skinny, shorn, pitifully flat-hatted boy-scholar—wrenched a sob from my throat.

"None of that," he said sternly. "The only men in Florence who allow themselves to weep are rich men felled by cupid's arrows, ones who write poetry to their unrequited loves. You are a tradesman. 'Cato the Apothecary.'"

We had agreed on my old nickname, as much for the similarity to my own name as by his fondness for the Roman statesman and philosopher.

I wiped the wetness from my cheeks and put on the red hat. When he straightened it I saw tears brimming in his eyes, but he held them back. He stooped and picked up the casket of books.

I peeked out the front door and found the street as deserted as the church cemetery at midnight. He placed the chest in the cart and said good-bye to his mule, who had served him well for so many years.

"Go on," he said to me, "before the light comes."

We did not embrace. After all, I was no more than a young scholar passing through the village who had visited the local apothecary. An elaborate scheme involving a sick aunt in a distant village had been devised to explain my sudden absence from Vinci. Caterina, daughter of Ernesto, had been an outcast, a persona non grata, for so long that no one would have cared anyway.

"I will write," I said and, taking up the donkey's reins, turned, catching the last glimpse of my father.

"Beloved daughter," I heard him say before clattering hooves drowned out his voice.

That morning I stole away from the only home I had ever known. Left behind my father, the house I was born in, a mountain village that had showered me first with love, then with scorn . . . and my sex. There was no doubt that of all of these I would miss my father most. The house was a house. Vinci, like any other small town, was filled with men and women quite as willing to be cruel as be kind. As for my sex, aside from getting Leonardo from it, when had it ever brought me joy?

I was very grateful, though, on a day of such deep severing that Nature had gifted me with warmth, just a few wispy clouds and enough breeze to cool my brow. As I made my way down the steep path away from the hilltop church, the castle with its ancient wall, and the houses that called themselves Vinci, I questioned my own sanity. *Had melancholy so unbalanced me that I would do such a thing as this?* No. That was impossible. Papa would have taken me in hand and stopped me.

But this elderly mule pulling the cart, were he to have an opinion, might have thought otherwise. Poor old Xenophon, trussed to the rickety carriage and led by the mouth by me, groaned with his heavy load. When the sun finally rose and I was visible to him, I thought he was eyeing me oddly. "Who is this stranger with my mistress's scent but the look of a lad?" I imagined him thinking.

My male disguise was a misery in two parts. The first was how cloistered I felt in the coarse gray wool tunic, with a fringe of white shirt beneath showing through at the neck. Second, and worse, was the fear of my disguise's failure—discovery that a Tuscan village woman was daring to deny her very sex and take up residence in the great city as a man, and a businessman at that.

But here I was. There was no turning back. And in truth, the adventure of it all was just beginning to dawn on me.

The road east from Vinci to Florence hugging the south bank of the river from Empoli to La Lastra was better than the north, which was hardly a horse trail. The farmers with their summer crops, and merchants bringing their cargos of raw wool and silk from the seaside port of Pisa to the city of fashion that Florence was, clogged the byway, so I was never alone.

Some fellow travelers were friendly, the farmers especially. They wished for conversation, gossip mostly, news from whatever town you'd just come from. Still nervous and unprepared to launch myself into the wide world as a man, I pretended shyness, and instead of talking waved and smiled and quickly lowered my head as though I had a great deal on my mind.

By my calculations and my father's map I was roughly two-thirds of the way to Florence when night fell. I pulled my cart and mule from the road and under a tree I made a crude bed for myself, with no fire. Though exhausted, I was barely able to sleep, and when the first rays of sun fell on my face I was up and moving.

As my grunting beast rounded a river curve I received the greatest shock of my life—first sight of the city of Florence, its enormous cathedral dome and three high towers squarely centered in a sea of red rooftops. Even the mule was stunned into stopping, his weary eyes fastened on this odd vista.

I prodded Xenophon to go, as my excitement had in that instant multiplied tenfold, so much so that my terror subsided a fraction. As we hurried on, more features of the great city revealed themselves. The river as it passed through it, more congested on the left bank than the right, was encircled by a wall of red ochre, its thickness ten feet or more, with a dozen stone guard towers remaining, placed all along its length.

Now I could see a few huge castles in the hills on the south side of the river, and to the north in Florence itself, amidst what had seemed at a distance an even mat of rooftops and churches of which there were more than a hundred, giant edifices that dwarfed even a three-story house. These must be the city palazzos of the wealthy families, the nobles and the famous merchants, bankers and lawyers whose true religion, Papa had told me, was *commerce*, not the Catholic church.

It was not until I passed a portion of the outer wall and came to the westernmost bridge crossing the Arno that I realized my time of reckoning had truly come. I could still turn back, spare myself the humiliation, and the jail sentence, and perhaps even torture I would suffer if I was found out to be a woman living as a man.

I admit I did pause at the brink of the Ponte alla Carraia. I watched the traffic fascinated, as I had never seen a bridge wide enough for two carriages to pass each other. Realizing the moment had come, I gave Xenophon a tug, and the cart lurched after us. We joined the procession of commerce and thus entered our new life in "the city that ruled the world."

*O*nce I had left the bustle of the bridge I found to my great surprise that the streets, both wide and narrow, were strangely quiet, almost altogether deserted. The houses, I could see, had been built many years before of gray or honey brown sandstone, and were attached, one to the other. Many of their third or fourth stories jutted out farther over the thoroughfares than their street or first floors, and the upper windows and loggias were, almost every one, gaily decorated in some way. There were brightly colored banners and flags, tapestries and family crests, long garlands of flowers, and even long braids of cloth of silver or gold. Yet there were no young ladies sitting in the covered balconies flirting with young gentlemen below in the streets, as my father had told me was the custom in Florence.

But as my mule and I clattered the cobbles of Via Borgo Ognissanti, past the church of Santa Trinita and along the river road, a sound was coming clearer and louder to our ears. While it slowed the beast, it only made my heart beat faster and pulled me ahead with excitement. It was a sound I had never heard in my life—the sound of human voices screaming and cheering, what must have been an enormous crowd, and the clattering of hundreds of hooves on stone, all of it at once.

As we approached even closer the mule's eyes went wide, and with a final ungainly rearing he sat down on his hind legs. He had had enough. I was close to the piazza and desperate to behold its excitements, but I was certain I could not make the animal budge from his terrified posture. Everything I owned was in the cart. Did I dare leave it unattended in this strange city, surely teeming with thieves and ruffians?

I made my decision. I had seen barely a soul since I'd left the bridge. I surmised that if there were thieves and pickpockets, they would be wandering amidst the crowds doing their dirty work, not roaming deserted streets. I would count on the gods of good fortune and leave my possessions only long enough to catch a glimpse of what lay up ahead in the yard of Piazza di Santa Croce—the city's largest square. I tried soothing Xenophon with a gentle hand on his snout and a look into his bugged eyes, then hurried forward, turning the last corner.

The spectacle before me was more wonderful than even my florid imagination could have conceived.

It appeared that every inhabitant of Florence was in the square, some sitting in risers on two sides, and the whole of the piazza, with the exception of a horse track around its perimeter, was jammed cheek by jowl with people in their Sunday best. The horses of the *pallio*, judging by the rising crescendo of voices, were in their last lap of the famous race, and as the roar of the hooves came closer I actually caught a glimpse of the horses' heads—mad eyes and foaming mouths, their riders arrayed in gaudy guild and neighborhood colors, slung low along their mounts' necks, whipping them or whispering encouragement.

A moment later a roar of both triumph and defeat rose to a deafening roar and the crowd surged madly, moving to fill in the racetrack and surround the winner of the *pallio*.

I found myself shaken, paralyzed, my heart thumping hard against my chest.

I was dearly tempted to stay and join the celebration, but I desired more to find my new home. Seeing the way there congested with revelers, I found that I could only move west again before moving north. My father's map, admittedly rough—he had not been to Florence in so many years—proved to be true.

I presently found myself in the Piazza della Signoria, where, unlike

the largely deserted street, there was much activity. It was being prepared for some other large celebration. None of the workers—carpenters
hammering a platform under the long loggia of the Palazzo della
Signoria, the seat of Tuscan government, nor the men hanging gay banners, or the ones upending tall flagpoles into holes set into the perimeter
of the stone square—took any notice of the wide-eyed young man, his
donkey and cart, as they passed. They all talked or shouted to each other
as they worked, exchanging good-natured insults and witticisms, a trait
that my father had told me was common to Florentines. They were
proud to be intelligent, well-spoken and shrewd. Even to people of the
lower classes, the greatest sin of all was stupidity.

I saw near the piazza's edge a pile of hay, and taking pity on Xenophon, I led him to it. As he began to eat I found myself suddenly
squirming. I steeled myself and went to a man lifting a heavy board
onto the risers he was building.

"I'm new to the city. I have to relieve myself," I told him quietly.

"Piss?" he said.

I nodded.

"Over there." He was pointing to the alley wall. I cursed myself,
worried that I had sounded like a woman.

I walked to the farthest end of the wall and turned my back on the
man, whose suspicious eyes I imagined were boring into me. Then,
lifting my tunic, I unhooked from its lace around my waist the small
horn-shaped device that my father had fashioned for me. Cupping the
large end over my naked vulva, I held my breath and urinated. The
water I made moved blessedly and without leakage from the catch-cup
to the smaller spigot, allowing for the stream of piss to shoot in a
manly fashion against the wall.

The carpenter must have been satisfied, for when I turned back
to my cart the man was back at work. I went to my contented-looking
mule.

"You have eaten," I whispered to him. "And I have publicly pissed.
Do you not think we've done well for our first hours in Florence?"

As if in answer he made a grunting sound deep in his throat, one that made me smile. *The beginning of a great adventure,* I thought. I was in Florence, and somewhere amidst the teeming throngs was the reason I had come.

Leonardo. My darling son.

In the cathedral square, the Duomo's enormous cupola boggled my imagination. I could see the Campanile and across the way the famous Baptistery, which had stood in that spot since Julius Caesar built it in Roman times. These sights called out to me to stop and stare at their awesomeness and importance. But I wanted desperately to find my new home and some privacy.

Moving out the Via de Servi and turning right on the Via Riccardi, I found myself on a long block of four-story houses, the street very narrow but clean. Nowhere so far had I found sewage running in gutters, nor pigs and dogs rooting around in kitchen garbage thrown from upper windows. Like all the other buildings I had seen since entering Florence, the houses were of light brown and gray stone, and their façades were uniformly modest, as though their inhabitants wanted no one to know whether what lay inside was rich or poor. It was a preposterous Florentine pretension of humility. For it was always said, "Better to be a Tuscan than an Italian. Better yet to be a Florentine than a Tuscan."

I reached the spot my father had marked on his map, and sure enough, just in the middle of a long block, set between a prosperous-looking bakery and a residence with a stout metal-studded door, was a gray stone building, its storefront nailed up with rotting boards. Its first-story windows were boarded as well, and the jutting second- and third-floor wooden loggias looked ready to fall down on my head.

Wasting no time, I went back the way I'd come, carefully counting the number of houses from the corner, then led my animal to the alley behind it. "Almost there, my friend," I said. There were stone walls interspersed at every house with a back gate, and I remembered to *count*, as a mistaken entry into the wrong garden would result in an unwanted commotion.

I reached what I believed was my own back gate, happily wide enough to allow my cart in. Removing from a purse hung inside my tunic the old rusted key my father had given me along with the deed, I found the keyhole and strove to open the ancient lock. Clearly the key fit. It simply refused to turn. With all the strength in my hands I tried and tried, to no avail. It was the first time, though it would not be the last, that I wished I *was* a man, with a man's strength.

The mule made a mournful sound. I was tempted to make one myself. Frustrated, I gave the gate an angry shove and, to my shock, it swung widely into the garden, the lock and key quite unnecessary for its opening.

I wasted no time, leading Xenophon and my belongings into the yard. There stood my house and an overgrown garden. I went right to the back door and that, too, gave way with a swift kick of my boot at its base.

I was not altogether unprepared for the small confraternity of rats, whose peace I'd disturbed, that came rushing at me with awful rodent squeals, and some the other way, farther into the house. My father had been right about it being a rattrap, but there was nothing to be done for the moment.

I spent the next hour emptying my wagon, glad that everything was packed tight in wooden chests against the horrible creatures, and happier still that I had only to pull the boxes *down* from the cart and drag them along the overgrown but still visibly paved walkway into the largely empty storeroom. It was in here that the rats had made themselves at home, and by the great mass of their droppings I knew they were many and had nested here for a long while.

Only after the cart was emptied did I venture into my new home. The door separating the storeroom and the shop opened easily, but with its front windows boarded up there was only light enough to see that the place was spun heavily with cobwebs. *So,* I thought, *spiders could be counted in good numbers as well as rats.*

I was pleased to see that, despite thick dust and the cobwebs, what had been old man Bracciolini's apothecary was reasonably intact. There were sturdy shelves on three sides, and a counter that ran nearly the width of the shop, leaving just enough space for a person to come and go through. Behind and under the counter were cabinets with doors.

When I swept the dust and grime from the counter with my hand I was delighted to discover it was made of the finest travertine marble, an unattainable luxury for my father, but one that Poggio had been able to afford.

Now eager to see my new shop in the light of day, I grabbed the broom I'd brought and hacked a path through the cobwebs, the way I'd seen country lads hack through undergrowth to clear it for a new field. Using the handle, I pried the first of the rotted boards off the large window. It was real Venetian glass, another Bracciolini luxury. Sunlight came streaming in. But when I wrenched away the last piece of wood I reared back in fright.

A face and body were pressed square up against the glass. It was more the sudden shock of it than the demeanor of the person himself. He was just a boy, no more than thirteen, lean and wiry, his dark hair in a bowl cut. He was smiling impishly, as though he'd meant to give me a fright. He was pointing his finger, as though to say, "Let me in." Recovering my senses, I went to the front door, unbolted it, and tried to pull it open. It was jammed tight.

"Stand back," I heard through the wood planks.

I did, and all at once with a crash the door flew open on screeching hinges. There the boy stood, beaming, very pleased with his success. I was glad that the force of his blow had not splintered my front door.

"Benito Russo at your service, signor," he said, and bowed politely at the waist. I returned the male bow, feeling a bit odd.

"Cato Cattalivoni," I introduced myself. Benito's voice, I quickly realized, was still in the process of changing from that of a boy, so mine was even more manly than his. "My master and uncle, Signor Risticante, is the owner of this house," I went on. "He and I are reopening the apothecary here."

"Splendid!" Benito said. "I am your neighbor." He pointed to the house to the right of mine. "Or I should say, 'we' are your neighbors. My parents, two sisters and grandmother."

"Have you lived there long?" I asked. I wondered silently if they remembered the previous owner, or his apprentice, my father, Ernesto.

"Several generations," he said absently and came in, uninvited. He looked around in wonderment at the cobwebs and the counter and shelves.

"We're to have an apothecary next door to us? That will suit my grandmother very well. She's always sick or complaining about something." He looked at the countertop where my hand had swept the dust from the marble. He picked a cobweb out of his hair. "Will you and your master clean it up by yourselves?"

"Actually," I answered, beginning to spin my own web of deceit to this talkative youngster, "my uncle will be several months coming. I'll be readying the shop and house myself."

"Yourself!" Benito cried. "You'll be dead of fatigue before he arrives! Let me help you. I don't begin work till November. I'm to be an apprentice in a silk dyeing shop. You can hire me for cheap."

I trusted the boy at once, liked his proximity to my house, as well as his age, for I thought him less likely to suspect my sex. On that count I had so far been unquestioned. The merchants along the road and the workmen at the Signoria seemed to have had no doubt of my masculinity. And now Benito appeared fooled.

"If you help me get my house and shop in order I will provide you and your family all of my apothecarial services for nothing, for as long as I live here."

Benito's eyes went wide.

"Signor," he exclaimed, and bowed even lower. "What a gift that would be!" His eyes were sparkling, no doubt musing on the honor and respect he would gain in his family by delivering such a windfall to them.

We worked for a while, Benito showing off his manly strength in lifting heavy crates. While he worked, he talked. I heard about the great families who ran the city—the Spini, the Tornabuoni, the Rucellai, the Pazzi, the Benci. And of course, the Medici. The festival—one that would not be finished for two more days—was in fact a celebration of the coming marriage of the Medici heir, Lorenzo.

"Everyone loves him," Benito said. "He'll no doubt succeed his father when he dies. Unofficially, of course."

I told him I was not sure what he meant.

"Well, Florence is a proud republic. We have no kings or princes. And Lorenzo is a discreet and modest man." Then his eyes twinkled. "But on the occasion of his betrothal to a wealthy Roman girl, he himself proclaimed a three-day festival to celebrate it. We Florentines are always happy for any excuse for a gaudy spectacle," he confided. "And no one throws a better one than Lorenzo and his brother, Giuliano."

There were many questions about my uncle and master, about whom I wove a splendid story of renown in Siena, calling up minutiae my father had fed me about the place—one I had never been, and where, thankfully, neither had Benito visited.

I was looking around the place, wondering where to start.

"I have a suggestion, if I might be so bold . . . ," Benito began.

"And your suggestion is . . . ?" I prodded him.

"That we leave off all work for today, and that you accompany me to the festival." I smiled my assent. "Splendid!" he cried. "But we should change our clothes. We're full of cobwebs and dust. And on a day such as today, all young men should be at their best."

I tried to look serious. "You have a point. Meet me outside in a quarter of an hour."

I was sorely tempted to stay and explore the upstairs rooms of my house, but I knew that could wait. A Florentine festival sponsored by the Medici heir on the occasion of his betrothal was an occasion not to be missed. I might even catch a glimpse of Leonardo.

My young friend Benito and I joined the throng of celebrants who were pouring from every house into the street, reminding me of rivulets and streams feeding through the Vinci hills into the Arno. Their mood was buoyant and jovial, and they were clothed in their finest. The women, cheeks aglow, breasts high in deeply plunging bodices, were topped with hair uncovered to show curled ringlets or intricately woven braids. Men wore, in the finest of textiles, an astonishing array of fashions: tunics, robes, capes, and doublets with hose. They finished their costumes with hats and turbans of sometimes alarming size and fantastical shapes.

Unlike the serious and grim-faced town fathers of Vinci, even the older men smiled and laughed as they walked, flirting openly with the women, young girls to old ladies.

As Benito and I with the rest of the city poured into the spectacle that was the Piazza della Signoria, there seemed a feeling of gay abandon, as though not a care in the world troubled a one of them. And yet, I saw the Florentines not as a vulgar or dissolute people, but as healthy and naturally happy. I had never in my life experienced such an explosion of color and cacophonous sound. As I had seen this morning, every window, roof, loggia, and parapet overlooking the square was crowded with celebrants and hung with a gorgeous array of banners and streamers, flags and tapestries fluttering merrily in the breeze. Every inch of the piazza teemed with revelers, tableaus, and musicians. There was a parade of miniature castles, gilded and glinting in the sun. Then, as a small herd of riderless horses crashed headlong into the crowd, I turned to Benito, crying, "What was that?!" but he'd been swallowed up by the masses.

Suddenly I caught the barest glimpse of a young man all the way across the piazza, a young man who might have been my Leonardo—wild-haired, even-featured and beautiful. He disappeared into the throng as quickly as he had appeared, and I found myself horrified to realize that I might not recognize my own son. I had not seen him for three years. Those years between thirteen and sixteen were the ones in which a boy grew and changed the most. Piero was tall, wide-shouldered, and well made, and even as a young boy Leonardo resembled him in those ways. As for his face, I reassured myself, if I was close enough to see that broad mouth, his fulsome lips and straight-toothed smile, the long straight nose and wide-set gray eyes flecked with gold, I would know him in an instant.

A loud trumpet fanfare thrust me out of my musing back into the chaotic piazza. The Palazzo della Signoria's stone front and tall rock bell tower could hardly be seen for all the silken banners fluttering around them. Under the palazzo's ground-floor loggia a platform had been erected, draped and canopied with costly brocades of blue and gold and white. Two long rows of high-backed chairs, ornate and thronelike, sat empty under the tent.

As I tried to see better what and who was under that loggia, I pushed shamelessly through the crowd till I was several rows from the front. Suddenly I felt a tap on my shoulder. I turned and saw Benito at my side.

"Glad you came with me?" he asked.

"More than glad. It would have been a crime to miss this," I told him.

"Look, Cato!" Benito pointed to the doorway of the Palazzo della Signoria, which had swung open and out of which, in a long procession, dozens of men emerged, all of them sober and dignified.

"Who are they?" I said to Benito as I watched them, one by one, take their seats and fold their hands on their laps. He explained they were the current members of the Signoria and the heads of each of the guilds. I could see in the richness or modesty of their dress the guild heads' visions of themselves. The bankers and the notaries were hung with thick chains of gold, rings of precious gems on every finger. The silk and wool men had attired themselves in simple fashion, but proudly displayed the best of their wares on their bodies. The carpenters and butchers and masons were stockier, more muscular under their robes. Their features were coarser, too, men who over the generations had not had the money or prestige to marry with the finest and most ancient Italian female stock.

As if my thoughts had suddenly turned to flesh, a noble*woman* now emerged from the Signoria door outfitted and bejeweled in a way I had never seen a woman adorned, opulently and dazzlingly elegant.

More trumpet blasts announced from the rear of the Signoria a host of fifers and standard-bearers, followed by heralds, pages, and men-at-arms. Each and every one of them was costumed dramatically.

"Lorenzo's designs," Benito said of their dress. "He takes a hand in every part of the festival's planning."

"Who is the woman?" I said to Benito, never taking my eyes from them.

"Lucrezia de' Medici," he said, "Lorenzo and Giuliano's mother."

The crowd began to cheer, if not halfheartedly perhaps reservedly, for the next person out the door, a man rather severely dressed in black, and bent over nearly double. His face, if it had been handsome, I could not see for the pain that was etched into every feature.

"Piero the Gouty," Benito offered, "Lorenzo's father. The Medici's Highest of the High. He doesn't have long to live."

"I can see that."

"He's none too popular," Benito said. "Certainly not so loved as his papa, Cosimo—he has been named Father of the Country. No one will admit that they long for the day that Lorenzo will rule."

Now the real show began. First came eighteen knights, all in flashing silver armor and military helmets, each, Benito told me, representing the great Florentine families. The armor, too, had been created by Lorenzo.

"Where are the friars?" I asked Benito. Even on Vinci's feast days, puny compared to this spectacle, the village holy men were conspicuous participants. Here, today in Florence, they were conspicuously absent.

"This is not a day for the friars, Cato," he replied, unable to hide the disdain in his voice. "The church has its own festivals, but not like this. Look, look! Here is the Queen of the Day!"

Enough talk of holy men, I thought and smiled to myself. Indeed, here came Lorenzo's bride, perhaps the loveliest creature I had ever in my life seen. If I had been a man, I think I would have fallen in love with her myself. Her hair was the color of the setting sun, falling in soft curls about her pale, rounded shoulders. Her features were delicately honed, the nose coming to a pretty point, the chin and cheeks a study in fine curves and perfect angles. Her eyes danced with delight.

And who wouldn't be delighted? She was robed and bejeweled as a princess in pale blue and white silk, seeded with a thousand pearls, and though I could not from that distance see the color of her eyes, I imagined them a perfect match to her gown. Her manner of transport was magnificent and stately; she was enthroned on a queen's gilded chair and, with the crowd grown silent in awe, carried high on the shoulders of eight uniformed bearers down a purple carpet to a place in the middle of the square cordoned off by velvet ropes.

She was set down facing the Signoria, the dignitaries under the loggia regarding her with nodding heads of approbation.

Suddenly the crowd stirred, then began cheering as out from behind the hall on horseback came a young man—he looked sixteen at the most, one of the handsomest men I had ever set eyes on. Short, pale, curly hair framed a nobly proportioned head, a chin and jaw cut as if by a razor. He had a regal, straight-backed bearing, offset by a boyish grin from ear to ear. He was waving to the crowd, who uninhibitedly adored him.

"Giuliano," Benito whispered, not bothering to temper his awe of this young man. "Lorenzo's younger brother. They are best friends and will rule together when Piero dies."

A fife and trumpet fanfare, louder and grander than all the rest, was joined by a sound I recognized as a roar. It was a louder human commotion than I had ever in my life heard.

Every person on the square, from windows, on the roofs and parapets, were cheering, and chanting a single name. "Lorenzo!" The cheering finally ceased and only the chanting remained. "Lorenzo! Lorenzo!! Lorenzo!!!"

Then he came. At first all I saw was a figure on a white charger, his

silk cape swirling around him, black shoulder-length hair, the long
white plumes of his cap arched out over his shoulders.

The horse and he seemed to be one as they rode down the purple
carpet toward "the queen." The mount was draped in red-and-white
pearl-encrusted velvet, and pranced in proud high steps. Lorenzo
wore a velvet surcoat of scarlet, and a flowing silk scarf gorgeously
embroidered in scarlet roses. He sat tall and dignified in his saddle,
carrying an azure shield of fleur-de-lis and in whose center nestled a
diamond the size of a duck's egg.

He did not wave his hand as his brother had, but the eyes with
which he surveyed the chanting masses were filled with such extraordinary love for them that such a gesture was altogether unnecessary.

When a woman from the crowd called out, "We love you, Lorenzo!"
the man flashed a smile so brilliant and heartfelt that I myself felt a
strange tugging in my breast. And when the people began to roar again
in their approval of him I found myself shouting with them.

I had never raised my voice like that before, never felt the sensation
of idolatry for a mortal man and, I realized, a young man at that.

While Lorenzo de' Medici was certainly older than Giuliano, he
looked not more than twenty-five. He was not handsome in the way
his brother was. His skin was a deep olive. The nose looked crooked,
almost sunken, the chin and lower lip perhaps a bit too pronounced,
and deep wrinkles in his forehead bespoke of a serious nature. But he
was tall, broad-shouldered, and slim at the hips. I could see his muscular legs, those of a horseman.

Now Lorenzo on his horse had passed us and was making his way
down the long purple carpet to "his queen." Frustrated to be watching his back, as well as a horse's ass, I grabbed Benito's arm and started
pushing my way through the crowd till we were in good sight of the
beautiful lady, who watched with admiration as Lorenzo dismounted
and with a flourish of his white cape bowed low to her.

A page appeared with a velvet cushion on which sat a crown that
seemed all to be made of large cut diamonds. Lorenzo took the circlet

from the pillow. The crowd hushed once more, and as he knelt before his wife-to-be, I heard for the first time the voice of Lorenzo de' Medici. It was deep, almost a growl, but he spoke with studied eloquence.

"You are the jewel of Florence and the queen of all of our hearts." Then he stood and gently placed the crown into the riot of her golden curls.

The crowd cheered again.

"What a lucky woman to be getting such a fine husband!" I had to shout over the noise to be heard by Benito.

"What do you mean?!" he shouted back. "That is not Lorenzo's betrothed. She is Lucrezia Donati, the most beautiful and beloved woman in Florence!"

"Where is his wife-to-be!?" I was very confused.

"She is on her way here from Rome! Clarice Orsini is her name. It's a very noble family, but the match is not very popular with Florentines! Romans are well known for their pride and snobbery! But the alliance brings soldiers and several great estates with it! And a six-thousand-florin dowry. Six thousand!"

The racket had lessened again, for Lorenzo was now singing to the newly crowned queen. There was a smile behind that voice of his, the odd amalgam of gruffness and gentility—the smile because the words he sang were bawdy and outrageous. But far from the crowd being shocked or dismayed by his verse, it seemed to make them love Lorenzo more.

"Don't tell me," I whispered to Benito, "he composed the song himself."

"How did you know?"

"Is there anything that Lorenzo de' Medici does not do splendidly?"

"If there is, I cannot think of it."

The song finished, the bearers heaved the throne on their shoulders and Lorenzo, throwing back his red-rosed scarf and cape, mounted his charger in one graceful sweep. I could tell he would soon be out of sight, and I wished to see him one more time.

With more brazenness than I thought I had in me I pushed forward to the edge of the purple carpet. Oncoming was Lorenzo, followed by the crowd and enthroned queen.

But I had, in my enthusiasm, perhaps jostled a stocky Florentine lad too hard, for now with a grimace in my direction he jostled me back. I was unused to roughhousing like young men regularly do, and I was caught off balance. With my scholar's cap flying off my head, I fell unceremoniously into the middle of the purple carpet flat on my back, right in the path of Lorenzo's charger.

Before I could spring to my feet I found myself staring up into the face of the Medici heir. He was smiling a dazzling smile, and his hand reached down to pull me up.

I lifted my arm and his strong hand gripped mine. I was on my feet in the next moment. I snatched my cap and placed it back on my head. Lorenzo, with a grin, straightened it for me. The crowd was delighted by this little scene. The great Lorenzo helping the hapless young scholar with grace and good humor.

Then with a wave to the queen's bearers that he was moving again, Lorenzo rode back for the loggia, where his mother and father were standing with Giuliano, waiting for him to join them, completing the Medici family tableau.

I stepped back and felt myself lost amidst the masses. I was aware of Benito speaking to me, tugging at my arm.

"Cato! He pulled you up! Straightened your cap! Acknowledged you!" The boy began dusting off my tunic, as though he was the servant of a fine gentleman. I noticed that many eyes were fixed on me, as though I had been blessed by God himself.

"I'm all right, really I am," I said to Benito, wishing for him to stop his fussing. "Tell me, is that food I smell?"

"Food? You think you smell food?" His whole face lit up and I was reminded suddenly of Leonardo and the insatiable appetite my son quite suddenly acquired the year he turned thirteen. "I will show you food!"

Benito began moving through the crowd to the perimeter of the square. "Stay close so we don't lose each other again!"

Now we had reached the edge of the piazza, where, to my further astonishment in a day of unending astonishments, was a long row of tables, each covered with a colorful tent and piled high with some Tuscan delicacy being served by a smiling Florentine woman. Separating each table was a barrel of wine and a vintner hawking the fruit of his vines.

There was nothing an Italian was more proud of than his wine, unless, of course, you counted his olive oil. But the oil was a given, used in every dish, in potions and poultices, and preserves and even to lubricate the skin. My father used to say, "Cut a Tuscan's vein and out is just as likely to pour wine or oil as blood."

"Food indeed," I said to Benito.

"What did you expect?" said Benito. "How can it be a festival without a feast?"

We walked down the row of tables deciding what we wished to eat first.

"And I suppose this was all provided by . . ."

"Look around you, Cato," the boy said rather dramatically. So I did as I was told. "There is not a single thing you can see, hear, taste, or smell in this whole piazza that has not been imagined, created, or paid for by Lorenzo."

My eyes had fallen on the canopy beneath the Signoria's loggia.

The core of the Medici dynasty stood together. The ruler's frail arms were slung over the shoulders of his two sons, of whom he seemed very proud. Then Lorenzo picked up his mother's hand, and with adoring eyes kissed the tips of her fingers. The scene tightened my throat, but what I saw next was like a sharp stake thrust into my belly.

Talking with the head of the Notaries Guild was Leonardo's father, Piero da Vinci.

Of course I knew that in moving to Florence there would be no way to avoid seeing him. He was a respected lawyer, "a notable notary," Leonardo had quipped in one of his letters.

I had determined to stay as far away from Piero as possible, as he was the one person most likely to recognize my identity. True, he had seen me almost never in the past ten years. I had grown from the girl he had seduced into a mature, work-hardened woman. Piero himself had seen less and less of Vinci in the years after Leonardo's birth, coming more often and finally moving to Florence, where his aspirations and ambitions could take flight.

It was possible, I concluded, that Piero might stare me right in the face and never know it was his once-young, once-beloved sweetheart. When I felt my guts beginning to churn I knew I should leave. I found Benito at a table serving quail pastries. His cheeks were stuffed with the delicacy and his eyes were watering—it must have been spiced with hot peppers.

"I'm going back to my house," I said. "I must at least make up a place where I can sleep before tonight. I've not even been up my stairs yet."

"Do you want me to come help you?" he asked with his mouth full. It was comical to see, but it was a sweet gesture of sacrifice from a boy I had met only hours before.

"Don't be silly," I called back to him. "Stay and enjoy the food."

"And dancing!" he shouted at my back as if to entice me.

I was tempted to say with a touch of sarcasm, "I suppose Lorenzo de' Medici choreographed the dances, too." Later I found out that he had.

I climbed the stairs that clung to the east wall of my house, finding them thankfully sturdy, and also found, to my surprise and delight, a reasonably intact and less than filthy sitting room on the first floor. There were two large windows in the front, which, when uncovered, looked down on the street, and a good-sized hearth on the back wall that looked down on my garden. From here I watched the mule busily clearing the brush, chewing contentedly and seeming completely at home in this new yard.

On the second floor I found what had been used as a kitchen, and a bedroom complete with an Italian's most prized possession—a family-sized bed with wooden canopy. There was no bedding, just a frame, and the dust in there was so thick that when I placed a single foot in the room a cloud of it rose up around me.

One more flight up I found, on the street side, a smaller chamber that once might have been used for a bedroom, but had since been converted by the elder Bracciolini to a study. There was an unremarkable desk—but one I was mightily pleased to see—and a wall of shelves that must have held books. I smiled, suddenly feeling more at home here, for the place reminded me of my father's house. Not all men had studies. Fewer still owned books.

There was a history of scholarship in the house. And a link with my father. Perhaps some of the volumes that had graced these shelves had been acquired or first copied by Poggio and Papa on one of their adventures, and brought as a gift to Poggio's father, my father's master.

But the greatest delight was yet to come. Across a tiny landing from the study I found a closed door. This bore a padlock, but it was so rusted that a blow with my broom handle pulled it off, hinges and all.

Papa had told me that my new home had once hidden a laboratory, for old Bracciolini, aside from his work in the herbal arts, had been an alchemist. He'd been Ernesto's teacher in both. So when the door creaked open and I beheld that most heretical of all chambers, I felt a thrill of delight, though not surprise.

There was little left of its equipment for an untrained eye to recognize the room's purposes. But I could tell. It had been placed on the top floor facing the garden, the most private room in the house. There was a lingering smell of sulfur and the sharp bite of mercury that permeated the walls and floor. The long tables were stained and burned in the same way my father's laboratory tables had been. And there, on the far wall, was the furnace—not a normal hearth or a brazier to give heat on a chilly evening. This was a proper fire-and-brimstone oven, one that once lit was tended constantly, with sacred fervor . . . and never ever let to burn out.

By now I had lost the sun and I was forced to carefully feel my way down the dark stairway to the ground floor and find a lamp to light.

By its glow alone I swept and mopped my bedchamber, being careful to remove every last spiderweb and rat dropping from the bedstead, and finally with some trepidation carried up a thin mattress, sheets, coverlets, and pillow to lay in its boards. The moment the bed was made exhaustion overtook me, and barely able to remove my outer clothes, I collapsed there and fell deeply asleep.

*I*n the next weeks my new young friend Benito was good to his word and helped me with the cleaning and refurbishing of the first two floors of my house. Of the rest he saw nothing. I had clandestinely carted all of my books and alchemical equipment to the third floor. The bedrooms, too, I determined to keep private.

The boy worked cheerfully, this being his nature, but also because having secured my services to his family in exchange for his work he had, indeed, raised his currency with them.

Wearing kerchiefs over our faces we disposed of the most disgusting tasks first, cleaning the storeroom and shop of their ingrained filth, tearing out walls and floorboards that were rotted away, concealing years of black mold. Benito was a more than adequate carpenter and replaced the rotten planks with wood donated by his father, the overage from a shed he had recently built in their garden.

I took special pride in my large glazed front window, which I washed with vinegar and polished to a glittering transparency. The shop shelves, floors, and walls were sanded smooth and finally given a fresh coat of paint in three different shades of green. The travertine marble counter, scrubbed with borax, showed itself to be the gleaming white glory of the apothecary. Then Benito built me rodent-proof containers for my storeroom.

I worried that my shelves would look bare with too few jars and bottles of remedies, but I cleverly conceived of displaying myriad bunches of herbs in the empty spaces rather than, like my father had done, hanging them in the storeroom. In this way I managed, by bringing the outdoors inside, to cheer up the look of the shop as well as improve its smell.

During those weeks, neighbors and passersby stuck their heads into the shop and I happily made their acquaintance. They were, I later learned, typical Florentines—friendly but wary, loathing stupidity and loving to gossip. Where in Vinci I had eschewed the practice of gossiping, now I embraced it. It was the best way to stay informed, and the people with whom I enjoyed this friendly chatter were likely, when I opened for business, to become my customers. And the more of them that came to believe my disguise now, the better.

All the talk in those weeks was of Lorenzo de' Medici's marriage, how his mother, Lucrezia, had made a special trip to Rome to spy on the sixteen-year-old prospective wife as she was coming and going to church, in order to decide on her appropriateness. The Medici matron had found Clarice Orsini's face too round and her neck too thin. The education she'd received had been ordinary, not nearly as fine as her three daughters'. Perhaps it was Clarice's shyness and modesty that caused the Orsini girl to "poke her head forward like a chicken" when she walked, my neighbor surmised. Lucrezia de' Medici had conceded that Lorenzo's prospective wife had pretty reddish hair, long graceful white hands, and a nicely shaped bosom. But in the end, my neighbor concluded, the size of her dowry was the deciding factor.

Despite a promise of many customers, I was not yet ready to open my apothecary. I had need of an outdoor sign, and I knew exactly where I would procure one. The thought made my heart race.

I would be going to the famous bottega of Andrea Verrocchio.

The confidence I had acquired in the past month from successfully passing as a man began to evaporate as I took to the streets on foot to visit my son. I had deemed it wise to keep both the move to Florence and my male disguise a secret from him, for no other reason than worry that the letters might fall into the wrong hands. I had no fear of Leonardo's response at seeing me in a tunic and cap. In the years since his birth in Vinci, the adversity and ostracism we had endured on one hand, and the joyful education we had shared on the other, had forged the deepest understanding between us. It was one that allowed for games and practical jokes—a bond that few mothers shared with their children.

He would recognize me in an instant and join the ruse with relish. For he missed me in his life as sorely as I missed him. I was sure of this.

What I did fear was my ability to fool Maestro Verrocchio, with his discerning artist's eye. Surely he could tell a man from a woman. But I had no choice. Today would set my course in stone. If I was found out, the humiliation and scandal would not simply be mine, but my son's as well.

I had to be strong, fearless. And I had to succeed.

As I made my way through the streets I was but mildly distracted by the beauty of the frescoes painted on the façades of the churches, at every corner shrine, their candles illuminating a Madonna and child painted by one of the great masters. I was coming to see that such displays were less a sacred art than Florence bragging about its world-famous artisans. Old Roman columns graced a minor piazza, or an ancient stone sarcophagus, now a water trough where horses stood and drank.

I arrived at the artisans district and was directed to Via Agnolo, a narrow but carefully paved street lined not with houses or palazzos but with one workshop after another.

For all his disreputable behavior toward his son, I thought, *Piero has done well by Leonardo in arranging this apprenticeship with Verrocchio.*

Looking down Via Agnolo I could see at a glance that one bottega above all was a hive of activity. I approached slowly, watching several young men loading an ornately carved and painted headboard on a horse cart, trying, with some difficulty, to avoid a clutch of boys playing with a ball, and chickens pecking at scratch on the pavement. Finally they lashed the bed head securely to the cart's rails and sent it on its way.

Standing before Verrocchio's bottega I saw its grand arched entry-
way, which, except for a heavy awning, left open the whole expanse
of whitewashed studio. Its vaulted ceiling stretched out in a long,
broad rectangle, with a smaller opening to a work yard. Some of the
studio's wares were on display in front—a gilded basket and a fantastically painted wedding chest, the scarf that Lorenzo de' Medici had
worn on the day of his betrothal festival, and next to it his brother
Giuliano's suit of armor.

Verrocchio was very much a favorite of the city's leading family.
Indeed, from all the artisans in Florence, he had been chosen to create
the tomb of Cosimo de' Medici.

The young men who had loaded the cart had gone back inside and
I could see now they were, each one of them, an apprentice in the
shop. Straightening my back and rising to my full height—now two
full inches above that with which nature had endowed me by use of a
lift in my slippers—I entered the bottega.

I could see a stairway at the back leading to what I presumed were
the living quarters above. On both sides of me rose the most astonishing
array of industry. My nose was assailed by dust and sweat and pungent
varnishes and solvents. The place echoed with hammering, clanging,
the hiss of white-hot steel meeting water, a metal point chipping marble. Strangely there were no human sounds. All the boys and young
men were working in concentration, or at least obedient silence.

One apprentice swept the floor with a wide broom. Another stood
at a workbench cleaning a vast array of paintbrushes, and next to him
an older boy ground colors at a large grindstone. The walls were vari-
ously hung with tools or sketches or carnival masks and death masks.
A wooden model of a small church stood on a turntable.

I watched as a boy plucked an egg from a chicken's nest box next to
a worktable, delivering it to another apprentice mixing bright blue
tempera. The egg was cracked into a bowl and added to the color.
Near him on a bench was another boy gathering onto a stick a bunch
of boar's bristles, fashioning a paintbrush. Near him was a youngster
covering a large wooden panel with white paint.

I studied every face, looking for my son, but he was so far nowhere among these boys. They were—here in the front of the shop—younger than Leonardo, no more than thirteen, the age at which he had arrived in Florence.

At an imperceptible demarcation in the studio, the age of the apprentices rose a year or two and the jobs at which they worked became more skilled. One was decorating a chest with a fire-breathing dragon, another applying gold leaf to the halo of a sweet-faced Madonna. A boy polished the round cheeks of a small bronze cherub. Another stood at a large panel laying the first colors onto a cartoon outline of what I could see would be a major painting of saints and angels.

Neither was Leonardo in this group.

The final third of the bottega held the most impressive level of artifacts. There was sculpture of every kind—bronze and marble and wood. Gold work and ironwork. There were portraits of ladies and gentlemen unknown to me, but clearly wealthy enough to pay for their likenesses to be painted by Maestro Verrocchio. Another man sat at a loom, threading glittering fibers through a long swatch of cloth of gold. Last there was a lad covered in fine dust, tapping away with his chisel at a marble slab, the subject and features of which were not yet discernible. I had been told that a bottega produced more than frescoes and statues, but never had I imagined that the world of the artisan was so broadly imagined.

But where was Leonardo? And where was his master, Verrocchio?

As I made my way to the far end of the studio I began to hear the sound of a lute being prettily played, with no accompanying voice. It was coming from the open back door, so I proceeded on. An unused anvil and a huge kiln stood untended, shimmering with internal heat. But when I peeked around the door I was met with a shock of the unexpected.

While the yard directly outside the back door was nothing more than a serious workplace, the other half was another world altogether. I might have been looking into a small wooded glen outside of Vinci. An ancient walnut tree shaded the better part of a high-walled garden that had been planted with shrubs and smaller trees, and the stone walls hung thickly with vines. There was even a tiny patch of "meadow" with grasses and wildflowers abounding. In a corner where two of the garden walls met, a rock waterfall sent cascades of crystal water bubbling down a tiny pebble-strewn stream, complete with ferns and moss!

Amidst this bucolic haven under the branches of the thick-trunked tree I could make out several young men lounging on the ground and an older, heavyset man on a bench, each with a sketchbook before him. Another man stretched out in the grass leaning on one elbow plucked at the lute. A platform was centered between them, and on it sat a grisly sight—the severed head of a long-haired and heavily bearded giant, or at least a clever likeness of such a head. Clearly it was Goliath.

But where was David?

I heard the older man call out, "That is the longest piss in Florentine history!"

The others laughed good-naturedly and then, from behind the walnut's massive trunk stepped a most beautiful youth, a thin sheet draped around him. Gracefully he bent to pick up a wooden sword lying in the grass, and in the moment before he let drop the drapery and struck his pose above the head of Goliath, I knew this perfect creature to be my son, Leonardo.

I was thoroughly transfixed, as though I had caught sight of a Greek god. He had retained the leanness of boyhood, but in the years since I'd seen him last his muscles had defined and hardened. His height, the shape of his legs, and the vertical cut of his loins were so like his father's that a breath caught in my throat. His cheeks, jaw, and chin still retained the round lines of youth. The mane of curly brown-gold hair curling around his face was angelic.

My son! I cried silently. *Leonardo!*

Wishing to gather my wits I pulled back through the doorway and stood as still as one of Maestro Verrocchio's statues. There I stayed, my eyes closed, one moment practicing the first words I would speak to the group in the garden, the next planning a cowardly escape.

"Surely you don't mean to stand in that spot the whole day."

The voice behind me was so close and so unexpected that I nearly came out of my skin.

"Whoa! Sorry, lad."

I turned and was greeted with the third shock of the day.

Lorenzo de' Medici stood behind me with an amused expression on his dark, handsome face. The look changed when he saw me. While I knew instantly who he was, he had only a vague memory of having seen my face. I could tell he'd not yet placed it.

I executed a small, respectful bow. He nodded at me with what appeared as equal respect.

"Cato, lately of Siena . . . ," I said. "You . . . at the celebration of your betrothal . . ."

"I remember now. You're the young man who threw himself under my horse."

I smiled at his easy humor and felt comfortable adding, "You straightened my cap."

He looked at me askew. "It could use straightening again."

I reached for it.

"I was joking."

This time I laughed out loud.

"Who are you here to see?" he asked.

"I . . ." I was altogether unprepared for this question, but I knew I could not afford to stutter.

"The purpose of my visit is twofold. I've come to have a sign painted for my shop . . . my master's shop," I added quickly. "And that's my nephew there, the model." I moved aside so Lorenzo could see into the garden. "He doesn't know I've moved to Florence. This is a surprise visit."

"You're Leonardo da Vinci's uncle?" he said, looking at me, too closely for comfort.

"On his mother's side," I said quickly. "You know him?"

"Everyone knows him," Lorenzo said. "He is the maestro's prized pupil." He saw my delighted expression. "Were you not aware?"

"I know that the boy is talented," I said, trying for a nonchalance that was difficult to maintain. "But he's modest about it."

"Leonardo? Modest?" Now it was Lorenzo's turn to laugh. "You really must not have seen him for a while. He's brilliant, sweet-hearted, levelheaded, and respectful of his master. . . ."

"But not modest," I offered.

"Nor humble," Lorenzo added.

I turned to look at the group sketching my son. "Do those traits trouble the maestro?" I asked, having forgotten for the moment that I was conversing with one of the foremost young men in the world.

"Not as much as they do his father."

I was grateful to be looking away from Lorenzo, as he would have noticed my discomfort.

"You know Piero da Vinci, then?" I asked.

"Not really, I've just heard Verrocchio speak of him." There was a brief silence before Lorenzo continued, rather gently. "The man treats his son with very little regard. But of course you know that."

"Yes," I agreed, "he does." I wondered if he also knew of Leonardo's bastardy. Chances were he did.

"What kind of sign?" Lorenzo suddenly demanded.

"Sign?"

"For your shop. Your master's shop."

I turned to face him. "Apothecary," I answered.

"Apothecary! Then one day you and your nephew will be members of the same guild."

I nodded. It was true. Physicians and apothecaries together with artisans were brothers in the same guild.

"What is *your* errand here today?" I asked, feeling suddenly bold.

"Coming to drag my friend Sandro out of here to visit a certain lady." He gave a wink and a grin. "Shall we go join our friends and family?" Lorenzo said.

"After you," I said, and stepped back for the Medici heir.

We passed through the outdoor workshop and moved, without pausing, to the green garden.

The man plucking the lute looked up and saw us first. He sprang to his feet and smiled at us. His face was long and oval, his sloe eyes brown and expressive.

"Botticelli!" Lorenzo bellowed at him, and I realized with a start that this must be the renowned painter Alessandro Botticelli. They embraced heartily. Then Lorenzo bowed to Verrocchio. "Maestro, you're looking well."

The heavyset older man, whose lips seemed too large and sensitive for his careworn face, began to rise from his chair.

"Do not get up, Andrea."

Verrocchio stayed put, gratitude for the respect shown him glowing on his features. The apprentices scrambled to their feet, however, with Leonardo quickly clutching the sheet to him. Everyone made their obeisance to the closest thing Florence had to a prince.

I could see my son gaping at me, unaware that his expression of surprise was as naked as his body was.

"This is Cato," Lorenzo announced. "A new apothecary in town."

I was struck by the sweet irony of the moment. Lorenzo de' Medici was introducing me, a humble village woman in the guise of a man, into his august society.

"Do you not recognize your uncle?" he said, turning to Leonardo. "He tells me it's been some time since you've seen each other."

"Uncle Cato," Leonardo said, moving forward, awkwardly tying the sheet around his waist.

I embraced him. He'd grown taller than I was in the years we'd been apart. The arms that encircled me were wiry and hard.

"I wanted to surprise you," I managed to utter without any crack of emotion, but the sweet, familiar smell of him nearly took my breath away.

"Surprise me you did, Uncle," he replied with the greatest restraint. But I could feel the core of him trembling wildly and his strong fingers gripping me.

So there, under the pleasant gaze of these great men of Florence, love and relief flowed between my son and me like a warm, silent tide.

"Bring some wine for our guests, Guido," the maestro said to one of the apprentices. He rose instantly and was gone. Verrocchio turned to me. "So where is your shop?"

"Via Riccardi," I said. "A pleasant neighborhood. I'm restoring the building. My master will be very pleased when he sees it."

"And doubly pleased that he hasn't had to do the restoration himself," Verrocchio added with a chuckle.

"I would like your studio to make me a beautiful sign," I said, worrying that I appeared overly serious amidst this rather jovial group.

He turned to Leonardo, who had dropped the sheet so the sketching could resume. I was struck again by the sight of him, as much by the utter grace of his form and movements as by his beauty. "Why don't we have you paint your uncle's apothecary sign, eh, Leonardo?"

He grinned at the idea.

"He's a good boy," Verrocchio said, then lowering his voice, added, "A genius. You see this garden. His idea. His design. His execution."

I nodded, attempting equanimity, while all the time I was burning with pride.

"He said he could not bear being away from his beloved countryside," the maestro continued. "A good thing, as we work here seven days a week . . ." He looked over at Lorenzo chatting amiably with Botticelli and raised his voice for all to hear. ". . . except for festival days, which, happily for Florentines, come more often with Lorenzo setting the calendar."

Smiling, Lorenzo pulled a bench over to Verrocchio's bench and sat, leaning into the artist, who, among all these men, was the least attractive, almost porcine in his features. "I'd like to discuss the plans for a new festival with you," he said.

"A new festival. And what is its theme? Religious perhaps?"

Everyone laughed at that, as though it were a well-worn joke.

Lorenzo gazed conspiratorially at Sandro Botticelli and said, "The Four Seasons and the Four Elements."

I tried to stifle my surprise. While I knew that Florence was the most secular city in all of Europe, Lorenzo and Botticelli's idea bordered on the pagan.

"It has possibilities," Verrocchio replied, clearly pleased with the idea.

Guido came with the wine, which was served all around. Botticelli joined Verrocchio and Lorenzo, and they sat with their heads together making joyful plans for their newest extravaganza.

I took the opportunity to go to Leonardo, who, I had noticed, was staring at me unabashedly, certainly wondering how it was that his mother was casually engaged in conversation with these men. I could hardly fathom it myself. With the garden so small and the market for gossip so large, we were forced to speak in an impromptu code. But then Leonardo had, as had I, been schooled from the earliest age in the art of subterfuge.

"How is your sister?" he asked me pointedly.

I smiled. "I stopped in Vinci on my way from Siena. Your mother is very well. Thriving, in fact. She sends you her love and told me to remind you to wash behind your ears."

Leonardo repressed a smile. "Mama loves to nag me about that."

Now I repressed my own smile.

"And tell me about my grandfather. How is his garden?"

"He says it is incomplete without you there tending the plants."

Leonardo's expression became more urgent. He carefully moved us away from the others, toward the rock waterfall in the corner of the garden.

"Maestro Verrocchio was kind enough to indulge my pastoral fantasy," he said quite loudly, and we realized our nearness to the water caused our voices to be thrown farther than we wished. After I had exclaimed, quite sincerely, at the work he had put into the waterfall and stream that looked as if it had been there since the beginning of time, we moved again, now to the tiny flowering meadow he had planted. We squatted and spoke in voices so low we were sure no one could hear.

"I cannot believe you're here like this," he said, unable to contain his glee. "You have always been daring, Mama, but you have outdone yourself this time."

"I was dying without you, Leonardo. And I was not ready for my life to end."

"Who is this 'master' of yours. The apothecary who has sent his student ahead of him?"

"He is Umberto . . . a figment of my imagination. Sadly, he will be dead within the year, leaving me everything."

Leonardo laughed at that. His smile was a work of supreme beauty. No wonder Verrocchio used him as a model.

"Tell me, son," I whispered, "tell me honestly. Are any of these men suspicious of me . . . my womanhood?"

He didn't immediately answer. That worried me.

"It is hard for me to be objective, of course." He spoke slowly and thoughtfully. "But I think, as Florence is presently a place of peace, whereby masculine warriors are little called for, gentle, refined, and scholarly men are deemed worthy, and young boys as pretty as girls are . . ." He hesitated. ". . . men's playthings. . . ." He looked into my face and studied me as an artist would his subject. "I think you are a passable young man. Work on keeping your voice in the lower range."

"I will."

"And let me put my hand to those lifts in your shoes. They should be more well-hidden."

"When can you visit me at my house?"

"As the maestro said, we work all the time. But you, my clever mother, have created the perfect opportunity." He saw my puzzled expression. "Your apothecary sign."

I beamed.

"I cannot believe you own a house in Florence."

"Remember your grandfather's employer, Poggio?"

He shook his head.

"I will tell you the whole story when we can be private."

There was a small commotion around Lorenzo and Botticelli, who were making to leave.

"I'm going, too," I said to Leonardo.

We stood.

"I want to kiss you and kiss you," I said, losing my battle with emotion.

"Mama," he said imploringly. "Just give me a pat on the back, like the fond uncle you are."

I did as I was told, and bidding a good afternoon to Leonardo and receiving his promise of designing and executing my sign, I departed just behind Lorenzo de' Medici and Sandro Botticelli. They were laughing companionably as they tried to maneuver through the back door, side by side, with their arms thrown around each other.

"After you, Lorenzo," said Botticelli, making way and executing so low and embellished a bow that it mocked the respectful gesture.

In his turn, Lorenzo outdid his friend in flourishes. "No, no, after *you*, Sandro."

Then they noticed me.

"Don't mind us," said Botticelli. "We grew up under the same roof. Silly young brothers together. Sometimes we act as though we haven't grown up."

I wondered at that. *Botticelli growing up in the Palazzo Medici?*

We walked along the center aisle of the bottega now, three pairs of eyes drawn to the crucible of creation through which we moved.

"Andrea is a forward-thinking maestro," Botticelli said. "He is the first in Florence to experiment with the Flemish technique. This uses paints mixed with oils rather than water. I'm beginning to like it myself. Leonardo has a brilliant future ahead," he added. "If only he can learn to concentrate on one thing at a time. His mind wanders."

"It always did," I said.

"I agree with Sandro," said Lorenzo. "I see him going far. He'll make you and his mother proud."

"I would hope, if possible . . . ," I said, trying to remain cool, "to keep the news of my arrival in Florence from Leonardo's father."

Lorenzo and Botticelli exchanged a look.

"That should be no problem," Botticelli finally said. "No one here is particularly fond of Piero da Vinci, and Leonardo is much loved, despite his bastardy."

"Perhaps *because* of his bastardy," Lorenzo added as we continued on. "The maestro himself is an illegitimate son. Men like Piero suffer from false pride. They forget that the highest nobles in Italy, the pope even, love and elevate all their children, whether they were married to their mothers or not."

"It doesn't help that Piero is a lawyer," Botticelli added. "By their guild's own laws, a bastard son is prohibited from taking up his father's profession."

"In the case of the divine Leonardo da Vinci," said Lorenzo as we reached the front archway at the street, "that is a blessing in disguise."

I was jolted twice in the space of Lorenzo's one utterance—reminded by the word "disguise" of my own dissimulation, and also by the great compliment paid my son by the Medici heir.

"Thank you both for all the consideration you have shown my . . . nephew." I choked. I had very nearly said "son."

"It has been a pleasure," Lorenzo replied. "I hope Sandro and I can visit you in your new establishment. I love apothecary shops. My crushed nose dulls that sense, but in such places I am sometimes able to smell."

"You should come soon then, before I open the place for business. So I can show you around. Without a stream of customers. We can spend more time talking."

"So you like to talk?" Botticelli asked with a sly grin.

I think I blushed. "I do like to talk."

Lorenzo smiled his handsome smile. "Then you have found yourself in good company. Other than riding and celebrating festivals and making love to beautiful women, talking is our favorite thing to do in the world."

"Shall we come tomorrow?" Botticelli said.

"Tomorrow it is," I said, hardly believing what had just occurred.

They went their way down the street, and I started back the way I'd come, though seeing little of what was before me. My mind was whirling so, with everything I had witnessed and heard, the people I had met, the memory of Leonardo in my arms again.

A pox on Piero! I thought suddenly. Even now he treated his only son with small regard. I remember his boasting that he had secured the apprenticeship by virtue of his "close friendship" with Andrea Verrocchio. Ha! The apprenticeship had only to do with Leonardo's genius. Verrocchio himself had used the word to describe him. But I refused to dwell too long on such remembrances. My father would always say they could cause the liver to simmer in its own bile, the guts to putrefy, and the heart to turn black and shatter.

So I pushed Piero from my mind.

I was filled with equal measures of contentment at having finally seen Leonardo—so happy and well appreciated—and excitement at the thought of the visit I would certainly get from Lorenzo de' Medici and Sandro Botticelli, who, though I hardly knew them, seemed to be men of their word.

At my house I began at once to clean the remnants of clutter from the renovations and prepare for their visit. I worried. Should I have benches or chairs for us to sit down on in the shop, or should I entertain them in my sitting room upstairs? They had not told me when they would arrive, so I wondered if I should fix a meal or some small delicacies. But I was a young *man* now, and too poor to hire a housekeeper or a cook. The meal could not be too sumptuous or well prepared or it would look suspicious. Neither could I shame myself in front of these great men with poor food.

I settled on a simple but delicious meal—an earthy Sangiovese wine, the creamiest white goat cheese, a loaf of good bread, and the baked compote of Greek olives, red grapes, olive oil, and balsamic vinegar, slightly seasoned with thyme, that Magdalena had taught me to make. It was my father's favorite and was sure to please my guests.

I swept the floor, poked with my broom into the ceiling corners for spiders. I opened the pots of several of the most fragrant herbs so their rich scents would mingle and permeate the shop to please the Medici's nose, he who loved the smell of apothecaries. And I made the decision to limit the visit to the ground floor, allowing me to place all my fervid preparations in the shop and storeroom.

I bathed that night, the cool water I had hauled up the stairs to my tub feeling wonderful against my warm skin. I lay back and by candle-light gazed at the length of my body, still skinny as a reed from my rejection of food. Finally released from their tight bindings, my now-smaller breasts were uncreasing and softening in the water. My arms were strong and the fingers dexterous from the hard and delicate chores of housewifery and this summer's labors. My legs were lean but retained their soft curves. Between them the womanly parts cast a dark, three-pointed shadow under the water's ripples.

This form had served me well as a woman. Now it must serve me as a man. Somehow, I thought, if I am to survive in Florence, I must begin to *feel* myself a masculine creature. Father had suggested that an elixir of bull testicles might provide me with the features of a male—a further shrinking of my breasts, a deeper voice, and perhaps even some facial hair. But the number of the poor beasts' stones I would need to make the extraction was so enormous it rendered the possibility null. I would instead have to rely on illusion, and my hitherto unknown talents as a mimic. As for any female venereal desires, they were long gone. I might even fool myself.

It was only Leonardo who worried me on this account. The sight of him today had caused an unbidden upsurge of motherly passion, a softening at the core of me. My shrunken breasts had, for an instant, ached the way they had in the moments before I'd put my baby on the nipple.

Well, I thought, if the loss of my womanhood was the price I must pay to bring Leonardo back to me, it was cheap. Already I had tasted the boundless freedom of living as a man—to walk where I wished to walk. To speak to whom I pleased, and however I pleased. In any event, there was no going back to my life as Caterina.

It was necessary that she die.

I inhaled deeply and, holding the breath deep in my lungs, slid down in the tub till I felt the water close in over my head. In a wild pagan baptism of my own design I let that woman seep out of me through the skin, pushed her through every pore, lungs ready to burst. When I finally exploded to the surface, the shout of my exhalation was the last gasp of Caterina de Ernesto da Vinci, and the birth cry of Cato the Apothecary.

My new life had truly begun.

*T*he next morning, clean and freshly bound, I stepped into my shop. A glorious and familiar aroma filled my nostrils. I smiled to think that soon my clothing would be permeated with the smell of plant life, the healing salvia and licorice and lavender, a balm to the senses, soul and body.

I took down the curtains I had hung temporarily over my street window and sunlight flooded in. I looked around. The apothecary was a pretty place with its green walls and bright white marble countertop, bunches of dried flowers in their soft colors peppering the shelves. It was slightly larger than my father's shop, and the ceiling here was higher, giving the room a lofty, almost grand appearance.

I took from a box beneath the counter a small casket I'd brought with me from Vinci. Inside was another gift from Papa, a little bronze bell that was meant to be hung over my front door. While waiting for my visitors I did not wish to stay idle, which I knew would only heighten my already-substantial nervousness, so I walked through my doorway into the storeroom to retrieve a hammer and nails and a bench to stand on.

When I returned to the shop, Lorenzo de' Medici was in the middle of the shop floor, his eyes closed, deeply inhaling the fragrance that I myself had recently appreciated. He was dressed so plainly, lacking all pretension in a tunic of fine brown wool, with no jewelry of any sort and a flat black cap that nearly disappeared against his long dark hair, that it did not surprise me in the least that the Prince of

Florence had come to this modest neighborhood drawing no attention to himself at all.

He was alone—Sandro Botticelli was nowhere to be seen. Lorenzo opened his eyes and saw me in the doorway, the bench I was holding crosswise blocking my way into the shop. The sight must have been comical because Lorenzo laughed aloud, a wonderful sound, and his strong white teeth flashed against his burnished olive complexion.

"Do you need a hand?" he said, looking at the bench I held.

"Not if I've got a brain," I said lightly and turned it so I could pass through the door. I tried not to fumble as I came out from behind my counter and set the bench and tools down. I bowed to him. "Welcome, my lord."

He bowed back. "Call me Lorenzo. All my friends do."

I felt suddenly bold, as I had when I'd first spoken to him at Verrocchio's bottega. "You already count me as a friend?" I said. "We've only just met."

"You are the uncle of the most talented apprentice in Florence, and you are a trained apothecary who has created a most inviting shop. . . ." He looked at me squarely. "If we are not already friends, I think we shall be."

"Where is Signor Botticelli?" I asked, trying in vain to stifle my pleasure at his answer.

"Sandro has been mysteriously locked in his apartments since you last saw him. He sends his apologies." Lorenzo spied the bell in its casket. "Would you like some help putting it up?"

I marveled at this man who was so easy in his ways, making a person of far lesser rank feel instantly cared for and important. I could see why the people of Florence loved him. I handed him the bell, the hammer and nails, and I picked up the bench again.

The morning passed very pleasantly, the two of us arguing about the correct position of the bell, and laughing at the number of nails we bent trying to pound them into the doorframe. I showed Lorenzo around the shop and storeroom, answering an unending stream of questions about the efficacy of several herbs and the making of potions and poultices for gout—a condition from which his grandfather and uncles had suffered mightily, one which was, even now, killing his father.

When I brought out the food I had prepared we sat on benches on either side of the marble counter and ate. He devoured the grape and olive compote with a genteel gusto that reminded me, with a silent ache, of my own father. I watched with fascination as he invoked one subject of interest after another, proceeding down a seemingly narrow path, only to take a sudden side switch, and another and another, all of which cleverly returned him to the main road of thought. As he talked, he smeared chunks of bread with the goat cheese, piled on the compote and popped the whole mess into his mouth. While he chewed, he encouraged me to answer or comment, or contradict him if I disagreed.

It was the strangest amalgam of appetite and intelligence I had ever witnessed.

At first we argued about several of the Virtues—Truth, Time, Fortitude, and Justice. His discourse became more openly Socratic, asking me pointedly ironic questions that would lead to more and more questions, so that at the end of it all, if not coming to any pat conclusion or solution, I would have nevertheless taught myself a lesson.

"At which university did you study?" Lorenzo finally asked, wiping his fingers on a linen towel I had laid between us.

I thought of lying but was terrified of getting caught. So I told the truth.

"We had no money for my education, but my father was a scholar. He was my only tutor."

Lorenzo straightened. "Would I know of him?"

"No, I don't think so." I stared at the tray with the remnants of our small meal. There was nothing left of it. Not even the cheese rind.

"You were hungry," I said, changing the subject.

"Have you any more of that?" Lorenzo pointed to the dish that had held the compote.

I chuckled. "You're a greedy fellow," I said.

He laughed that laugh that I was already coming to love. "I know what I like," he replied.

"I'll see if there's more in the jar," I said, standing up and moving to the doorway with the dish. "My neighbor, Signora Serrano, makes it. I wish I could ask you to my sitting room but it's still a shambles," I called after me as I started up the stairs.

"Never mind," I heard at my ear. I was startled to see Lorenzo at my side. "You should see Sandro's rooms." He was following me up the steps. "Everyone indulges 'the artist.'"

I was holding my breath, praying that everything was in order in my sitting room, and wondering at the novelty of a young man following me to my private rooms, a man none other than Lorenzo de' Medici.

On the first floor he gazed around for a moment, then headed for a pretty embroidered hanging that had come down to me from my mother's family. "Why are you staring?" he said, turning back to me. "I thought you were bringing us more of Signora Serrano's delicacy."

"Yes, yes," I said and climbed to the next floor.

When I returned a few moments later with the news that we had eaten every last grape and olive, he was standing at the front window with his back to me. He was hunched, looking at something he held in his hand. When he heard me on the stair he turned. There was a look of amazement on his face.

He was holding a book.

"You have a copy of the *Asclepius*," he said.

I blanched. "I guess I must," I said, "unless you brought it with you." It was a poor joke.

His laugh was different this time. Darker. No longer jovial.

"This is a Hermetic text," he said.

"And in some eyes, heretical," I added. "Though many men read it."

"But they read the Latin translation. This is in Greek. You are reading the *Asclepius* in Greek."

"So it appears," I whispered. This book was one of those treasured volumes that Poggio Bracciolini and my father had transcribed so many years before.

"Your father must be quite a scholar," Lorenzo said. He was gazing at me quizzically, as a child would a wooden puzzle.

I wished for a way to steer him from this thought path, one that felt dangerous to my new identity. Then he spoke.

"I would like you to come to my house and sit at my father's table. The family will be there. Sandro. A few others. Two evenings from now. . . . Why are you gaping at me?"

"Am I gaping?"

"Wide enough for a frog to hop between your teeth."

"You are inviting me to the Palazzo Medici. Anyone would be awestruck."

"You, Cato, have just spent an entire morning discoursing with me on a wide variety of scholarly subjects. And you read the *Asclepius* in Greek. I do not think it odd to have a man such as yourself at my dinner table."

"All right," I managed to mutter.

"I'm going now," he announced and embraced me briefly. Then he started for the stairs. He turned back with one of those brilliant smiles. "You see, I was right," he said. "We *have* become friends."

I was still in a state of disbelief two days hence when I locked my shop and strode—a new mode of ambulation for me—down the Vias Capponi and Guelfa and turned onto Via Larga, an exceptionally wide thoroughfare, though one that exuded dignity and quietude, with houses on both sides, some of them large and elegant.

I came then, on my right, upon the Monastery of San Marco, with its stark façade, where, from within, I could hear many voices raised together in the chanting of the psalms. Past that there were several modest homes and a quality silk shop without a sign, as though those patrons who needed to know its location had no need of advertisement.

I knew I must be nearing the Palazzo Medici and expected to see guards at its perimeter. But in the next moment the edifice was looming large—again on my right—and there was not a soldier or guard anywhere in sight.

I could see, at the end of a huge three-storied city mansion, crowds of men standing under and around its loggia that turned the corner at

Via Gori, and sitting on stone benches built into the outer wall, talking loudly and gesticulating enthusiastically in making their points. Others stood with heads bent together, conversing with quiet urgency.

They were negotiating. There, under the corner loggia of the Palazzo Medici, men were doing business.

Now I could see others were entering and leaving through a grand front doorway on Via Larga. I moved close enough to touch the building. The ground floor had been built like a fortress with stone blocks so rough-hewn they looked as if they had just been chiseled from the quarry. Above this, the wall of the first floor, studded with a row of high rounded windows, was finer cut stone. The third, with even more windows, appeared smooth and polished.

Facing the wide-open grand entrance and marveling at its orgy of commerce, I was further surprised to see that the inner courtyard, a square bounded by graceful columns all around, boasted a statue of a naked man on a pedestal, one that could easily be seen from the street.

With no one stopping or questioning me, I passed through the door and emerged into the courtyard with the three stories of the palazzo rising four-square around me. Inside, above the powerful arches and columns, was a row of windows, and above that a railed terrace.

To the right of the entrance on the ground floor guildsmen came and went through an inner door, whose sign above read simply BANCO.

But of course, I thought, *the Medici are bankers.* Where better to house the Florentine branch than here at the family fortress?

Drawn to the bronze statue, I saw it was the figure of a boy no older than Leonardo, and like my son modeling for Verrocchio, at his feet was the ghastly severed head of a giant. *This must be another artist's rendition of David with the slain Goliath,* I thought.

Though I had seen little sculpture in my life, the genius of this art-ist was apparent to even my untrained eye. But except for the sword he carried and the stone for his slingshot, he was not at all as I had imagined David of the Old Testament. He wore a brimmed hat, with girlish hair that fell to his shoulders, and standing with hand on hip at a jaunty angle, he looked more tipsy from wine than having just be-headed a Philistine giant. He was strangely effeminate.

"The great Donatello," I heard Lorenzo say behind me. I had come to recognize my new friend's voice. "His *David* is the first freestanding statue created in a thousand years. He was, of all the art-ists my grandfather patronized, his most beloved. They asked to be buried next to each other . . . and were."

My mind raced. *Would Lorenzo de' Medici someday patronize my Leonardo? Would his art grace the walls of this palazzo?*

I turned to him. "You invited me to supper at your 'house.'"

"This *is* my house. Come upstairs and I'll show you." He tipped his chin at the line of merchants at the banco door. "They'll soon be leaving to have their supper. Then we'll reclaim the ground floor."

I followed him up a broad, straight stairway. "I loathe the banking business," he told me. "Of course we made our fortune as bankers—to kings and merchants and popes. But I have no interest in money for money's sake." He turned to me. "Does that seem odd?"

"Very."

"I have no facility for it either. Thank goodness Giuliano likes num-bers. We'll rule together someday. He has his strengths. I have mine."

I thought of the handsome sixteen-year-old I'd seen riding before Lorenzo at his wedding festival. Giuliano seemed so young to rule. But then, so did Lorenzo. He was barely twenty.

We reached the first floor and at once I was impressed by the quiet serenity that enveloped us. Just a story below was a seething financial marketplace. Yet here we were, as Lorenzo had promised, in a home.

Not, of course, just any home.

Every available space of wall, every niche, every inch of floor was itself a work of art in marble, gilded plaster, or finely carved wood. Monumental ceilings soared far above our heads. There were tapes-tries, paintings, sculptures, bas relief medallions, and exotic Ottoman carpets. I could not decide where to look first.

Lorenzo decided for me. He steered us into the first door at the top of the stairs, a salon that, by my rough calculations, stood above the open-air public loggia on the corner of Via Larga and Via Gori.

"This is where the family gathers," he said, "and where, in bad weather, we entertain."

It was an enormous chamber with an azure and gold ceiling of staggering height, its many windows flooding it, even this late in the day, with enough light that all of the precious artifacts adorning it were clearly visible.

"Have you heard of the Pollaiuolo brothers?" Lorenzo asked.

I shook my head.

"Come look at their work." He guided me to the first of three large paintings that graced the salon's walls. "They are friendly rivals of Verrocchio. Aside from your nephew, their bottega boasts some of the best young talent in Florence."

"But this is amazing," I said, staring at its naked, beautifully muscled man, his warrior's pelt headdress flying out behind him. One upraised arm clutched the club with which he would momentarily bash in the brains of a many-headed beast, one of whose sinuous necks he clutched in his other hand.

"It is *Hercules and the Hydra*," Lorenzo told me.

Two others by the Pollaiuolos were similarly alive with action and naked men. All the paintings and statues I had ever seen in my life had been of a purely Christian nature. These in front of me were mythical paintings, from Greek tales that my father had told me as bedtime stories. Ones that I was told never to share with other children.

But when I turned to Lorenzo to make the observation, I found him staring quite peculiarly at the rippling-muscled Hercules and perceived, for the briefest moment, that my host was embarrassed. When he felt my eyes on him he said quickly, "Come. There's much more to see."

He took me out into the hall above the courtyard again and we made our way to a set of massive carved doors. I could smell incense wafting up from the cracks beneath it.

"Is this a chapel?" I asked, intrigued. "*Inside* your house?"

"The first of its kind," he answered. "The pope had to give us a special dispensation for it." He swung open the doors and in we went. Here was a spectacular mural that surrounded us on three sides and climbed to the top of the high vaulted ceiling. My head spun with the fabulousness of the colors alone, no less the scene that the artist had rendered.

"What am I seeing here?" I said.

"Gozzoli's *Procession of the Magi*."

He led me first to the west wall. I had to crane my neck to see the details all the way to the gorgeously gilt ceiling, but I was determined not to miss a thing. Here, before a bright white mountain range that I could not discern as snow or ice or marble, was an immense procession indeed, all of the men on horseback and on foot. But there were animals, too—huge spotted cats—one of them oddly riding pillion behind a boy on horseback, and a great falcon standing on the ground.

"Who are these people?" I said, attempting to take in the complex and meticulously rendered faces and clothing, the weave and folds of the textiles, the facets of the gems, the luster of a silver spur. Every feather in the plumage of the birds, every petal of every flower, and each tree hanging with ripe fruit was in itself an ingenious work of art. The leaves of certain plants appeared to be painted in solid gold.

"Who they are," Lorenzo began, "is a story within a story. It is, after all, Gozzoli's painting of the three Wise Men journeying to the birth of Jesus. Ten years ago, when my grandfather and father hired him to paint the fresco, it was the fashion that models for the biblical figures should be men and women the artist knew and admired."

"Their patrons?" I suggested.

"Patrons and families and friends. Important figures of the day. Even the artist himself. You can find Gozzoli three different times in the fresco. This is the Holy Roman Emperor as the Wise Man Melchior," Lorenzo said, pointing to an old man whose headdress resembled a crown. "And here is Balthasar, the Wise Man from the East. Gozzoli used for his model John Palaeologus, the Eastern emperor. Both rulers were in Florence in 1439—it was quite a spectacular occasion—trying to bridge the schism between the two branches of the Catholic church. It ultimately failed. . . ."

"Constantinople was conquered by the Turks four years later," I offered.

"Quite right. But the true outcome of the visit was wholly unexpected and even more stupendous. In John's entourage were some of the greatest Greek scholars and thinkers and theologians of the time. During that conclave a great passion for classical learning was born. Florence was buzzing with debates between the best minds of Eastern and Western thought. It was how and when my grandfather's obsession for gathering the art and philosophy of ancient times began. After everyone left he sent out scouts like Niccolo Niccoli and Poggio Bracciolini to find the lost manuscripts of antiquity."

I was tempted in that moment to reveal my father's connection to Poggio, but I held my tongue.

"Things in Florence were never the same again," Lorenzo finished.

"Tell me about this one," I said, moving to the east wall. This was by far the most crowded and detailed of the three frescoes, with dozens of men attending six men on horseback as they rode down from a castle at the top of the high white mountains. A dog chased a man on horseback, who himself chased a deer.

"Well, here you can see my family." Lorenzo smiled at me. "No surprise. We were Gozzoli's patrons."

"This looks to be your father." I pointed to a broad-cheeked man in rich red robes on a white horse. I felt myself suddenly embarrassed by my familiarity. "I saw him at your wedding festival."

"Ah, the day you threw yourself under my horse." Lorenzo had a way about him that made me feel at ease. "You are right, though. That is my father, Piero. And following right behind him on a brown horse in robes as humble as a monk's is my grandfather, Cosimo."

"And where are you?" I asked.

This time Lorenzo's smile was wry. "I am in two places, actually. Here . . ." He pointed to a very young man on a magnificently caparisoned white steed. Unlike his father and his grandfather, he was clothed in royalty and wore a large bejeweled crown. The boy's features were fine, almost pretty.

"This is the idealized version of Lorenzo de' Medici as, I suppose, the artist expected the ruler of a great republic should be." Then he pointed to another face nearly lost amidst a gaggle of scholars, all easily identified by their tall scarlet caps. "This is me as well. The *real* ten-year-old—jutting lip, squashed nose and all." Lorenzo was matter-of-fact when he said this, with not a hint of injured vanity. "Listen, there's something I want to show you before dinner."

Lorenzo seemed on fire now. I followed him back down the stairway to the ground floor and its square colonnaded courtyard.

It was as Lorenzo had said it would be—emptied of the bankers, merchants, negotiators, and hagglers. Several servants were quietly sweeping the marble floor and another was polishing the heavy wooden doors that looked as though they could hold back a small army. It was, here in the Palazzo Medici, as serene and domestic now as it had an hour before been chaotic and mercenary.

We crossed the courtyard diagonally to a single unobtrusive door. But what was to be found inside it was anything but ordinary.

It was a magnificent library.

The tall fitted cabinets and shelves of inlaid cypress and walnut filled every inch of the four walls from floor to ceiling. They looked and smelled freshly constructed and finished. Many ornate pedestals had been built to accommodate large manuscripts. I turned to Lorenzo to find on his face an ecstasy in which tranquility and excitement were balanced in equal parts.

"Until this year the collection was lodged at the Monastery of San Marco. These are the books and manuscripts my grandfather and my father collected. Recently I've acquired some myself." He looked around, beaming. "Where do I begin?"

I found his ardor infectious. "The earliest," I suggested.

"Good. The earliest." He didn't have to think but a moment. He crossed the chamber and opened a stained-glass cabinet door. Then he withdrew from the shelf, with something akin to religious reverence, a scroll, the antiquity of which was clearly apparent. He placed it on a massive table and gestured for me to sit down before it. He unrolled it with a delicacy in those strong, muscular hands that seemed impossible.

I silently read the title, in Greek. I was hardly breathing.

"Is this . . . an original?" I finally said.

"Yes."

I saw in front of my eyes words that had been inscribed fifteen centuries before. It was not a work that my father had ever translated or possessed, though he had told me of its existence. I read silently the opening lines of Sophocles's *Antigone*. Lorenzo stood behind me, quietly inhaling my delight. I could have sat there for hours, reading this legendary play, but a few moments later I rolled it closed, slowly and with great care.

"I've a Greek treatise on surgery," Lorenzo offered. "Or perhaps you'd like to see a manuscript of Cicero's letters. Or Tacitus. I have two of his. All the classical and early Christian literature. . . ."

I turned and looked up at him. "May I come back again, when I have more time?"

He smiled broadly. "Of course! Here is the beauty of it, Cato. This library, like no other in Europe, is open to the public. All scholars are welcome."

This was a staggering thought.

"Knowledge, Herself, has her home here," he intoned reverentially.

"That's beautiful, Lorenzo."

"I wish *I'd* said it. It was one of my tutors, Angelo Poliziano, who did." Lorenzo moved to a shelf upon which stood a row of bound books—these which had been printed in the new style, on a press with moveable type—and lovingly ran his fingers across their spines. "This house is the nurse of all learning, which here revived again."

"And who said *that*," I asked gently.

"I did," he replied, unable to conceal his pride. "I fancy myself as something of a poet, though I have everything to learn."

"What better place for you to be, then? In the belly of the nurse of all learning."

"In at least one way," Lorenzo said slowly, seeming to think as he spoke aloud, "I've turned into my grandfather. I would, had I no responsibilities to family or state, spend my entire fortune on books."

"Even more than art," came an unexpected voice from the library door.

We turned together to see Sandro Botticelli leaning against the doorframe, a jaunty grin on his long sensual face. He looked altogether at home in this place of magnificence, and utterly pleased with himself.

I found myself smiling at his presence. I liked this audacious man. I said to him, "So to Lorenzo, politics and art are lesser occupations than the collecting of books?"

"That is a gross understatement," Botticelli replied. "He is *obsessed* with books, as Cosimo was. I would go looking for my friend to play ball with, search all over, only to find the two of them in a corner of the San Marco library, poring over Plato's *Republic*, the old man pointing with a gnarled finger at a difficult passage, and Lorenzo translating with a look of such transported joy you would have thought he was making love to a woman . . . except he was ten years old."

Lorenzo laughed at that.

"I'm glad to see you here, Cato," Botticelli went on. "Another good mind is always welcome at the table. The more voices, the fiercer the arguments."

"I'm delighted to be here," I said, "though I admit to an utter state of awe."

"How can one not be awed?" Botticelli continued. "Can you imagine how it was for me, a working-class boy of fifteen being taken under the wing of Cosimo de' Medici, the greatest man in Italy, and being raised like a son in his wonderful family? Then, the most divine woman, Lorenzo's mother, became my most generous patron. If there is Heaven on earth, I swear it has been my life so far."

The sudden sound of a gong being struck three times reverberated authoritatively through the palazzo.

"That is our dinner being served," Lorenzo said. "Shall we?"

With that, we three companionable fellows walked shoulder to shoulder back out into the central courtyard and toward a rear doorway.

"Say hello to Hadrian," Botticelli quipped, acknowledging a marble bust of the infamous Roman emperor in a niche above the door.

"He is Sandro's favorite sodomite," Lorenzo added with an indulgent smile that left me wondering about what other indulgences were acceptable in this household.

We exited the palazzo and stepped as if into another world. Sheltered from the bustle and stark stone of the city, here between ivy-covered walls, was a living paradise—Verrocchio's garden a hundred times over. Footpaths wound through a riot of flowering bushes, patches of blossoms and grasses, short and tall. Artfully pruned trees and others as wild as nature had made them shared the garden with a pair of strutting peacocks and what sounded like an entire flock of songbirds trilling ardently. Through the greenery and splashing fountains I caught a glimpse of a large, masterful bronze statue—a woman about to behead a cowering man. This was no simpering Madonna, I thought. "This way," Lorenzo said. "We're dining under the loggia."

The south wall of the garden was dominated by three sweeping stone arches separated by ancient marble columns in the Greek style. A moment later we'd passed through the arches to be confronted by a high-vaulted chamber and an immense dining table, perhaps the largest single piece of furniture I had ever in my life seen.

It would have easily seated forty, but places were set only at one end—I counted eight. Though the silver filigreed candelabra and salt-cellar would have paid for a whole new section of Vinci to be built, the place settings surprised me with their simplicity—terra-cotta plates and goblets, no finer than would be found on my father's table.

The other diners were flowing in through all three archways now. There was a young woman who, I surmised, must be Lorenzo's wife, Clarice Orsini. My friend Benito had been right; the newest member of the Medici clan had a palpable air of snobbery about her. She was tall, though not as tall as me, with a pale moon face on a long thin neck and a headful of tightly curled hair, more red than blond. She was not unpretty, but the aloof tilt of her chin, and her lips, which seemed perpetually pursed, made me sorry for Lorenzo the instant I set eyes on her.

Giuliano and Lucrezia de' Medici clutched either arm of Piero. First Giuliano seated his mother, then together with Lorenzo the boys helped their father to his chair at the head of the table. The ruler of Florence grimaced as his knees bent to sit.

Giuliano and Lucrezia took places on Piero's right and left, Lorenzo and his wife next to Giuliano, and I across from Lorenzo at their mother's side. Sandro Botticelli sat next to me. Next to Clarice was an empty place setting. No one spoke of it.

"This is my new friend, Cato Cattalivoni," Lorenzo announced, sounding very pleased. He introduced me in turn to his mother, father, brother, and wife.

"Will you make a blessing on our table, Lucrezia?" Piero asked his wife in a voice rough with suffering.

We all closed our eyes as she prayed.

She spoke in a lovely, melodious tone, and suddenly I felt a pang of longing, almost to the point of physical pain, for my own gentle mother, whom I had never known.

The blessing was over and the servers were bringing in wooden platters of steaming loin of veal with sour orange relish, and ravioli in a fragrant saffron broth. The chicken with fennel was equally delightful, and an herb and mushroom omelet was redolent with mint and parsley and marjoram. This would certainly be a feast, but it was, I realized, one of the simplest food, none that Magdalena had not served my father and me a hundred times.

Suddenly I heard my name spoken. Lorenzo was addressing his

parents. "Do you remember that fabulous mechanical sun and constellation that Verrocchio and his apprentices erected for our third wedding feast?" His mother nodded. "Cato's nephew, Leonardo da Vinci, designed it. Cato has just opened a wonderful apothecary on Via Riccardi."

"Really it is my master's shop," I demurred. "He'll be joining me presently."

"You are modest, Cato. You yourself refurbished the place and made it a thing of beauty."

"Whosever shop it is, we are delighted to have you at our table, Cato," Lucrezia said, leveling me with a warm and welcoming smile. I could see that her two front teeth crossed a touch at the bottom, but it only increased her charm.

"Oh, I so loved the sun and stars!" Clarice cried, sounding more like a little girl than a woman. "We had three feasts," she told me across the table, "one more splendid than the last. My in-laws built a great ballroom out into the Via Larga, just for the occasion. We had fifty dishes at each feast." And she added pointedly, "Served on the *best* gold plate!"

"Clarice thinks us very strange for eating simple fare on stoneware when we dine as a family," Lorenzo told me, trying to suppress his amusement. "In fact, the first time her mother came for a visit, she was insulted by it."

"Well, it is strange, husband. And it was positively embarrassing when instead of sitting with our guests at the wedding feast, you stood up and *waited* on them."

"That is nothing for you to be embarrassed about, Clarice," Lucrezia said. "Lorenzo has a fine sense about what is right and proper in any given situation. He has since he was very young. Do you suppose his father would have sent him at the age of sixteen to visit the new pope if he had—"

"I was seventeen, Mama."

"Sixteen when you went to Milan as a proxy at the wedding of the Duke of Sforza's son . . . ," she insisted, "and on the way, investigated our banks in Bologna, Venice, and Ferrara. And you are quite right, my darling." She smiled at Lorenzo. "You *were* seventeen when your papa sent you to Rome to wrest a concession from the pope for our family to work the alum mines in papal territories."

"Your brothers advised me all the way," he said to his mother. He seemed embarrassed at the praise being heaped on him in front of me. But Lucrezia was not finished.

"Well, my brothers were not present when you visited that appalling creature in Naples." Lucrezia addressed me directly now. "Don Ferrante, the ruler there, is renowned for his extreme cruelty and violence. He is positively determined to rule the whole of Italy. My husband sent Lorenzo to discover the man's intentions."

"And I never did," Lorenzo demurred.

"But you fascinated the man. Charmed him. And came to an understanding with him that has held Tuscany in good stead with Naples ever since."

"Please, Mama," Lorenzo begged her.

"I know how to silence her," Giuliano said with a wicked grin.

"No, son," she pleaded, appearing to know what was coming. She began to flush pink.

"Our mother," he began, "is the most accomplished woman of the century."

"A noted poetess," Lorenzo went on, pleased that the conversation had veered away from himself. "She has written in *terza rima* a life of Saint John the Baptist, and a brilliant verse on her favorite biblical heroine, Judith."

"That big-boned woman in the garden about to decapitate Holofernes," Sandro told me.

Lucrezia, sincere in her modesty, sat with downcast eyes, knowing she could not quiet the boys and their litany of her accomplishments.

"She is a friend and patron of artists and scholars," Giuliano boasted.

"And a businesswoman of some merit." This was Piero who had chimed in. "Do not forget the sulfur springs at Morba that she purchased from the republic and turned into a successful health resort."

"Enough! All of you! I shall never brag about any of you ever again," she announced with comic solemnity. There were murmurings of mock approval all around the table. "Though it *is* a mother's right," she added, as if to have the final word.

I smiled inwardly, agreeing with her entirely. It was indeed a mother's right to brag about her children. To glow with the pride of their accomplishments. But here at this table I was witnessing a remarkable happenstance—children that were reveling in their mother's achievements.

I suddenly noticed that despite Piero's enjoyment of this family banter, the patriarch's eyes were closed. Giuliano, too, had observed this.

"Papa!" the younger son cried. Piero's eyes sprang open. "Why were you sitting there with your eyes closed?"

He smiled sadly at the boy. "To get them used to it," he said.

There were cries all around of "No, Papa!" "Don't say such a thing!"

Lucrezia grabbed his sore-knuckled fist and bit her lip. She looked at me imploringly.

"Have you anything for pain, Cato? All of my husband's physicians have thrown up their hands with it."

I looked around, momentarily unsure about talking of so intimate a subject at this table, but I could feel all around me the raw love and concern of family for family, and no less affection in Sandro Botticelli's eyes than in Lorenzo's or Giuliano's. *Manners be damned,* I thought. I leaned toward Piero.

"Is there a repression of urine?" I asked, and he nodded yes. "Frequent fevers?"

"Almost every day," Lucrezia answered for him.

I was silent for a time, recalling a decoction my father had once made for Signor Lezi's condition, one that closely resembled the Medici patriarch's. It had not cured the gout, but had considerably lessened the man's fever and suffering.

"If your sons"—I smiled at all the young men, Sandro included—

"will come to my shop tomorrow, I will send them home with something that I promise will help you."

Lucrezia bit her lip and blinked back tears of gratitude.

"Thank you, Cato," Lorenzo said. "We all thank you." He grinned. "First thing in the morning we'll be descending on your apothecary like a pack of hungry dogs."

Now everyone was smiling. Even Piero looked hopeful.

"Forgive my tardiness," I heard from one of the garden archways. We all looked up to see a sweet-faced man of perhaps thirty-five, hurrying to take his place across the table from me, next to Clarice.

Lorenzo nodded at me. "Let me introduce you to our beloved tutor and longtime family friend, Marsilio Ficino."

I was startled, to say the least. Ficino was a legendary scholar, one of the greatest writers and translators in the world. "Silio," Lorenzo went on, "meet our new friend, Cato the Apothecary."

I detected pride in this introduction, and was pleased that my new identity was more than accepted. I sat a bit taller in my chair. This evening that had begun as extraordinary was becoming fantastical. I, at the Palazzo Medici offering medical advice to the patriarch of Florence, and now meeting Marsilio Ficino! *Would my father believe me?* I wondered. Then I remembered what he had said when he'd given me his cache of precious books—that I would need them when I was in the company of great men. *How had he known?*

My mind had wandered momentarily, but when I refocused it on the table I found that the discussion had turned to a most fascinating subject, and I prayed I had not missed a single thought. Lorenzo was speaking in the most reverential tones of an ancient text recovered six years before that had been given to Ficino to translate.

"Do you remember how eager my grandfather was to have the translation finished?" Lorenzo said to his tutor.

"'Eager,'" Ficino began with a gentle smile, "would never begin to measure Cosimo's desire for the completed manuscript. He was *rabid*."

Botticelli, Lorenzo, and Lucrezia chuckled at the memory.

Piero nodded more solemnly. "He was determined to read the entire *Corpus Hermeticum* before he died, and you, Silio, realized that dream for him."

The *Corpus Hermeticum*? By its title I knew this to be a Hermetic text, but it was one my father had told me nothing about. I wondered if he knew of it himself.

"How long did it take you to translate the Greek into Italian vulgate?" Lorenzo asked with a wry smile. "Six months?"

"Four," Ficino answered, then became more serious. "We all knew he was dying. How could I disappoint him?"

"Forgive my ignorance," I said, "but I am unaware of the *Corpus Hermeticum*." All eyes turned in my direction.

Lorenzo spoke up, addressing the group. "Cato has read the *Asclepius* . . . in Greek."

Ficino nodded at me, pleased. I felt heat rise in my neck. I hoped it would not rise further, causing me to blush like a girl.

"It is not yet published," he told me. "But if you know the *Asclepius*, then you know the words of its author, Hermes Trismegistus. The *Corpus* is a before-now-uncovered text of that same great Egyptian sage."

The astonishment must have been apparent on my face.

"Like the *Asclepius*, it illuminates the magical religion of the Egyptians," Ficino explained.

"Though it goes more than a little further into it," Lorenzo added.

I had to work to keep my mouth from hanging agape. It shocked me that these high men so openly discoursed on a subject the church insisted was heretical.

Sandro Botticelli interjected with great animation, "Hermes goes into quite some detail about the use of magical images and talismans for spiritual development. He talks about statues that can be made to *speak*."

Clarice cleared her throat so loudly she might have been choking. When we turned to her she was flushed with indignation.

"Well?" Lorenzo demanded. "What is it you wish to say, wife?" I did not sense much affection in his voice.

"Only that . . . all this talk of magic and astrology and talking statues . . . ," Clarice began.

I realized that these conversations must be commonplace around this table.

". . . is *blasphemy!*" Lorenzo's wife looked to her mother-in-law for help. "Is it not?"

"Clarice is quite right," Lucrezia said with a stern edge, but I sensed a patronizing note as well. The mother of this family was famous for her religious piety, but first and foremost she was an indulgent mother. It was proving difficult for her not to smile when she said to her boys, "You all do have a whiff of sulfur about you."

There was laughter at that.

"All we wish for is intuition of the Divine without the aid of a savior," Ficino insisted.

"That is more than a touch heretical, don't you think, Silio?" Lucrezia said with great affection.

"Drawing the influence of the stars down into statues by astral magic, as our master Ficino does, is even more so," Lorenzo added. Now I was certain he meant to annoy his young wife. Lorenzo continued his argument. "These are legitimate practices of philosophers, Mama."

Lucrezia considered the statement as Clarice steamed.

"You must remember, my dear," said Marsilio Ficino, "that the most Christian Augustine was himself *reading* Hermes. Taking him seriously. Even if he disagreed on certain points, he could not have thought the man too much of a heretic."

"He's right," Lorenzo added. "The wisdom tradition Hermes speaks of can be traced in an unbroken line to Plato himself. And who can deny Plato's wisdom?"

"In fact"—Ficino turned to me again—"we now believe that Hermes was a contemporary of Moses himself."

"Really?" I was truly startled at this revelation and could not wait to write my father of it.

"Really," Lorenzo agreed. "We have even begun to discuss the question of whether Hermes *was* Moses."

"I'm going to bed." It was Piero. He had heard enough of high philosophy for one evening, it seemed. Or perhaps the pain had simply overtaken him. His hands were flat on the table and he attempted to push himself to standing.

"Wait, Papa!" Botticelli cried, standing in his place. "Please, I have something to show you."

Piero's face softened, and a pleasant expectation crinkled his mouth. He relaxed back in his chair.

Sandro stood. "Don't anyone move," he said and dashed from the table, "except you, Giuliano. Come help me!" The younger brother followed Botticelli, and they moved toward a closed door that appeared to lead into the palazzo from the loggia.

A moment later, to the sound of crunching on the marble floor, they returned, rolling on a wheeled contraption a huge, paint-smeared sheet covering a rectangle that looked to be six feet high and twelve feet across.

Facing us all, the artist beamed. He carefully removed the cloth and stood aside. Every jaw in the room loosened and fell. Then there was silence as a dozen eyes drank in the splendor.

"I call it *Birth of Venus*," Botticelli said.

The first sight of it was simply startling. It was blatantly pagan and openly erotic, and an unquestionable statement of its maker's genius.

A woman, magnificent in her nakedness, was stepping lightly from a half shell at the edge of a placid sea onto a fecund shore. Her features were delicate and proportioned as if by the hand of the Creator. The color of her skin was pale, tinged with roses, but so fine in texture that one could almost see through her body. Venus's hair was glorious—red gold and so thick and long and flowing it draped the whole length of her torso, where, holding it with one hand, she modestly covered her pudenda.

So deeply drawn was I to her image that it was only by virtue of a hank of that lovely hair blown sideways from her head that I became aware of other figures in the painting. On the left in the air, amidst a storm of flowers, hovered two winged wind gods—one male, one female—entwined in each other's arms and with puffed cheeks, creating the breeze around the goddess of Love.

To the right of Venus was another figure, a woman—perhaps Spring—who in her pretty floral dress held aloft a posy-embroidered cloak with which she seemed to be urging the newborn goddess to cover her nakedness.

But my eyes could not long stray from Venus herself. She was slender, and the one breast not covered by her right hand was small, but her belly and thighs were prettily plump and rounded. Only her left arm seemed oddly shaped—too long, and almost disconnected from her shoulder. But nothing diminished the overall beauty of face and form, and her expression of unutterable sweetness.

I think Botticelli had not expected from the viewers this profundity of emotion, this stunned hush.

"Do you see what I have done, Marsilio?" he said to Ficino, breaking the silence. "How the image holds a reflection of Idea? How I have used the greens for Jupiter, the blues for Venus, gold for the sun. Is she not a perfect talisman to draw down the power of the planet Venus, the very life force of Heaven, and store that echo . . . that taste . . . that substance of the divine Idea of Love, for our use?" His hand was clutching his own heart, and his eyes were limpid with tender emotion.

But the boys' tutor was quite speechless. His lips moved as though he was still trying to put his thoughts into words.

"My darling boy," Lucrezia finally said, "you have done far more than paint a magical talisman. This is a masterpiece for all time."

"I would venture that she is the most beautiful woman ever painted," Lorenzo offered, "ever in the history of the world."

"What incantations are needed to bring her to life?" Giuliano asked in a hushed whisper. "I want to make love to her. Instantly."

Everyone laughed at that, and the spell seemed all but broken . . .

except that I caught, out of the corner of my eye, Lorenzo staring at me. He was, I think, unaware I had seen him.

"Come here, Sandro," Piero said to the young man whom he and his own father had raised from a boy. His voice was stern and serious. Botticelli went to the patriarch's side and knelt at his feet, laying his head on one swollen knee. The older man's gaze fell on Ficino.

"This is your influence, Marsilio. I see it. I hear it. All your lessons of spirits and occult forces, magi controlling the influences of the stars . . ." Everyone was still. Afraid to breathe. Piero looked up at Botticelli's panel.

"This painting . . ." His voice was choked with emotion. ". . . it makes me want to live another day."

A sob escaped Lucrezia's throat, and she clutched her husband's arm. There was a general outcry of relief and celebration. Sandro began kissing Piero's hands in gratitude. The rest of us stood from our chairs and edged closer to the painting to study its perfection.

Clarice was clucking with quiet indignation to her mother-in-law over the total nakedness of Venus on her clamshell. I overheard Ficino and the Medici sons' conversation.

"I've always told you," the boys' tutor said, "that images can be used as medicine."

"Perhaps as strong as an apothecary's," Lorenzo suggested.

"Indeed," their teacher murmured appreciatively. "Indeed."

CHAPTER 11

" *U*ncle Cato!"

I looked up to see my son standing just inside the apothecary door, in exactly the same spot where Lorenzo had surprised me several weeks before.

Of course the bell we had put up together jingled, but I had been so engrossed in consulting with my new customers—Benito and his grandmother, Signora Anna Russo—that I failed to hear it. My surprise and delight must have been instantly apparent in my expression, for Anna turned expectantly to meet my "nephew." I just prayed that my confusion at being addressed as uncle, and not "Mama," was less obvious.

"Leonardo," I called cheerfully to him, my husky masculine voice already becoming second nature to me. My shop had been an instant success, what with the very real need for a neighborhood herbalist, as well as profuse gossip about my talents spread all around by my young friend, Benito. The moment I had opened my doors—even without a sign—I had been overrun with customers with every sort of ailment from warts to agues to infections to female maladjustments. A preponderance of my patients were women who confided to me that they had never felt so comfortable talking of "personal matters" with any man before. In no time, ladies and girls were coming from different Florentine neighborhoods, even some from across the Arno.

With all that business and counseling, my new speaking voice and persona had developed. But more than anything, the friendship of

Lorenzo and the acceptance by his family—though I did not confide this to my neighbors or customers—did more for my confidence in this new life than anything else.

The potion I had mixed for Piero de' Medici's gout had, of course, not cured him, but thankfully it had relieved the worst of his discomforts. For this Lucrezia had been eternally grateful. After that she had sent for a veritable stream of everyday remedies and cosmetics, with the occasional request for Sandro Botticelli's pigments. I hardly dared to think it, but the Medici matriarch was becoming my patroness.

Leonardo was gazing around at the shop, his eyes fixed on the lofty ceilings. "I like your shop, Uncle."

Benito had gone directly to Leonardo's side, a wide grin plastered on his face. He'd been nagging me about meeting my nephew, who was just a little older than him.

"It's not really Cato's shop," he told Leonardo. "Or so says our new apothecary. But I can tell you that when the old man arrives he'll have a hard time wresting customers away from your uncle."

"My great-uncle Umberto would have a hard time wresting a worm from the mouth of a dove," Leonardo said in a half-jocular, half-serious tone. "He's already sixty-eight and quite feeble."

Bless this child of mine, I thought. *He is helping me set the stage for "my uncle's" demise.*

I came out from behind the counter to give Leonardo a manly hug, then formally introduced Benito and Signora Russo. They were equally charmed by him, Anna remarking quietly to me that such a handsome boy was going to make some nice girl very happy one day.

"Come outside and see your sign," Leonardo said.

"My sign," I said rather stupidly, having forgotten my secondary excuse for having barged in unannounced at Verrocchio's studio three weeks before. "Of course. My sign."

All of us piled out the door and Leonardo began unwrapping from heavy canvas a long narrow sign that read, simply, APOTHECARY, in shades of green and gold. The lettering itself was bold and elegant, and a border surrounded it—a chain of flowers and plants, each of which I recognized as the herbs and medicines I used in my pharmacy. The leaves of yellow chamomile flower were interwoven with the stem of sage and some of its petals encircled the slender stem of basil and parsley, and on and on, never the same plant twice. I was moved deeply by Leonardo's work and forced myself to stay dry-eyed as Leonardo threw up a ladder and he and Benito manhandled the sign up the ladder, installing it above the window.

A crowd of neighbors gathered. There was much good-natured chatting and laughter, and many compliments to the artist, which Leonardo accepted with grace and not a little pleasure. Benito told everyone who arrived that the artist was, in fact, my nephew.

Once the sign was up it looked wonderful. As the ladder was taken down everyone applauded and Leonardo took a bow. I could see how pleased he was with his artistic effort, and also with the public approval of my neighbors.

I had been feeling warm and full, but as I watched the crowd disperse I felt my heart lurch with the thought that Leonardo would be leaving, too. He must have seen my expression.

"I thought I'd spend the rest of the afternoon here, Uncle." There was no one around to hear us, but we remained cautious. "Maestro Verrocchio has given me the day off."

"The whole day?" I said, surprised at the artist's generosity. Masters of all the trades were well known for working their apprentices half to death.

"And the evening as well," he added.

"Oh, Leonardo . . ." My eyes were filling with tears.

"Let's go in," he suggested, and opened the door.

Once inside I placed the CLOSED sign in the window and turned to him. He was looking at a table I had set up for selling pigments.

"Four lire for an ounce of azurite. That's a good price."

"Let's go upstairs," I said. "Out of sight."

He followed me up the steps, pausing to gaze into the storeroom.

"Hurry," I said. When we reached the first-floor salon I turned to him and threw my arms around him. His embrace of me was just as fierce. We stood and wept for joy and relief for several minutes, unable to speak. Finally we parted and beheld each other's tearstained faces, which made us laugh.

"Come, sit down," I finally said.

"I don't want to sit down. I want to look around. See what you've done. This is amazing!" He was examining the books, the tapestries, the furniture, all of which was familiar to him. "The shop is extraordinary. The proportions, the colors you've chosen. . . . And look at you! You're a man!" He laughed again. "How did you do it?"

"I have my secrets," I said, teasing him. "As you will no doubt have from me."

"Never," he said, teasing back. "Not from my mama."

"Come up again. There's more." He followed me up another flight. "How is Grandfather?"

"Very well . . . but very lonely, I'm afraid. First you gone. Now me. He is left by himself in a village that has treated us very badly. He is talking about traveling."

"Traveling? Where would he go?"

"The East. Perhaps as far as India."

Leonardo threw back his head and let out a long exhale. "The East . . ."

"He thinks he has a buyer for two of his most valuable manuscripts. Their sale would finance a splendid journey."

Joy lit my son's face, and not a little envy. "One day I shall travel to the East," he said.

I had led him up, pausing only briefly on the third level to glance into my bedroom and the kitchen. I think he half knew what was to be found on the top floor. We paused before the locked door.

"Mama . . ." His look was imploring, mischievous.

I unlocked it and swung it inward. He followed me in. I heard the breath expelled from him. Then there was silence. When I turned, his eyes were closed and the fingers of his right hand were pressed between his eyebrows.

"This is so dangerous," he said of my alchemical laboratory.

"No more dangerous than my pretending to be a man."

"I'm not sure of that."

"You don't disapprove, do you?"

"Disapprove! No, no, Mama! I'm awestruck. I'm flabbergasted." His eyes grazed over the tables piled with flasks and beakers, stills and pelicans. The alchemical furnace was burning with quiet intensity in one corner.

"I love you so much," he said. His face grew red and his eyes overbrimmed with tears. "You have done this for me. Risked everything to be near me."

I smiled. "You're worth it, Leonardo."

This wrenched a small laugh from him. "I swear, between your heresies and mine we shall both burn at the stake."

"And what are *your* heresies?" I said. "You're seventeen years old."

He looked suddenly shy and refused to answer.

"Well," I said, "I'm going to pack us some lunch, and we'll take out the cart and mule. . . ."

"Not old Xenophon?"

"Indeed. He will be very pleased to see you. We will ride into the hills across the river, and you will tell your mama what kind of trouble she can expect you to be getting yourself into."

"I'm so glad you're here," he said.

As we walked together through the city, leading the mule on foot, Leonardo talked without stopping. We conversed with the ease we had always shared while he grew up, and as though we had never lived a day apart from each other.

It had made him smile to see that Xenophon really did recognize him, and he stroked the beast's nuzzle, speaking to him like an old friend. I'd forgotten how much my son loved horses, even those as broken-down as this one. It was lovely to see how closely he observed the creature as they reacquainted themselves—Leonardo cocking his head, or pulling back just so, as if he were fixing the image of the mule in his memory for a later work.

The only time we grew silent together was at the busy northern corner of the Palazzo della Signoria. We both knew this was the location—quite a prestigious one—of Piero da Vinci's house. Once we had passed I asked the inevitable question.

"Do you see your father often?"

"Almost never," he said with a lift at the end of the short phrase that was Leonardo's attempt to prove that Piero's disregard of him was not painful.

"Have you met the new wife?" I asked.

"Francesca? No. But I hear she is just as pretty and quite as infertile as Albiera was."

"It must have been difficult for Piero," I said, carefully measuring my words as well as my emotion, "to lose his father and his wife within a year." I chose not to speak of Leonardo's rift with his paternal grandfather. Antonio da Vinci had never warmed to his grandson.

"How is my uncle?" Leonardo asked with sincere interest.

"Nothing bothers Francesco as long as he can visit his orchards and vines and sheep. He is the best-natured man I have ever known."

"Does he know of . . . ?" Leonardo indicated my clothing.

I nodded. "Only he and Papa and Magdalena."

The teeming Mercato Vecchio, with its fruit and vegetable stands, fish, meat and cheese stalls crowded and noisy, was difficult to negotiate with the cart, so we went very slowly. Though Leonardo shouted out greetings to many young men and nearly half the merchants we passed at the marketplace, we did not stop to shop or gossip, wishing only to put the bustle of the city behind us and lose ourselves in the countryside.

But on the Ponte Vecchio itself—the bridge lined with some of the city's most beautiful craftsmen's shops, all built of stone—Leonardo and I were hard pressed not to stop and ogle at the wares. Many were goldsmiths' places, and the candlesticks and saltcellars and filigreed plates and goblets were a glory to behold.

South of the river was the Oltramo district, far less populous than the city proper. We climbed into low, verdant hills almost immediately.

Later we settled in a tiny cleft in a hilltop, as if nestled between the breasts of a voluptuous woman. With the mule munching contentedly on sweet grass, a gentle breeze caressed us as we gazed in awe at the great city sprawled below us. From here even the red Duomo cupola looked no larger than a halved walnut shell, and the tallest towers little squared-off sticks.

It was a joy beyond comprehension to be private, in the beauty of nature, with my Leonardo, who thrilled me with his manliness and confidence in his new world. The last time we had been together he'd been a gawky pubescent boy stumbling over his big feet, and self-conscious for his lack of facial hair and the ragged squeaks in his changing voice.

Though he still had a fresh look about him, he was formed into something undeniably masculine. His voice had grown deep and rich. I could not take my eyes off him, and delighted in his every word.

"You always were remarkable, Mama," he said, chewing thoughtfully on a crust of fragrant rosemary bread, "but now you astonish me. Not in Florence two months, and already a friend of the Medici."

"I owe that to you, son. I made Lorenzo's acquaintance at the bottega."

"Acquaintance is one thing. A seat at his dinner table is quite another."

"It *was* extraordinary," I told him, pleased at remembering. "Sandro Botticelli unveiled the most marvelous painting. And I still haven't recovered from the conversation." I felt that I should lower my voice, though I knew we could not be heard by a soul. "They are the foremost family in Italy, perhaps the world, yet they spoke of the most dangerous ideas. They savaged Pope Pius for his treatment of Cardinal Platina." Leonardo looked baffled. "The librarian at the Vatican," I said. "He was imprisoned and tortured for his pagan beliefs."

A sly look slid like a cloud's shadow over my son's face. He reached into the leather satchel he'd brought with him.

"I want to show you something," he said, and drew from the bag a large folio made of heavy black cloth. It was thick with vellum pages. Carefully—his strong, well-made hands working with the delicacy of a lace maker—he untied the ribbon that held the folio together, laying it open for me to see.

The first page was instantly recognizable as a study of dogs, a dozen or more in every imaginable pose. They would have filled the page completely but for the small masses of writing between the images. Though unreadable, I recognized them instantly as Leonardo's back-to-front script.

He smiled to himself and turned the page over so I could see the next. This was the portrait, in red chalk, of a young woman. She had the sweet, faraway look of a Madonna, but there was a hint of mischief in her smile.

I was overcome, for here again was proof that in three years Leonardo's already-prodigious talent had multiplied several-fold. He turned the page again. This was less easy to discern. There was a single image and a volume of writing all around it.

I leaned down to see better and found myself shocked at the sight. It was a frog laid open, eviscerated. No, that is wrong. All of its organs were still in place, with only the skin peeled back. I had never seen such a thing. I was looking inside the creature, at its internal organs.

"What does this say?" I asked, pointing to the unreadable writing near the frog's flayed belly. I realized there was urgency in my voice. Perhaps it was fear.

"I describe the heart there, and how it differs in texture and color from the bowels."

"And what about this?" I demanded of a dense paragraph with small arrows aimed at the feet. He put his head closer and silently read his own backward writing.

"I am questioning why a frog has webs between its toes, and why the webs between people's fingers and toes are so much smaller."

"But *who* are you questioning?" I asked, bemused.

"I don't know," he said. "I always had you or Uncle Francesco or Grandfather to ask about such things. I still have the questions . . . but no one to answer them." His face flushed very suddenly. "I love Master Verrocchio. He's so kind and forgiving, but I would not think of bothering him with such things. You understand," he said imploringly, "don't you, Mama?"

"Of course I do," I said quickly and gestured for him to show me the next page. But I was genuinely and inordinately touched by his sentiment, and suddenly saw into Leonardo's new life in Florence. How, despite his genius and his fortunate surroundings, he was still, after three years, adrift in an uncertain sea. There were friends, and a kindly master, but a dearth of people he could deeply trust.

I hoped he hadn't noticed my lips quivering to stave off a mother's overbearing emotions. I think he *did* see—for he observed all the world so meticulously—but he fixed his eyes on his next drawing, allowing me the privacy of sentiment.

"Leonardo," I said, staring down at a page I assumed to be the same frog, this time its back laid bare. The muscles and the column of his bony spine were rendered in impossible detail.

"Drawings like this . . . the questions you ask. They are . . ."

"Heretical?" he said simply.

"In the extreme."

He looked me square in the face and smiled. "Now where would I have acquired such dangerous tendencies, I wonder? And the people you are keeping company with now. . . ."

"You must be careful, Leonardo. You are not a Medici. You have none of the protections they do."

"I will." He no longer smiled. "I will be very, very careful, Mama. I promise. In fact, I brought my drawings for you to hide at your house. I seem to be attracting more attention than I like at the bottega. And there is no privacy."

"Your secrets are safe with me," I told him. "We will lock them away with mine, on the top floor."

Leonardo looked away, over the ocean of red Florentine rooftops. "Having you here in the city . . . ," he began, but paused, seeming to collect himself. "It is the happiest day of my life."

*I*t seemed too bitter an afternoon to be playing outdoors, with snow still left in small piles on the ground. But it was Sunday and the churches had emptied. It was, I supposed, a time when young men always gathered for games, the more rough-and-tumble the better.

As I came into the pastoral flat between two low hillocks near the northeast wall of the city, I saw twenty-five noblemen at play together. In the scrum, faces set in stern or even angry grimaces, they were tossing a hide ball between them. It was a fast game. Feet were flying, hands were darting, poking, reaching. Much grunting and shouts of triumph, fury, or disbelief at a fumbled play were heard from the writhing mass over which the faint, steamy cloud of body heat was rising.

Lorenzo was easy to pick out. He was the darkest, in both hair and clothing. It seemed to me, watching him wield his thick, muscular body like an angry bull, that he was the fiercest combatant as well. Giuliano was still a boy compared to his brother, though what he lacked in strength he made up for with raw energy. Sandro Botticelli was here, but I did not see Leonardo.

With a final crescendo of guttural satisfaction and defeat, the game finished and the men separated, not into two teams but into fifty good-natured friends, laughing and knocking arms, and clapping each other's shoulders.

Lorenzo caught sight of me almost instantly and, breaking away from the crowd, strode in my direction.

That smile again. . . .

"I'm pleased you came, Cato," he said, "though you missed the best game of *calcio* I've played since I was a boy."

To my great surprise, from that first dinner at the palazzo I'd received a steady stream of invitations to share Lorenzo's company—everything from holiday masses at the cathedral, which I gracefully declined, to public festivals, where I became one of the Medici family's entourage, which I most happily accepted.

"You're only slightly battered," I said, noticing a scrape on his forehead and smudges of mud on his chin and tunic front.

"Perhaps we can stop at the apothecary for a cleansing poultice," he said familiarly.

"Come earlier next time and you can play." This was Giuliano, who barged between us, knocking shoulders. As usual he'd taken no time in joining the conversation.

"I fear I'll never play *calcio* again. I had a bad fall from a barn window and injured the head of my leg bone. I'm barely able to ride."

"My brother," Giuliano proclaimed, saving me from an embarrassing moment, "is having a romance with his horse."

"Tell me more," I said, giving Lorenzo a sidewise grin.

"They're together constantly," said Giuliano. "Lorenzo insists on personally feeding Morello, who stamps and whinnies and dances around at the sight of him."

"The horse has good taste in men," Lorenzo told his brother.

"And if Lorenzo, for more than a day, is unable to get there and act as stable boy, Morello grows *ill*." He turned to Lorenzo with all seriousness. "When you were in Naples the beast nearly succumbed."

Several others of the young men had joined us and now, with no words spoken, they trudged and bumped with rude grace back toward the city.

I think it was Lorenzo who started the singing, but in no time everyone had joined in. It was a bawdy song about a hairy girl who, despite her hirsuteness, was a perfect lover. Everyone knew all the words, and finished by clapping themselves in their armpits and falling over themselves with laughter.

By now we were in the city streets, picking out a house of ill repute or a rich palazzo, and singing loudly at the window till a girl opened it to encourage us, or a matron to scold us.

Sandro Botticelli scooted between Lorenzo and me, locking arms with us on either side. "Have you any new verse for tonight?" he asked his adopted brother.

"A line or two," Lorenzo answered modestly.

"That'll mean an epic poem," Sandro ribbed. He turned to me. "He's already famous for his sonnets, you know."

"Is that so?" I said, smiling.

"He wrote a slew of them as a precocious youth," Botticelli continued. "Love poems to the most beautiful woman in Florence. They were disgustingly sentimental."

"Fie on you!" Lorenzo laughed, jabbing Sandro in the side. "Stop here," he ordered very suddenly, and at once the group obeyed him, as a military patrol would attend its captain. Then, in a quavering voice more filled with passion than tune, he began to sing to a closed second-story window:

> *How beautiful is youth*
> *So soon it is over and gone . . .*

The others took up the song as a chorus, parroting the lines. By the time they were through, the window had opened and a very pretty young woman stepped out onto the loggia. Despite the frigid air, she wore just her tight-waisted gown, the top of her creamy breasts pale and exposed in the moonlight.

"Who is that serenading me?" she called down to the raucous group that had suddenly gone very still. "Come, tell me who you are! I cannot see your faces, but I *think* I hear the scratchy croak of a Medici."

Suddenly a snowball was arching through the air, and with a soft splat it landed squarely in the girl's cleavage. She let out a yelp, sending the young noblemen into convulsive laughter.

I heard Giuliano's surprised exclamation. "Lorenzo, you're mad!"

I was shocked to realize that so refined a gentleman as I thought Lorenzo to be would have done such a thing. I held my breath, wondering what might come next. A scolding. The lady's quick disappearance from the loggia. An angry parent at the door. I was afraid to look up.

The next thing I knew a snowball had landed on the head of Sandro Botticelli. Now there were mock cries of outrage from the men. There was scrambling to find piles of snow to throw up at the girl, and she was now simply pushing the white stuff from the loggia rail down onto our heads.

She was laughing gaily till we heard a gasp. She peered down, her face and bosom dripping, and called, "You're all terrible!" Then she darted back inside.

"'Oh nothing, Mama,'" Giuliano mimicked in the voice of the young woman, "'I'm just taking the night air!'"

Everyone roared as we all hurried away round the corner. Giuliano and Sandro paired up ahead. Lorenzo and I walked together.

"Weren't you just married?" I said to him, genuinely interested, yet aware I might be treading on dangerous ground. "Is this how a newlywed is meant to behave?"

"It's permissible," he answered, caught off guard. "More than permissible. Expected. Surely you're no stranger to courtly love. And then there is Platonic love." Once these last words were out of his mouth Lorenzo grew distinctly uncomfortable as he tried to clarify. "I love my brother more than I ever will my wife. I love Angelo Poliziano and Sandro Botticelli more than I ever will my wife."

He seemed to collect himself. "Clarice was 'given to me' for reasons that are political and military. She'll be the mother of my children, and I will bear her great affection for that, and of course I will love my sons and daughters. But my wife shares none of my intellectual"—he hesitated—"or my spiritual passion. I had hoped for more in that regard." Then Lorenzo smiled broadly. "But no matter. I am the luckiest man in the wide world. You will never hear me complain about my marriage again."

We had, in our pairs, arrived at the Mercato Vecchio. A great crowd of men, women, and children had already gathered in the market square and were chattering expectantly, slapping their arms against the cold. In the center, beyond the masses, I could hear a clatter of hooves on the cobblestones. A temporary pen had been erected there, and from the sound of it, it held a half dozen horses.

As Lorenzo and I made our way forward through the crush, a loud explosion concussed my ears and all at once the sky was illuminated, as though a thousand stars had exploded overhead—fireworks.

The oohs and aahs of the people with every gaudy display were coming fast and furious, and now Lorenzo and I stood at the central pen. The beasts were wild-eyed at the commotion around them and the exploding lights above.

Then someone opened a gate in the pen and steered into it a single horse. I could see it was a mare and realized instantly that the ones waiting for her were all stallions. The crowd stirred, its attention drawn away from the fireworks to the show about to begin on the ground.

The mare's scent instantly inflamed the male horses, who began, with a chorus of whinnies and snorts, to bump against one another and vie for nearness to the female. When light again blazed overhead I saw the fire reflected in the mare's terrified eyes. The strongest of the stallions mounted her then, and the Florentines erupted into cheers. He thrust again and I found myself unable to tear my own eyes away from the lathery chaos of horseflesh before me, the mixture of raw animal pleasure and pain.

Then I caught sight of Lorenzo at the edge of the crowd. He was standing with a servant I recognized from the family palazzo. I could not hear the man's voice, but from Lorenzo's slack jaw and the dull pain in his eyes I knew a tragedy had befallen the Medici.

I pushed through the onlookers to my friend's side. He turned to me. "Will you find Giuliano and Sandro?" he pleaded. "It's our father." Distracted, he looked away. "I have to go. Now."

"I'll find them," I said. "Lorenzo . . ." He turned, looking back to me, stunned, like a bludgeoned fish. I put my arms around him and pulled him to me. "I'm sorry."

"Papa . . . ," he whispered, then disappeared into the crowd.

I went to find his brothers.

*T*he cavernous Chapel of San Lorenzo, like all churches, echoed and amplified every sound made within its soaring walls. But this day, utter cacophony reigned. The place was devoid of its Dominican monks and friars in their daily plainsong and prayer, but was instead frenetic with stonemasons, wood- and metalworkers pounding, chiseling, and sawing with great abandon.

It pleased me that I recognized so many of the faces, for they were all master craftsmen and apprentices from Verrocchio's bottega. Conferring with the maestro himself was Lorenzo, and now, to my joy, I saw Leonardo enter from a back door carrying over his shoulder lengths of thin, braided metal wire.

I sat well back in a pew, aware of the strangeness of my surroundings. I had not stepped foot in any religious establishment, save the small chapel at the Palazzo Medici, for many years. The beauty of San Lorenzo's architecture and the fabulousness of its decoration could not ameliorate for me the hypocritical sanctity of the place. I had no patience for the Church of Rome or anything it stood for. I wondered how Leonardo, himself staunchly pagan, was faring in these surroundings.

I watched as Lorenzo clapped Verrocchio on the shoulder and escaped from the din out the back door. Following him, I made my way up the side aisle so quietly that the busy artisans, including Leonardo, took no notice of me. There would be time to see him later.

Outside I found myself in the quiet of the monastery's courtyard and saw that Lorenzo had taken a seat on a stone bench near the central fountain. I sat down next to him.

He turned and gave me a smile, warm but lacking the sparkle I'd become accustomed to. "I've missed you," he said. "Mama tells me you're well. The shop is thriving."

"No little thanks to her."

There was such gravity about him now, I thought, and it seemed that in the ten months since I had last seen him, he had aged ten years. But would not I, too, be grave if my father had died after a long and painful illness? If I had become the most powerful nobleman in Florence? And here, today, Lorenzo de' Medici was attending to the business of Piero's tomb—the commission he had given to Verrocchio's workshop—one that he, as the eldest son, must insure would properly honor the man who had served the city well, if not long.

But there was more to Lorenzo's distracted sadness than that. I was sure of it. He had written, asking me to meet him at the church, reminding me that if I came I would see my dear nephew as well.

As if I needed luring, I thought.

Lorenzo sighed.

"What are you thinking?" I asked him gently.

He laughed, but the sound was anything but cheerful.

"I'm thinking about the people who died in Volterra. The women raped. The orphans made. I'm thinking how their deaths and misery came at my hands, and now lie hard on my conscience."

I was groping for words. All of Florence had heard of the sack of its neighboring village of Volterra by a mercenary army.

"Why is it on your head?" I asked him, afraid of sounding ignorant or ill-informed. But I had truly heard nothing in the local gossip that implicated Lorenzo de' Medici in the massacre there.

He grew silent again, thinking hard. I did not press him and finally he began to speak. He had the sound of a man in a confessional admitting his sins to the priest.

"When that delegation from the Signoria came to me after my father died, they told me they were commissioned by six hundred Florentine men, all of whom wished me . . . begged me . . . to take on Piero's mantle and rule Florence."

I knew *this* story. It had become the most popular piece of gossip, near legend, when it had happened.

"I told them I was unfit. Too young—only twenty-one. Told them I lacked vital experience." He paused before he continued. "They refused to take no for an answer. I thought first of Giuliano. That of course he would rule with me. He is only seventeen, yet . . ." He pressed his lips together and stared straight ahead. "Pairs of brothers ruling together is the way it has always been done in my family. In Florence. My great-grandfather Cosimo with his brother Lorenzo. My father with Giovanni. Who was I to turn my back on so beloved, so expected, a custom? But how could I, with my anger, my intolerance, my vindictiveness, my extravagance—and my brother still a green lad—hope to keep peace in Italy?" He squeezed his forehead between his fingers. "I looked at the men of the delegation and I saw they were asking that I take on an impossible task."

"Why impossible?"

"Because Florence is a republic, not a kingdom, Cato. And they were asking me to become a king. But a king without a crown. Without a treasury. Without an army. Somehow I, at twenty-one years of age, should understand how to lead not just Florence but reign with the dukes of Italy and the pope in Rome. To treat with the highest rulers in Europe. The Sultan of the Ottoman Empire . . . and do so as a *private citizen*!"

I sat still, considering Lorenzo's words. I had, of course, never thought of his rule in this way.

"And then, but a few months after, came Volterra." His olive features suddenly looked ashen. "I made a grave mistake, siding with the owners of the alum mine . . . and not with the villagers. When they defied my ruling I allowed a violent *conditori* to station an army of mercenaries outside the village."

"You did not give him the order to *attack*, Lorenzo. Everyone knows that."

"The army should not have been stationed there in the first place! That was *my* error. My youth. My inexperience." He shook his head. "My pride."

"Relinquish your post, then," I said.

"No!" he quickly cried. "You don't mean that."

"Of course I don't. You were born to lead, Lorenzo."

He sat, his elbows pressed into his knees, his chin resting between the palms of his hands. The posture was so human, so lacking pretension, that it endeared him to me even further.

"I am the *cappa della bottega* of Florence," he said. "The foreman of the shop. I must be good at what I do, and prevail in this role for which Providence has selected me. The Florentine military is weak, so we must survive other ways—by our financial dominance. Our mercantile strength."

"This is not beyond your capabilities," I told him. "You have a genius for diplomacy."

He considered this. "Even if I do, I must make amends for Volterra. Somehow."

"Build an orphanage there," I said. "Send the widows a pension."

"And what do I do for the ruined girls?"

Ruined, I thought. *I had been "ruined" in a small town.*

"Send them tutors," I said.

"Tutors?" This took him by surprise.

"If they've lost their reputation, let them have an education."

He smiled. "Spoken like a true scholar." It was the first time that day I had seen a spark of joy in him. He thought about my idea. "Plato would have approved. He believed that Athens wasted the talents of half the population by not using women in government and military work." He thought for a moment more. "I've already begun reviving and endowing the university of Pisa. It's fallen on hard times. I could hire tutors from there, and from the university here in Florence. Send them to Volterra." He eyed me appreciatively. "I *like* the way you think, Cato."

"There's no greater compliment than that," I said. "To me. To my father." I felt myself reddening. Though Lorenzo spoke of the mind, and had surely sought my counsel today, that strange spark between us had, in the space of a single conversation, reignited.

A commotion of voices at the church's back door was a welcome diversion from our heavy and uncomfortable conversation. It was the gang of Verrocchio's workmen, each carrying a small sack with his midday meal.

Leonardo must indeed have noticed me inside, as he made directly for the bench where I sat. He muttered "my lord" and bowed with the grace of a fine gentleman to Lorenzo, who returned the greeting with a respectful tilt of his head.

But when I stood to embrace my son I felt an odd tension in his muscles and realized in his tongue-tied silence that followed that Leonardo was starstruck in the presence of Lorenzo de' Medici. He could hardly believe that his once-disgraced mother—albeit in the guise of a man—could claim friendship with such a high personage. The very ruler of Florence. I so wished Leonardo to be at ease with Lorenzo.

"What have you got in the sack?" I asked him.

"The maestro's cook sends us bread and cheese and wine, and if we're lucky, a portion of stew." He opened his bag and brought out the brown half loaf and a large square of pale yellow cheese. Without hesitation he broke these up into three parts and handed them all around. Then he peered into the sack again and removed a stoneware crock and a spoon. "It took some doing to convince her to leave the meat out of mine," Leonardo continued, offering the crock and the spoon to Lorenzo, who accepted it, dipping his bread in the stew.

"No meat?" Lorenzo inquired.

"I don't eat the stuff, nor do I eat fish or fowl. Anything with a face on it."

"That's extraordinary," Lorenzo said, then handed me the crock.

I ate a spoonful, then said, "It's also heretical according to the church fathers."

Lorenzo sighed. "The church fathers . . ." He murmured the words, then said no more. I thought it best to change the subject.

"Lorenzo has a horse called Morello, who is as devoted to his master as his master is to him," I told my son.

Leonardo's face lit up instantly. "Tell me about him," he demanded of Lorenzo, then gave his full attention to the answer.

"He's a beautiful beast, chestnut with four white feet and a star of white on his forehead. He holds his tail in a proud arch, and his legs are like steel. Most of all I love Morello's head—just magnificent—long and handsome with black liquid eyes . . ."

Utterly rapt, his eyes closed imagining the horse as it was described, Leonardo smiled. "I have a passion for all living creatures, but none do I love more than horses. There is such a dignity about them. So much strength and so much sweetness in a single package. One can commune very deeply with a horse."

Lorenzo nodded, feeling the truth in Leonardo's sentiments and, I thought, suddenly understanding his heart. "Have you a horse of your own?" Lorenzo asked.

"No, I've no time to give to a horse. And no money to keep one. I ride whenever someone will loan me a mount." He smiled in my direction. "And I commune with my uncle's mule. We're old friends."

"I have a stable full of beautiful animals, Leonardo," Lorenzo said. There was such matter-of-factness in the statement, I thought, with not a trace of gloating or ostentation. "Please feel free to ride any of them."

"Except Morello," Leonardo said with a teasing grin.

"Except Morello," Lorenzo agreed. He laughed, and I with him.

I could not have been more pleased with the outcome of this meeting if I had written the dialogue myself.

"What's all the commotion?"

We looked up to see one of the other apprentices standing above us. He asked Leonardo, "You coming carousing with us tonight? Visit the prostitutes?" He grinned wickedly. "Girls or boys. Your choice."

My son flushed with embarrassment, and even I had a difficult time keeping a straight face. "Of course," Leonardo answered. He seemed to have regained his composure. "But not too early. The maestro gets cross with us if we haven't finished our work."

The boy moved on to invite other apprentices to the night's adventure.

"Well," Lorenzo said to me as he stood. "Shall we go and see what progress has been made on the tomb without a crowd surrounding it?"

I rose to his side. "*Ciao*, Leonardo."

"Uncle . . . ," he said and nodded a good-bye.

"Fare well tonight," Lorenzo instructed him with a conspiratorial wink. But when my friend's eyes met mine he looked quickly away.

"I shall do my best," Leonardo called after us as we moved toward the chapel door.

"Don't forget to visit the horses!" Lorenzo called back.

I had never seen Leonardo so nervous before. He, and the younger of the bottega's apprentices taking orders from him, were rushing around the nave of the still-empty silver-gray and pillared interior of the Church of San Spirito, perfecting last-minute details on the set for this evening's *sacre rappresentazione*, "The Descent of the Holy Ghost to the Apostles." This performance, overseen by Giuliano de' Medici, was meant as a spectacular climax of the state visit to Florence of the royal family of Milan—four weeks of insanely indulgent entertainment.

Duke Galeazzo Maria Sforza was an Italian tyrant known far and wide for his appalling cruelty. A myriad of stories had circulated in tavernas and over backyard fences in the past weeks. One about the poacher that Galeazzo had had executed by forcing the man to eat whole the hare he'd caught on ducal land—fur, teeth, and claws included. How he raped his courtiers' wives and enjoyed ripping men's bodies apart with his bare hands.

Why, the opinionated citizens of Florence argued loudly over my apothecary counter, *was Lorenzo seeking such a despicable man's friendship?* But even the simplest Florentine understood the importance of alliances.

"His wife, 'Bona,' is the French king's daughter," one of my customers had observed.

"A poke in the pope's eye," said another. "Sixtus will see that our friendship with Milan is unbreakable. No better way to show strength than that."

"How does it look, Uncle Cato?" Leonardo had come up behind me.

I regarded the realistically painted wooden mountains that stretched across the front of the tabernacle. I opened my mouth to speak.

"Just wait. One moment more," he told me, then gave a signal to a thirteen-year-old apprentice standing to one side of the set. The boy promptly disappeared, and all at once I heard the metallic grinding of gears.

To my amazement the mountains began to move, first to the left and back to the right.

"Tonight," Leonardo said, his eyes sparkling, "with lights flashing as brightly as lightning bolts, and the loudest, most ungodly noises you've ever heard, it should look as if an earthquake is happening amidst a storm."

I shook my head in wonder at the effects created by my son's latest *ingegni*. "It is the most fantastical thing you have ever done," I said sincerely. "And that, Leonardo, is saying a great deal."

He smiled with pleasure. The wide-eyed village boy had come so far so quickly. Within five years under Verrocchio's tutelage he had graduated from paintbrush cleaner to trusted assistant to First Apprentice. His master had never once chosen jealousy over advancement. Leonardo's first assignment on a major work, *The Baptism of Christ*, was a single little angel holding Christ's robes. The maestro himself had completed the tortured figures of Jesus and the Baptist in the River Jordan, then given his young student full flight with the oils he had recently learned to use. The resulting figure, a celestial child with his head thrown back over his shoulder, all rose and honey skin tones, and ethereal blond curls, was recognized at once as a minor masterpiece. So moved was Verrocchio by Leonardo's angel that in a stunning admission of his own inferiority he'd let it be known he would abandon his own work with oils, leaving that art to its true maestros. His first loves, gold working and overseeing his bottega, would thereafter suffice. Leonardo's work on that single angel had demonstrated so staggering an originality and depth of feeling that my boy's reputation in the world of Florentine artists was established, and once and forever sealed.

The visiting Milanese royals had been in Florence a full month now, during which time I had seen little of Lorenzo. He was spending all his time proving his worthiness to his ally of the north. Leonardo and Giuliano were constant companions, however, for it was that Medici who provided the approval and the florins for every spectacle and pageant that had been planned for the Sforzas.

Indeed, now Giuliano arrived at San Spirito, ahead of the guests who would soon be filling the church. As I stood in the back he entered and headed down the long central aisle, straight for Leonardo, who at once began pointing out to his patron how the evening's scenario would unfold. As the pair of them put their heads together I caught glimpses of Giuliano's face and was reminded how beautiful a man he was becoming. He'd lost nothing, I was happily reminded, of his sweetness or boyish charm.

Suddenly their jovial laughter rang out in the church, thundering amidst the massive columns and monstrously high arches. My own heart expanded with the sound, and as I watched the apprentices light a thousand candles, throwing Leonardo and Giuliano into golden light, I knew that I could not have wished for a finer friend for my son.

Before long the huge doors of San Spirito banged open and hordes of Florentines and Milanese entered. They had traveled on foot and horseback and in coaches south from the Palazzo Medici, across Ponte Santa Trinita to this church on the other side of the Arno.

As Lorenzo strode up the center of the cavernous church followed by the Milanese nobles, he spotted me and brought forward a young man looking to be no more than fifteen. He was small and muscle-bound under his velvet doublet, a young tough in fine clothing. It was his complexion, though, that was his most outstanding feature. It was dark olive, to the point of looking brown.

"Cato, meet Ludovico Sforza. Vico is Duke Galeazzo's youngest brother."

As I executed a brief formal bow I felt a twinge of premonition, as if I were seeing this young man in my future.

"What do you think, Cato?" Lorenzo said, playfully elbowing the Sforza boy. "Is Vico even swarthier than me?"

"He looks to have enjoyed the sun more than most," I offered, unsure of how familiar I should be.

"I love to bake in the sun," the young man said, having taken no offense whatsoever. "I slather olive oil on my skin and it turns me this color."

"Vico *Il Moro*," Lorenzo jested.

"The Moor," Ludovico repeated. "I like it. It fits."

More people crowded in and Lorenzo, finding his wife and mother, took one on either arm and gestured that I should join his retinue at the front of the church. I did follow, but cut off by a group of raucous young men overeager for the best viewing, I found myself half a dozen rows behind my friends. It seemed an eternity before the enormous crowd settled and the first eerie strains of pipe and lyre music commenced.

Then suddenly with the violence Leonardo had promised, the mountains began to move and rumble, and the sky filled with a band of angels, who were men and boys hoisted high and flying through the air on all-but-invisible ropes and pulleys. Explosions like thunder rocked the air, and a brilliant light flashed, then quickly faded, almost as real as bolts of lightning.

I heard women around me shrieking with fear and delight at the spectacle, and I guessed that more than a few men were quaking in their boots.

The story of the descent of the Holy Ghost—here a tall, gaunt creature in flowing tissue robes and a golden spiked halo—down into the presence of twelve cowering apostles was played out amidst wooden painted clouds and smoke billowing from behind the mountains. The effect was so gripping, so terrifying—even for a nonbeliever like myself—that no one realized that the smoke was *real*.

Fire had broken out behind the set.

All at once Leonardo's painted scene burst into flames. People shrieked in panic and stampeded back toward the doors behind them.

I caught sight of Lorenzo and Giuliano. Their eyes met and locked in brief but fierce concentration of purpose. They were altogether calm and seemed to be of one mind, as though such a catastrophe was as commonplace as a game of *calcio*. With a few signals of hand and head they leapt into action.

Giuliano sprang forward through the thickening smoke to the front row, grabbing his mother and sister-in-law, Clarice, and pushed them ahead of him to the side of the church. Lorenzo spun on his heels and like a furious shepherd sliced Bona, Galeazzo, and Ludovico Sforza from the chaotic mass now surging to the doors, and herded them in the same direction as Giuliano had taken the Medici women.

Determined to follow them I moved to the right but was violently plowed into by a man twice my size, and suddenly found myself on the marble floor, trampled underfoot by men and women screaming and fleeing. The air was thick with acrid smoke.

I tried to rise and was knocked down again. My eyes burned and I began to choke. Flames rose in columns all around me. But as the wooden mountains, completely consumed by fire, began toppling toward me in a nightmarishly slow fall, a pair of strong hands grasped me roughly under the arms and tugged me backward.

"Mama!" was all Leonardo had time to say before the set, with a horrific roar, collapsed entirely, exploding into a plume of burning wood fragments and a rain of molten embers.

Clutching one another and cradling our heads from falling debris, he led me, gasping and blind from the terror, through a doorway in the side of the church.

A moment and a lifetime later we were gulping fresh air and rubbing the pain from our eyes. Once I knew we were safe my thoughts sped like a loosed arrow to Lorenzo, shocking me with the intensity of my fear for his life.

A moment later he was there, soot-smudged and altogether un-hurt.

"All right, you two?" he said with utter calm. But I could see in his expression the same panic I had felt in the moment before he'd appeared. "Come back to the house later," he pleaded, then left us.

My friends were all safe, and miraculously the fire that destroyed much of San Spirito claimed not a single life.

It was a night I would never forget.

Companies of Night

*T*he weather had turned warm and lovely. My existence, while having settled into something I might call comfortable, was never quite routine. But then how could living a man's life in a woman's body ever be routine?

This day, having borrowed Benito's family horse—Xenophon too stubborn to be coaxed into the harness anymore—we clip-clopped past the last of the stone houses and headed northwest along Via Faenza into the countryside.

I passed by small landholdings with modest cottages worked by their owners and kin. But here and there I could see spread out before me what had lately become the newest fashion—great tracts of land owned by the wealthiest families of Florence, their gracious villas surrounded by orchards and vineyards, immense barns, herds and flocks of farm animals, all tended by small armies of hired laborers.

Observing the contrasts of the two circumstances, I was catapulted suddenly into musings about the contrast of my own existence. The one constant blessing was, of course, Leonardo. It seemed as if the Fates had consistently rained down blow after violent blow on Caterina, the woman of Vinci, but they had nothing but gracious smiles and blessings for Cato, the apothecary of Florence.

I pondered the rights I now owned as a man. I no longer had to read the Stoics to bolster me against the barrage of ugliness and petty gossip aimed at a fallen woman in a small town. I was free to move about in city streets and markets, alone if I chose. I could speak as I wished, in any tone I liked, and I could study as I saw fit. My opinions were heard and considered with respect. I debated in all manners of discourse, from medicine to animal husbandry to politics, with no one naming me a witch, a shrill housewife or a freak of nature.

But what would it take, I wondered, *to thrust me from Paradise to Hades? The removal of my breast bindings and the drawing in of my bodice? The loosing of my hair and the softening of my voice?* It seemed absurd that such inconsequential actions would deprive me of all the freedom, all the strength and standing in the world that I had recently won. But it was, I was sorry to concede, all too true.

Save Lucrezia Tornabuoni de' Medici, matron of the wealthiest and most enlightened family in Europe—the rarest of all birds, revered as much for her mind as her mothering—the lot of even the happiest of women, those with gentle, loving, well-to-do husbands and many healthy children, was nevertheless one of constraint, submission, and subservience. Their thoughts, unless of Christian piety or domestic virtues, were neither sought nor spoken. And those with cruel, ignorant, or drunken fathers or husbands were subjected to lives no better than a slave's.

The ritual bath in which I had submerged myself the night before Lorenzo's first appearance at my shop had, indeed, opened a portal into an altogether new life. I had undergone a birth as profound as Leonardo slipping from my womb into Magdalena's hands.

Birth, I mused, playing the word in the soft recesses of my mind. *Rebirth. Rinascimento.* How many in this life are so fortunate as to be granted a new beginning such as this? How many even consider such a thing as possible?

I thought of my destination this day—another blessing. Lorenzo had invited me for a brief holiday at his family's country villa, Careggi. I looked forward to seeing his mother, Lucrezia, still in mourning for her husband, and the handsome, winsome Giuliano. Clarice would certainly be there with her and Lorenzo's infant son, Piero, and daughter, Maddalena. Perhaps Sandro Botticelli would take time from his painting to join us. I smiled, thinking of my petty longing for the simple but excellent meals I would surely enjoy at the Medici table. And the quiet beauty of the countryside, which I missed, living in the crush and bustle of the city.

Lorenzo's directions, written as a map, brought me at length to a crossroads marked by a stone pillar carved simply with the well-known "six balls" that symbolized the Medici—these represented medicinal pills of a family whose earliest ancestors had been doctors—and an arrow pointing up a narrow, tree-lined lane.

The dappled sunlight filtering through the branches and falling on my arms and lap and horse's back lent a magical quality to my approach to the long, gracious white stone house, simple but for a second-floor loggia spanning its entire length. There was an olive orchard and a pasture of grazing cattle on the left, a vast vineyard and a field of flowers that looked more like a wild mountain meadow than the garden of a rich and formal home on the right. *Genius,* I thought. *Pure genius.* The illusion of pastoral simplicity amidst opulent glory.

And then a most welcome sight to my eyes—Lorenzo standing at the doorway of the house, all smiles, arms opened wide in welcome. My heart soared at the sight of him. That which others saw as ugliness, I could only see as beauty. The swarthy complexion was exotically handsome to my eyes. The pugnacious chin simply strong. The crushed nose a testament to his manliness. Were I a woman still, I would have wished him for a lover.

"You found us with no trouble, I see."

"And what a place to find," I said, sweeping my arm to extol the wild garden and the orchard and the vineyard.

"My favorite in all the world," he said with sincere reverence. "I am finding that in my poetry, nature is the greatest of all inspirations."

"Even greater than love?" I challenged.

He began to unharness the horse from my cart. "For the moment, yes. But then again, I have yet to find a great love." He led the horse to the pasture where the cattle were grazing and, opening a gate, let him in. "The woman of my sonnets was not really mine," he confessed. "More a figment of my imagination. An ideal . . . Come, Cato, grab your bag. I'll show you to your room."

I took my satchel down from the cart and followed Lorenzo into the Medici villa.

Two great marble staircases rose in identical curves to the first floor. The vestibule was flanked by a great salon on the right and a dining room on the left. The furnishings were simple and informal, and I was reminded of the dining utensils at the city palazzo. To my surprise I saw no house servants at all. In fact, the place looked altogether empty.

We took the steps to the right, passing half a dozen niches in which were displayed works of antiquity—an old Roman mosaic of a woman's head, a graceful marble hand, perhaps all that was left of an ancient statue.

Lorenzo nodded to another niche, where a chubby naked boy with wings clutched a dolphin almost as large as he. "From Verrocchio's bottega," he said. "I see some Leonardo in it."

My heart swelled with the knowledge that my son was, in so many ways, entwined with this noble family.

Climbing another staircase to the second floor, Lorenzo showed me to a bedroom. I saw nothing of its furnishings, as I was instantly attracted to its double doors, ones that opened out onto the villa's forward loggia. I went to them and flung them wide, stepping onto the covered overhang, gazing out at the vast expanse of rolling green from a height that allowed a great distance to be viewed. From where I stood, nothing of the city could be seen at all—an illusion, I thought. So close was it . . . and yet so far. This was to be my room for the next several days. What a privilege it was!

"Thank you, Lorenzo. This is wonderful."

"I thought you'd like it. Month after month of city stone and marble, no matter how elegant, can be stultifying. And you were a country boy growing up."

I wanted to throw my arms around him for his kindness, but instead flung my bag on the large plainly covered bed and began to empty it.

"There's a place for your things," he said, pointing to a painted chest with a pitcher and a bowl on top. "You can wash away the dust of the road." I saw he wore an enigmatic smile.

"Is your mother here?" I asked. "Giuliano? Your wife?"

"No," he answered, that smile growing more and more mysterious. "This weekend you shall be meeting my *other* family."

"What family is that?" I said, but Lorenzo was already halfway down the hall, calling back to me:

"Come to the back garden when you've freshened up. You'll find us out there."

I splashed the cool water on my face and was suddenly struck by the novelty of the moment. Here I was, standing alone in "my" room of a Medici palazzo, its private door opening onto a splendid loggia, cheeks dripping, a pure white towel at my fingertips. The bounty of my life, it seemed to me, was a bottomless cornucopia.

I dried my face and closed the door for privacy, then changed into clean linen. I took a brush to my hair, neatening it, and chose to leave off my scholar's cap. It seemed a stiff affectation in this place. I put on a fresh robe and opened the bedroom door. The second-floor hallway was quiet and empty as I stepped out.

The gardens behind the Villa Careggi were different from the front—quite formal, a new style the Italians had lately affected. It was symmetrical, with careful rows of hedges and shrubs and bursts of blossoming flowers. But beyond this perfectly formulated courtyard were two objects that seemed in this setting at once extraordinary and altogether fitting.

One was a tree, both ancient and imposing in height, with a massive trunk spreading muscular boughs that groaned in a draping canopy. It was so large and thick with greenery it appeared more as a vegetal behemoth than a tree. If it had had a voice it would have shaken the very earth with its sound.

The other object was a man-made structure of unearthly beauty. It was a round temple, in the style of the Greeks, all of graceful white marble columns and a perfectly globular golden dome.

I was drawn to the tree, however, as there were voices and laughter coming from its direction. Gravel crunched under my soles as I took the winding path through the symmetrical perfection of the garden. I stood before the verdant leviathan, awed by its age and majesty, then beheld the cluster of men beneath its shaded canopy.

They sat, or lay sprawled comfortably on rich Turkey carpets in an exotic patchwork of colors, dotted with decanters of wine, ceramic bowls of grapes, boards of cheeses and breads, and bowls of deep green olive oil for dipping.

One by one they looked up and saw me. Silence fell, and all that could be heard was the wind knocking branch against branch, and from a nearby pasture the plaintive bleating of a young goat suddenly quieted as it found its mother's teat.

"This is my friend Cato," I heard Lorenzo announce. "Some of you know him. The rest of you, by day's end, will be glad to have made his acquaintance."

It was a stunning introduction, one that I felt quite sure—despite my normally confident bearing—I could hardly deserve. After all, in this company I recognized, besides Lorenzo, the genius translator, priest, and physician Marsilio Ficino; the respected poet Angelo Poliziano, who was said to be in love with Lorenzo; and Vespasiano da Bisticci, Florence's premier bookseller.

Now stepping forward to place an arm around my shoulder, Lorenzo made my reintroduction to these men with the simple grace of naming. Then he began with the ones I did not know.

Leon Battista Alberti was the most elderly of the assembled, and the one Lorenzo introduced to me with the deepest reverence and formality. The moment I heard his name I was riveted to the spot. This was the very oracle of scholarship and culture in Florence. The "avatar of grace," the prince of erudition. He had written authoritative books on architecture, painting, sculpture, and the art of living itself. "Artistry," he was known to have declared, "must apply to three things—walking in the city, riding a horse and speaking." He had also published on the properties of light and optics. Nothing, however remote from ordinary learning, was hidden from Alberti's genius. But he was a paradox, too, an amazing athlete, said to have once jumped over a man from a standing start. Of all the great men in Florence, this was the one whom my Leonardo admired the most.

"I am deeply honored, signor," I said and was rewarded by a kind smile.

"Meet 'Gigi' Pulci," Lorenzo said of a ruddy-faced and almost corpulent man. "He is our favorite bawdy poet."

"Amusing and sardonic," Pulci corrected him with a friendly grimace.

"All of those and more," Lorenzo cheerfully conceded. "And here is another. Antonio Pollaiuolo—the greatest master of painting in the city."

"I've always admired your Hercules series in the Medici salon," I told him. "My nephew, Leonardo da Vinci, deeply respects your work with the human form."

Pollaiuolo, a man who seemed as muscular as the characters he painted, nodded to me with a pleased expression.

"Cristoforo Landino . . . ," Lorenzo said of a tall, skinny man whose smile revealed several missing teeth, "who you of course know by reputation as a professor of rhetoric and the translator of Dante into the Tuscan tongue. And here," Lorenzo said, walking me around the tree to a brown-robed scholar whose head was balding and whose shoulders seemed rounded from too much study, "is Count Pico della Mirandola."

This, too, was a name I recognized. My father had stood in awe of the man for his brilliant translation of the book of Jewish mysteries— the *Cabala*.

"Again, I am honored," I said, feeling overwhelmed at the extraordinary brilliance of this company, and beginning to wonder at the reason for such a rich and varied gathering of minds.

"Come, sit with us," Lorenzo said, clearing a space for me on a cut-silk Ottoman carpet at the knee of Alberti, whose skin was wrinkled with age but whose clear green eyes blazed with fine intelligence. "We were discussing ancient Athens—the Athens of Socrates and Plato, and its similarities to modern Florence."

"Similarities and *differences*," Gigi Pulci insisted.

"The same in how Florence has attracted the greatest philosophers, artists, scientists, and writers of the Western world, and offered them generous patronage," said Cristoforo Landino with a tone of authority.

"The same in its climate of cultural achievements and open-mindedness to new and original ideas," Ficino added.

"Athens also put the entire male population of Kione and Melos to death, and sold their women into slavery," Lorenzo interjected in a mournful tone, "not unlike your illustrious leader"—he looked down at his feet—"who allowed Volterra to be besieged and ravaged."

"It was not your intention," Angelo Poliziano quickly said. "It was a blunder, one for which you are making amends."

"The Greeks had a public theater, as we do *not*," Bisticci the bookseller offered. "When they had disgraced themselves in those massacres, they had Euripides to write a brave play about it—the *Trojan Women*."

"We in Florence have only a repressive church with its inquisitions and heresies," Pico said.

"True." It was Pollaiuolo speaking. "But here we are—thinkers, writers, architects, artists—finding ways, even if they are hidden symbols in our paintings and the sculptured walls of our cathedrals, in the mathematics of our music, to display the messages and the mysteries that we all hold so dear."

I thought then of Sandro Botticelli's *Birth of Venus* and the pagan mythical secrets embedded within his images of feminine beauty and nature. He was not present this day, but I knew without asking that he must be a welcome member of this "family."

"Let us not lose our cheerfulness," Ficino urged his companions, "which is a most becoming attribute of a philosopher."

"If you keep harping at us that cheerfulness and pleasure are the highest good and the fruition of knowledge," Gigi Pulci shot back, "we shall all become *joyful.*" He uttered the last with so dolorous a tone that everyone laughed.

"Come," Ficino said, getting to his feet. "It is time we began our meeting." The others stood as well, straightening their tunics and stretching their joints.

Their meeting? I thought. *How much more of a meeting was there to be?* The answer became more apparent as the men began to wander down a farther gravel path in the direction of the round Greek pavilion. I saw Lorenzo, his arm around Poliziano's shoulder, gesturing to me with a tilt of his chin to follow.

Hanging back, I noticed that all amiable chatter had ceased, and what had begun as a casual stroll had, as it reached the edifice, become a stately, single-file procession. Lorenzo opened the tall double doors, and one after another the illustrious Florentines disappeared from sight.

Lorenzo was waiting for me, bringing up the rear, with that mysterious smile again. "Welcome to the Thinkery," he said. "The Temple of Truth."

I stared at him perplexed.

"Enter at your own peril," he added with real gravity now. "It is the most dangerous chamber in all of Europe."

I stepped across the threshold and he followed, pulling closed the doors, then bolting them behind us.

Before me was a scene I could never in my wildest dreams have conjured. The fluted columns of the circular space and the walls that connected them were of the purest and most finely polished white marble I had ever seen. There was a solidity, a permanency about the place, and yet it was suffused by a sense of ethereal translucency. It was lit from above by a skylight in the arched dome, as golden within as it was without. In the center of the floor was a round pool of crystal-clear water, and in its center a torch that burned with the look of a fierce eternal flame.

The men had retained their silent single file and were moving slowly and with the greatest reverence around the perimeter of the temple, itself lined with marble benches. I joined the train behind Pico della Mirandola, and a third of the way around the circle found myself confronted by a niche in the wall, one that displayed a bust of a man in the Greek style. Even before I saw his name inscribed in the stone pedestal I knew it was Plato. The finely carved marble statue had been crowned with a wreath of fresh laurel, and I could hear Pico murmuring a quiet *reverence* to the long-dead philosopher.

But the parade continued and, another third of the way around the circle, I had come to a second niche and its inhabitant, a great and elderly sage by the sight of his long, curled beard. The inscription read "Hermes Trismegistus." I felt my breathing run shallow and my skin grew clammy. *These men dared worship the thrice-great Hermes!*

Pico passed it and took a seat on the bench beyond. With Lorenzo behind me, my eyes fell on the last icon. The outrageousness, in a Christian world, of the first two had prepared me, I believed, for anything. In fact, I was anything but prepared.

It was a full-length statue of Isis.

Pressed into the niche on every side and at the feet of the Egyptian goddess of magic and healing, motherhood, virginity, and sexuality were fresh bundles of flowers and fragrant herbs. Someone had made a garland of peonies and hung it around her neck.

So paralyzed and confounded was I at the sight of her that only Lorenzo coming up behind me and whispering in my ear to sit did finally move me from my stance before the statue.

I watched Lorenzo make the subtlest obeisance to Isis before taking a seat on the bench several feet from me. All the men, I could see, were perfectly spaced. The eyes of the gathered were wide open and fixed on the flame in the fountain. No one spoke. No one moved but for the gentle rising and falling of chests, and occasional blinking. Thus the contemplative hush grew to a length that should, in any other circumstance, have proven unnerving. But strangely, it grew more comfortable. Almost companionable.

And then without a word being uttered, as if by an inaudible signal given, the men suddenly broke their reverie. Postures relaxed, gentle laughter was heard, and quiet conversations began.

Marsilio Ficino stood, his eyes sweeping round the temple and gazing warmly at each and every smiling face. I found myself surprisingly and happily at ease in the presence of such unspeakable greatness.

"Welcome, all," he said, "to Plato's Academy of Florence, and the Confraternity of the Magi."

The Platonic Academy! I was thunderstruck. Of course there were rumors about in the city of secret religious societies—"companies of night"—of every persuasion. But of the one that was said to worship at the altar of "the Perfect Man of the Greeks," only the faintest of whispers were uttered. Such practices were, to the church, the height of heresy and the depth of depravity.

"We have with us today," Ficino went on, "a guest in our midst, Cato Cattalivoni, a scholar and apothecary. He comes to us by the highest recommendation of Lorenzo de' Medici, and if, when we're through with him . . ." Ficino smiled and I heard good-natured chuckling all around. ". . . he so chooses, the honorable Cato will become a brother in our quest for Universal Truth."

"Here, here!" several men cried out.

Ficino sat and Lorenzo began speaking, though he remained seated on his bench. Despite the gravitas of the circumstance, his tone was as natural and friendly as it was in any of our private conversations.

"My grandfather Cosimo, in 1438—eighteen hundred and sixty-six years after Plato's birth—founded the Academy. The books and manuscripts of the ancients were just then beginning to flow in from the East, and the educated and curious-minded men—many of them humanists, many of them clerics—were eager to explore the ideas of antiquity. The previous centuries in Europe had grown so dark, so bleak, plague-ridden and superstitious. And the church was in every corner of every household, terrifying men, women, and even little children with the horrors of hellfire and damnation . . . for the sin of simply being alive.

"Then Grandfather discovered Silio," Lorenzo continued, gazing fondly at Ficino, "and had him begin the translation of *all* the works of Plato. Poggio Bracciolini, Cristoforo, and Pico here worked very hard on their translations as well." He smiled at Bisticci. "And Vespasiano, bless his heart, made the selling of books into an honorable trade. Of course, now we have Silio's translation of the *Corpus Hermeticum* to guide our work."

"Tell Cato about the *original* Academy," Gigi Pulci demanded.

"Why don't you tell him, Gigi?" Lorenzo relaxed back on his bench.

"In the three hundred and eighty-third year before Christ's birth, at the age of forty, Plato the Greek visited *Italy,*" Pulci announced with the greatest pride. "We do not know much about what he saw or studied, but we do know that when he returned home, he was inspired to begin his own college of scholars and teachers and students. . . ."

"Italy inspired Plato himself!" Poliziano cried to the approval of all.

"With one purpose alone," Pulci continued, "to dedicate themselves to every sort of intellectual study—philosophical, mathematical, astronomical, biological, medicinal. And as we now revere the Greeks, we have come to understand that they revered the Egyptians."

Landino continued from there. "Of course philosophy was Plato's first love. And his earliest years and dialogues defended the memory of his beloved teacher, Socrates, against his many detractors."

"And murderers," Leon Battista Alberti added with great passion. "Imagine being put on trial and executed by the state for simply teaching young Athenians to think for themselves and speak the Truth. The irony is that Socrates had been hired by those young men's *own fathers* to tutor them."

"So the Athens that we so revere was not, in fact, the Ideal State?" I asked, suddenly finding my voice.

Several men began to answer at once, but the melodious voice of Antonio Pollaiuolo prevailed. "Democracy was attempted, but was ultimately scorned by men as wise as Plato himself. Other forms of government—oligarchy and plutocracy—were even more miserable failures."

"Yet Lorenzo is enthralled by Plato's 'Perfect State' in the *Republic*," Poliziano insisted. "Wishes to fashion Florence after it."

"Guilty as charged," Lorenzo announced. "But look here, we are veering away from our general introduction of our Academy to Cato toward politics, when it is philosophy that truly brings us together."

"Quite right," Ficino said. Now he came to his feet and began to walk slowly around the fountain, speaking with deserved authority. "Philosophy, we believe, is man's highest calling, a mystical and esoteric initiation for the chosen few. In the tradition of Plato we have cultivated a taste for fine argument. We esteem conscious inquiry into knowledge and reality. We strive to leave ourselves open to new influences, and remain ready at all times to reconsider our opinions."

Ficino had completed his circuitous route and now stood before me. I was suddenly struck by the privilege of receiving a lecture by the very tutor of Lorenzo de' Medici. Ficino's voice grew stern.

"We of the Academy do recognize our enemies. They are irrationality and immorality. Foolish thoughts and conduct." He pulled me into his intense gaze. "A life lived without questing for Truth and for Virtue, Cato, is one unworthy of living. Some of us, Pico first and foremost"—he nodded in Mirandola's direction—"attempt to reconcile the pagan and occult teachings with church doctrine and the Scriptures. But we have, all of us, become devoted to the Hermetic belief that man is *not* a miserable creature, born to original sin and dependent on God's mercy for salvation. We agree that man is a divine being trapped in an imperfect world. Hermeticism elevates the soul of man, where the church tramples it into the dirt!"

And so it went, my indoctrination into this remarkable fraternity, one whose lineage, like golden threads wove back and back into the unbroken fabric of antiquity. A brotherhood of the brightest stars in the universe of intellect.

I remember much of what I heard that afternoon, but I recall with even greater clarity how, at every turn, I silently blessed my father. Without him and his rigorous teachings I neither would have held a seat within that illustrious circle nor been able to comprehend the discourse or to occasionally add a comment or disagreement into the mixture.

And it was that day, too, in which I fell in love with Lorenzo de' Medici, in every way that a soul can do. There was gratitude, certainly, for his belief in my person, for his patronage allowing me entry into his world. There was admiration for all that he was as a man, a leader who wished to rule by the highest principles, a poet with a sweet and gentle heart, a man for whom the natural world and its mysteries were supreme.

But above all, there was love.

Whether he felt the same for me was immaterial. Requited or not, proclaimed or unspoken, my feelings were set in stone as pure and white and translucent as the marble of the Truth Temple walls. He was "my Lorenzo" now, as surely as my son was "my Leonardo."

Hours had passed in conversation, and I was aware that sunlight no longer streamed through the temple skylight. The cold marble was chilly on my bottom, and a restlessness among the men sparked an almost impromptu blessing to Plato, Hermes, and Isis, and with no further ado, the gathered filed out into the early evening light.

There was laughter and camaraderie as we crunched our way down the gravel paths through the formal gardens to the darkened villa. Several men stopped along the way to relieve themselves, and I suddenly realized my own need. I found a hedge, and with my "horn" began watering it.

"A treat, eh?"

I startled so violently at the voice near my shoulder that the device came completely out of my hand. I grabbed it quickly but my piss sprayed wildly, and embarrassingly, from left to right.

"Whoa, sorry!" Lorenzo laughed as he began to relieve himself at my side. "I hope it's not our meeting that makes you so jumpy."

I tried to recover my aplomb. "Not the meeting, but the *member* that snuck up behind me and . . ." Instantly, I regretted my choice of words, but Lorenzo graciously refrained from playing on the pun. Instead he went silent and finished quickly, giving me a friendly pat on the back before disappearing.

A close call, that.

When I'd stowed my horn and straightened my robes I went to join the others at the back door, where Lorenzo led us all into the shadowy house, though not the salon or dining room, but to the kitchen.

As there were no cooks or servants, everyone went to work as though it were the most natural thing in the world. Gigi Pulci lit wall torches and began building a fire along the length of the wide kitchen hearth. Several chickens and as many hares had already been plucked and skinned, and Lorenzo, standing at the workbench, rolled up his sleeves and himself oiled them with his bare hands. Then he skewered them onto a long rod, which he handed to Poliziano, who set it on a spit over the fire.

Landino and Mirandola were silently slicing tomatoes and shucking peas. Cabbage was being chopped with great industry by Pollaiuolo. Bisticci was elbow-deep in seafood, cleaning piles of cockles and river crabs, gudgeon, mullet, grayling, pike, and turbot, and heaving them into a massive iron pot. Even old Alberti was busy fashioning ravioli from sheets of dough and bowls of creamy white cheese.

"Cato," I heard Lorenzo call to me. "Don't just stand there gaping. Make us some of that marvelous compote. It can't be that difficult. In the cold cupboard you'll find grapes and olives." He pointed to a shelf crowded with bottles and jars. "Oil and vinegar are there, and all the herbs you should need. And a pot . . ." He knelt at the side of the hearth, where cook pots and pans were piled. With something of a racket he pulled out a good-sized crock and thrust it at me.

"This is a rather large vessel," I said, trying to keep a straight face.

"I can promise you there won't be a spoonful left by night's end." He stood and gave me a lopsided grin. "How did you like your first session in the Thinkery?"

I was at a loss for words.

"I shall have to *think* about it," I finally said.

Lorenzo laughed. "Get to work," he ordered, and started cracking open a mammoth pile of walnuts.

"The next topic is Death," Silio Ficino announced suddenly and with little ado, as though we were still gathered around the eternal flame overwatched by Plato, Hermes, and Isis, and not engaged in oyster shucking and ravioli making.

"That really is rather a broad palette, don't you think?" Gigi Pulci said as he scraped a carrot.

"Let us make it personal," Ficino said. "About our own deaths. For example: I wish to die . . ." He took a moment to collect his thoughts. ". . . believing in my heart, as well as in the words I write, in my own goodness and divinity."

There was silence, aside from the chopping and clanging, as the philosopher cooks deliberated and cogitated.

Cristoforo Landino spoke next. "I wish to die in the knowledge that my body shall dissolve, but thus dissolved, I am transformed."

"Here, here!" someone said. "Well spoken," said another.

"I wish to die believing I have finished my work," Lorenzo said with quiet dignity, "and that my beloved Florence is safe."

There were murmurs of approval all around.

"I wish to die in my beloved's arms," Poliziano said, unable to keep his longing eyes from straying toward Lorenzo.

"I wish to die inside my favorite courtesan," Gigi Pulci announced, loudly sucking a grape into his mouth and eliciting the hoped-for laughter.

"I . . . ," Vespasiano da Bisticci began, waiting for the guffaws to die down before continuing, "wish to die with the most books in my possession."

To this there were shouts of mock disdain, but then Lorenzo cried, "We shall have a race to the finish on that one!"

"Once dead," Alberti intoned with a seriousness that quieted the room, "I wish to find myself in the company of great souls—Plato, Hermes, and Moses among them."

There was quiet contemplation after that, till Antonio Pollaiuolo spoke simply. "I wish to die neither in fear nor in pain."

There were grunts of agreement all round. I became aware I was the only one left to speak.

"I wish to die happy," I finally said.

There was silence, and I suddenly feared the sentiment lacked all profundity or meaning. Then I felt a gentle hand on my shoulder. I turned and saw Ficino, father of the Platonic Academy, smiling a warm smile.

"A man after my own heart," he said.

From the corner of my eye I saw Lorenzo beaming with pride.

It was the finest moment of my life.

"As you have so graciously invited me into your *sanctum sanctorum*," I found myself saying, excited by the memory of Papa opening his to me for the first time, "I would like to make you aware of a chamber three floors above my shop."

Everyone stopped their culinary tasks and attended me. Lorenzo, who had come no higher than my sitting room, was particularly bemused.

"What kind of chamber, Apothecary?" Bisticci asked, playfully suspicious.

"Well, it has, till now, been a *secret* chamber." I was having a difficult time trying not to smile.

"Would it, perhaps, be a place that Hermes himself would find agreeable?" Ficino asked hopefully.

"More than agreeable," I said, completely surrendering to my joy. "Positively elemental."

I watched Andrea Verrocchio hurrying toward Leonardo and me from down the street as we approached a building that housed, according to a large, beautifully rendered sign, THE FLORENTINE PAINTERS CONFRATERNITY.

I said to Leonardo in the baritone that still amused him, "Are you ready to join the Artists Guild?"

"It's hard to believe. It feels like yesterday that I arrived in Florence a skinny boy."

"You're still too skinny," I said very quietly, unable to control myself. "You don't eat enough."

"Mama!" he whispered back, afraid I'd be overheard babying him.

I laughed at myself. "I won't say another word."

"Look," Leonardo said as his maestro joined us, "there's old Filippo Lippi going in."

"And Domenico Ghirlandaio behind him," Verrocchio added.

My heart started pumping a little harder. These were legendary names in the Florentine art world. Ghirlandaio had been Sandro Botticelli's master before his more mature apprenticeship with Verrocchio.

"Come," Andrea said, herding us through the doors into the waxed-wood-smelling vestibule, "let us see who else is here."

If we had hoped to be in the company of greats we were not disappointed. Already standing before a table in the largely empty chamber, where the artists club registrar—a pale young man with wide eyes made even larger by the company he found himself in—pointed in an open book, Sandro Botticelli was signing his name. Standing behind him waiting for their turns were Antonio Pollaiuolo and his brother, Piero, Lippi and Ghirlandaio at their backs.

On a bench someone had placed a carafe of red wine and some lovely, very fragile Venetian goblets, ones that I recognized as having come from the Palazzo Medici.

As we took our places behind the Pollaiuolos, the artists greeted each other with happy embraces. I was introduced to those I did not know. *They were signing on to be members of a confraternity,* I thought, *but they were already brothers.*

Antonio Pollaiuolo stepped up to sign, first laying down thirty-two soldi, the price of membership. "You see, this is what you get," he said to the registrar, indicating the small mob of artists behind him, "when you close your books for three years, then open them again."

"Oh, Maestro, we are so honored by your presence . . . ," the young man replied, shaking his head in wonder, ". . . all of you."

"Don't let *him* sign," Botticelli said, pummeling Leonardo's arm. "He's a baby."

"I may be a baby," Leonardo quipped, giving Sandro an imaginary uppercut, "but I know a thing or two about perspective."

The other artists groaned with pleasure, preparing for the most enjoyable of all pastimes—a verbal joust.

"Have you seen his trees in *The Birth of Venus*?" Leonardo said. "They're flat as flounders!"

Botticelli grinned wickedly. "Da Vinci's fluffy little mutt in *Tobias and the Angel* is so ethereal you see right *through* it."

"Oooh!" "Low blow!" "Come, we can do better than that," I heard the artists muttering delightedly.

"The angel in your *Annunciation* looks like he's chasing Our Lady out of the room. She seems ready to throw herself, in despair, out the window!" Leonardo cried with obvious exaggeration.

"You be careful, you snippet," Filippo Lippi chimed in. "That is my apprentice you're trouncing."

"Actually, he's *mine*," said Verrocchio, grabbing Botticelli by the shoulder and pulling him to his side.

Everyone laughed at that and suddenly it was Leonardo's turn to sign the register. He bent down and smiled at me as I removed the thirty-two soldi from my waist pouch and handed it to the registrar.

"Everyone needs an uncle like you, Cato," Antonio Pollaiuolo said quite seriously.

There was murmured agreement.

Then Verrocchio said, "His father should be here. He ought to be ashamed."

"That's all right, Andrea," Leonardo said. "I wouldn't want his sour puss mucking up our happy occasion anyway." He put on so convincing a bright face that I almost believed him. Maybe it took a mother, I thought, or someone else whom Piero da Vinci had hurt so deeply, to see that stubborn flicker of pain in his son's eyes.

"Have I missed all the fun?"

Everyone turned to see Giuliano de' Medici burst through the door, smiling. He headed straight for the bench. "Why aren't we drinking yet?" He started pouring wine.

"We were waiting for you," Botticelli said.

Everyone gathered around Giuliano and took a full glass from him. He eyed Leonardo with playful suspicion. "I've heard the loveliest little piece of gossip," he said.

"Let's hear it," Verrocchio urged.

It always fascinated me what scandalmongers men were, when it was women who were always blamed for such things.

"Bring Leonardo closer in, so he can hear," Giuliano said. "Oh, that's *right*," he said, as though to himself, "it's about *him*."

Leonardo's posture changed. He looked like a turtle trying to withdraw into its shell. But he allowed himself to be pulled into the center of this group of his friends.

"You know that portrait of young Ginevra Benci?" Giuliano slyly asked.

"She's not so young," Botticelli responded. "She's more than fifteen."

Leonardo pleaded with his eyes for Giuliano's mercy.

"It's a beautiful painting." This was Antonio Pollaiuolo. "I think it's Leonardo's best to date."

"It's no wonder," Giuliano went on, ignoring my son's silent and desperate request. "He knows her very intimately."

Everyone made loud exclamations of feigned shock and moral outrage.

"This is a bit dangerous, Leonardo," Filippo Lippi said. "She has a rich husband."

Leonardo had turned an alarming carnation pink.

"*And* a lover," Botticelli added. "Silio Ficino's friend Bernardo Bembi."

"Ginevra and Bembi are *Platonic* lovers," Leonardo said unexpectedly, then fell silent, shocking everyone with his veritable admission of guilt.

I was pleasantly dumbfounded. My son was sleeping with a woman—admittedly a questionable choice considering how prominent was her husband and how notorious her "love affair" with Bembi. But Leonardo's lover was not a prostitute . . . and not a young man, either.

"All of you tell me," Leonardo said, clearly shifting the attention away from himself, "is it any more scandalous than Giuliano keeping a mistress . . ." He paused dramatically. ". . . and getting her pregnant?"

There were shouts and whistles.

Giuliano pouted in Leonardo's direction, outdone but not unhappy with the revelation.

"To the happy father!" Botticelli cried, raising his glass in Giuliano's direction.

Leonardo smiled with pleasure at his small victory. Then Sandro lifted his glass in his direction.

"To Leonardo, whose safety from two jilted men we pray for!"

Everyone laughed and raised their glasses.

"Salute!" they cried in unison. "To Leonardo!"

CHAPTER 17

"Silvery Water," Lorenzo pronounced.

"Divine Water," Silio Ficino countered.

"Mercury," Pico della Mirandola intoned with the seriousness of a tutor, "was first known as Water of the Moon."

"Milk of the Black Cow," Lorenzo offered.

"Never heard that one," Vespasiano Bisticci said as he moved to light the charcoal burner under the cylindrical glass *kerotakis*.

"Wait!" I ordered. I had been perusing an open manuscript that looked to be a thousand years old. I went to the apparatus that stood on the workbench in the center of my alchemical laboratory and placed a small quantity of metallic powder on a screen at the upper part of it.

It was the middle of the night and this a surreptitious gathering of men leading double lives.

I gestured for Pico to quickly close the top orifice with a solid hemispherical cover.

"Seed of the Dragon," Lorenzo suggested. "It is by far the most poetic."

"*Bile* of the Dragon describes mercury better," Pico insisted.

"Depends on the dragon," Bisticci quipped.

Everyone laughed at that, but the moment the bookseller put a flame to the charcoal, we all crowded around the *kerotakis* and quieted. Five sets of eyes fixed with utter fascination on the glass cylinder and the quantity of quicksilver puddled at its closed bottom.

As it heated, it began bubbling. Ficino was visibly trembling. I could hardly hear the sound of breathing in the deathly quiet attic room. Then suddenly the silvery element vaporized, leaving nothing behind at all in the bottom of the cylinder.

Though we could not see under the solid cap at the top, we knew—or at least hoped—that the vapors were attacking the metal powder.

"Now we must be patient," I told everyone.

"How long?" Ficino asked.

"I'm not sure. The text does not say how long *melanosis* takes to occur."

"We're fortunate to finally have a laboratory for our experiments," Silio Ficino said, smiling at me.

"You're looking very dubious, Pico," Lorenzo said, addressing his friend.

"I am not convinced of the value of practical alchemy," he replied. "The great excitement about seeing minerals changing colors. I thought we all agreed that true alchemy is the transmutation of the spirit, not of base metal into gold."

"We do," Bisticci agreed. "But is there anything more fascinating than watching a substance, by the simple application of heat or the addition of another substance, change from black to white to the iridescent colors of peacocks' feathers, to yellow, then purple, then red?"

"Or to test Aristotle's theories that the four elements may indeed change form?" Lorenzo added. "Philosophy is the pinnacle, Pico, but experimentation is glorious. Come, admit it. You're just as curious as the rest of us." Lorenzo turned to me. "Where do you stand in this argument, Cato? It is your laboratory, after all."

I had recently "killed off" my master and uncle, Umberto, who had graciously left his apothecary to me.

Now my eyes fell on a small but lovely painting I had hung near my furnace. It was one Leonardo had recently gifted me—the figure of a beautiful old woman in flowing red garments, her hair pulled up in a knot on top of her head. I nodded toward her.

"That is the Chinese goddess of the Stove," I told my friends. "She is the divinity in charge of cooking and brewing medicines."

"*And* alchemy," Bisticci added. "She is the goddess of Alchemy. I have a painting of her in one of my manuscripts from the East."

"Where does one science leave off and the other begin?" Lorenzo mused.

"Some call vegetal alchemy the Small Work, and mineral the Great Work," Pico told us.

"No, no," Bisticci argued. "The Great Work is something altogether different. It is finding the elixir to prolong life for eternity."

"You're *all* wrong," Lorenzo insisted. "The Great Work is a *sexual* phenomenon. The mystical and physical and ecstatic melding of the male and female souls into one."

"You're a hopeless romantic!" Ficino cried.

"That I may be," Lorenzo answered, "but we do have reports of Nicholas Flamel and his beloved wife, Perenelle, achieving that state of grace in Paris on January seventeenth, 1382."

The celibate Pico rolled his eyes. "And where, pray, would a male adept today find a female adept with whom to . . . meld?"

"Point well taken," Lorenzo agreed. "But one can always live in hope."

"Look!" Bisticci cried.

We all turned back to the *kerotakis* to see a dark liquid dripping down the inside of the glass cylinder. With delicate fingers, Silio Ficino removed the small dome on its top and turned it over. We peered down at its concavity.

There was an unmistakable black substance coating the inside of the dome.

"We have achieved *melanosis*," Bisticci intoned triumphantly. "First changed mercury into vapor, and that vapor changed iron powder into *melonin*. It is the first step toward transmutation."

Everyone was silent, awestruck. Even Pico held his sarcastic tongue.

"This day we become brothers," Silio Ficino declared, "in an extraordinary fellowship stretching back two millennia." He closed his eyes. "Let the secrets of the universe open themselves to us." Then he took the dome and held it under a torch on the wall window, examining it closely. "What is the next procedure, Cato?" he said.

I moved back to the manuscript and followed my finger across the page. "Calcination," I told them, looking up from the book. "The next color we wish to produce is white."

Lorenzo beamed at me and I found myself smiling back. Then our gazes locked and I knew suddenly that this joy was something more than the shared success of our experiment or even admiration for my skills. I grew flustered and turned away to watch Bisticci clap Ficino on the shoulder and embrace Pico.

But the moment had seared itself into my mind and memory. It terrified me and thrilled me all at once. There was something between Lorenzo de' Medici and Cato the Apothecary. It was comic. Tragic. Magnificent. Impossible. He was feeling something for me as I felt for him.

And there was nothing, nothing in the wide world that could be done about it.

"All right," I said, willing myself to calm. "Someone go fetch the double-necked beaker."

I had never in my life straddled a horse, nor even sat to the side like a lady upon one's back. After all, I had never been a lady, and once a man, was a pretended invalid. But Lorenzo, determined as he was to have me go riding with him, insisted on finding a way that I—with "the head of my leg bone still a feeble thing"—should find comfort on the back of a horse.

He took it upon himself to consult both a physician and a saddle maker, and then one day, quite to my surprise and chagrin, presented me with a deeply padded contraption with a high back for support, and short stirrups in the Spanish Gineta school, which, the doctor had told him, would hold my injured hip at a painless angle. All Lorenzo wished was that I would try it. If it pained me, he would press me no more to ride.

I was a weekend guest, once again, at Villa Careggi, though this time Lorenzo's "first" family was in attendance, the members of the Platonic Academy nowhere to be seen.

Even more delightful was the presence of Leonardo, who found great pleasure in Giuliano's company. The feeling was mutual.

It was hardly dawn when loud pounding woke me from sleep—I had again been given the room that let on to the loggia. In my nightshirt and bare feet I dragged myself to the bedroom door and, opening it, found Lorenzo and Giuliano bursting with lust for the day.

"Dress yourself for riding!" Lorenzo cried. "Or shall we do it for you?"

"I think I shall do it myself," I said, feigning outrage and slamming the door in their faces. I heard laughter from without, and sagged with relief to be alone for the task. I quickly made water and re-bound my breasts, very tightly and all the way to my waist, as I had no way to know what the jouncing of a horse might do to those appendages. I put on breeches and sturdy boots that Lorenzo had provided me with, and a broad-brimmed hat, so that when I was done—though there was no looking glass in the chamber—I imagined myself as a very different young man than the tunic'd, red-capped scholar that I normally was.

The sun had just peeked over the eastern hills when the three of us reached the stables. It was with the greatest joy to be greeted by the sight of Leonardo pulling tight the cinch round the belly of a stunning bay stallion, and dressed for the ride.

A stable boy led out two horses that I quickly recognized—one was Morello and the other Giuliano's favorite, Simonetta, whom he had named after his first mistress. Now that he no longer "rode the woman," he would say, he enjoyed fond memories on the back of her equine namesake.

A moment later an elderly stable hand brought out an old girl already wearing the special saddle that had been made for me.

"It's been a long time since you've ridden, Uncle," Leonardo said. "Do you think you'll remember how?"

Frankly, I was terrified. I braced myself for both the lies I would have to tell and the experience of opening my legs to straddle a huge moving beast.

"You will all forgive me if we go at this slowly," I said. "Very slowly."

"No, no, Cato," Lorenzo assured me and grew immediately compassionate. "We will pretend as though you have never ridden before." He gestured to the old stable hand, who brought forward a step-up. "Is it your right or left leg?" Lorenzo asked.

"My left."

"Good. Then you should have no trouble lifting your right over the back of the horse. Try that." He came up the steps with me, and, guiding my left foot into the stirrup, grasped me by the waist and slid me up and over the saddle.

I grunted once for effect and sympathy.

"Are you all right?" Lorenzo cried with alarm.

"Yes, yes. Just a tiny twinge." But I was well settled in the contraption, and the high stuffed back felt wonderful. Indeed, the spread of my legs over the back of the horse, while an unusual posture for a woman, felt quite natural, even comfortable.

The stable hand fixed my right foot in the other stirrup, and the steps were pulled away. I looked down from my mount to see three beloved faces beaming up at me with utter delight. Lorenzo and Giuliano were triumphant. Leonardo's expression was priceless. I could not tell if he was on the verge of laughter or tears, but he was shaking his head from side to side, muttering, "Uncle, Uncle . . ."

"Let's be off then," Lorenzo cried, and mounted Morello in a graceful sweep.

Leonardo and Giuliano swung up into their saddles and, flashing a wickedly competitive grin between them, raced away together, neck and neck, leaving Lorenzo and me in the dust.

"He's still such a boy in some ways," he said, putting the reins in my hand, "but having him rule at my side, that has been a real joy."

Lorenzo trotted away, beckoning me to follow. I felt the horse move under me, a rhythmical sway, and was surprised to feel hardly more fear than I did bouncing on the seat of my cart. I knew that the mount Lorenzo had chosen would do me no harm. I did my best to pretend I was learning to ride once again, and not for the first time.

My old girl caught up to Morello. "Giuliano is a wizard with numbers," Lorenzo continued. "Something I am most assuredly not. I've happily given over much of the banking business to him. As for the provisioning and organization of our feasts and spectacles, I leave that to him as well, and he thrives on it. Do you not agree he is the darling of Florence?"

"Everyone does love him. It seems to me that you perfectly complement one another."

"That is true. Where I am weak, he is strong. Where I have neither interest nor time, he is fascinated and consumed with those details."

Morello picked up speed and my horse followed. I was proud of my steadiness and carriage on my first day of riding.

"Best of all," Lorenzo went on, "my brother is extraordinarily faithful to me. His loyalty is unimpeachable. To know that someone like Giuliano is at my back is the best sleeping draught that I could hope for. I think you should grind him up and sell him, Cato. You'd make a fortune."

"Speaking of potions," I said, "my father has sent me a crateful of treasures from the East. Indecipherable books. Herbs. Spices. Shriveled mushrooms. Small idols and textiles. Even a mummified cat he found in Egypt."

"I would like to meet your father one day. He must be extraordinary."

I smiled inwardly, knowing how true this was. "More fascinating than the material gifts are the letters he writes," I said. "He has spoken to many wise men and scholars. Men who hold great traditions in their heads. Many secrets. They speak with great reverence of an intoxicant—*Soma*, they call it—that produces ecstatic visions. The visions upon which all of the Hindu religion is based. When drunk, it made poor men feel rich and free. Life became radiant, immortal. But the plant from which it was made is now lost. Just a memory."

"It reminds me of the Eleusinian Mysteries of the Greeks. For two thousand years they performed an initiation ritual in a temple outside of Athens. Some unknown spirits were drunk, not unlike your *Soma*, and this produced the profoundest of religious, mystical feelings, a kind of frenzy. But it's all very unclear, for no one would speak of it or write of it . . . on pain of death. And knowledge of the spirit they drank—gone." Lorenzo turned to me and smiled. "So here we are with neither *Soma* nor the Eleusinian elixir to excite ecstatic visions. Only the tantalizing memory of them."

"Sadly so."

"How is the ride so far?"

"I haven't a pain anywhere. The saddle is brilliant."

We had gone a distance north from the villa and out through a north gate in the city wall. As the path widened out into a wider road Leonardo and Giuliano—two of the most handsome and vital young men I had ever laid eyes on—came racing back toward us. We went on together, four abreast.

"I had the strangest dream last night," I told them. "It gives me chills remembering it. In it I am a woman."

"That's odd in itself," Giuliano said, though Lorenzo had fixed me with a fascinated gaze.

"I gave birth," I continued, "not to a baby, but to a demon that began devouring me, one body part at a time."

"That's horrifying!" Leonardo cried.

"Wait, I'm not finished," I insisted. "I'm all but eaten, but before the monster can consume my head, I feel a surge of strength and purpose. I open my mouth wide—very wide, my jaws seem to unhinge—and I devour the demon in one bite! This wakes me up . . . and I find that I need to take an enormous shit."

Everyone fell apart laughing at that, and then we fell silent.

"What is it, Giuliano?" Lorenzo asked. "You have a strange look in your eyes."

"I had a dream last night, too." He began to recite it with great reserve and thoughtfulness that, for him, was unusual, as though it was of great significance. "I was walking on the Ponte alle Grazie during a fierce storm. The dream was so real I could feel the hard rain pelting my face and arms. Thunderbolts lit up the night like day. Clouds of sand, boughs and leaves were all flying around together along the river's edge. Then it became a terrible whirlwind of sand and gravel that rose to a *great* height, broadening out at the top like a monstrous mushroom that caught up the roof of a palace and then carried it away!" Giuliano's eyes were glittering, and it seemed he himself was caught up in the storm of his own storytelling. "While I was terrified by all this violent agitation, I decided, quite recklessly, to peer over the rail of the bridge. What I saw horrified me. The Arno—"

Giuliano stopped, groping for words. "The Arno was *seething*, one monstrous mass of swirling water. I thought to myself, 'Move away. Run. Run from this place!' I tried, but my legs would not carry me. And suddenly . . ."

I realized I was hardly breathing. I could not tear my eyes away from the boy and his nightmare.

". . . the bridge gave way beneath my feet! The next moment I was submerged. No, *not* submerged, for I was half in and half out of the water, being swirled and thrown about this way and that in a current that was wild beyond all imagining!" Giuliano went silent again for a moment, then whispered, "I died in the dream."

"That is impossible," Lorenzo said. "You cannot die in a dream."

"I know," Giuliano said very quietly. "I know. But I did die. I drowned in the deluge. Before I awakened—for I was shocked awake—all the world went black, and I knew, somehow, I was a dead man."

Leonardo looked stricken. He leaned over and placed a tender hand on his friend's arm. I saw tears glittering in Lorenzo's eyes. The moment was so terrible that I thought I must save it.

"Don't tell me," I ventured in the lightest voice I could muster, "when you woke, you had to take an enormous piss."

Everyone roared with relieved laughter. Then the two younger men took off like a shot, perhaps to dispel the last remnants of Giuliano's nightmare, leaving Lorenzo and me riding companionably side by side, the mounts walking at a leisurely pace. We were silent for a very long while.

"I have always been a lover of women," he said suddenly, taking me by surprise. "Of course I have 'loved' many men before. . . ."

Everything screamed in me, "Look away! Do not meet his eye!" But here was my dear friend, making what I was sure would be a desperately difficult pronouncement. I turned and gazed directly at him. In that moment I learned how true was the adage that the eyes were the windows of the soul. For I fell deeply inside of the man, and he was joined with me likewise.

"But I have never been *in love* with a man . . . before you, Cato."

Time stilled. All sounds around me were magnified—the horses clopping, insects buzzing, the air blowing past my ears.

I knew I had to speak, answer him. All of those silent, heartfelt messages I had felt, but feared to admit had been sent, had indeed been real. I wished with all my heart to tell him that my feelings matched his perfectly. But how on earth could I?

"I want you to know," I said, trying to remain strong and sure in my inflection, "that I know the burden of finally understanding a thing that you want, *desperately want*, and realizing it is just out of your reach. It is a pain that has no description, yet is one that is keen as the pain of loss."

He was silent, but I knew he had heard my words clearly. Heard and believed me.

"I love you, Lorenzo. You know that I love you very much . . . ," I finally said.

He smiled at me then, the smile that warmed me so. The one I adored. "But for the time being," he finished for me with infinite grace and humor, "I should steer my course to the ladies."

I hoped that my relieved exhale was not too loud or insultingly pronounced.

"I think that best," I said, hating my words.

We had never broken the gaze between us for the whole eternity of that exchange. But now it was best finished. He turned and looked ahead.

"Are you up to riding a little faster? A trot perhaps?"

"I would like to try," I said. "I hope one day I can gallop apace with you." I grinned at him. "Race you."

"Nothing would please me more."

Nothing would please me more than falling into your manly arms, I thought. *Taking your dear face between my hands and kissing those cheeks, the chin, eyelids. The rich wide mouth. Running my fingers through your thick black hair.*

"Anything I should know about trotting?" I said instead, trying to lighten the mood.

"You should push into your stirrups, putting weight into your feet to keep your bottom from hitting the saddle." He was very brave in light of my rejection, and I loved him all the more for it. "There is a rhythm to it that is unexplainable. But you'll learn it soon enough. It should prove natural. Move your knees forward more. Keep a tight hold on the reins."

He leaned over and laid open my hands, flattening them with his fingers. Into my outstretched palms he carefully laid the reins, and wrapping them around my fists once, closed them over the leather.

"You will tell your horse what you wish by your carriage and the movements of your legs—squeezing and releasing, a well-placed heel on a rump. The animal *wishes* you to command her."

"If I trot, will I have had a proper ride?" I said, looking into his eyes.

"Most assuredly. Very respectably."

"You give the signal then. If I fall behind you . . ."

"I will be right there," Lorenzo said, holding my gaze. "I will never let you fall."

"*Let* me get us some *sfogliatella*, Mama." Leonardo whispered the final word with the utmost caution, though no one could possibly have heard him in the uproar around us in the Piazza Santa Croce. The Pazzi, a mighty family of Florentine bankers and one of the Medici's great rivals, was taking great pleasure in publicly celebrating the betrothal of Carlo Pazzi to Lorenzo and Giuliano's sister, Bianca. It had been a three-day circus of parades, fireworks, outdoor feasts, and dances, all of which the *paterfamilia*, Jacopo Pazzi—tired of always being outshone by the Medici—had insisted on paying for . . . every florin of it.

"If I eat another bite I'll explode," I told my son.

"The table with the pastries is right there," he insisted. "I'll get two and we can take them home for later."

He disappeared in the direction of the food, and I smiled to myself. Leonardo was as dear a man as he had been a child. So thoughtful. So loving to his mother. It was all I could do to keep myself from grabbing him and covering him with kisses, as I had when he'd been a baby. He retained a certain quality of that boyishness even now, that desire to please me.

He returned with the delicacy wrapped in his handkerchief and opened it to show me the two-layered crusty baked pastries in the shape of a lobster's tail, its creamy white filling oozing out the sides. I touched one. It was still warm.

"You spoil me, Leonardo."

He towered over me now, having attained his full height. Leaning down, he said quietly, "That is what all good sons are meant to do. But you make it a pleasure."

A deafening blast of trumpets silenced the crowd. As I had seen on my day of entry into the city, now came a procession of the families of the betrothed—the Medici and the Pazzi—to sit in state under a gloriously fashioned tent of royal reds and blues, and embroidered with the families' coats of arms.

I smiled to see Lorenzo, Giuliano, and Lucrezia all looking splendidly elegant for the occasion. Bianca had had the misfortune, as a woman, to be endowed not with her mother's sweet features but the swarthy complexion and hooked nose of her father.

The Pazzi were, to my eye, all very plain and undistinguished, neither ugly nor beautiful. But they all wore the same haughty expression, as though the audience they had this day assembled to feed and entertain and witness the family's magnificence was hardly good enough to lick their boots.

When Lorenzo and Giuliano flanked their sister and with kisses on both cheeks made a show of presenting her to her Pazzi groom, the crowd erupted into wild cheers.

Leonardo and I were so caught up in the happy occasion that when I heard the next voice booming over the ruckus to quiet the onlookers, I felt my guts clench. I knew without looking that Leonardo, too, must be experiencing a flood of emotion.

It was his father, Piero.

He now stood under the canopy between the two Florentine clans, gorgeous in the garb of a nobleman, but wearing the thick gold chains that distinguished him as a lawyer. He had come up in the world, I thought, surely an employee of the Pazzi, as Lorenzo steadfastly avoided using his notary's services, out of deference to Leonardo and me.

Piero was in excellent spirits, for here he was, the center of all attention in Florence, the greatest families in the city behind him and the populace before him, hanging upon his every word.

"It is my pleasure and my great honor," he began, "to be here before you today."

My heart began pounding, and I cursed that organ for its unbidden fluxes and flutterings. I felt Leonardo grasp my hand and I squeezed it slightly, not passionately, hoping to quell whatever uneasiness might be surging through his soul.

Then, quite unexpectedly, Piero turned and nodded to one corner of the tent canopy. A lovely young woman with pearls strung through her golden curls, as lavishly attired as Piero himself—and clearly pregnant—stepped shyly to his side.

I felt a sudden chill run through me. It felt as if I was standing with my son in the middle of a road with a carriage and a four-horse team barreling toward us, my legs unable to move or take us out of danger.

"I am Piero da Vinci. This is my wife, Margherita"—he grinned brazenly—"and our first child."

The crowd loved it and began stamping their approval. I saw Lorenzo scowl. He knew we were here in the audience.

"My family and I . . ." Piero gazed possessively at his third bride. ". . . wish all of the blessings under Heaven to this match. As a Notary of the Republic of Florence I do hereby announce the betrothal of Carlo della Pazzi and Bianca de' Medici, to later be blessed and sanctified by the church."

I felt Leonardo stiffen at Piero's utterance of the words "my family," so blatantly and publicly, excluding his only son—already a known figure in Florentine society—from his blood circle. It was an excruciating slight.

Done with his introduction, Piero gestured, almost rudely, with his chin for Margherita to step back, which she dutifully did. Piero held out his hands to either side. Carlo and Bianca came forward and each took one. Then with the greatest solemnity, Piero placed their hands together.

"In the eyes of the laws of this republic, you are betrothed."

The citizens of Florence cheered. I felt Leonardo slip away from

me, but I was determined not to lose him in the crush. I followed him
to the edge of the piazza, where the onlookers had thinned, and rushed
after his hurrying form. Tall as he was, his shoulders were hunched and
his head hung between them as a mule that has just been whipped.

I came to his side and slipped my arm into the crook of his elbow.
"We're going home," I said.

He didn't speak and he didn't resist. He just came along, as though
purged of all will. I unlocked the apothecary door, and he went in
ahead of me, climbing the stairs two at a time to the second floor.
When I reached him he was sitting on a bench near the window and
staring down at the street, though I doubt he was seeing anything but
a dark chasm of despair.

"My darling boy . . ."

"Because he did not see fit to marry you . . ."

"In his defense, Leonardo, your father *did* wish to marry me. No
matter what happened after, you were conceived in love and passion.
Piero simply did not have a spine stiff enough to fight for me. For us."

"Like a snake," Leonardo said with the greatest bitterness. He closed
his eyes. "I wanted to kill him today. Squeeze the life out of him."

"You have every reason to hate him," I said. "But remember this.
'He who takes the snake by the tail is afterward bitten by it.' Your father has left us behind. He has no use for us. And he is bound for
glory. I think it wise to stay out of his path. If you block his way or
anger him I fear he will strike out at you. He still has the power to
hurt you more than by simply ignoring your existence."

He was looking at me with a sudden curious intensity. "How has it
been for you, Mama, all this time? You, the most female, the most
maternal of women, living as a man?"

I realized I'd scarcely allowed myself to dwell on the subject. I decided I would not think too deeply before answering.

"In almost all regards it has been miraculous," I replied. "The most
astonishing years of freedom."

"But the fear of being discovered?" Leonardo pressed, incredulous
at my nonchalance.

"Fading. I think that I am a better actor than I ever dreamed. And sometimes . . ." I fell quiet then, boggled at the next words I would speak. "I even feel myself a man."

My son, who was so hard to surprise, was shocked into silence. His expression of bafflement was priceless. But I had said all I wished to for the moment.

"Shall we have our *sfogliatella*?" I suggested.

Leonardo removed the handkerchief from his pocket and laid the pastries on the table. "I'll get us some wine," I told him and went upstairs to the kitchen. When I returned a few minutes later I saw that he had laid the sweets aside and had covered the table with drawings. As I came closer, curious to see, he put out a hand to stay me.

"These are . . . different, Mama. I don't want you to be worried."

"Worried? What could worry me?"

He stepped aside. I stood over the table and looked down. It took a moment for my mind to comprehend what my eyes were seeing, but when it did my hand flew to cover my mouth.

Leonardo had taken a leap forward in his anatomical drawings. A very great leap. These were not the innards of small animals with their organs exposed. In metal point on blue paper, these were finely rendered drawings of human beings, or parts of human beings. Full dissections. Here a skull with every bit of flesh removed down to the bone. Here was a skinless human leg, fully realized with striations, and attachments and a sense that at any moment they might *move*.

But the renderings were only a part of each page's makeup. Where the anatomical drawings left off, Leonardo's backward scrawl began. Though I could not easily read the words, I knew without being told that they must be his explanations of what he had observed and drawn.

"Leonardo . . ."

"You don't have to tell me, Mama. I know it is dangerous."

"But do you know *how* dangerous? Pope Sixtus has hired on a torturer called Torquemada to carry out persecutions on all manner of sinners and heretics. This inquisition is already beginning in Spain with the Jews, many of whom are fleeing. Lorenzo plans to open Florence's gates to them, but that will make this city and the people in it even more suspect in Rome's eyes." I knew I must sound desperate. "You must take care, Leonardo. Please!"

He fixed me with a mild, indulgent smile. "I cannot let slide so valuable an experience as the corpses. To see the human body like this"—he swept a graceful arm over the drawings on my table—"is a priceless gift from Nature. I am seeing the very causes of life, Mama! I have seen into the *brain*. I have followed the path of a nerve that stretches from behind the eyeball to the back of the skull!"

He touched me with a gentle finger on the back of my head. His gaze softened. "I have never been more alive . . . than when I am closely examining the dead. That sounds horrible . . ."

"No, not horrible. Odd, yes. Outrageous, yes. But wondrous." I looked down at his anatomical drawings. "These are wondrous!"

He smiled at me. Then he took me by the shoulders and planted a kiss in the center of my forehead. "I will be careful. Take every precaution. I will *double* my precautions. Triple them!"

"You tease me now."

He became very serious then and made me look into his eyes. "No, not teasing. Not in the least. I know what you sacrificed for me to be here, now, in Florence, in the company of the greatest men in the world! I will not endanger myself. I will not endanger you. I promise. Mama . . ." He hesitated with a strange look on his face. "What is between you and Lorenzo?"

"What is between us," I began, "is very complicated."

"Complicated?"

I threw my head back and gazed at the ceiling. Leonardo was the only person in the world with whom I could be my true self—who knew me as a woman, a man, a mother, an uncle, a patron, a friend.

"Lorenzo is in love with me," I said. "With Cato."

Now it was Leonardo's hand that flew to his mouth.

"You're not laughing at me, are you?"

"No, not laughing. Covering my flabbergasted expression." He tilted his head in a way he did when observing the subject of a draw-ing. "Are you in love with him?"

"Oh, Leonardo, how could I not be?"

"Does he know?"

I shook my head.

My son heaved a great sigh. He understood all at once the implica-tions, the complications, the impossibilities, the pain and the ridicu-lousness of our plight.

"I take it this is one 'regard' that has proven less than 'miracu-lous.' "

I felt hot tears suddenly welling. Leonardo saw and placed his hand on mine.

"Surely you can confide in Lorenzo. He is a great man."

"That is why I *cannot* confide. You and I are already in terrible danger should my disguise fail. Lorenzo carries the burden of all Tus-cany on his shoulders. Should a friend of his be revealed as a . . . a . . ." I looked helplessly at my son. "What *am* I?"

"A hermaphrodite," he said, pleased with his answer.

"Yes," I agreed. "That will do for now."

Both of us smiled. It was as though a weight, like a heavy woolen cloak, had been lifted from my shoulders. I had shared my secret—unique and delightful and unbearable as it was—with my be-loved child.

"So have you any more?" I asked of the drawings.

"More?" He picked up his satchel and grinned wickedly. "Oh, Mama, you haven't seen the least of them."

CHAPTER 20

"Cato, come quickly!"

It was nearly evening when a wild-eyed Benito bolted in through the front door of my shop, setting the bell to frantic ringing. I looked up from my grinding mortar.

"It's Leonardo. He's been arrested!" Benito's expression became even more panicked. "He's being held by the Office of Night."

My arms fell to my sides. I tried to compose myself. This was an office of the church—the "Conservers of Morality." Leonardo's arrest by these people could mean only one thing.

Benito wished to accompany me but I begged him to stay behind, close up my shop and tell no one what he knew. It was a futile request, I realized. News of this kind traveled quickly through the city.

I made my way through the city with the greatest haste, hardly letting myself think, for the thoughts were too dark, too beastly to contemplate.

When I arrived at the building a crowd had already gathered outside. I pushed my way in and saw before an official desk manned by two robed friars—one severe and lugubrious, the other puff-cheeked and florid—four groups of men talking with terrible intensity within themselves. These must, I realized, be the families of the others arrested with Leonardo.

I was shocked when one of them looked up from his conversation and revealed himself to be Lorenzo. He came to me at once, his concern impossible to conceal. It was a struggle almost beyond measure to maintain my male demeanor. I was Leonardo's *mother*. He was in desperate circumstances, and I had never, since coming to Florence as a man, felt my femininity so strongly as I did in this moment. Yet I steeled myself and spoke as Cato.

"Is it sodomy?"

"It is."

"Why are you here?"

"My cousin Lindo Tornabuoni is one of the others charged. And another is my uncle Bernardo Rucellai's illegitimate son."

I knew the name Rucellai. Everyone did. Theirs was a very great family in Florence, rivaling though not equaling the wealth of the Medici.

All I could do was shake my head in confusion.

"Three others are involved as well—two goldsmith's apprentices and a doublet maker. The youth they're said to have abused is another goldsmith from a good family."

"Those speaking for the accused step forward," the lugubrious friar intoned.

Everyone crowded around the desk. Beads of perspiration trailed down the cheeks of the fat-faced priest as he read from a document in his hands.

"Bartolomo di Pasquino, Arturo Baccino, Lindo Tornabuoni, Tommaso di Masini, and Leonardo da Vinci are charged with the lewd and degenerate vice of practicing sodomy on one Jacopo Saltarelli, not yet seventeen. They have been denounced anonymously by a virtuous citizen. . . ."

"Anonymously?!" one of the relatives cried with great indignation. "Then how do you know he or she is virtuous?"

"Silence," the fat priest ordered with icy disdain, then continued as if he had never been interrupted. "By means of a letter dropped in a *tambura* drum—'the mouth of truth' in the Via Motola." The *tamburas* were drum-shaped boxes placed around the city into which citizens deposited written accusations of their neighbors of both municipal and religious infractions.

I could feel the family members bristling around me. Only Lorenzo stood calm and strong at my side.

The other priest now spoke. "A hearing will take place tomorrow at noon. You will return then to see—"

"We will see them now," Lorenzo said with unflinching simplicity. He stepped forward to face the friars, who had apparently not, till then, seen who stood among the relations of the accused.

The two clergymen leaned in to confer with one another. The pale, long-faced one tried with little success to not tremble. "The guard will take you to them."

"Hold steady, Cato," Lorenzo said as we were led through a wooden door past several official-looking offices and in through a second door, this one massive and made as much from iron as wood, and bolted shut from the outside.

The Office of Night prison hallway was dim and frightening. There were dismal barred cages on either side of us, peopled in the front cells by women who must have been prostitutes. Farther back we found six young men, two to a cage.

Leonardo was sitting with another young man, dressed all in black, behind bars, sharing a rude bench. The guard unlocked the door and Lorenzo and I were allowed in.

The black-frocked man, Tommaso di Masini, stood and embraced Lorenzo, muttering, "Thank goodness." Leonardo barely looked up. I saw with alarm that for the first time in his life he had the appearance of a beaten dog.

"Nephew," I said. When he did not rise I took Tommaso's place on the bench he'd given up. "Leonardo." I spoke his name softly, as I would to a person seriously ailing. "Are you injured. Ill?"

"No," he said in a haunted tone, then glanced around. "But I am here in this terrible place. . . ."

Thankfully, Lorenzo spoke up. "You will not be for long, Leonardo. None of you will."

Hope gleamed in his eyes. "Can we go with you now?"

I marveled at Lorenzo's calm as he said, "Not till tomorrow, after the hearing. At noon. Then you'll be freed. I promise you."

Leonardo shook his head. "I cannot stay here the night." Panic was rising in him. He looked at Lorenzo pleadingly. "We're in a *cage*."

"I know. But you're not alone. Your friend is with you. And you'll be strong for one another." He held Tommaso's eyes now. "Will you not?"

Tommaso nodded.

Leonardo was crumbling inside.

My heart broke for him. I took him into a manly embrace, stifling the truest of my own fearful emotions.

"Trust Lorenzo," I whispered.

Now the jailor was at the door. We took our leave. Lorenzo had a quick word with his other cousin in a separate cell, and when he came out we left the place.

We walked in silence for a while, my mind in a whirl of fear and despair equaled, I was sure, only by Leonardo's own. Lorenzo was maddeningly calm.

"I'm very suspicious," he finally said. "Of the four boys arrested, two of them are related by marriage to the Medici. I'd wager the motive here is political. The others arrested, like Leonardo, were unwitting casualties." Then he noticed my condition. "Cato, you're trembling."

"Am I?"

He stopped and grabbed me by the shoulders, turned me to face him. "You love that boy very much, don't you?"

My voice cracked as I said, "I promised my sister to protect him." I was struggling to keep my upwelling female attributes from overwhelming the male.

"Did you know Sandro Botticelli was similarly accused?" I shook my head, thinking it better not to speak. "Our lawyers got him released the next day. As will these boys be. You have my word. By tomorrow evening Leonardo will be back in Andrea's bottega."

I forced a brave face. Lorenzo let go my shoulders and we continued walking.

"The hypocrisy is maddening," he said. "Plato's idea of love between men is as acceptable in Florence today as it was in ancient Athens. It has been and still is practiced by the greatest emperors and kings. Some believe it is a cause for *pride* among men of worth. Yet something like this can happen when idiot priests denounce it from their pulpits."

"The irony is," I said, finally finding my voice, "that Leonardo had fallen in love . . . or at least lust, with a woman."

"So I heard. Though I understood Ginevra Benci recently broke his heart."

"What about the scandal, Lorenzo? Leonardo's reputation?"

"People will talk for a while. Such things are the sweetest fodder for gossips. But it will pass. Look at Sandro. He's no worse for the wear."

We'd come to the corner where we would part. I wanted so much to bring Lorenzo home with me. To pass this terrible night with my dearest friend. Take comfort from his strength.

"I wish I could come to the apothecary now," he said, reading my heart, "but there are arrangements to be made."

"Of course," I said.

"Go home. Try to sleep. Be at the Office of Night at noon." We embraced stiffly. Then he pushed me to arm's length. "You know I'll do everything in my power to protect him."

"Thank you, Lorenzo."

He turned to go. "Tomorrow, then?"

"Tomorrow," I called after him.

Despite Lorenzo's assurances, the hearing was no less than a Dantean Circle of Hell.

All the accused men, as well as the victim of their alleged sodomy, Jacopo Saltarelli, were standing trial for their "violence against nature," as the prosecutor, one Fra Savonarola, had endlessly repeated to three ecumenical judges behind an ornate table, a crowded room of relatives, and vicarious spectators. The monk was small and very darkly complected with a huge hooked nose and fleshy lips. The heavy eyebrows covered a great deal of his forehead, but nothing softened the hard gleam of vindictive fury in his eyes.

"These are diabolical creatures!" he shouted, jabbing a finger in the direction of each man in turn. "A wretched crew of heretics so filthy and perverted they might as well have carnal knowledge of Satan! Sodomites, sodomites, one and all!" the prosecutor shrieked. "Look at this man—if one can call him a man." He pointed to Tommaso di Masini, who wore a tasteful black tunic with a fashionable collar so tall it hid the lower part of his face. His hair had been plastered back against his head with gum arabic.

"See how he wears devilish black. And there is a good reason for this. The man, a bastard of the Rucellai family"—the prosecutor paused for his slur to be well accounted by the audience—"is a self-styled master of the occult. A *magician* . . ."

I heard shocked whispering behind me.

". . . who goes by the name Zoroastre!" The prosecutor continued, scanning the faces in the audience. "Do you know who Zoroastre is, good people? His is a pagan *god*! A god of the Turks!"

I heard a woman weeping, and wondered if it was perhaps Tommaso di Masini's poor mother. I myself was close to weeping.

"And this boy"—Fra Savonarola glowered fiercely at Jacopo Saltarelli—"already at sixteen a piece of homosexual scum. He, too, wears all black. And has dozens of regular customers in his prostitute's trade."

"I am not a prostitute!" Saltarelli shouted back, his face flushing crimson. "I am a goldsmith's apprentice!"

"Silence," Savonarola hissed, then turned, to my great horror, in Leonardo's direction. "And this young dandy," he began.

"I object, Your Grace." A tall, slender, and distinguished man of middling years came to his feet and with a deep, level voice addressed the three friars who sat in grim-faced silence. This must, I realized, be the lawyer Lorenzo had hired, probably a longtime friend and Medici supporter.

"If you notice," the lawyer said, allowing himself a small smile, "I, too, am wearing black. And I am neither a magician nor a prostitute. I respectfully submit that the prosecutor should reread Aristotle's principles of syllogistic logic."

Fra Savonarola spluttered with outrage, "I have no need to read the heresies of the Greeks, who themselves were all homosexuals! Every law of God and man that one needs to know can be found in the blessed Scriptures!"

"But in any court of law, whether it be God's or man's, one is bound to have *evidence* of the crime being committed. Is that not true?" He looked directly into the judges' eyes. Then he swiveled gracefully on his heels and smiled at the audience. There was murmured agreement.

"Of course evidence must be shown," the lawyer continued. "Something more than one anonymous man or woman's accusation dropped in a *tambura* drum. That anonymous person . . ." His pause now cast subtle aspersions on the faceless, nameless denunciation. ". . . may have a personal complaint with one of these young men . . . or with someone in their family that has nothing at all to do with the reason for this charge. I ask the prosecutor, before another vile word is spoken out against my clients, to provide this much-reputed office with signed statements from witnesses to the alleged crime."

The prosecutor's lips were working in furious agitation.

"You do have signed statements, do you not, Fra Savonarola?" the silver-haired lawyer asked.

The judges seemed to be squirming in their seats. One muttered, "Evidence, Friar. Provide your evidence."

The man seemed ready to explode. "These young *sodomites*"—he fairly spat the word—"were only yesterday arrested. I have had insufficient time to gather my written statements from witnesses, and the criminals' own confessions."

Confessions? My mind reeled. *Leonardo tortured for a confession?* Indeed, all in the hearing chamber began grumbling.

"There will be no confessions," said the men's lawyer with calm confidence. "Without signed statements or other proof of their guilt, all of these fine young gentlemen of Florence will walk out of this hearing with me today."

The middle judge was as perturbed with his prosecutor as with the Medici lawyer's inarguable defense. But he was unready to completely forgo the public humiliation of six potential heretics.

"The accused are hereby discharged . . . ," the judge began. The perceptible sounds of relief rippled through the room. ". . . *on condition*," the cleric continued, his voice booming with pomposity, "that the case be brought back to the drum to be reheard in two months' time."

"Unfair!" one of the relatives cried from behind me. "You condemn them to two months of Purgatory!"

The judges stood and, herding the chastised prosecutor before them, left through a side door, pulling it closed with an angry crash.

But the families were already celebrating their sons' freedom, temporary as it was and shadowed by the threat of another public airing. Everyone was embracing.

Leonardo came to my side. He was terribly subdued, unsmiling. "Can we go, Uncle Cato?"

"Yes, of course we can. But first you must thank Lorenzo, and the lawyer who spoke on your behalf. I see them over th—"

"Please. Let me out of here. I cannot breathe."

Leonardo's distress was evident. I made way for us through the crowd of well-wishers, stopping for no one until we were out the door.

We were met by the most welcoming and cheerful of sights. Verrocchio and a dozen of his apprentices were waiting, all smiles, for their brother. They took Leonardo in their arms with hearty backslaps and genial ribbing. I detected the faintest hint of a smile as he allowed himself to be led away.

Before they rounded the corner he turned back and caught my eye.

In his world of pain there glimmered a single ray of gratitude, and another of thanks.

I raised my hand to wave, but he was already gone.

The second hearing had, with no further evidence of guilt from the prosecutor Savonarola, come to nothing. All the young men, including Saltarelli, had been "absolved" of the crime of sodomy.

But the scars those two months had left on Leonardo's spirit ran deep. As I watched him and his friends be dismissed from the bench, I saw that much of his innate joy had drained away. The smile was subdued between the growth of beard and mustache he now affected. It covered the handsomeness of his jawline and the sensuous curve of his lips, but that, I knew, was exactly what he desired.

A disguise. A mask. Anything to hide his shame. Shame that his reluctant absolution by the church fathers could never erase. In Leonardo's mind his reputation had been permanently and irrevocably sullied.

As the doors opened and families and friends piled out into the sunshine, Lorenzo and I followed a few steps behind Leonardo, who was—as had become his habit—alone. I saw him heading for Andrea Verrocchio, who had proved a steadfast friend through the ordeal. But another figure was suddenly barring my son's way, looming before him like an angry god.

It was his father.

I could not see Leonardo's face. I started toward him but Lorenzo stayed me with a hand on my arm.

"Do you not think this is Leonardo's fight?" he said.

I sighed heavily and together with Lorenzo stepped back to a place out of Piero's sight, but within hearing of father and son.

"How could you, Leonardo? What have I ever done that you should dishonor your family so horribly? How can I possibly hold my head up in society now?" Piero straightened his fine doublet and glared with disdain. "If your grandparents were alive they would soon be dead of humiliation. As for me, I'm not really surprised. You are simply acting according to your deepest nature—the bastard son of a whore mother that you . . . aaigh!"

At Piero's cry I chanced a glimpse and found Leonardo's large hand wrapped around his father's neck. Piero was trying to pry away the viselike fingers.

"You will not speak of my mother so," Leonardo whispered with Herculean restraint, then released Piero. Many eyes were fixed on the pair of them now. Verrocchio had taken up Leonardo's back. Lorenzo was moving forward, I with him.

The maestro spoke directly to Piero. There could be no mistaking the disgust in his expression. "Your child is illegitimate because of you, Piero da Vinci, not for some sin of his own."

Piero looked stricken at Verrocchio's words. He opened his palms to the artist. "Andrea . . ."

"Do not call me by my given name. You are no friend of mine. And why would you wish to be? I am a bastard son, did you not know?"

Lorenzo and I moved into Piero's sight. He knew instantly that the ruler of Florence had just witnessed this public humiliation by the much-loved Verrocchio, but his eyes grazed my face without recognition.

Piero glared at Leonardo and, trying to salvage a bit of his dignity, made his final thrust. "My wife has given me a son. A *legitimate* son. Praise be to God." With that Piero swiveled on his heels, pushed his way through the gathered crowd, and disappeared.

I still could not see Leonardo's face but his posture straightened suddenly, as if a rod had been pushed up inside his spine. Without a word he took a step forward. The cluster of onlookers parted for him, like the waters of the Red Sea for Moses.

And in a moment he, too, was swallowed up by the crowd.

"I cannot understand the cruelty of parents toward their children," Lorenzo said. "And for such a beautiful soul as Leonardo."

I was straining in the direction my son had gone. Lorenzo stayed me with an arm around my shoulder. "I think he needs to be alone."

"I'm afraid that now he will always be alone."

"He has you, Cato," Lorenzo said with a consoling smile, "and all of the Medici behind him. He is a man who knows how to survive. Surely you know that."

"I do. Sometimes I need to be reminded."

*L*orenzo and I were both right about Leonardo. He did survive the devastation of the sodomy charges. But more and more he became a solitary man, one consumed less by his loves and lusts for women or men and more for his artistry, invention, and experiments.

He was making a name for himself in Florence, eccentric as he was. His foibles were tolerated, even indulged. And blessed Lorenzo, along with Giuliano and Lucrezia, began a quiet, almost secret patronage of Leonardo as an artist of which few were aware.

I'd seen little of him in the months following the trial, and I missed his company. Taking myself to Verrocchio's bottega one Sunday afternoon, I was told I could find my nephew at the hospital of Santa Maria Novella.

The nursing nuns all knew him by name and directed me to a stairwell leading down worn stone steps into the hospital's cellar.

It was dark and damp and felt like the bowels of the earth—not a place I would wish to spend my time. But Leonardo was here, and I was determined to see him.

At the end of a long hallway I saw the door to which I'd been directed, and opened it. A waft of frigid air struck me, and in the next moment the smell of the place knocked me back on my feet. *Rot and death,* I thought. *How can Leonardo, who so loved the fresh scents of rivers rushing through spring meadows, exist in such hideous environs?*

But there he was, his back to me, hunched over the center of a long table. Resting upon it, though canvas-covered, there was no mistaking the head and torso of a corpse. Indeed at the far end, the feet and calves of what appeared by their delicacy to be a woman were undraped and glaringly naked.

To his left were two smaller tables, upon the first of which was spread open his folio and some pieces of red and black chalk. On the other was a row of metal knives and clamps and saws.

A kerchief that must have covered his nose and mouth was knotted at the back in his long wavy hair. He worked with such rapt concentration he did not hear the loud creak of the heavy door.

"Son," I said, and he turned with a start.

He looked beyond me into the deserted hallway. "Mama," he said and smiled awkwardly. "I would say, 'Welcome, come in,' but"—he gestured helplessly at the body before him. "You should close that door."

"Is it awful?" I asked, doing as he told me.

"No," he said. "It's . . . breathtaking."

In his satchel he searched for and found another kerchief and a small vial. He sprinkled a few drops from the vial onto the cloth, and even through the stench I could smell lavender oil. He handed it to me, and I placed it around my face. A saving grace, I thought. The way such onerous work was possible.

He gestured me forward to the corpse's feet. I fully expected a gruesome dissection, but nothing could have prepared me for the sight of a fully pregnant woman, her great belly flayed open, her womb parted and the child within lying in deathly peaceful repose.

I failed to stifle my gasp. Never in a thousand years could I have imagined such a thing. Far from being speechless, I recovered quickly and became a fountain of questions. *How did she die? How old is the fetus? Is this the placenta? Where is the umbilicus? Is it male or female?*

Leonardo patiently began to explain, unflinching, as he touched the miniature limbs, moving them aside with the tenderest care to reveal the genitals.

"Big *cazzo* for a little man," he quietly joked, trying to put me at ease. "Can you see the fingernails? They're so tiny." His voice was filled with wonder. He turned suddenly to his folio and with red chalk filled in a missed detail in several sketches of the fetus.

I looked closer and I could see the plastered-down tendrils of silky hair.

I burst into tears and turned away, pulling off my mask.

"Mama, I'm sorry," Leonardo gently said, coming to my side and removing the kerchief from his own face.

"Why am I weeping?"

"Dead children always make you weep."

"I suppose they do. Leonardo," I began, allowing my eyes to fall on the corpses of mother and child.

"You don't have to say it. I know this is madness."

"And done so carelessly." I knew my voice was becoming shrill. "One question to the boys at the bottega and this is where I was led. The Office of Night let you slip through their fingers once. A second arrest for necromancy . . ." I shook my head. "The best Medici lawyers will not save you from that."

"But how else can I learn? How do I study the physical nature of man?" he asked with almost childlike sincerity. "How muscles make limbs move? Cause expressions in the face? The few men who teach anatomy ignore what they see before their eyes and instead spout off verbatim what has already been taught and written by the Greeks and Romans. Why bother doing dissections at all?" He was growing more passionate. "Experience is *everything*!"

"My darling boy," I began, but he was on fire now, hardly hearing me.

"In another cadaver I found a tree of nerves that descends from the brain and the nape of the neck, stretching along the spine and into the arms and legs! On that same body I dissected the hand. I was not content to see the structure but wished to understand its *workings*, so I took threads and wires and used them to replace the muscles. When I pulled on them, they moved the fingers!"

I was silent, but my expression must have been drawn with concern.

"Mama, please, you must be happy for me. I know it is all grotesque, but it is marvelous beyond compare!"

"I am happy for you," I said most unconvincingly. "But do you spend all your time here, with the dead? What of your friends? Have you a lover?"

He looked away as he spoke and though the words were chilly, his voice was turgid with feeling. "Love is a hell of which fools make their heaven. It is poison with a sweet taste. A death having the appearance of life."

I knew he was quoting Petrarch, but I let him go on.

"And lust? It slows the intellect, and all that comes of it are disappointment and sorrow." His voice trembled. "Those who do not restrain their appetites . . . place themselves on the same level with beasts."

"Leonardo . . ." My voice was pleading. "You've been wounded by the church. . . ."

"Damn the church!" he cried, wheeling around to face me.

I placed a hand over his mouth and begged his silence. He placed a hand over mine and, curling my fingers into a fist, kissed them and brought them to his heart.

"I'm all right, Mama. This is enough for me now. More than enough. And I'll be careful."

"You always say that."

He smiled. "You'd better go. I don't have much time here before they . . ." He looked down at his dissected subjects.

"I understand," I said quickly and made for the door, turning back before I opened it. "Come visit me, will you?"

He tied on his mask and turned back to the mother and child. "If you make me a vegetable stew," he said.

I was no longer a stranger to the sumptuous sleeping chambers of the Medici brothers. Many nights we would gather—the family friends or sometimes the Academy fellows—sprawling across the canopied bed, perched on chests or sitting amidst pillows on the carpeted floor to drink wine, play musical instruments, and sing. We would listen to Lorenzo or Poliziano's or Gigi Pulci's newest verses and hurl good-natured insults as well as abundant praise in their direction . . . or simply talk, as men do, into the wee hours of the morning.

This time it was different. It was the Sunday afternoon before Ascension Day and we were dressed for church and gathered in Giuliano's room. He was in bed, laid up with a leg not yet healed of a fall from Simonetta, who had reared up at the sight of a snake in the road. My poultices had almost finished their work on the gash across his thigh, but a cracked rib had punctured a lung, and his breathing continued pained and shallow.

Still, on this day, he wished desperately to be joining his brother and their friends at the Duomo.

"You must rest, Giuliano," Lorenzo ordered him tiredly, for he had said this a hundred times already.

"I don't want to rest anymore. I've already missed the banquet for Raffaele, and now I'm going to miss the sight of beautiful young ladies in their church finery. Silio, hand me my blue doublet."

"No," Ficino answered simply. "You're staying in bed. Your mother is worried about you."

Giuliano sulked. "And tell me again why we are bothering to pay for an expensive celebration of a seventeen-year-old brat?"

"Because the brat is a beloved nephew of our *dearest* Holy Father, and he has just been made a cardinal. Angelo," Lorenzo said to Poliziano, "why don't you go see how he is progressing?"

The pope's nephew, Raffaele Sansoni, was even now down the hall in the Medici salon, changing into his vestments for his first public appearance at the cathedral.

As Poliziano sauntered out of Giuliano's room, he muttered so we all could hear, "For once I agree with Giuliano."

Lorenzo looked thoughtful. He had been angry at Pope Sixtus's treatment of the family, recently handing the Medici control of the Curia's finances over to the rival Pazzi bank. It was all part of Rome's greater plan, Lorenzo was sure, to take control of the far too independent Florence.

"Things *have* been different since Sforza's assassination," he said, almost to himself. Lorenzo referred to Galeazzo, the much-reviled Duke of Milan, who had been, if not Lorenzo's friend, the strongest of Florence's allies in the north. "Sixtus believes that now with an eight-year-old boy as duke and a female regent governing him, Milan is in total disarray, and Florence therefore weakened."

"You think the pope's spies don't know you are playing both sides of Milan?" Ficino asked.

"What? That I am giving Bona and her young son support at the same time I'm offering friendship to the boy's uncle?" Lorenzo laughed bitterly. "The Vatican spies know *everything*."

I had never busied myself with politics, but Lorenzo had, of late, been consumed with the subterfuge swirling through the courts of Rome, Milan, and Naples, for the downfall or survival of Florence was at stake . . . and the sovereignty of Italy itself. He spoke freely of these matters with all of his close friends.

The boy's uncle of whom Lorenzo spoke was Ludovico Sforza, the most ambitious of Galeazzo's five ambitious brothers. Ludovico, now known by all as *Il Moro*, the Moor, had been sent into exile by the widowed Bona, she fearing that his naked desire to wrest control from her son was greater, by far, than all his uncles' combined.

Had Lorenzo to choose, *Il Moro* would become Milan's next ruler. They were friends, and the man would prove an ally as strong as Galeazzo had been.

"Give Lorenzo a little credit here," Sandro Botticelli insisted. "He knows a thing or two about diplomacy. If he thinks it is a good idea to entertain the pope's nephew—he *is* rather a beautiful boy. . . ."

Giuliano punched Botticelli in the arm, and the artist jostled his friend in such rough play that the bedridden Giuliano groaned in pain.

"Then I say we show him a good time," Botticelli finished.

The door opened and Ficino returned. "He's ready."

Botticelli stepped forward and smiled lasciviously. "I like a man in a red dress."

Everyone laughed and moved to the door. I stayed behind at Giuliano's bedside.

"I'll change your dressing when we get back," I told him.

"Good man, Cato," he said, smiling up at me.

I went to join the others.

Raffaele Sansoni was indeed a handsome young man with the earnest expression of the scholar he had, until recently, been. He'd studied at Lorenzo's new University of Pisa and looked far too young to be wearing the red cardinal's robes and skullcap. We surrounded him now as we made the brisk four-minute walk from the Palazzo Medici to the Duomo, keeping the conversation cheerful, for the boy was clearly nervous about his first official High Mass in the great Cathedral of Florence.

With throngs of worshippers coming from every side, we were nearing the immense front doors when nature called in so urgent a way that I had no time to announce my separation from the group, and slipped into the alleyway beside the Duomo. With the horn I did my business, then leaned back against the wall. I had never lost the distaste I felt for the inside of a church, and now I wondered if I could take my leave unnoticed, later making apologies to Lorenzo. I stayed a few minutes more, ruminating whether my distaste for the institution was stronger than my affection for Lorenzo. He so enjoyed his friends around him at a public occasion.

I decided, with a sigh, to go in, and thus stepped from the alley into the street. My attention was immediately drawn by male laughter coming from Via Larga, the direction from which we had, only moments before, arrived.

It startled me to see Giuliano limping along, flanked by two men, one of whom I recognized as Francesco Pazzi. The other I did not know. They were draped in a friendly way over Giuliano. Pazzi appeared to be tickling him.

Something was vaguely unsettling about the scene. Giuliano should have been in bed, I thought. And Francesco Pazzi seemed far too familiar with him, kin by marriage though he was. I tried quieting the voice inside. My mothering instincts were getting the better of me, I decided. I steeled myself and, turning, stepped through the tall, magnificent doors of the cathedral.

The mass had already begun.

I could see above the hordes of the faithful, standing crushed shoulder to shoulder, that young Cardinal Sansoni had been successfully delivered to his place on the high altar. Lorenzo and his friends were near to the ambulatory at the north end of the choir, quietly respectful of the gaudy ritual being played out before them.

I turned, hoping to see Giuliano enter, and was relieved when he did come in, alone, to take a place at the south end of the choir.

The priest had given the honor of elevating the host to the visiting cardinal. When Raffaele lifted his arms and intoned, *"Hoc est enim corpus meum,"* the sacristy bell began chiming. At that, men doffed their caps, and to the sound of many thousands of rustling garments, the entire congregation of the faithful fell to their knees.

Once again something in me rebelled against the sanctimoniousness of the place, and I hesitated kneeling for the briefest moment. In that very instant I saw from the corner of my eye a tiny flash of light, and turned to look behind me.

I saw Giuliano quite clearly, for he, too, was still upright . . . but the expression on his face was something terrible. A moment later I saw the flash for what it was—sunlight glinting off Francesco Pazzi's sword as it fell through the air above Giuliano de' Medici's head. Other men had descended like a pack of ravenous wolves and were stabbing him again and again.

I shouted "No!" but my voice was drowned amidst shrieks of pain and outrage now coming from the *front* of the choir, near the high altar.

Lorenzo!

I pushed through the chaotic crowd and saw a glimpse of him. The sight was strange to my eye, for his neck was bloodied, and with his cloak wrapped clear round his arm he was fending off dagger blows from a brown-robed priest!

Angelo Poliziano appeared from behind and sank his own blade into the friar's back. Lorenzo drew his sword as Botticelli, Ficino, and other friends surrounded him.

I wished desperately to help him but I found myself pushed back by the panicked masses surging for the cathedral's doors. I glimpsed Francesco Pazzi racing to intercept Lorenzo, who now leapt like a young stag over a painted screen at the choir, heading toward the new sacristy behind the altar. His friends took on the assassins in a frenzied battle that ended, suddenly—the moment they saw Lorenzo safe at the sacristy gate. They ran to join him, leaving several attackers down, and Francesco Pazzi standing blood-soaked and utterly damned in the center of the cathedral floor.

I watched with a soaring heart as Lorenzo and company slammed the gate with a resounding crash that echoed through the high cavernous arches of the Duomo. Then Pazzi was running past me like a wild thing, out the church doors, and I found myself alone.

All but for Giuliano, who lay inert in a pool of thickening gore.

I went slowly forward, knowing that there was nothing to be done for him. I knelt at his side and saw the skull split nearly in two halves, the blue doublet in tatters, the body beneath it like freshly butchered meat. When I tore my eyes away from the sight of him I saw a man hanging incongruously from the ladder of the organ loft.

It was Sandro Botticelli, staring down at the horror that had been wrought upon his beloved family. Even from that height he must have seen that Giuliano was beyond help. Our eyes met, but I had no voice at all. I just stretched my arms beseechingly, though for what I besought I did not know.

Then Botticelli was scrambling down the ladder and disappeared back into the sacristy.

I removed my cape, placing it over my fallen friend. Unarmed as I always was, I stood guard over his poor body should anyone dare come to further desecrate it.

A moment later I saw a pack of men rushing past the open cathedral door. I glimpsed Angelo Poliziano, bringing up the rear, swiveling fearfully to look behind him, before he, too, disappeared from sight.

And there I waited, hour after hour, seeking some sense in this senseless murder, weeping and whispering curses in the house of a vengeful god.

After standing guard over Giuliano's body at the Duomo I had finally come away, leaving the sisters of San Gallo to tenderly remove him. I had arrived at the Palazzo Medici so dazed I hardly saw or felt the mob milling around me. When I came to my senses I saw they were men—from the oldest to the youngest—each of them armed and now surging toward their ruler's home to defend it with their lives.

A rumbling had grown into a roar as Lorenzo stepped out onto his balcony, his red brocaded doublet stained even darker at the left shoulder, a blood-soaked bandage tied around his neck. As he raised his hand the cries grew louder and I heard myself with the others shouting his name as a chant—"Lorenzo! Lorenzo!"

Oh, that he lived!

There was no way to describe the agony that was painted across his features. His posture was upright and proud, but the soul inside that fragile shell must have been sagging and withered. He had lost his brother—"the better half," he used to tell us. He could hardly quiet the crowd, but finally his words rose above their din.

"Citizens of Florence," he began, his voice more strong and steady than I could have imagined it to be. "We have suffered a great loss today. My brother . . ."

Even from a distance I could see his expression crack and fold with the torment of exerting such excruciating control. The crowd was whining and snarling in anticipation of the next words spoken.

". . . Giuliano is dead."

The howls of rage and agony grew to a roar, and the seething mass began to move, outward and away from the Medici balcony.

"No, stay!" Lorenzo shouted from where he stood. "Good people, you must listen to me!" He waited till they quieted and stilled. "I implore you, for the love of God, moderate your actions!"

"The Pazzi are responsible for this!" someone in the crowd shouted back at him. "Will you tell us otherwise!?"

"I will not tell you that. But I can say that magistrates even now have some of the mur . . ." He stumbled at the foul word. ". . . murderers of my brother in their custody. The others are being sought as we speak. Justice will be done!"

"That's right!" a young man cried out, thrusting his sword into the air. "And we'll be the ones doing it!"

The sound of that affirmation was deafening.

"Take care!" Lorenzo's voice was raw with anxiety. "In our frenzy we must not punish the innocent!"

"Giuliano was innocent!" an old man near me raged. "And now he's in pieces on a cold marble slab!!"

"Please, please . . ."

But Lorenzo's words were lost as the crowd began to disperse, though not into four directions. The bulk of them, swords and daggers and clubs raised high, were heading ominously south, in the direction of the Palazzo Pazzi.

Angelo Poliziano had come to the balcony then, and with a gentle hand on Lorenzo's shoulder, drew him inside.

When the crowd had gone—except for a large self-appointed guard that surrounded the palazzo's perimeter—I sought entrance inside to tend to my friend's wounded neck. I knew there would be little I could do for his torn and bleeding spirit.

All was chaotic inside the palazzo, the ground floor thick with family, Medici supporters, Signoria members, and clergy. I climbed the broad stairs to the first floor to find the main salon door open, and went in.

It was a scene of the most ghastly despair. Male friends and relations, many of them shouting, some of them still weeping, stood in small clutches peering nervously out the windows to observe the streets. A larger contingent had gathered around Lorenzo and Lucrezia. I found it horribly ironic to see them all here beneath Pollaiuolo's paintings of Hercules engaged in violence and killing, and wondered if, despite Lorenzo's deeply felt instinct toward peace in his republic, brutality and mayhem were now its only fate.

It was hard looking at Lucrezia, knowing only as a mother could know that unutterable pain of losing so beloved a child, that the very heart of her had been wrenched from her breast. When finally I braved a look I saw the alarming pallor of her cheeks, red-rimmed eyes sunken into dark sockets, mouth a press-lipped slash across her jaw. She had aged immeasurably in a few hours.

Lorenzo, though he tightly clutched her hand, was speaking with great passion to the men who had become, suddenly, his *consiglieres*— Ficino, Landino, Poliziano, Bisticci.

I saw Sandro Botticelli standing, looking altogether helpless, behind them. The agony etched in his features was excruciating. I went and stood beside him.

"Tell me about Lorenzo's wound," was all I could think to say.

"The flesh is sliced clean. No deeper than that." Botticelli's eyes, always sparkling, were dull and dead. "Young Ridolphi insisted on sucking it out, fearing poison on the blade." Sandro looked down at his feet. His voice was raw and ragged. "Oh, Cato . . . Lorenzo knew nothing of Giuliano's murder until we brought him here. No one dared tell him in the cathedral. He thought . . . he thought Giuliano was still in his bed, safe from all harm. When Lorenzo was secured here he told me to bring him his brother." Botticelli covered his face with both hands and choked into them. "It was *I* who told him Giuliano was dead!"

He began sobbing loudly, shoulders heaving. I put my arm around him and brought him into a corner, allowing him to weep like a small boy in his mother's arms.

"Oh God!" he cried.

At this, Lorenzo looked up and for the first time I caught his eye. He held my gaze steadily as the others talked to him of strategy and revenge, till finally he was drawn away by the urgent voices of his counselors.

Finally I was given leave to tend the stitched dagger wound with my medicines. We spoke not at all, Lorenzo staring straight ahead with glazed eyes. Only heaven knew what horrors he was reliving . . . or imagining.

When I finished, my hand lingered on his neck perhaps a moment more than necessary. Before I could remove it he grasped my fingers and held them tight. In that strangely private moment we mourned Giuliano, and Lorenzo thanked me for my ministrations. But I knew I had failed to offer any real comfort, for there was none to be had.

With the others I stayed in the salon throughout that day and night. I offered both Lorenzo and his mother a potion of poppy and valerian to calm them. Lucrezia accepted it gratefully, but he refused it. He needed his wits about him, he told me, and every bit of the furious humors that were coursing through his veins. That way he could act against his enemies, as an arrow shot from a crossbow—powerfully and with a true deadly aim.

In the weeks and months after, when the full extent of the conspiracy became known, the mood of Florence changed forever. Certainly there had been family feuds that had torn the city apart, and many murders. But never had one beloved by so many died such a cruel and premature death.

The conspirators were found to be members and adherents of the widely respected Pazzi family. A Florentine archbishop named Salviati had been revealed as the grand conspirator. For weeks after Giuliano's death, mobs swarmed and rioted in Florentine streets. Every other day one or another of the culprits was caught and taken to the Signoria, where their savage punishments were meted out to cheers and jeers, sometimes laughter. But many grown men sobbed as the wound of their young leader's loss was ripped open again and again.

Worse, we learned that the Holy Father himself had taken part in the assassination plot. Florentines felt such an unfathomable rage at their spiritual master that some eighty men died for the killing of one.

But that was not the last betrayal. Sixtus, infuriated that his conspiracy had failed to bring our city under his control, had taken the diabolical step of condemning Lorenzo and the citizens for daring to hang the "ecclesiastical person" of Archbishop Salviati. Calling Florentines "dogs led to savage madness" he had, unbelievably, excommunicated them, one and all. He'd forbidden that mass be said. No baptisms or burials would be recognized. St. John the Baptist Day—the most sacred and beloved of all Florentine religious festivals—was to be canceled.

There seemed to be no end to the savagery of Rome.

For many months I saw little of Lorenzo, his limpid dream of Florence as "the New Athens" shattered with Giuliano's death and Rome's campaign to crush Tuscany's will. The bullying pope insisted that

Florence "atone for its sins," and Lorenzo was ordered to appear in the Holy City.

All of these edicts were defied.

Don Ferrante of Naples proved an unfaithful ally, too willing to treat with Pope Sixtus against Florence, even sending his Neapolitan armies to join the Roman guard in open battle against Florentine troops.

Then, in a display of diplomatic bravado that stunned even his staunchest admirers, Lorenzo stole away from Florence on a moonless night and laid himself—body and soul—at the mercy of the tyrant in Naples. "This war was begun in the blood of my brother," he had written to the Signoria before he left, "so it may be that by my blood it must be concluded."

His friends were all sick with worry that the evil Don Ferrante would do him harm—imprison or even murder him.

But in the end Lorenzo came home to us—happy, healthy, riding a magnificent gift horse from Don Ferrante—an honorable peace treaty with Naples in hand. The whole population came out in a riot of gratitude to welcome their hero. He had saved them from war. The shouts and trumpet blasts were deafening. Strangers embraced each other in the streets.

It seemed as if all the affection heaped upon the two brothers now fell as an avalanche of love and pride on the one who still lived. From the moment he stepped through the western gate of Florence, my dear friend was ever after hailed as Lorenzo *Il Magnifico*. Even without a crown on his head all the world, it seemed, looked to him as a force to be reckoned with.

And I had never before been so much in love.

*I*t was very late, but I had been inundated with demands for the remedy for a lung fever sweeping our quarter. Though its symptoms were thankfully not plaguelike, still there was terror of the plague, and the first few customers that had used my concoction of feverfew and mallow had seen miraculous relief.

Several days earlier I'd gone to the herbal importers on Via Salvia and emptied their shelves of these dried flowers, then ground masses of them till my wrist hurt and my eyes were bleary. In my laboratory I'd distilled, then calcinated them into a fine powder. Now I was finally folding a few grams into paper envelopes and sealing them with wax. Tomorrow the apothecary would be mobbed with customers clamoring for the medicine.

It was tedious work, this part was, and my mind strayed as it often did to thoughts of Leonardo. It was hard not to worry about my son, for he'd recently left Verrocchio's protective wing and struck out on his own. He had taken himself to live in the bottom two floors of a house on Via da Bardi with little space, and even less good light for painting. Upon beginning his tenancy he'd immediately run afoul of his landlord, when, without permission, he had unceremoniously knocked out the front wall of the ground floor for a window.

Then he'd brought to live and work for him Tommaso di Masini, the bastard son of Lucrezia's brother. Now since the Saltarelli affair he was known as Zoroastre. He seemed a kindred spirit with Leonardo, clothing himself only in linen so he would not, as he said, "wear anything dead" on his body. Even after his public humiliation at the sodomy trial he had never abandoned his black attire and so was believed by many to be a magician of the Occult Arts. Leonardo had no money to pay the young man for grinding his colors and his excellent metalworking skills, but the young man seemed less interested in wages than friendship with another young eccentric man steeped in the dark side of Florence.

Leonardo had become melancholy, and even refused a few small commissions Lorenzo had offered him, insisting nonsensically that this was charity. Instead he accepted a commission that had been arranged by his father—a large painting of *The Adoration of the Magi* for a city convent. There was no cash payment to be made. The whole ridiculous proposition reeked of Piero's disrespect of his eldest son. Still, I expected that Leonardo, once at work, would produce a splendid painting.

I could not have been any more surprised when I visited him at San Donato seven months into his contract to find him reclining lazily in front of the panel near a large pile of logs, staring up at his work and gnawing on a heel of bread.

The painting could hardly be called more than a colorless cartoon, with its charcoal sketched figures—some sixty of them—that included not only the Virgin and baby Jesus in the center, but the three Wise Men, who appeared as ancient wraiths, gaunt and corpselike, and seemed to be groveling at the feet of the unfinished Madonna and child, clawing at them with bony fingers.

When he saw me in the chapel he did not bother to stand, and greeted me with little more than politeness, which, along with the paucity of his work, worried me more than angered me, for I took these to be a measure of his depressed condition.

"What is this pile of wood?" I'd asked, needing a start to the conversation.

"Payment," he told me in monotone, and sniffed sharply. "I painted the monastery's clock. This is how I was paid."

That exchange had been the high point of our conversation. I had reason to worry about my son, but unlike Cato the Apothecary, whose potions alleviated his customers' suffering, I had no way to heal what ailed Leonardo.

I had just finished sealing the hundredth paper packet of the fever powder when I heard a tap on the apothecary window. I looked up to see Lorenzo looking in at me. He wore the strangest expression, one that was quite unrecognizable.

I went around and unlocked the door. He came in, though hesitantly. Since Giuliano's murder he, like Leonardo, had been bedeviled by the deepest melancholy. But Lorenzo was as disciplined as a soldier, trained to quash such emotion. Now I could see pain and discord splashed across the canvas of his features.

I closed the door behind him.

"Come upstairs," I said gently.

In my salon I pulled the front curtains closed, but when I turned back he was right there—inches from me. He was still. Hardly breathing. Yet his presence was large, his scent—musk and rosewater and wool damp with perspiration—made me suddenly lightheaded.

"Cato," he whispered hoarsely.

With all the courage I owned I met his gaze and held there, unflinching. It seemed to unhinge him. His face crumpled. Tears welled in his eyes. Then he grabbed me and clutched me to him. The noise he made was a strangled moan.

"Forgive me," he said. "I cannot, I cannot . . ."

My arms rose to encircle his waist. "Lorenzo . . ."

"I have never *ever* been with a man," he said softly in my ear, "nor do I believe have you."

"My friend . . . ," I began.

"I am your friend, Cato, but I have feelings for you that surpass every form of friendship I have known. Every form of love. I've tried to forget them since you rebuffed me that day in the country. I have lavished affection on my children. Been unerringly kind to my wife and my mother. Funneled all my passion into the Republic of Florence."

He laughed miserably. "I've been going mad, and nothing I do will banish you from my thoughts."

I was shaken body and soul by Lorenzo's remarkable confession.

"You need to come with me, Lorenzo," I finally said.

I pulled out of his embrace. His look was pure confusion. "Just come with me," I said, taking his hand.

I led him up another flight of stairs. We stood then, face-to-face in my bedchamber, mingled love and fear, natural and unnatural yearnings rising in vapors around us like chemical steam in a glass beaker.

He raised his hand to touch me, but I shook my head "no."

Then I lifted my tunic and threw it aside. My shirt was next.

I saw him staring at my linen-bound chest, and without a word I began the unwrapping. His jaw fell open, for he saw at once what I had been hiding, and as the bindings dropped to the floor the look on his face changed from agony to amazement to joy.

My breasts, freed from their long imprisonment, plumped into soft curves. He reached out. Touched them, wonderingly, proving them real.

"My name is Caterina," I said. "Leonardo is my son, and you, Lorenzo . . . I have loved you from the beginning."

He was silent for the longest time, just staring at my face as though seeing it for the first time. Recognizing it.

Then he threw back his head and roared with laughter.

The heaviness in my heart—the cumulus of all the years of secrets and lies—began to lift. Then it was airborne, like a cloud of black smoke from a chimney that rises and finally dissipates into clear air.

I reached out and began to unbutton Lorenzo's doublet. "So have no fear, *Il Magnifico*, we are not sodomites," I said, suppressing my own smile.

He barked another laugh. But then his expression changed. He grew serious. Taking my face in his hands, he drew closer and placed his warm lips over mine.

I think I had waited my whole life for that kiss, so rich with tenderness and celebration, the kiss that pitched suddenly into wanton desire. I felt lost in a flurry of hands clutching, caressing . . . moans of hungry pleasure . . . clothes falling away . . . skin on skin. . . .

We sought the bed and fell back on it together.

"Caterina," he murmured, trying the sound of my name in his mouth. His breath warmed the hollow of my throat. He brushed my nipple with his tongue.

"Aaah, Lorenzo, Lorenzo, so sweet . . ." I lifted his face to mine. The hard lines of pain and loss had already softened. "You are my love," I told him.

He smiled his beautiful smile.

"And you are mine," he said. "You are mine."

Madmen and Holy Relics

I had kept secrets in my life, most of them difficult, painful, or damaging. But the subterfuge of hiding the truth
that Lorenzo de' Medici was my lover was altogether
delicious.

I walked with a new spring in my step and customers asked me
why I was constantly humming. Even Leonardo, who had, since the
Saltarelli trial, worn his misery like a heavy cloak, found his mother
so blatantly cheerful he emerged from the darkness long enough to
inquire as to the reason.

Of course I told no one but him. It delighted my son to an unac-
countable degree, a fact I found baffling. I had in my safekeeping a
growing hoard of his notebooks and folios, all of which he allowed me
to peruse. And from the time I admitted my love affair with Lorenzo,
more and more did I see evidence of Leonardo's obsession with strange
sexuality and even more with hermaphrodites. He filled pages and
pages with them.

That is how he sees me. The half man, half woman was a classic
theme of the occult. It took its name from Hermes, the symbol of the
masculine god, and Aphrodite, the penultimate goddess of femininity.
When joined into one, the creature became a perfect blending of the
male and female persona.

One sketch he called *Pleasure and Pain*, but I saw it differently. The
naked lower torso was male in every way, but the body split into two

figures above—one old and frowning, the other young and limpid. He described them on the page in his left-handed scribble both as men, but the youth was a pretty girl, and the elderly man sprouted one round, womanly breast.

In another drawing he depicted a cross-section of upright coitus. Here the soft-featured feminine figure with long curling hair to midback had a penis stuck erect into her partner, and the partner with a large bulbous breast herself seemed to have a cock as well. *The Witch with a Magic Mirror* was blatant—a male face on the front of the head, a female face on the back.

More disturbing were his drawings of the female genitalia, which, uncharacteristically for Leonardo, were incorrect anatomically, and more than that, strangely grotesque. Lipless vulvas were black, gaping maws, flanked by tight, angry muscles of the groin.

I once chanced to question him, having long before lost all embarrassment as his mother, and he answered me with barely a hint of emotion.

"In general, the woman's desire is opposite a man's. She wishes the size of his cazzo to be as large as possible, while he wishes her parts to be small. So neither ever attains their desire. And do you not think, Mama," he continued with the greatest sincerity, "that genitals are hideously ugly?"

I laughed at that. "I never thought of them that way," I admitted.

"I believe if it were not for the faces and adornments of the actors," he said, "and the impulses sustained . . ."

"You speak of love?" I asked.

"Love. Lust. Whatever you like. Without them and a pretty face I think the human race would die out completely."

"Leonardo!"

"You asked."

"So I did," I agreed.

But I never asked again.

Far from finding any part of Lorenzo ugly or the act of lovemaking futile, I had come completely alive in his arms. He had a strong, well-made body. His legs and buttocks particularly fascinated and delighted me. The muscles were plump and perfectly defined, the smooth skin tawny. His chest was firm under a mat of black hair, his nipples small and quick to answer my insistent nibbling.

Leonardo would have thought it amusing that I found the shaft of Lorenzo's sex a staunch and elegant creature. And that though he lacked a talent for painting or sculpting or working gold into masterpieces, he had truly perfected lovemaking into a fine art.

In my bed, pleasure was his passion. Pleasure in every form and fancy. I'd known pain with Piero, but Lorenzo would never hear of it. Within weeks of our discovery of one another there was not a crevice, a surface, or a sweet spot we lovers had not explored and delighted in. There were French ways and Eastern ways, exotic unguents he provided, and herbal concoctions I had only, for the first time, prepared. We laughed as much as we moaned in ecstasy. We ate meals in bed. Read books in bed. Shared every secret and fear and every wild dream to which we had ever dared aspire.

My male disguise, Lorenzo told me, made him hard. Now, to be in the public presence of "Cato" meant hiding an erect cazzo. He imagined me naked under my tunic and hose. Could barely wait for the moment we would stand in my private chamber and he would untangle me from my linen bindings, reveling in the moment my breasts would spring forth and he could take them into his mouth to worship my long-hidden womanhood.

There were other explorations. My laboratory was our private playground. We would pore over the texts of the *Corpus Hermeticum*, deciding which alchemical experiments might interest us. We would busily gather the materials needed, then with one of us calling out the steps from the book, the other would execute the procedure with flasks and *kerotakis* and burners and descensories. Sometimes the step required more than two hands, so the reader would race from manuscript to workbench and back again for a word or phrase forgotten. There were explosions and failures and unexpected discoveries.

Lorenzo endeared himself further to me with his nearly obsessive stoking of the alchemical furnace. He marveled that I, single-handedly, had kept the thing burning continuously since my coming to Florence. He loved my stories about keeping Papa's fire alight as a young girl, and wept when I told him of the one time, that terrible night in Vinci, when I had let it die out. He would be a slave to the furnace whenever he visited me, he promised. Anything he could do to help me he would do, he said, for I was an inspiration to him.

I, an inspiration to Lorenzo de' Medici, I mused. *How extraordinary.* But then I thought, *I am* four times *blessed.* Il Magnifico's *lover. Privileged mother of a genius. Beloved daughter of a kind and generous father. "Brother" to the finest minds in Florence, perhaps the world.* After a painfully inauspicious beginning, life and all its graces had been bestowed upon me, as treasures are laid at the feet of a great queen.

There was one final jewel held out to me by Lorenzo. One evening as I happily toiled in my laboratory he sat back on a stool, legs stretched out before him, his fine linen shirt white against his olive skin. He spoke my name, as always he did, with the warmest inflection of love.

"Caterina," he said. "Do you recall the night we were all here together, Silio and Pico and Vespasiano working with quicksilver?"

"I do."

"We talked of the Great Work."

"Yes, and we all disagreed what the Great Work was, if I remember correctly."

"I have come across some books in my library," he said slowly, "and some writings by Pico and Silio."

I found a stopping place in the sublimation procedure and gave

Lorenzo my full attention. He spoke slowly, choosing his words with care.

"They all seem to arrive at a similar conclusion. That true alchemy takes place within the confines of the human body. That the act of love is the bridge between heaven and earth. It is the highest sacrament possible, and that only through the sexual act can the soul achieve enlightenment."

"I think most would call those outrageous assertions," I said.

"Most would. Most have not had the opportunity to read *The Erotic Papyrus of Egypt*, either."

"Nor would they dare." I smiled. "What does that appallingly heretical text tell you?"

"That the most sacred ancient Egyptian rites were sexual. But Dante—and who among us questions Dante?—he tells us in *Fidel d'Amore* of achieving intellectual and mystical harmony through sexual love."

"And . . ."

"And our very own Marsilio Ficino writes of 'altered states' where in a climax of all the senses, the soul achieves reunion with the Divine!"

I went and stood between Lorenzo's outstretched thighs. He pulled me to him.

"I have a copy of *Abraham and the Jew*," he said with no little mystery in his voice.

"*Abraham and the Jew*?" I said with an amused smile and, leaning down, gently took his earlobe between my teeth.

"It was the book used by Nicholas Flamel and Perenelle the night they accomplished the Great Work."

"I see." Now I sought a nipple through the thin white shirt. He groaned. "And I suppose you would like for us to strive for the same goal," I said.

"You will be the bride of a god, and I the lover of a goddess." He lifted my tunic and slid my hose down over my hips. "Complete

union . . . ," he whispered breathlessly, "with one's beloved other half."
Then he lowered me onto himself.

"Tomorrow," I told him.

"Tomorrow . . ." His sigh was long and contented. "Tomorrow is
soon enough."

*A*n invitation to the city palazzo had been delivered by a Medici page, who'd been instructed to receive my acceptance then and there. Clearly, declining this request was unacceptable.

As I strode into the central courtyard at the appointed hour I saw, to my surprise, all the members of the Platonic Academy standing in genial clusters waiting to be called to dinner. A moment later the family descended the staircase, Lucrezia on Lorenzo's arm. Clarice and her eldest daughter, Maddalena—not quite a beauty at twelve—Piero, who took the stairs alone looking disdainful and haughty, and the plump thirteen-year-old Giovanni.

Dinner was a genial enough occasion, but the moment the final course was finished, Lorenzo stood and invited his fellow philosophers to repair upstairs to the grand salon. We settled ourselves in comfortable chairs and began talking among ourselves. But when the door opened it was to everyone's surprise to see Lorenzo ushering his mother in before him.

Sandro Botticelli stood and gave Lucrezia his seat. I could see a look of especial delight on the face of Pico Mirandola, whose unpublished manuscript of *The Witch* Lorenzo had recently shown me, a story revolving around an Italian cult presided over by a goddess, and whose theme was feminine power. Silio Ficino seemed similarly delighted by the inclusion of a woman into the hitherto all-male Academy. But really, I thought, it was not altogether strange, for Platonists did, in fact, revere Isis, and Lucrezia de' Medici was the most remarkable woman in Florentine society—a scholar, a poetess, a patron, and mother to *Il Magnifico*. *Why shouldn't she join our ranks?*

Everyone voiced their sincere welcome as Lorenzo stood to face us.

"Tonight we will dispense with all ritual and formality," he began. "There is trouble afoot, my friends, and we must be prepared for it. Of course we are mourning the death of our beloved Pope Sixtus. . . ."

Lorenzo paused briefly to allow for his irony to be acknowledged, then continued. "The election of the new pontiff, Innocent VIII, was sadly out of our control, as Rome has given us no purchase in the last years. How Innocent intends to rule is a mystery, though I believe he could never be more of a threat to us here in Florence than Sixtus was."

Lorenzo opened a parchment and looked down at it, as though to refresh himself of the contents before he spoke again. "I have here a letter from Roderigo Borgia, now a cardinal and high advisor to the Holy Father." Lorenzo smiled to himself. "Roderigo calls our new pope 'a rabbit of a man,' one with few convictions who is easily swayed. But Cardinal Borgia warns us to be on our guard." Lorenzo's voice became very solemn now. "Innocent has endorsed the publication of a German book entitled *Malleus Maleficarum—Hammer of the Witches*."

He handed the letter to his mother, who folded it carefully and placed it in her lap.

"The disastrousness of this endorsement by Rome cannot be overstated. The book has already precipitated a wave of witch burnings in Europe, which will no doubt weave its tentacles south into the Italian peninsula and further enflame Queen Isabella's Spanish Inquisition."

"What can be done?" Pico asked.

"Florentines are the most tolerant people in Europe," said Poliziano. "Milan and Pisa can be counted on for sensible restraint as well."

"We have our printing presses and our booksellers." He nodded to Vespasiano. "We will counteract the madness through the written word and in the universities."

Murmurs of general agreement swept the room, but I was watching Lorenzo's face, and there was yet something troubling him.

"Have any of you heard the sermons of a young Dominican friar who has recently begun to preach in our city? His name is Savonarola."

I looked at Lorenzo disbelievingly. *Was this the same man who had prosecuted Leonardo for sodomy?*

"I've heard him," Landino said. "He's an ugly little gnome—big nose, meaty lips. He is a rousing speaker. I'll admit that. But what he preaches is ridiculous. He is telling the people of Florence to abandon their luxuries—fine clothes, wine, perfumes, ladies' powders and paint. He wants us to abolish carnivals and horse races, gambling and card playing. No one will heed him."

"There's more," Lucrezia said. Everyone turned to listen. I had not seen her this somber since the death of her son. "This man believes he is divinely inspired. He insists that God is speaking through him, telling the people of Italy that the sensual pleasures are destroying their souls. He is calling for the destruction of all 'wanton' works of art. Those of a nonreligious nature, of pagan themes, classical themes—so many of the masterpieces you have created—he is insisting they be destroyed."

"Destroyed?" Botticelli cried. "Destroyed!"

"He's a madman," Ficino said dismissively.

"Prostitutes he calls 'those pieces of meat with eyes,'" Lucrezia told us. "He wants all sodomites burned alive."

I felt a clenching in my guts at those words.

"The people of Florence need to frame a new constitution, this friar tells us, and be governed not by man but by the laws of God alone," she continued. "If Florentines do not mend their ways, they will be dreadfully punished in the fires of hell and damnation. Only a return to the simplicity of the early Christian church can save them."

"I cannot believe the people of Florence will be swayed by such lunacy," Pico said.

"Nor can I," Ficino agreed.

"You must remember one thing," Lucrezia offered in a command-ing voice. Everyone turned to regard her with the deepest respect. "People, even the most rational of them, are fickle creatures. The slightest breeze can sway them. They are driven most volubly by their *fears*. I can see this friar one day stoking their fear of damnation into a great fire."

"But the greater threat at present," Lorenzo said, "is Pope Inno-cent. My mother and wife and I have discussed this at length, and concluded that some sacrifices will have to be made to restore a bal-ance of power with Rome."

"What are you saying, Lorenzo?" Sandro Botticelli demanded, dread suffusing his voice. "Has not this family already sacrificed Giu-liano to the perversions of one wicked pope?"

"These are not outright losses, Sandro. They will bring as many blessings as hardships."

"What is your plan?" Ficino asked Lorenzo.

He sighed. "A betrothal. My daughter, Maddalena, to one of the pope's sons. And Giovanni's appointment to a high office of the church."

"He is only thirteen," Pico Mirandola observed. "What high posi-tion in Rome could you possibly seek for him?"

"Cardinal," Lorenzo said simply.

An uproar of incredulity unsettled the room.

"Listen to me," Lorenzo said, quieting everyone with calm author-ity. "I count Cardinal Roderigo Borgia as a friend. He, in turn, has a close ally in the papal offices—Ludovico Sforza's brother—also a car-dinal, who will help us overcome all obstacles to Giovanni's appoint-ment."

There was quiet and not-so-very-quiet discussion among the members.

"Please, everyone, listen to Lorenzo," Lucrezia begged.

"The Fates have happily cooperated in these endeavors," Lorenzo went on. "I recently received an invitation to travel to Rome to meet with the pontiff and all the European heads of state."

"Is this safe?" Landino demanded to know.

"Cardinal Borgia promises it is. Innocent wishes us to view some sacred relics that have come into his possession. But of course he wishes, above all, for the rulers of the Christian world to come groveling. See him in all his splendor."

"I don't like it," Poliziano said.

"None of us likes it," Ficino insisted. He fixed Lorenzo in his affectionate gaze. "But we all hold Lorenzo in the highest possible esteem. We trust him to do what is best for Florence. What is right." He turned his eyes to the faces of his Platonic brothers. "Do we not?"

"We do!" came the chorus of voices, mine raised louder than anyone's.

"A marriage into the papal family, and a Medici cardinal." Lorenzo smiled with confidence. "Consider it done."

*J*t was to my great surprise and even greater delight to be invited by Lorenzo to accompany him to Rome. "His physician and advisor," he would call me. Physician was true enough. I had begun treating him for the first symptoms of gout that had been plaguing him—occasional soreness in the joints of his thumbs and big toes, a feeling like broken glass grinding inside them, he told me.

By then I was proficient as a horseman, quite enjoying my cushioned saddle, and even attempting a short gallop, if not a race with Lorenzo. But most of all I relished the chance to spend time away from the narrow streets and mountains of cut stone that were Florence. It was a lovely summer journey with my favorite companion south through the green and rolling Italian countryside, with none of our friends or Lorenzo's counselors, and only a small company of *conditores* to guard us along the road.

As for the Great Work, we had—Lorenzo and I—been attempting a spiritual joining in my bed, but the thing always eluded us. Somehow, too much attention was paid to pleasuring each other's bodies for any protracted striving toward a Sacred Initiation, an Alchemical Wedding.

Lorenzo had for months been bringing books to my house from his—those from the East that smelled of patchouli and incense. One that was called *Kama Sutra* showed Indian men and women entwined in sexual postures that, when attempted by the two of us, left us collapsed in a heap, laughing till tears flowed. *The Erotic Papyrus of*

Egypt, translated first into Greek and then into Latin, had, we decided, been transcribed by a prudish monk, for most of the passages that should have provided its readers with actual techniques used by the gods and pharaohs for Oneness with the Universal Divine were either blank spaces or had been rubbed out of the text.

Our one triumph, a joining of intellectual study and physical ecstasy, was discovery of the "rosebud." It was a symbol found in numerous medieval churches and cathedrals. At the tip-top of their doors' archways leading inside—doorways that were shaped very much like vulvas—was carved a rose. That delicate stone flower corresponded perfectly with the small fleshy bud at the pinnacle of every female cleft, that tiny organ of sexual joy—the only part of the human body, a man's or a woman's—whose sole function was pleasure.

It was a mystery. Had the church, the one that preached that women, through their original sin, had brought filth and shame and degeneration into the world, been founded on the principle of female ecstasy?

But the melding of body, intellect, and soul slipped from our grasp again and again. That Lorenzo had brought with him on this journey to Rome his copy of *Abraham and the Jew* became less a means for fulfillment than a source of merriment. And in the evenings, when we had stopped for our rest, *Abraham* remained tucked away in Lorenzo's trunk as we found high pleasure, if not spirit, in each other's arms.

I had never traveled before, save my one-day journey from Vinci to Florence, so Lorenzo delighted in showing me the sights he most loved—like the village of San Gimignano with its hundred tall towers. He said Florence had had many more of these ancient keeps in the past, but had torn them down to make way for modernity. South of Siena cattle grazed in the low rolling hills capped with jagged volcanic rocks.

Most evenings we slept in either flea-bitten inns or the more comfortable tent our guards erected for us. Our one-night stay with the monks in the Abbey of Monte Oliveto Maggiore compared as a luxury.

Finally we were in the countryside north of Rome and traveling the Via Flaminia down toward the city. Here our *conditori* became wary, as the place was notorious for the bandits that regularly terror-ized travelers and pilgrims. But luck was with us and our passage through the campagna was peaceful and uninterrupted.

Lorenzo, however, now began to prepare me for the hellhole that was the "City of God." It was, he said, no more than a tenth of the size it had been in the days of the empire, and what was left were the ruins of that pagan stronghold. It had fallen on hard times since the days of the Great Augustus, when it was accepted as the center of the known world, and not so long since the Catholic church had again made it its home after years in France.

Still, nothing could prepare me for the shock of the place. Having entered from the east we rode back down toward the Tiber through the famed Seven Hills of Rome, these dotted with only the occasional run-down farm.

The streets—anything but the broad avenues described by the Ro-man writers—were hardly more than alleys, and filthy ones at that. The piazzas were no better than garbage heaps, the stench of human excrement and rotting entrails wafting up from them as though they were cesspits.

Small neighborhoods huddled around broken-down churches, and even the larger homes had crumbling walls and heavy gates closed tight. Loggia and stairways jutted into the road, making it nearly im-possible to pass. Most of the people in these places were themselves ragged. Nearly every woman we saw was a prostitute.

Up ahead we saw a vineyard—a sight for sore eyes. But as we rode past I could see, poking up from between the green rows, ruined walls.

"The Palatine," Lorenzo murmured, "or what is left of it."

I remembered this had been a neighborhood of fine palaces in im-perial days. One was Nero's. It was said to have been covered in gold.

"See the cattle grazing?" Lorenzo asked and jutted his chin toward an overgrown field full of sheep and their shepherds. Strangely, pieces of once-towering arches and ruined walls and half-buried columns rose up here and there among them. "The Forum," he said. "Seat of ancient Roman government."

Thankfully Hadrian's Pantheon had been spared ruination, as the Temple of the Gods—a round dome larger even than Brunelleschi's cathedral in Florence—had seven hundred years before been converted into a Christian church.

The Colosseum had not fared so well. The gladiatorial stadium, even in its pitiful condition, I could see rose on a scale so massive it was hardly fathomable. More terrible than the marketplace of farmers, butchers, and fishmongers who hawked their wares between its arches were the masons who mindlessly hacked and hammered at the curved marble walls and the grimy slaves that pushed the pilfered blocks onto carts and carried them away.

"So this is the city from which Clarice looks down upon us?" I said. "From where is bred her snobbery and ostentation?"

"It's hard to believe," Lorenzo agreed. "Poggio always called Rome a wild wasteland." He sighed. "Every time I visit I feel my heart aching for the glory that was lost from here. Imagine what the great men whom we study would think if they could see their beloved home now."

As we approached a bridge over the Tiber, I could see the tall marsh grasses growing on the banks and inhaled the stink of dead fish. Rumbling ominously in front, beside, and behind us were cart after cart of stone quarried from the ancient ruins.

"Where is it all being taken?" I asked. "Who is the thief of antiquity?"

"Our host, of course. Innocent is in a frenzy of building. He's determined to pick up where Pope Nicholas left off with his plans to renew Rome and the church to their former glory. I'm sure he'll speak of it . . . endlessly. What he will never say is that Saint Peter's Basilica—that most hallowed monument—is built on Caligula's killing fields and cemeteries, the graveyard of thousands of butchered Christians. Even now packs of wolves come down from the hills and dig up their bones."

"Very holy," I observed.

Lorenzo smiled.

But all the squalor of the streets evaporated as we crossed the river and entered the Vatican compound. Instead there were clouds of dust stirred by the industry of construction. Virtually every building face was crisscrossed with scaffolding. Huge piles of stolen marble stood waiting for dressing by an army of stonemasons.

The towering doors of the Papal Palace opened. Priests and bishops lined up along its polished marble hall to welcome *Il Magnifico* to the holiest house on earth. I had wished to hang back for that entrance but Lorenzo insisted I stay by his side.

Coming forward to greet us were a pair of red-robed cardinals, their three-cornered birettas on their heads. I saw from the corner of my eye that Lorenzo was smiling with recognition. Our salutations were, by necessity, measured and steeped in ritual, but as the two led us away from the vestibule and up a majestic white marble staircase, its sidewall hung with massive tapestries, the introduction to Roderigo Borgia and his cardinalate brother, Ascanio Sforza, was as natural and friendly as four men meeting in a taverna for a night of wine and women.

"You see those boys there?" Roderigo said, pointing to a pair of youths walking side by side in the first-floor hallway and dressed in rich velvet tunics and jaunty caps. "They are two of Innocent's offspring. We have seen many Holy Fathers become 'Unholy' Fathers, but before this, never one who openly housed his children in the Vatican."

"That speaks well for the man," Lorenzo observed mildly.

Ascanio smiled. "I understand you're adopting Giuliano's son by his mistress."

"Medici blood." It was all Lorenzo had to say—understood by everyone.

We'd come to a fantastically gilt and carven door. Roderigo opened it and showed us in. It was an apartment fit for a king, with two separate sleeping chambers joined by an ornamented salon.

"I'll send in tubs and attendants for your baths," Ascanio Sforza offered, "to get the road grime from your pores."

All at once the pleasure of my surroundings transmogrified into a threat.

"Very kind of you, Cardinal Sforza," I said, hoping to keep my tone calm and even. "But a wash basin will do nicely for me. I've a skin condition that worsens if I soak in a tub. But Lorenzo . . ."

"By all means, send me a tub," he finished for me. "But no attendants. My physician here will see to my needs."

"Very well." Roderigo moved to the door, Ascanio following. "Someone will be sent to fetch you for the evening meal. The Dukes of Savoy and Milan have already arrived. Our rider tells us that Maximilian's cavalcade should be here momentarily. The French king has sent his regrets, along with Edward of England."

"Louis is too old to travel," Ascanio said.

"And Edward of England too fat," said Roderigo. "All that gluttony and debauchery."

With that they were gone. Lorenzo bolted the door behind them and immediately took me in his arms.

"So tell me, physician, what is to be done with this rod that grows stiff between my legs at the first mention of a king's debauchery?"

"I cannot be sure," I said with a lazy smile. "But I would guess it will need examining."

A page came to collect Lorenzo and me as the sun went down over Vatican Hill. I could hardly keep my eyes off my lover, for I had not seen him so resplendent since the day of his wedding festival. He wore black velvet—a doublet trimmed with ermine, the puffed sleeves large and slashed to reveal fine ruffles of cloth of silver silk. And he wore diamonds—fist-sized clasps at both shoulders, in rings on his fingers and a row of them hanging like teardrops from the rim of his black velvet cap.

Lorenzo, in all the years I had known him, had shown nothing but modesty in his dress and manner, but this night he was changed. Bold. Confident. Strutting and peacocklike. *Necessary,* I thought. *Necessary to display his might and his wealth to this new pontiff.*

He'd even urged me to assume less severe garb than a scholar would for this visit, and having had several attractive doublets made for me, took great delight in helping me dress. When I admitted it felt strange for the first time in my life to display my legs in nothing but a pair of hose, he insisted I was "a fine-looking man" in all my parts.

We were shown to a dining hall so massive and so opulently appointed that the Medici garden loggia was a peasant's table in comparison. No ladies had come. And no children were present.

This was a meeting of men who ruled the world.

Maximilian, tall and rangy with the strange pugnacious Hapsburg chin, owned an empire that spread across the entire European continent. His demeanor was the easy grace of one whose noble family bloodline snaked like a river too far back into history to imagine ever finding its source.

Jacque, the Duke of Savoy, had a long oval face, tight red curls and eyebrows so severely arched he looked at all times surprised. The Savoys, too, were an old and powerful family that held the high Alps joining France and Italy in its powerful grip.

The two cardinals, Roderigo and Ascanio, stood to greet us, and when they regained their seats, I saw with a shudder of delight that Ludovico *Il Moro* Sforza, now a solid young man, inhabited a place at the table. It seemed apparent by *Il Moro*'s presence here that his sister-in-law, Bona, had lost her regent's control over the Duchy of Milan.

"Vico!" Lorenzo cried with sincere joy.

The two embraced. Ludovico recalled meeting me in Florence, but even more memorable was Leonardo's fantastical *sacre rappresentazione* at San Spirito and the fire from which we had all escaped with our lives.

"His Holiness," a page announced, and we all stood.

Innocent was tall and, I thought, rather handsome, though I could clearly see that meekness about him that Roderigo had called "rabbitlike." His gaudy robes and jewels were expected, but the way he moved his hands, as though every gesture was an onerous benediction, I found irritating.

One by one we made our obeisance. I was only too aware of my hypocrisy as I knelt and, taking the soft perfumed fingers in my own, kissed the papal ring. I wondered then as Lorenzo did the same if he loathed that necessary act. If he saw in his future an ally, or a murderous enemy as Sixtus had been.

The pope bade us all sit and, clapping his hands twice, began the parade of servants bearing the first course of what I imagined would be many courses—an open pigeon and prune tart smelling of nutmeg.

With Roderigo and Ascanio greasing the wheels, conversation flowed easily. It was plain how deeply Innocent depended upon the counsel of his cardinals. For all his flourishes he barely had an opinion of his own. But the pair of them were clever, and tactful in the extreme. Never once did they stray toward condescension or hubris. And every chance they had, they made much of Lorenzo and his beloved Florence, as well as the beauty of Milan's steadfast alliance with them.

The pope hinted half a dozen times that he hoped Lorenzo would send him some of our city's "excellent artists" for his many projects, but Lorenzo was tactfully evasive about granting that wish, at least until he had made the point for which he had come.

"Queen Isabella's Inquisition that has sent thousands of Jews fleeing from Spain is troubling," Lorenzo said. He fixed Innocent in an intense gaze. "And the witch burnings that are occurring with ever greater frequency since the publication of *Malleus Malificarum* perhaps moreso. These are signs of a coming catastrophe in Europe, Your Holiness."

Innocent began to splutter with anger and confusion. He had never imagined so blatant an attack on the first evening of his entertainments.

"I'm sure Lorenzo meant no offense, Holy Father," Cardinal Sforza offered quickly.

Cardinal Borgia, too, was ready with a soothing balm. "I believe what our friend Lorenzo is saying, Holy Father, is that he dearly wishes that your reign and reputation are never besmirched by such calamitous events as he describes."

I watched as the pontiff's features slowly settled and calmed. "I have no wish to be remembered as a murderer, a persecutor," he said.

"Of course you do not," Lorenzo said, his demeanor softening. "You wish to be remembered as the pope who brought peace and justice to the world. The pope who restored Rome to its former glory. And you *will* . . ." He smiled broadly. ". . . with the help of Florence's greatest artists and architects, whom I will gladly send you."

Now it was Innocent who was smiling, an alarming sight, for the man's teeth were brown and rotten.

But Lorenzo's point had been well made. He had rallied strong support from the two cardinals who controlled the pope. And he had, for the moment, made the Holy Father a happy man.

Perhaps there were other skirmishes to be fought, but this evening had begun successfully.

Next morning the pontiff was all abuzz, hurrying us through the meal and the obligatory tour through his domain. First we viewed the former pope's chapel, the one he had named "Sistine" after himself. I found it very boxlike and uninspiring. Innocent did, indeed, need the talent of Florentine artists to bring him greater glory.

We were then taken in to see the vast basilica in the shape of a cross—the one Innocent desired to rebuild. Now it was simply a thousand-year-old church, a cavernous space with five columned aisles jumbled with chapels and oratories and shrines. Frescoes and mosaics, precious gems inlaid into molded silver and gold. Statues and crypts of various martyrs were buried within its walls.

All of it left me cold, but then when had a church done any more than chill my soul? Innocent, however, waxed effusively of his grandiose schemes. "Pope Nicholas," he intoned, sweeping his ringed fingers in a majestic arc around the cathedral, "wished a reborn Basilica of Saint Peter. A temple so glorious and beautiful that it would seem a divine, rather than a human, creation. Sadly he died before he could see his dream fulfilled. I shall take up that mantle."

He led us to a circular, chest-high wall in the center aisle of the church, where its two arms crossed. "Here," he cried, "here lie the remains of our beloved Simon Peter, upon whose bones the very church was founded!"

I hoped my smile, as the Holy Father gazed at us all, was passably sincere, as my sentiment was wickedly cynical. But what he wished for us most to see were his precious relics. He was like a child with a new toy, gathering us to follow him down some stone stairs to a belowground hallway.

"Behold," Innocent intoned and swept his arm around the small, low-ceilinged chamber illuminated by flickering wall torches. There were three crypts—two of them long and thin, one square and small—all tilted at an angle so that their contents might be easily viewed. "The Sacred Regalia of St. Maurice," he said.

The pope moved to the first long box of polished cedar lined with rich purple velvet. Inside lay what looked like a common lance, though very old, its metal blade as pitted as the wooden handle was shrunken and splintery.

The sight of the weapon that so enthralled the Holy Father left me cold, and though I dared not say as much, I had no knowledge whatsoever of St. Maurice or his importance in the Christian pantheon.

Lorenzo stood with Maximilian and the Duke of Savoy staring down at the other long box. I came to their side.

"What is in here, Lorenzo?" I asked.

"It is the 'Spear of Destiny.'"

Pope Innocent glided up behind us and in the most reverential tone said to me, "It is, my son, the very spear that pierced Christ's side as he hung upon the cross. It makes me weep to look upon it." He sniffed loudly and wiped at his cheek, though it looked very dry to me. "Can you not feel the pain of our Lord? That point of steel, *that very blade* touched the flesh of Jesus Christ. Hastened his death and resurrection, and thus our salvation. But come, there is more to see."

As we repaired to a second chamber in the basement hallway, we were joined by Cardinal Borgia. The Holy Father seemed relieved at having "his brain" attending him.

Inside the second chamber was a single case within which was a smallish piece of yellowed cloth, its reddish-brown markings crudely arranged in the shape of a face.

Before this relic Pope Innocent knelt momentarily before flinging out his arms and extending his legs, then flopping his great belly on the stone floor in complete prostration.

"The Veronica," Roderigo Borgia said in such a cynical tone that we who were standing eyed each other incredulously. "This is the cloth that the good woman of that name used," he continued, "to wipe our Lord's face as he staggered under the weight of the cross on his way to Calvary. Can you not see the imprint of his features?" The cardinal gestured with two fingers for the rest of us to join the pope in his full prostration.

There was nothing to be done but obey. I knew that Lorenzo felt as ridiculous as I did, but we managed to keep straight faces as the pope droned a benediction into the floor.

The showing over, we were all invited by the pontiff to stroll through his private garden. Lorenzo and I were only too happy to oblige, sincerely awed by the rare and exotic flowers and trees that had been collected from the four corners of the known world for Innocent's personal enjoyment.

We had bent down to sniff the fragrance of an African striped fuchsia when the Duke of Savoy sidled up behind us. He spoke quietly.

"Did the Veronica impress you?" he said.

Lorenzo and I stood facing the man and closed our ranks for privacy. "The truth?" Lorenzo asked.

"What else, my lord?"

"Not only a fake, but a pathetic one at that. Perhaps I'm spoiled by the artisans of Florence, but I know a dozen who could have executed a much better one."

Roderigo Borgia had made his way toward the three of us.

The Duke of Savoy stepped aside and allowed him into our discreet circle. "The Shroud of Lirey has been in our family for one hundred years," he said.

"A shroud?" I asked. "What is the nature of this shroud?"

Savoy lowered his voice to a whisper. "The full-length winding cloth of Jesus with his image divinely imprinted on it."

The rest of us were silent, quietly urging the duke to continue.

"Its authenticity cannot be disputed. Thousands of pilgrims and clergy in hundreds of showings have seen it and accepted its veracity."

"Hundreds of showings?" Cardinal Borgia said. "Imagine the small fortune the Savoys have enjoyed from a single holy relic in their possession."

The duke seemed offended by such a suggestion. "The Lirey Shroud has not been seen in public for twenty-five years." The timbre of his voice became even more shrill.

"Why is that?" Lorenzo wanted to know.

Savoy bristled, appearing besieged by the questioning. "I cannot say why. But I believe our family's fortune is sufficient enough so that profiting from a holy relic is not our concern." He glared at Cardinal Borgia. "And I think, Roderigo, that you should perhaps examine your own Christian faith. Cynicism seems to be your guiding principle these days." With that he nodded politely to us all and moved away to view a butterfly-covered shrub.

"A full-length shroud. Curious," Lorenzo observed.

"Unseen for twenty-five years. More curious still," said Roderigo. "I happen to know the Savoys are, in fact, in dire need of money."

I regarded Cardinal Borgia with interest. His support of Lorenzo was intriguing. *But,* I wondered, *was it sincere?*

The answer came that evening at the dinner table, where all of us had again gathered. From the time we had been seated I had had the eerie sensation that one does in the still moment before a lightning strike.

The Emperor Maximilian rose and lifted his goblet. His tone was gracious and proud. "I am delighted to announce a betrothal—my own—to Bianca Sforza of Savoy." Certainly expecting this, the Duke of Savoy stood and lifted his glass as well.

"To my niece," Ludovico *Il Moro* proclaimed with a smile, and stood to join the others.

Now Lorenzo and I followed, as did Cardinals Sforza and Borgia.

The pope, with a show of self-important pomposity, remained seated but nodded his approval, then raised a pontifical hand in the direction of Maximilian and Savoy, and bestowed a long Latin prayer. The man was clearly enamored of his own benedictory repertoire.

Once everyone was seated again Savoy clapped his hands and a servant brought forward a small framed portrait. "Bianca is still a girl. Not yet ready to marry," he said, passing the painting around, "but once she is, it will cement an alliance between the great houses of Savoy and Hapsburg."

I chanced a peek at Maximilian, who tried unsuccessfully to stifle a sour look at the allusion of equal footing between the two families. The Hapsburg dynasty was a vast empire by anyone's standards, the Savoys a respected but limited regional duchy.

At that moment the portrait of Bianca reached us. I held it and Lorenzo and I gazed down at the youthful face, pretty enough, with graceful hands. I was startled by what I was seeing and knew that Lorenzo had seen what had caught my eye. Though in her fingers the Sforza girl held a flower—as was typical in portraits—there, just above her wrist, was a symbol embroidered into her sleeve. *A symbol that was as out of place on a Christian duchess's gown as a wing would be on a cat.*

Then Lorenzo took it from me and, passing it to Ascanio Sforza, stood.

He was always so tactful, so diplomatic, and I wondered at the timing of his announcement. It would certainly eclipse Maximilian's betrothal to Bianca of Savoy. It must be his express purpose, I thought. Another show of Florentine strength.

"I wish to propose another marriage," Lorenzo said, sweeping his eyes around the table, allowing the anticipation to build. When his gaze stopped and fixed on Innocent, the Holy Father sat back in his chair with curious anticipation.

"I wish to propose to you, Your Grace, the hand of my eldest daughter, Maddalena, to your son, Cibo."

The man looked stunned, I thought. *The pope's bastard son marrying into so illustrious a family as the Medici.*

With both hands Innocent beckoned his cardinals to his ears. The whispering went on for what seemed an eternity. Finally he waved them away. He sat silently, for as long a moment as he could manage before blurting, "I accept!" Then he graced us with his great rotten-toothed smile, and everyone raised their glasses with loud *"Salutes!"* Some of these exclamations, I noticed, seemed more sincere than others.

Roderigo Borgia stood. He was imposing with his steely gaze and thin-lipped smile. "We of the church are deeply grateful for the long and faithful friendship of the Medici family. And now it is time to reward them for their service."

There was nervous shifting in the chairs around me. I did not dare meet anyone's gaze.

"I hereby nominate Giovanni de Lorenzo de' Medici to the cardinalate!"

There was, for a brief moment, dead silence in the room. Then a commotion of voices.

"He is only thirteen!" Maximilian cried.

"Far too young," the Duke of Savoy added, barely controlling his anger.

"I second the nomination."

All eyes fell on Cardinal Ascanio Sforza, whose face was stern and impassive.

Pope Innocent was looking from one to the other of his cardinals. Their nomination was preposterous. And yet . . .

"Thank you, Your Graces, for your vote of confidence for my studious and deeply pious son," Lorenzo said. "A boy who has, since his youngest days, desired nothing more than a life of religious devotion."

My Lorenzo, my perfect lover, I suddenly realized, *is a blatant power broker, a political creature—one agreeable to familial sacrifices, even deception to further his broader objectives.*

The pope squirmed in his chair. "Giovanni is too young in years to wear the cardinal's hat," he objected, lacking all conviction.

There were murmurs of agreement from Maximilian and Savoy, though Ludovico Sforza remained still, his gaze impenetrable.

Though his eyes stared straight ahead, I could see the pope absorbing the approbation of his cardinals on either side of him. "But if he will go and study Canon Law at the University of Pisa," Innocent continued, "three years hence he will be welcomed to Rome and be seated amongst his brothers in Christ." The pope put his hands together and lowered his head.

Each and every man, whatever his opinion, now bowed to the will and word of the Holy Father. It was done. Giovanni de' Medici in three years' time would become the youngest cardinal in the history of the Catholic church.

"Lorenzo," I began as we undressed together in his sleeping chamber.

"Yes, my love."

"Before he started for home, my father sent me another chest of treasures." I was quiet as I unlaced the back of his doublet.

"I assume you're going to tell me what was in it."

"Aside from the usual, there was a small wooden box, and inside were sticky black balls the size of a fingertip."

"Poppy?"

"In his letter he told me this resin was from the *cannabis* plant. Hemp. In the East, rope is made from its fibers. But in this form it is called *hashish*."

"What does one do with *hashish*?" Lorenzo asked. Down to his shirt and stockings, he lay back on the canopied bed, nestled amidst silk coverlets and feather-stuffed cushions.

"Well, prepared in myrrh and wine, it is used as an anesthetic."

"Do you think it would help my gout?"

"It might," I said. "But it is also a . . . euphoriant."

"A euphoriant?" Intrigued, he propped himself up against the gilded headboard.

"Itinerant monks in India use it quite habitually. They claim it causes visions, wild dreamings. It gives them limitless powers of divination. Scythians used to gather in a tent around a pile of red-hot stones and throw the hemp seeds on it. Herodotus said the vapors transported them into paroxysms of joy."

Lorenzo smiled. "I hope you brought some of these sticky balls with you."

"No," I said, and watched his features deflate. Then I turned away. "My father said I should bake the resin into some confections, with honey, for the stuff tastes very bitter." When I turned back to him I wore a mischievous grin and held a small dark cake in one hand.

"Caterina, you devil!" He grabbed me and pulled me down on the bed.

I broke the thing in two and handed him a piece.

"We eat this as a sacrament," I said, becoming serious.

"Should we pray?"

"Perhaps so."

"But to whom?" Lorenzo asked with the innocence of a child.

I thought a moment. "To all the gods of Nature," I said.

He laughed. "Very pagan for the holiest house in Christendom."

"My father said that in India, many believe Jesus lived there for a time," I whispered, even knowing no one could hear me. "They say he is buried there. In a tomb. My father saw it."

Lorenzo, free of mind as he was, appeared shocked at such a notion. He took a deep breath. "To all the gods of Nature, and Philosophy and everything that is divine in man"—he smiled warmly at me—"and woman."

He placed the cake in his mouth and I did the same.

"It is slow-acting when eaten," I said.

"Have we time to make love before the visions come?" he asked.

"I don't know." I bent over and whispered in his ear, "Perhaps the visions will come *while* we're making love."

"What would your father say to this?" Lorenzo said as he laid his hand over my breast.

"That he wished he had had a *hashish* cake to share with my mother."

He kissed me and we began the sweetest, most unrushed of all the joinings we had ever known. Every movement was soft, tender. The touch of our hands and fingertips light and glancing. Limbs glided over limbs as if oiled. Strange, how desire rose so slowly in us both. No urgency pressed us forward. Kisses were long and lazy, peppered with swift darts of the tongue and tiny bites. Our mouths pressed lightly together, the only movement the breath from our nostrils a warm even flow across our lips.

Time stilled. No sight or sound outside our bodies existed. We floated on a warm cushion lighter than air. When finally he entered me it was slippery and luxuriant. I think that with our senses in such a state of exultation we had forgotten the intoxicant we'd taken, and it was only when I watched Lorenzo, in the simplest of movements, bring his hand to my cheek, that I saw the world had altogether changed.

The arc of his movement had slowed to such a degree, and the shape and color of his fingers had grown so defined in my vision, I was instantly obsessed with them. I took his hand in mine and held it before my eyes. There on its back was a whole *landscape*—myriad crevices, bony ridgelines, a forest of fine black hairs. Veins like riverbeds in which suddenly I saw running blue floods beneath the skin. I looked at his face and found it wonderstruck. He opened his mouth to speak, to tell me what he saw, but he was speechless.

Then all confinements of the flesh seemed to fall away, the form of my body lost in limitless sensation.

We came slowly apart so we could lie on our backs and stare up at the chamber ceiling, a glory of painted cherubs in the clouds—all blues and pinks and purples and greens. But the colors were nothing we had ever seen before—they glowed and glittered like sun-struck sapphires and amethysts and emeralds and rubies. And they were moving, the cherubs were *moving*! I could swear I heard their laughter as they darted in and out from between the clouds.

When I turned to Lorenzo this time I found he had risen from the bed, naked, and was standing stock-still, gazing at a wall torch. Moving was difficult—my limbs were heavy and lumbering, and every bare footfall on the carpet felt ponderous and important.

But now at his side I saw what he saw. The flame was more than a globule of dancing luminosity. It was fluid gold, and its movement a sinuous, frenzied dance.

We drifted helplessly in a sea of radiant light and all the color born of light. Fragments of images flew at us and receded, as did a confusion of sounds like angels singing from a long way off. Speech was impossible. Broken words and groans and sighs were all we could manage.

We slowly came into each other's arms, and like an answered prayer we melted one into the other. Melded mercury and sulfur. Alchemical eros. Our breath was the hissing of molten rock, our hearts pounding in one single rhythm. In the moment we climaxed together we were convulsing volcanoes. Great waves crashing. Stars exploding in the blackness of the heavens.

At dawn we found ourselves lying across the bed, sunlight streaming across our mellowed flesh. We had never slept, but it felt as if all Lorenzo's strength had flowed into me as, I imagined, mine had into him. I turned my head and found him gazing at me, a look of boundless triumph in his eyes.

"So that is what they mean," I said.

He nodded and smiled with perfect rapture. "I think it is. I think that is what they mean."

The rest of the visit was wholly uncomfortable, for our blissful state did never entirely recede from us. We knew we'd profaned the sanctity of Christ's bastion with our pagan and appallingly heretical rites.

So Lorenzo and I kept our distance from one another and hardly dared to meet each other's eyes.

But much good had come from our journey to Rome. Roderigo Borgia's and Ascanio Sforza's enthusiastic forwarding of Lorenzo's interests reaped handsome rewards. While Innocent would not retract his endorsement of *Malleus Malificarum*, he did finally agree to soften the church's stance on the persecution of witches. More important, the cardinals' incessant whispering in the Holy Father's ear proved such a potent bridge to trusting Lorenzo that all the Curia business dealings thereafter would, it was announced, be directed to the Medici Bank.

As we mounted our horses for the journey home, Roderigo Borgia came to bid us farewell. He and Lorenzo embraced heartily.

"Good-bye, my friend," Lorenzo said. "You have done me countless honors."

The cardinal smiled. "I've heard it whispered in these halls that now the pope sleeps with the eyes of Lorenzo the Magnificent."

Lorenzo swung up into his saddle and spoke to Roderigo. "May his confidence ever be well founded." As we rode away side by side he turned and said to me, "Oh, that Innocent had seen what *I* had through those eyes."

"It would be a different world," I said.

*L*ife in Florence resumed in a normal state for a brief time. Lorenzo worried himself endlessly on his decision of when and how to tell our brothers in the Platonic Academy of the shattering initiation he and I had experienced under the Vatican's roof. There were still members intent on reconciling our esoteric beliefs with the Holy Scripture, and there were few, if any, who would openly blaspheme the Catholic church.

"But is not the illumination we shared in Rome the very enlightenment we Platonists have been seeking all along?" Lorenzo demanded with rhetorical fervor again and again. "Incontrovertible proof of our own divine nature?"

"It is, Lorenzo. Without a doubt it is. But you understand these men better than I. Only you know whether they can make peace with the truth."

"How do you define that truth?" he would ask me with the intensity of an inquisitor.

"That neither prayer nor study nor meditation can so readily bring us into the presence of the Divine as ingesting a bit of sticky black resin from India."

"Uugh!" he would cry and pound his fist on the wall.

While Lorenzo argued with himself, I quietly baked the *hashish* into small cakes and invited Leonardo to my home for a quiet dinner, just the two of us.

I explained the substance that his grandfather had sent me and then

I bade him eat the confection, though I did not partake. Watching his expressions—the gape-mouthed gasps of wonder and delight, the fleeting moments of fear, his spontaneous singing and laughter, and tears of grateful understanding of nature's mysteries finally unveiled before his eyes—these were as gifts to me.

He would later insist that besides life itself, the *cannabis* cake was the finest gift I had ever given him. And he begged me for all I could spare, for since that first initiation, he said, the visions and dreams had exploded, and now ideas and designs, colors and shapes and perspectives were running riot in his brain.

"Even more intensely than before?" I asked incredulously.

"If it is possible," he said with a laugh.

"I hope one day soon your grandfather comes back from his travels so you can tell him how well his gifts have been used."

"It doesn't sound like he has any intention of returning, what with the new wife and another adventure every day."

Indeed, Papa had married, and his happy though infrequent letters had come from every corner of India.

"Maybe we shall visit him there," I suggested kiddingly.

"When do we leave?" Leonardo said.

It was market day, and needing a few things for my kitchen, I headed up Via Larga toward the Mercato Vecchio. I always enjoyed strolling past the Palazzo Medici, whether I was an invited guest or not. But as I strolled past the doors of the Monastery of San Marco, I stopped. It being Wednesday I was surprised to see a crowd spilling out the doors of the chapel. *What could be happening on a Wednesday?* I wondered.

I went inside.

I had never seen the place so full, nor had the audience ever been so silent. But a sound was filling the place—the sound of one man's voice.

It was the voice of doom.

From so far back he could hardly be seen, he was just a dark figure punching the air with his arms, but the shrill voice was familiar, and the words were loud and clear.

The preacher was Fra Savonarola.

"Ye women who glory in your ornaments, your hair, your hands, I tell you, you are all ugly. The ancient literature and art your humanist husbands hold so dear are pagan! Those authors are strangers to Christ and the Christian Virtues and their art is an idolatry of heathen gods, a shameless display of naked women and men! I hold in my right hand the sword of the Lord!" he cried in a hard, high-pitched voice. "People of Florence, I tell you now and will tell you again and again that by your evil ways do you risk the black cross of God's almighty anger!"

I left shaking my head, incredulous that so many were flocking to listen to such nonsense from a mad young monk. Lucrezia's warnings about the dangers he posed seemed impossibly exaggerated. Since our visit to Rome Maddalena and Cibo had wed, and Giovanni had begun the three-year study in Pisa that would guarantee his cardinal's hat. The Medici ties to the Vatican were secure.

Savonarola was quickly forgotten as I reached my shop and home.

Many nights our Platonic friends would gather in my third-floor laboratory, as much for conversation as for alchemical experiments. Lorenzo and I had not yet revealed our experience with the resin cakes, and neither had we repeated our explorations into the Divine. He and I did, in the privacy of my home, experiment with remedies for his gout, which, despite my ministrations, was worsening. Never had I known a man to suffer pain with such dignity and good humor. I only grew to love him more.

My age was beginning to show. My breasts lost their roundness and succumbed to gravity. Lines appeared at the corners of my mouth and eyes, and the face that peered back at me from the looking glass seemed someone else's—not my own.

Il Magnifico, meanwhile, was rising to the height of his diplomatic powers. European rulers sought Lorenzo's advice. Turkish potentates sent him lavish gifts. And Roderigo Borgia kept his word, insuring that the Medici Bank in Rome oversaw the Curia's substantial financial interests. Friends and rivals alike called Lorenzo de' Medici the "needle of the Italian compass," and all believed it was his repeated interventions that kept peace on the peninsula.

Even Florence had regained some of its joy after Giuliano's murder.

Too, life was good in our circle of family and friends. My days were happily filled with family pleasures and dispensing healing remedies to grateful neighbors. Nights were for Lorenzo, studying, exploring, and making gentle love in the comfort of his arms. For the Platonic Academy there were heavenly weekends spent at Careggi's Thinkery and sessions in my alchemical laboratory debating and experimenting with the best path to Divine Enlightenment.

It was beginning to feel, again, as though all was well in the world.

*T*ra Savonarola had continued his sermons, preaching of hell and damnation, but they were clearly the rants of a madman, one of whom the fickle citizenry would certainly tire. And there was gossip—unfounded and impossible to believe—that gangs of white-robed boys calling themselves "angels" were roaming neighborhoods, knocking on doors and relieving Florentines of their luxuries—books and tapestries, wine, and all profane paintings and sculpture.

But these were nothing but preposterous rumors.

One late afternoon I visited Leonardo at his studio, bringing with me a savory vegetable pie and quantities of herbs that he had requested to make dyes—elder leaf for green, mignonette for yellow, and woad for blue. They were needed for the commission he had received to costume the entire Rucellai family for this year's Carnivale. They would be arrayed as the whole pantheon of Greek gods and goddesses, complete with fabulously hued robes and gowns, masks, shoes, shields, gold and silver crowns and scepters.

But when I arrived at the bottega, sun streaming in through the huge front window where Leonardo had knocked out the wall, I found he and Zoroastre—through whose Rucellai family connection they had received the commission—busily at work on costumes of far less frivolity and gaudy colors.

"What is this?" I asked Leonardo of the subdued gray textile sleeve he was sewing. "What's happened to the gods?"

"I suppose they've absconded to Mount Olympus," he said lightly and unperturbed.

"My father changed his mind," Zoroastre said, looking quite disgusted. "He's requested a more biblical theme for Carnivale. Moses and Rebecca and all the silly 'begots.'"

I very much liked Zoroastre, who my son proclaimed was a rare combination of good-natured charm and dark mystery. He never whined or complained no matter how shaky their circumstances. I sensed the young man harbored a passion for alchemy, but he was sensible enough to realize such interests must be hidden from public scrutiny.

"Our old friend Savonarola is finding more and more religious consciences to prick," he said.

"How this time?" I asked.

"You know that flood on the Arno several weeks ago?"

"A horrible tragedy," I said, remembering the stories I'd heard.

"Well, it wasn't simply a freak deluge upriver from the city that swept a dozen children and some nuns to their deaths. . . ."

Leonardo finished for him. "It was God's punishment for the sinful extravagances of Florence. That 'He' would take children—orphans no less—and the Brides of Jesus was a sure sign of an anger so terrible that 'He' drowned even these innocents."

"'The guilty sinners of the city must hold *themselves* accountable,'" Zoroastre added. "That's what my father heard the friar say in Sunday's sermon."

"That's preposterous!" I cried.

"Worse," Leonardo said, "it was an orphanage supported by the Medici, so Lorenzo was, of course, personally to blame."

"You'd think Florentines were too smart to believe such rubbish," Zoroastre complained. "My own father! But no." He held up the shapeless gray robe he was stitching. "From Jove to Jehosephat."

I just shook my head, refusing to dwell on such idiocy, and went wandering about the studio—a smaller version of Verrocchio's bottega, yet no less fantastical—to see the current commissions in their various stages of completion. A tombstone carved with angels; a gilt and prettily painted bedstead awaiting attachment of its scalloped blue velvet canopy; a pair of small bronze satyrs mounted atop marble pedestals.

"Look at what I'm doing for Lorenzo's library," Leonardo called to me. "Just behind you."

I turned and found a smallish wooden panel painted with a scene from antiquity. Amidst Greek columns and cornices and Cyprus trees sat a white-robed older man, and a young man at his knee. I knew without asking that they must be Plato and his beloved teacher, Socrates. Their faces, as was the custom, were those of the patron's family members. In this case, Cosimo de' Medici as Socrates, Lorenzo as Plato.

"He will love this, Leonardo."

"Do you really think so?" he asked almost pleadingly.

It never failed to amaze me how much approbation a man of so much genius continued to require. "I'm sure of it. And what an honor to have a place in the library. It is his most beloved room in the palace." Then my eyes fell on the bottega walls around the panel. They were tacked up with dozens of sketches—a subject to which I was no stranger, though I found them still somewhat shocking.

They were human dissections. Limbs, skinned faces, skeletal spines, male genitals. Here was an elderly man, there a little girl.

"Nephew," I said, beckoning him to me. "Is this wise? Your studio is a public place." I spoke more quietly. "Let me take them home and put them with the others."

He fixed me with a rare annoyed glare. "I'm tired of hiding who I am. This is what my mind has wrought in studying Nature." He gazed at the panel for Lorenzo's library. "Socrates spoke the truth of Nature. Is he so hateful a model to emulate?"

"Of course he isn't," I answered, failing to add what we both knew had been Socrates's tragic punishment for truth telling. I whispered now. "That is enough from your nagging mother. Why don't we eat our supper?"

The streets were quiet as I walked home. I thought about Leonardo. He was, more than any of us in the Academy, a profane and heretical man. My son was the epitome of all that the church feared most. More than the stylish clothes and ornaments that every Florentine affected, it was his secretest thoughts and his strange behaviors that set him most dangerously apart—his blatant refusal to hear the mass or take communion, his human dissections, his love of men as well as women, even his refusal to eat the flesh of animals.

He enjoyed proclaiming on every Good Friday that "All the world is mourning today because one man died in the Orient," and that he would rather be a philosopher than a Christian. He was obsessed and spoke loudly and openly about freedom of the mind, freedom from tyranny and repression, the freedom of flight. He had, of late, become famous in the Mercato Vecchio for strolling amidst the stalls, till he came to the place where a merchant sold caged songbirds.

He would inquire of the cost for the lot of them, and whatever the price, he would pay the seller. Then one by one he would hold the tiny wooden cages to his chest and open their doors. They shot from their confines like tiny-feathered cannonballs, disappearing in seconds. Others—and he wept when he described these creatures—were dead and stiff in their cage bottoms. They had not been sick birds, he insisted. Their souls had simply succumbed to the torture of imprisonment, and only then had their bodies given up life. I could see the pain in his eyes, the terrible memory of how close he had come to losing his own freedom—a fate much worse than death.

The sound of voices roused me from my thoughts, and up ahead I saw a flash of white disappear behind the corner house. I cursed myself for inattention to my surroundings with all the strange rumors about, true or not. I looked and saw that many more windows were shuttered, the streets more deserted than usual. Yet something, now that my awareness was piqued, was clearly and ominously afoot.

When I turned the corner I saw at the door of a fine house a dozen barefoot boys in white robes tied at the waist with rope. They were carting out the front door a pile of women's silk gowns, a fine painting, and a box of cosmetics, all the while singing "Hosannas." I froze where I stood, staring at the scene quite disbelievingly. Then the "leader"—a pimply faced lad of sixteen—came out the door with a husband and wife in their nightgowns. In the boys' frantic looting a silver-framed looking glass fell from the box and broke on the street. One angel picked up a stone and in a frenzy smashed it again and again till it was nothing but tiny shards.

I could not fathom the expression on the faces of the man and woman at the door, for they stood watching the pillage of their lives without rage, or even resignation. They were nodding their heads in acceptance and then, to my horror, the wife began singing hymns along with the boys! As the ruffians left I heard the husband shout after them, "God bless!" The leader yelled back, "You are Godly citizens! You will be spared from the fires of hell!"

I found myself staring not at the devilish boy brigade disappearing down the long street but at the couple, who, with sincerely beatific smiles on their faces, turned and reentered their house, shutting the door behind them.

That is when I heard it. A woman, screaming.

I froze where I stood, but the scream became a woeful wail and then pitiful sobbing. I hesitated a moment longer, knowing in some part of me that a dreadful future lay ahead with that wailing woman. But the future was inevitable. It must be faced. There was simply nowhere to hide from it.

Around the corner I came upon the frightful scene. That same band of Savonarola's white-robed angels were kicking and beating the still figure of a man lying on the cobbled street. Other boys restrained a woman. One of her hands outstretched to the man, trying to go to his aid. With her other hand she attempted to cover her exposed bosom. Yet another child with a gold braided headband, an obscene excuse for a halo, taunted her with a panel of lace that I recognized as the frontpiece of her gown—something they had certainly ripped from it moments before.

I rushed forward and heard the boys now, chanting to the woman,

"Harlot, filthy harlot!" and she pleading, "Let me help my husband!" To my horror I saw a pool of blood widening around the man's head—his skull must have cracked upon the cobblestone pavement.

So intent was the vicious gang on its prey that I was kneeling at the man's head in the midst of them before they even noticed me. He had a terrible wound at his temple.

"What's this!" a boy screeched at me. "Who do you think you are?"

"I can help this man," I said, trying to stay calm as I felt the threatening crush of bodies around me—perspiring young flesh and a brush of white cotton on my cheek.

"What business have you on the street at this ungodly hour!" one of the youths shouted at me.

Blood and ire rushed to my head and I spoke as I felt, without fear but much fury. "I have every right to walk in Florence at any hour I please. It is you, filthy devils, who've no right to injure a man and harass a helpless woman!" I was gently turning the poor victim's head, which appeared to be cocked at an unnatural angle. "Now move back, and if there's one among you with a shred of decency, you will help me take this man to my shop, where I can help him."

The boys went quiet suddenly, and all I could hear was the terrified woman's sobs.

One of the boys hovering over my head ventured meekly, "Where is your shop?"

"On Via Riccardi. It is an apothecary."

"Apothecary!" I heard another angel cry, and suddenly felt a stinging blow at the back of my head. Outraged, I turned finally to look up. It was the pimply faced leader. A fist flew, and knuckles met the bones of my cheek. I fell backward, stunned though not insensible.

"You're nothing but a sorcerer!" he shouted at me, then hauled off and kicked me in the side.

I could hear the woman groaning with despair.

"We'll take this one in," the ruffian announced. Then he grabbed the lace panel from the smaller boy who held it, and dipping it in the comatose man's blood, smeared the woman's face and bare breasts with it.

"May God forgive you for your sins," he hissed at her, gesturing for his friends to lift me up and follow him. He marched ahead of them singing the *Te Deum* as I was hauled, by the hellish angels, struggling and terrified, to a dark and uncertain destiny.

There was a morbid irony that my place of incarceration was the same as Leonardo's had been for his sodomy arrest. The Office of the Night had been appropriated by the new and even more vicious religious authority in the city—Fra Savonarola and his minions. Where before in the receiving chamber for vice offenders had sat two friars behind a table with at least a pretense of dignity, now there was nothing but row upon row of crude benches filled with dazed and bloodied "sinners." Lining the walls were more of the appalling angels standing at attention. The air reeked of fear and desperation, and as my captors pushed me down on a bench and told me to keep my mouth shut, I heard shrieks of pain from beyond the door where I knew the prison cages to be.

They were torturing people, I suddenly understood. This was far worse than anything I could have imagined. Not simply a rounding up of luxuries to be burned for proving a purer devotion to Jesus.

The Inquisition I thought only in Spain had found its way to Florence.

The gossip about Savonarola we had believed to be preposterous had been true. How blind and foolish and soft we had all allowed ourselves to become! It was not that we'd forgotten the friar. We had simply and dangerously underestimated him. With our heads and shoulders in the clouds, our minds grasping for the stars, we altogether failed to see that Florence had begun smoldering at our feet.

I'd hoped that having been brought in last to a full room of the accused would have given me time to formulate a defense of sorts, but within moments I heard a gravelly voice call out, "Bring the Apothecary!"

I was hauled to my feet and pushed through the doorway and down the corridor, through that second metal door and into the prison hall.

With a shove I found myself sharing a cage with three other men and a woman. Unlike the prostitutes I had last seen in these cages, this was a cultured lady in an elegant velvet gown, with a gentleman I suspected was her husband. She sat on a bench staring and dead-eyed. Patting her hand in distracted consolation, the man himself appeared as a victim of rough handling.

Two other prisoners sat with glazed expressions on the cell floor. As I sat down next to the beaten man he said without prompting, "All we did was object to their taking a masterpiece from our home. The boys, those terrible thugs, they began to rip hangings from our walls, smash our Venetian glass."

The two others were silent. Never did the sound of torturing cease, only quieting briefly before reaching a new crescendo of agony.

No matter how I tried, I failed to direct my mind into any semblance of order. All I knew was that I would in no way draw Lorenzo into this horror. All his strength would be needed to hold Florence together in the coming years. Thoughts of how it would be when they discovered I was a woman disguised as a man came to me often, though I refused to dwell on them, too dreadful to contemplate.

And so when a jailor came flinging open the door and calling, "Apothecary!" I stood to meet my fate with no more plan than a foolish boy setting out on his first night of drunken debauchery.

I was taken down the hall to a small windowless chamber lit by a single torch, and tied tightly to a chair facing away from the door—strapped at the chest, my hands near the bend of my hips, and my calves to the chair's legs. Restrained as I was, I suddenly thought of Leonardo and finally comprehended his mania for freedom. Clutching at any small comfort, I found some knowing that whatever became of me, Lorenzo would send my son away from this horror.

Perhaps it was this knowledge that gave me a modicum of strength.

I heard the door open behind me. *I will meet my torturer now,* I thought. *Look into the face of the Florentine citizen or Dominican friar who, on the base and corrupt orders of his church superiors, through obscene practices inflicted upon me and other innocent prisoners, will lose his soul and the very essence of his humanity.*

But when my torturer came around to face me I saw to my great shock that it was Fra Savonarola himself.

This close, he was truly hideous to behold. I cannot say which of his features inspired such revulsion in me—whether the large, liver-colored lips, the huge misshapen nose, the green eyes glinting with hatred, or the great bushy black eyebrows that seemed all of one piece. I smelled his putrid breath as he leaned down close to my face and began ranting a venomous sermon of God's punishment for those who blasphemed him.

When he paused to breathe after an endless vindictive monologue, I opened my mouth and spoke four words. "What is my crime?"

He looked confused. Then he beckoned to someone behind me and a robed monk came and whispered in Savonarola's ear.

"You impugned the authority of my sacred brigade of angels," he said.

"Your angels had just beaten a man senseless. He may be dead," I replied, using every iota of courage I owned. "And they pulled a front-piece from a lady's gown, exposing her breasts most immodestly. This did not seem to be the work of the God of whom you so righteously speak, Fra Savonarola."

He brought the lesser monk to his ear again. From his expression it was hard to know if the angels on the streets of Florence were acting within or outside the preacher's orders. One last whisper in Savonarola's ear.

"So, you are an apothecary?" he accused.

"That is my trade. I was not aware healing the sick was a sin. Is it not a reason why we so love Jesus? I thought he believed in one man easing another's suffering."

His liver lips quivered with disdain. "So you dare hold yourself on a plane with our Lord and Savior?"

"I love my fellow man as well as I love God."

"That is blasphemy!" he shouted, spraying spittle across my face. "Mankind is scum at the feet of Jesus! Unworthy of your love!"

I thought to say, *Jesus loved mankind enough to sacrifice his life for it!* but I held my tongue. It was useless trying to best this mediocre mind in a senseless debate. It was more important to live another day.

I began slowly and thoughtfully. I had, after all, become a master of deceit. I remembered Papa's belief that it was better being a living hypocrite than a dead truth teller. "Perhaps you have opened my eyes, Fra Savonarola. Shown me another way of thinking."

This seemed to please him. I saw the slightest upturn of his lips. "Then you will henceforth leave the healing of men to Jesus Christ," he said.

I knew at once what he was suggesting, and I foundered for a sensible response. I had gone very cold.

"So you will close your apothecary," he said, more a command than a question.

I looked into those eyes and saw behind them a demon lurking, one with not a shred of sanity.

"Yes. I will." I felt my throat tightening, my chest burning.

He gestured to his assistant.

"And you will tell this good friar the location of this devil's den of yours so that within the month, when my angels come to call, they will find the place abandoned. Altogether."

"Yes."

"And the poisons you call medicines will be deposited in the Piazza della Signoria, consigned to the bonfire's flames."

I came close to breaking then. The words choked me. All I could do was nod.

"Tell me," he demanded, placing his face close to mine.

"Consigned to the flames," I whispered.

"Better than this body," he said, thumping me on the chest atop my breast bindings. He fixed me with an odd look, and I froze, terrified that he had felt an unusual thickening there. I strove to appear calm, to reveal nothing.

"Have you English henbane in your shop?" he asked, and I nearly died with relief.

"I have some," I said.

"Send that to me. I understand it keeps a man coherent while he is being . . . 'convinced' of his heresies." Savonarola made for the door. "Let me not see you here again," I heard him say behind me. "The next time it will not go so easy."

CHAPTER 29

I asked Lorenzo to call a special meeting of the Platonic Academy at the Palazzo Medici. Lucrezia had by then become a regular member. Now, in the first-floor salon, everyone sat on the edge of their seats as I, pale and shaken, told my story.

"What is happening, friends?" Vespasiano Bisticci cried when I had finished. "What is happening to our beloved city!"

There was a general outcry in the room.

"There is more." Pico della Mirandola quieted everyone with a voice of dread. "In yesterday's sermon at San Marco, but a few doors from here, Savonarola leveled his harshest criticisms against the Medici . . . and against us."

The room went silent.

"He named Lorenzo as a tyrant, insisting that he and his 'pagan-worshipping minions' turn their backs on Aristotle and Plato, who were now, themselves, 'rotting in hell.' Lorenzo, he demanded, must repent his sins or God would surely punish him."

"My mother warned us," a sober Lorenzo said. "Before we went to Rome she spoke to us about the power of fear. I do not myself understand how levelheaded people can so readily relinquish reason, scorn intellect and open-mindedness to replace it with a single man's threats of eternal damnation."

"How widespread is this plague of idiocy?" Gigi Pulci asked.

"What we all until this evening ignored as rumors, we now know

to be actual occurrences," Antonio Pollaiuolo said. "So we must assume that the entire city is in the grip of insanity."

"And Pico's account of yesterday's sermon," Poliziano added, "must
be viewed as a threat to every one of us in this room."

No one could speak, so terrible was the thought to which, a moment later, Ficino gave voice.

"We must temporarily suspend all meetings of the Platonic Academy," he said in a tone so aggrieved it might have been the announcement of the death of a friend. But he went on bravely, ignoring the
dolorous sighs and moans of his friends. "We must remember that the
teachings of our masters can never be truly silenced. They will live in
our hearts and the secret recesses of our minds, and in those thinking
men and women who come after us."

"It is not enough, I'm afraid," Vespasiano Bisticci said. Everyone
turned to him to listen. "If we are to save our lives, our books, our art
and antiquities, we must first of all hide them in safe places. . . ."
There were murmurings of agreement. "But we must also . . ." Our
friend paused as though he knew the words he was about to speak
were unsavory. ". . . appear to Savonarola, his army, and the Florentines who take his words as God's law, to be similarly converted to
this reprehensible religious fanaticism."

There were shouts of disagreement and outrage.

"Publicly disavow Plato?" Gigi Pulci cried. "The writings of our
great classical teachers?"

"If we mean to survive this mania, yes," Ficino answered bluntly.

There was silence again as everyone digested our leader's proclama-
tion as if it were the toughest gristle.

"I have an idea," Sandro Botticelli said slowly. "I will paint a spectacularly profane work and then make a very public show of sacrificing
it. Each of us, as difficult as it may be, must do the same. Meanwhile,
Lorenzo and Vespasiano should begin making arrangements to protect
what is most dear to us—the books, the antiquities—from this army of
demons."

"That is easily accomplished," Lorenzo said, and Bisticci agreed.

"It may still be insufficient," Pico said. "We are philosophers. Savonarola will not be content with the relinquishing of material treasures." He paused, as though gathering strength. "My writings, particularly those to do with the *Cabala* and Hebrew magic, are to these people among the most despised works that exist. It is true in Rome as well. I've been summoned by Innocent's commission to answer their charges of heresy. My *Apology* brought me very close to the Bishops of the Inquisition."

"Let us be honest," Ficino said with a much-needed touch of levity, "your *Apology* was nothing but a brilliant defense of your occult theories. It was bound to make Rome furious."

"In any event," Pico insisted, "I will recant and repudiate my magical beliefs. . . ."

"Pico, no," Gigi Pulci pleaded.

But Mirandola finished what he'd begun, ". . . then take my vows as a monk and retire from public life."

I saw tears glistening in Lucrezia's eyes, and Lorenzo looked stricken. He set his gaze on me.

"Cato," he said gently. "For all these years your neighbors have seen the smoke from your laboratory's furnace billowing up from your rooftop every single day, in the coldest winter and the warmest summer. They see me and all of us coming to your shop late at night. Some of them must know what goes on in your house. Till now they have chosen to ignore it, shown tolerance. But all that has changed. It will only take one person to inform on you. You are an alchemist. Not a title you'll wish to own in the coming years."

I felt cold overtake me, and a subtle trembling that I hoped no one could see beneath my robes. "I must dismantle the laboratory," I said to him.

"If you wish to live to see your nephew grow full into manhood," he agreed.

The gathering dispersed with tears and embraces in the colonnaded courtyard. Promises were made of finding every surreptitious device for keeping informed of the others' well-being. As Botticelli and Pol-laiuolo huddled together making plans of their own, Lorenzo steered me into his library. I gazed around, wondering with a keen ache if ever in my life I would see again so magnificent a collection of man-kind's intelligence.

"You have done so much in your life to protect Leonardo," he said. "But I fear Florence is no longer a safe place for him. He is already far outside the bounds of acceptable society. The man is an avowed *atheist*. To the small-brained zealots he will prove to have the most dangerous mind of all."

"What are you suggesting, Lorenzo? Where could he possibly go?"

"I will have to write to him, but I believe *Il Moro* would be de-lighted to have Leonardo at his court in Milan."

"Milan!" The thought of Leonardo so far from me tore at my heart.

"Caterina," he whispered urgently, "if he stays here they will burn him at the stake." He peered out the library door. Everyone else had gone. He pulled me farther into the room and kissed me, but when he released me I pushed back into his arms.

"How can this be happening?" I said. Of course Lorenzo's plan would save Leonardo's life, but how would I live without him? He had been my reason for coming to Florence and now, though my ex-istence was a broad, many-limbed tree, he was still the rich earth into which my roots were deeply grounded.

"There is no limit to fear that a mind can be induced to entertain," Lorenzo said. "So few people understand they are good. The church has taught them too well that they are evil and need punishment for their sins. The friar plumbs the deepest of their guilt and terror. We are in for the darkest of times, my love. The darkest of times. We must dispense with ideals for the moment and look to survival."

Despite his outrage at my treatment at Savonarola's hands, Lorenzo believed that any resistance in the current climate was futile. It must look as though my compliance was complete and altogether sincere.

He sent a small cadre of house servants to help me with the disassembling of the apothecary and laboratory. I watched as my world was taken apart bottle by bottle, shelf by shelf. The most precious of my herbs and spices and tools of those trades were carefully crated and hauled back to Vinci, as any of the Medici palazzos and country houses might soon enough fall under scrutiny. But boxes and boxes of medicinals, potions, and poultices that might have been used to help my friends and neighbors were piled at the front door for their discarding.

I carefully packed up all of the notebooks and folios I had been keeping of Leonardo's, making sure that chest was never out of my sight.

The belongings and furnishings of the first and second floors—bedchamber, kitchen, and salon—were trundled down the stairs and carted across the city to a pleasant house Lorenzo had bought for me on Via Tornabuoni, which we affectionately called Castella Lucrezia. It was small and sadly lacking a garden, but quite enough for me—without an apothecary or alchemical laboratory—to comfortably live.

When the place on Via Riccardi was finally bare and Lorenzo's servants had taken their leave, my grief was terrible but I refused to cry. I had loved my shop. The sight of it. The smell of it. The comings and goings of my friends and customers. The hub of harmless gossip. The potions invented. The healings accomplished. The advice and wisdom proffered, and just as often received. But most of all it had proven the place that perfectly expressed my being, my identity in the city of Florence—Cato the Apothecary.

Who would I be without it?

But there was no time for mourning. Lorenzo had written to Ludovico *Il Moro* in Milan and secured a position for Leonardo in the ducal court there. He himself was packing up his bottega, arranging for the release of certain of his apprentices to other studios, and making traveling arrangements for himself and Zoroastre, who would be moving north with him.

Benito came to move me into my new home. Together we unpacked my dishes, he carefully handing each one to me to wash and dry before placing them on the shelf.

"You know, Benito, you and your grandmother had best watch your tongues."

"Or what?" he asked. "Savonarola will cut them out? He is a little man with an even littler cazzo. That makes him a bully."

"But he is dangerous."

"That is why I'll refuse if they come recruiting me for his new army."

"You're a bit too old to be an 'angel,'" I said.

"And not nearly stupid enough."

"What have you told them?" I asked, alarmed but trying to remain calm. I had never admitted to Benito all I had seen and heard during my confinement in Savonarola's Office of Night prison. Perhaps he was yet unaware of how serious a directive or summons from the friar had become.

"That I will not serve him," Benito said. "That I've a family to help support."

"You must take care with the Dominican."

"What would you have me do?" he said. "Work as one of his monkeys?"

"No, of course not. But find a way to humor him. Even *Il Magnifico* is loath to openly defy the man."

"He drove you from your home, your shop," Benito said, all levity gone. "We lost the best neighbor we ever had. I hate him. I'd like to see him burning atop one of his own bonfires."

A few nights later with all the stealth we could manage, Leonardo, Lorenzo, and those of the Academy who'd met at my house with some regularity gathered in the third-floor chamber. The curtains were tightly drawn so not even the faintest candle's flicker could signify our presence there. The beakers and flasks, the ancient books and treatises, the stores of mercury, sulfur, and cinnabar were long gone from the tables and shelves. All that was left to distinguish the place as a laboratory was the alchemical furnace that, with its brilliant eternal fire, had illuminated our fumbling, stubborn perseverance to learn and discover the mysteries that Nature would allow her humble servants to know.

Every heart was heavy, every mind awash with turmoil as one by one we threw handfuls of damp earth from my garden onto the flames. They struggled valiantly, as a dying man gasps desperately for the last few breaths of life.

We were utterly silent in this, our unthinkable act—the smothering of the precious child we had together birthed and nurtured in the fecund womb that was Florence. I think part of everyone died as water and earth took their triumph over air and fire. The stove grew cold, its magic suddenly extinguished.

Then wordlessly, each clutching a candle to see us down the steps, we left my house, and with angry hammer blows boarded up the broad apothecary window and door. In wrenching sadness, we went our separate ways.

Lorenzo and I had gone to see Leonardo off to Milan. Standing together in his empty, echoing bottega, he gathered me into his arms.

"Don't cry, Mama," he whispered, "please don't cry." But then his broad shoulders heaved and he pulled me tighter, and his own weeping began. "Look how you have watched over me. Protected me." His voice broke with emotion. "All these years. And now Lorenzo. What friends you are. So beloved . . ."

"My darling boy," I murmured, trying hard to be brave. "I haven't the words to express what I wish for you. For your future. Perhaps Hermes said it best." I closed my eyes and saw the sage's words as they had been written in the ancient text.

"'Contemplate the world and consider its beauty. See that all things are full of light. See the earth as the great nurse that nourishes all terrestrial creatures. Command your soul to cross the ocean, to be in India. In a moment it will be done. Command it to fly up to heaven. It will not need wings. And if you wish to break through the vault of the universe and to contemplate what is beyond, you may do it. Believe that nothing is impossible for you. Think yourself immortal and capable of understanding all—all arts, all sciences, the nature of every living being. Mount higher than the highest height. Descend lower than the lowest depth. Imagine that you are everywhere—on earth, in the sea, in the sky, that you are not yet born, in the material world, adolescent, old, dead, beyond death. If you embrace in your thoughts all things at once—times, places, substances, qualities, quantities—you may understand God. The intellect makes itself visible in the act of thinking, God . . . in the act of creating.'"

"Mama . . . ," he said, tears glistening in his eyes. I knew that every word spoken had penetrated to his core. And I could see his love for me etched, with the pain of parting, in his beautiful features. Finally he released my hands, holding my face with the tenderest look. "Will *you* be safe? Perhaps you should come to Milan."

"I cannot leave Lorenzo," I said. "His illness is growing worse."

Leonardo smiled. "You mean your love is growing deeper."

I nodded, my eyes wet, my heart threatening to burst with that truth.

We walked outside together, where Lorenzo was waiting with the horses and wagon he had gifted Leonardo. Zoroastre finished tightening the canvas that covered the transport's bulging load and climbed into the driver's seat.

From a distance I watched Lorenzo and Leonardo embrace. They spoke momentarily, words I could not hear. But such affection suffused their faces, and such sadness, that I was forced to turn away, lest I weep and draw unwanted attention to what was meant as a simple, manly farewell.

Leonardo mounted the fabulous bay stallion he had named Giuliano and led the way down Via da Bardi, Zoroastre and the wagon carrying all that was left of my son's material life in Florence rattling after him.

Leonardo never looked back.

Lorenzo came to my side then. "He will thrive under *Il Moro*'s patronage, Caterina. He will prosper. It has been hard for Leonardo to live in the same city with that blighted father of his. In Milan he'll become a man in full."

"Defeat at the whim of a mad priest," I said. "It is a hard pill to swallow. There must be something we can do. Something to pull that monster from his evil pulpit."

"I feel Florence as I do my own body," Lorenzo said. "And she is very ill. She will grow sicker and weaker before she heals. But there is a cure for what ails her, and we *will* find it. I promise you that. I'll give everything, *anything*—my last breath—to save this city. Out of that unsavory creature's bonfires will come the spark of an answer. An idea. And we will bring him down, my love. We will bring him down."

CHAPTER 30

*L*orenzo's promise seemed an empty one on the day I brought my apothecary wares to the Piazza della Signoria. A crowd, a large one, had gathered there. And it was strange and terrible to see. The Florentines I had come to know had merrily gathered for festival days, spectacles, and even High Mass in their richest, most colorful silks, taffetas, and brocades. Men affected long point-toed shoes and held their heads high in fabulous rainbow turbans. Women's bodices were fantasies of embroidery, their hair intricately curled or braided with pearls and lace.

This, today, was a sober gathering. A veritable funeral crowd for all the blacks and grays and browns they wore. Not a flash of red or green or peacock blue was to be seen. No cloth of gold. Nary a slashed sleeve, nor burnt-orange hose. I saw no one smiling, and the only sounds were somber, muted whisperings.

But it was, after all, a funeral. A funeral pyre—Fra Savonarola's "Bonfire of the Vanities." The people had gathered round the largest one yet, a great pyramid twenty feet tall of their willingly sacrificed luxuries. As I drew my cart closer I saw a vast trove of treasures—fine Turkey carpets, antique tapestries, intricately carved chairs and mother-of-pearl tables. Books—there were hundreds of books. Paintings and statues. Adding my jars of herbs and unguents to the mountain, I could see masses of gold trinkets, silken shawls, Spanish lace *mantillas*, jeweled chains. There were dozens and dozens of mirrors, large and small, as though the friar's call had gone out that not just the vanities themselves but the means by which to view them must also be put to the torch.

Now from the direction of San Marco came a company of singing angels in their flowing white garments, and behind them a double row of tonsured monks in brown robes, each of them bearing a simple wooden cross. Following behind came Savonarola himself, he carrying a torch burning with a dark, oily flame.

The crowd silenced themselves further on sight of him and assumed a humbled, almost shamed demeanor. It made me more wretched, I thought, to see how this once-proud people now cowered and shrunk within themselves than even to have to lay the healing fruits of Nature on this terrible altar.

The new Prince of Florence came very close to me as he moved to the pyre. In fact, his green eyes briefly fell on my face, but if there had been recollection of the sinful apothecary whose shop he had ordered shut down, there was nary a flicker of recognition. He stood with his torch arm outstretched and glared into the crowd.

"Wicked, wicked, wicked!!" his voice rang out above our heads. "Piled before you are the symbols of your souls' degradation. There are demons, tiny demons that skip along the threads of silver on your sleeve, *incubi* who hide in the folds of your silken gown, Devil's familiars who lurk behind your looking glasses mocking your pointless vanity! Your evil ways shall be punished, people of Florence, and Satan's minions will triumph if you do not heed the voice of God. Do you hear me?! I have come to help you hear Him, for He does speak to me. Oh, He speaks in my ear and what He says again and again is 'Repent'!"

With that, he thrust his torch into the pyre. By the smell of pitch and oil I knew that the pile of goods had been well doused, but the way the mountain of goods exploded so quickly and violently into flames was shocking even to me.

"Watch how the fire burns!" Savonarola shouted. "See the demons burning before your eyes! Oh, repent, sinners! Repent or die like Satan's minions in these flames!"

Voices around me took up the chant, at first meekly, then gaining strength and fortitude. "Repent! Repent! Repent!!"

A pretty young woman came forward from the crowd, terror in her eyes, holding out from her body a heavy gold and gem-studded necklace as though it were a poisonous serpent. "Oh, God, I have sinned!" she shouted and flung the necklace onto the bonfire, then fell to her knees weeping. More men and women and even children rushed forward with their offerings.

I could hardly take my eyes from the friar, a red, writhing wall of flames behind him, those repugnant lips twisted into a gleeful smile.

A commotion began, and I turned to see the crowd parting behind me. A figure walked through—someone well known, I imagined, by the way the spectators respectfully retreated. When he reached the infernal bonfire I saw it was Sandro Botticelli. Like everyone else he wore a costume of subdued shades—a gray and black tunic—long and covering the shapely legs he'd so loved to display in varicolored hose. He carried under his arm a gilt-framed painting. At the front he turned to face the crowd and with decisive force thrust it high over his head, moving it from side to side for all to see. People gasped and groaned and others hissed at the sight. It was Botticelli at his pagan best—a naked Greek goddess fleeing in fright from a lust-ravaged satyr.

"God forgive me for the abomination of my art!" he shouted above the frenzied crowd. "I have sinned, but I will sin no more!" I watched as he spit the words from his mouth but I saw, as no one else could have, the lie behind his eyes. Brave or cowardly, this was the necessary deceit that would spare Sandro his life, ensure his survival in the coming years.

A triumph beyond measure for Savonarola. The Dominican strode to Botticelli, who fell heavily to his knees and bowed his head to receive a blessing. The priest raised his hands to heaven. "Even the most vile of creatures can see the error of his ways!" he cried. "Behold this sinner's redemption!"

The crowd roared its approval. I heard people weeping all around me. "He is saved!" a man behind me called out. "Oh, let me be redeemed!"

"But there are some," Savonarola shouted above the fray, "some who are beyond redemption! Some who will not bow to the will of the Lord! Who blaspheme His name, who spit on the cross!"

There were dangerous murmurings in the crowd, and I felt a thrill of terror pass through me. Something horrible was about to happen.

The sound of young, innocent voices singing hymns heralded a new parade of boy angels marching into the square. But this brigade surrounded other figures. Here were half a dozen men, their hands and feet bound in chains, their faces beaten and bloodied, terror in their eyes. As they reached the fire the angels parted to flank these helpless citizens.

One of them was Benito.

My knees jellied and my voice, as sometimes happens in a nightmare, altogether failed me.

"Look upon these creatures!" Savonarola railed. "They once were men, but now they have let the darkness overtake them! They are the Devil's own! Their hearts and brains are black and crawling with maggots!"

As I watched in growing horror, six wooden crosses in the shape of an X were hauled before each of the prior's victims and propped at an angle. The men were tied ankles and wrists, spread-eagle facing the crosses. Then six hooded henchmen carrying iron-pronged whips took their places before these poor souls and ripped their shirts down to their waists, baring the flesh that I knew, within moments, would be nothing but raw, bloodied meat. I cursed myself for not having warned Benito more strongly. For not having told him my story of arrest.

"Save these sinners!" Savonarola shouted. "Save them!"

As the first violent blows fell I felt a defiant "No!" welling up in my throat. I lunged ahead, but before I'd covered an arm's length, I felt myself plowed into with such force I was thrown to the ground. A hand covered my mouth, muting my cry.

Sandro Botticelli's body lay atop my own, his mouth at my ear. "Cato," he whispered desperately. "Don't be a fool. You will only make it worse for him."

Without another word Botticelli hoisted me to my feet and dragged me through the assembly of docile sheep.

By then we were running through the streets, praying to reach our unspoken destination before madness overtook us. The Palazzo Medici loomed. *Safety,* I thought. *Lorenzo. Sanity. Love.*

Sandro and I wheeled round the corner and into the central courtyard. There stood Donatello's *David*—beautiful, effeminate, profane. This family, beloved Medici, would be square in Savonarola's sights.

No safety here, I thought. *No safety at all.*

A Good Conspiracy

*S*ometimes there is a grace that attends life . . . when all is possible and the dawning of every day promises a new adventure—the way it was when I first arrived in Florence. Other times we simply survive, placing one foot before the other, waiting for a door to appear before us that, when opened, might thrust us headlong into an unexpected destiny.

After Leonardo's departure whole years passed with head-spinning swiftness.

To my great joy, he thrived in the fashionable city of Milan. Honors, not scandals, were heaped upon him by *Il Moro* and his people. He was named Official Court Painter, Revels Master and Engineer. And gone was the constant reminder of a father who wished his bastard son had never been born. Selfishly I longed for the warmth of Leonardo's company, the sight of his handsome face, and that mad glint that came into his eyes when he'd had another of his wild ideas.

In Florence it was a time of war. The battlegrounds were not the streets and piazzas but the soul of the city itself. The enemies not two armies but two men. *Il Magnifico* and Savonarola. There were no more festivals, save somber religious processions. Neighbors informed on neighbors, children on parents. Beauty, culture, and learning had been stripped from society. The joy Florentines once felt was replaced with fear of eternal damnation. I made do in Castella Lucrezia, though life there was a mere shadow of my former existence—a time when I was a respected citizen and a useful neighbor in the greatest city in the world.

The avenues were unnervingly quiet as I made my way toward the Palazzo Medici. What few people I saw made no greeting and would not even meet my eye. My destination was not the palace this day, but a special place adjacent to it—one that Lorenzo had created after the sudden and unexpected death of Clarice. It was a passing that Lorenzo mourned more for his children's mother and the dutiful Italian wife she had been than for any loss of love or passion between them.

As I pushed open the heavy doors to the Medici Garden I heaved the deepest of relieved sighs, for this was nothing less than an Eden. Planted lushly and decorated with stone fountains and the finest of the family's antiquities, it housed a school for up-and-coming artists. Here, the paintings and classical sculptures might need restoring. Others were meant only for teaching and inspiration. Amidst a stark city of pain my love had built a sanctuary of beauty and creation.

All along the garden's perimeter were covered cubicles with young men hard at work in clay and stone. A maestro strolled from student to student making his comments.

I could see that Lorenzo had already arrived. He stood beneath a massive marble Hercules with his eldest son, Piero—now twenty-four— the only one of the Medici children of whom Lorenzo despaired. The daughters had been married. Another boy made cardinal. But the snobbery inherited from his indulgent mother, his arrogance and frivolity deeply worried his father, as Piero would one day rule Florence. Lines of frustration creased Lorenzo's face as his son absently plucked living leaves from a rosebush and let them fall at his feet.

"We may, as you say, be the greatest family in Florence, but we are not royalty," Lorenzo insisted. "We are simple citizens, Piero, like any other in the republic."

"You want me to believe that we're no better than hide tanners or silk dyers?"

"That is exactly what you must understand in your deepest heart! A hundred years ago our ancestors were charcoal burners. We made good in this city, but if we lose our humility we are no better than the tyrants Savonarola preaches we are."

Lorenzo's eyes rose to a window of the Monastery of San Marco that shared a wall with the Medici Garden, overlooking it. He had believed it a stroke of perverse irony to have built the school so that the newly appointed prior of the order—Savonarola himself—was forced to look down on the "Devil's Playground" from his first-floor office.

"Look where your republican ideals have gotten us," Piero said with a petulance that angered me.

I came to their side. "How can you so disrespect your father?" I said, surprising even myself. "He's managed to keep five rival Italian states in a fine and measured peace. Foreign potentates curry his favor. Even Pope Innocent is kept pacified and subtly controlled. Your papa is the world's greatest diplomat, yet you have no need for his advice."

"I'd say I'm going out with my friends," Piero said with a sneer, "but in Florence there is nowhere left to go. Oh, unless one wishes to go to mass." He bowed perfunctorily to Lorenzo and did not bother a good-bye to me, then left the garden, slamming the heavy doors behind him.

Lorenzo could barely manage a smile at me, so distressed was he. "The boy is a disaster," he said quietly. "There is a weakness in him. Not of the body, like my own. Of the spirit."

Lorenzo spoke truly of his health. It was beginning to fail. None of my remedies seemed to halt the cruel progression of crumbling joints and unrelenting pain. Whenever we could we traveled to mineral waters. They eased the agonies for a time, but his duties always drew him back to Florence, and there was never a time that he refused to heed that call.

"I've had a letter from my father," I told him. "His Indian wife has died."

"I'm very sorry."

"He's always so brave, but I'm hearing homesickness in his words. I have nightmares of him dying in a strange land, alone and unloved."

"Will he come back, do you think?"

"He's always said he has no use for Vinci. I hope if he returns he'll come here. I can make a home for him."

"Come, let me show you something cheerful," Lorenzo said. We went to a cubicle where a short young man with a squashed nose and a fierce intensity was tapping with a chisel on the finely wrought face of a small marble faun.

It was the Buonarroti boy—Lorenzo's latest discovery. I knew that the young sculptor meant more to Lorenzo than a source of beautiful work for the Medici houses. Perhaps as a balm to the hurt of an unloving heir, he had recently adopted the artist, given him a room at the city palazzo, a salary, and an honored seat at his table.

"Michelangelo, show Cato what you've done."

The boy smiled up at his patron with naked admiration and love. "Well," he said, "when Lorenzo first saw me at work on the faun he poked fun at it because I'd given the creature a tongue and a mouthful of teeth. He said, 'Don't you know old people never have all their teeth?'" Michelangelo stepped aside and we peered at the faun's face. One of its front teeth was conspicuously missing.

"He knocked it out the moment I left," said Lorenzo, suppressing a smile.

"It is one thing to have a generous patron," Michelangelo said, his eyes fixed humbly on the ground, "and quite another to have a wise one."

"So it is," I agreed, and we went on to enjoy the loveliness of the garden. I chanced a look up at Savonarola's window and thought I saw a shadow suddenly disappear from behind it.

Lorenzo had seen it, too. "They say this place gives him fits," he said, eyeing the classical statues in its center. "All these naked young Greeks."

"He needs more than a fit," I said, unable to hide the bitterness in my voice.

Lorenzo's eyes grew unfixed, wandering. "What is needed," he finally said, "is another good head on this problem."

"I take it you know exactly on whose shoulders this head sits."

"Oh, yes. And I think the choice will suit you very well."

"So she is seriously considering sending the Genoese navigator west to find a new route to India?" Lorenzo asked with more than a touch of skepticism.

Roderigo Borgia, sharing a mineral bath with us in the ancient ruins at Chianciano Terme, dunked his head beneath the sulfurous hot waters and came up dripping before he answered. He was still a vibrant man at sixty, even more so shorn of his stiff cardinal's robes, his long black hair slicked around his head, the thin lawn shirt clinging to his chest. He had agreed to meet us in this Sienese spa, away from the prying eyes of Rome.

"Isabella's mind is made up. Ferdinand is unsure. So it is just a matter of time before this Christoforo Columbus sets sail. And of course she is very preoccupied at the moment."

"She will really banish all the Jews from Spain?" Lorenzo asked, scowling.

"My countrywoman is set in her beliefs," Roderigo answered. "If her Inquisition cannot rid her of the Jewish 'swine,' then she will have it another way."

"Surely there is something you can do, Roderigo."

"When I am pope, perhaps."

"Will it be soon?" I asked. Despite the sulfurous odor, I could not help but luxuriate in the pool that was so old the Romans had built colonnades around it as a monument to *their* ancestors, the Etruscans. "I understand Innocent's seizures are happening more frequently."

"He's got the constitution of a bull," Roderigo said. "He may outlive us all."

"Certainly me," Lorenzo joked, but I knew there was more than a grain of truth in his jest. We were spending more and more time away from Florence, desperately seeking relief from his symptoms and pain. Mineral waters and mud baths. Caves that blew warm air from inside the earth to be breathed. Foul-tasting waters that were drunk to induce the excretion of liver bile. And soaks at *Sant'Elena* for his kidneys. I forbade him to drink red wine, to which he acceded—though cursed me to high heaven—and all meats, which he staunchly refused to give up.

Still, when the pain and inflammation grew excruciating my poor love was too ill to eat anything at all. Then I would sit with him, forcing him to sip warm water infused with the juice of lemons. I applied to his joints poultices of juniper leaves soaked in ley and thickened with powdered elm bark. These provided some relief, as did the curative waters, as long as we could stay awhile.

But Savonarola's madness had completely poisoned the minds of our fellow Florentines. By the time Piero, who'd assumed the day-to-day responsibilities of ruling Florence, had sent word to his father that San Marco's prior had thrown into his latest Bonfire of Vanities a pair of sodomites and a female prostitute, and no one had objected—Lorenzo had already written to Roderigo Borgia and requested a meeting.

The cardinal had been delighted to come, as Rome was in the midst of a blistering summer. Between the stink of the streets and the dust in the air thrown up by Innocent's many building projects, the place had become unbearable. The thought of a cool Tuscany hill village pleased him as much as seeing his old friend Lorenzo.

Ascanio Sforza had agreed to stay behind to act as Roderigo's eyes and ears at the Vatican during this crucial moment in the papacy. Innocent was, indeed, dying, and all but a few of the sixteen cardinals who would choose the new Holy Father were content with the thought of a Borgia pope. Despite his whispered reputation as a pagan, he had proven, after thirty-five years as the head of the Curia, to be a brilliant administrator, fair-minded and popular with the people. Should anything of import occur in Roderigo's absence, Ascanio would send a courier posthaste.

"So what are we to do about this madman in your city?" the cardinal asked, taking his glass from the tiled edge of the tub.

"Stop him," I said. "Bring sanity back to Florence." In my years at

Lorenzo's side I had found my voice and could speak with authority to any man, even one who would, within the year, wear the papal tiara. "If his influence should spread outside of Tuscany to the rest of Europe, all its leaders will face the same scourge as Lorenzo has."

"What is the prior's weakness?" Roderigo asked. "Where are the chinks in his armor? That is where we will find our solution."

We were quiet as we pondered, steam rising up around us.

"He is dishonest," Lorenzo said, breaking the long silence. "So desperate is he to appear supernaturally blessed that he forces his friars to reveal to him the confessions of their parishioners. Then he inveighs about these citizens' sins from the pulpit, pretending he gained his knowledge by divine revelation."

"He steals confessions and makes them public?" Roderigo muttered incredulously.

"I think in his mania he has come to believe he *is* God," I said. "One of the San Marco priests loyal to Lorenzo told me he saw Savonarola kneeling at the feet of a crucifix saying to the wooden Jesus, 'If you lie, I lie.'"

"And he has begun to preach the Apocalypse," Lorenzo added.

"Really?" Roderigo seemed intrigued by this. "Does he claim to be a prophet?"

"I've heard he calls himself the 'Prophet of Doom,'" I said and grimaced, then added, "And he has prophesied Lorenzo's death and the death of Innocent in the same year—1492."

The cardinal was nodding thoughtfully.

"What is it, Roderigo?" Lorenzo asked.

"There is a prohibition in the church against false prophets," he replied. "Here is a man who believes himself infallible, who is a cheat, and who is breaking a serious ecclesiastical rule. I believe," he said with the hint of a sly smile, "that we have the beginnings of an answer."

We had rented the whole of the grand villa of Solana, and except for our own servants were thankfully alone on the premises and therefore able to speak freely at our table after the evening meal. Lorenzo was blessedly pain-free after his soaking mineral bath and was as sharp and decisive as I had ever seen him.

"Then we will lay a trap for Savonarola," he said, "proving him to be a false prophet. When he breaks canon law he will be chastised and prohibited from continuing to make his prophecies."

"But in his arrogance he will defy the church," said Roderigo, continuing the line of thought, "and the church, in reply, will throw its full force down upon his head."

"But what are the prophecies?" I asked. "And how do we place them inside the man's head?"

Lorenzo's eyes seemed to gaze into the future. "I know the way we will suggest them. Let us try to discover the first of them. The others will come."

As we sat quietly at the long table I was reminded of the last time we three had shared a board. It had been at the Vatican. The night Giovanni had been nominated for the cardinalate and two marriages had been announced—Cibo's with Maddalena, and Maximilian's with Bianca Sforza of Savoy. A picture began forming in my head. A memory of that night. All of us around the pope's table. A surprising detail.

"Lorenzo," I said. "Do you remember that portrait of Bianca Sforza as a girl?"

He thought a moment, looked into my eyes, and grew very still. I could tell he was flying back in time. We were sitting side by side in Innocent's lavish dining room, Bianca's portrait held between us.

"Yes," he said. "Her sleeve."

"Tell me," Roderigo demanded, intrigued.

Lorenzo squeezed his forehead between his fingers. "It is convoluted and not altogether formed in my head. Tell him something, Cato. You know my mind."

I smiled inwardly, realizing how well I did know this remarkable man's mind. "It is just a seed, Roderigo. The tiniest seed. But there are two people who live in Milan who are our friends. Who will wish to assist us in our plan. And using their talents . . . and with their co-operation, we might indeed find our way to eradicate a certain vermin from our midst."

Roderigo cocked a wicked grin and poured himself another glass of wine. "Move closer, my friends, and let me hear what you have to say. There is nothing I enjoy more than a good conspiracy."

"My heart is pounding so hard it feels as if it will burst from my chest," I told Lorenzo as we passed through the gate in Milan's south wall. Though I could not deny that age was every day taking its toll on me, the thought of seeing Leonardo again after nearly a decade was making me feel young again.

We rode together in the comfortably appointed closed carriage Lorenzo used for traveling. It had taken us three days to journey from Chianciano, and my love was tired and sore from the constant jouncing on bumpy roads.

I parted the window curtains and saw that the city—strange for one of such importance to be far from any river or lake, or even perched atop a hill for safety—was teeming and noisy with life and commerce. The place seemed a random network of streets, unlike the straight and orderly ones of Florence. Here they were narrow and dirty. The houses of gray stone and tawny brick were some of them centuries old, others built with lovely new façades, and all interspersed with prettily laid-out gardens. Now and then we'd bump across a bridge over a narrow canal.

"Look to your right, Caterina."

I did and saw a fine modern building with a sign that announced BANCO MEDICI. "Will you tell the driver we will not be stopping here?"

I did what I was asked.

Indeed, this visit to Milan was secret to all but a few. We drove several blocks farther and entered a large square.

"Prepare yourself," Lorenzo said. "The Duomo is quite astonishing."

Despite his warning my mouth fell agape at the sight of the mammoth edifice, not simply its color, a whitish rose marble, but the intricacy of its design. The tall spires and buttresses were all lined with narrow pinnacles that looked like French lace. It couldn't have differed more from the austere exteriors of Florentine churches. It might have been something imagined in a *hashish* dream.

"The Goths' influence," Lorenzo whispered. His voice had grown weak.

"We are here, my love," I said. "Leonardo's house is right on the southern edge of Cathedral Square."

Moments later our small cortege had pulled across a moat, through a gate in some fortified walls to a large cobbled courtyard. This was surrounded by porticos boasting a long stable house, and shadowed by a tall stone tower. It was, as Leonardo's letters had told, the old ducal palazzo, now deserted by *Il Moro* and given as a home to my son. Despite its dilapidated appearance and lacking the buzzing activity of a noble court, its colonnaded courtyard was astonishingly grand.

Leonardo's bottega, I thought, *in a duke's palace!*

"Mama?" I heard his voice outside the carriage and threw open the door. A moment later I was in his strong embrace, inhaling the clean scent of rosewater. My heart calmed instantly. But it was not until he had pushed me to arm's length that I had full sight of him—those sweet, melancholy eyes, the lush, shapely lips, high-boned cheeks and nobly slender nose. His hair was gloriously wavy, worn loose and long. I always censored my urge to remonstrate with Leonardo about the full beard he insisted upon keeping. All that hair, I thought, hid the rest of his handsome face. And how prosperous and fashionable he looked! Tall and broad-shouldered, his beautifully tailored doublet was deep yellow satin, his calves shapely in hose a shade lighter than above. And he wore, for the first time I remembered, simple gold rings, one on each hand.

"You're still a handsome man, Uncle Cato," Leonardo loudly proclaimed, as Zoroastre came out to greet us. The apprentice, still affecting all black in his dress, helped Lorenzo out of the carriage and gave instruction to the drivers for unloading our trunks and seeing to the horses.

Leonardo and Lorenzo embraced. I saw my son's face crumble with sorrow to feel the pain my lover so clearly suffered. But when they parted Leonardo was all smiles, for he knew very well Lorenzo would never brook the slightest pity for himself.

"Come, let us show you around," Leonardo said, and with Zoroastre at his side, led us through a grand front doorway. It was an enormous place with high ceilings and several wings sprawling away from a central corridor.

"For a time, *Il Moro* had Duke Gian and Isabella living in the north apartments here," Leonardo said. "They were strange housemates. Angry—for good reason, I suppose—to be banished from the royal residence to live with the court painter."

"And all the while the rightful ruler of Milan," Lorenzo added.

"And now?" I asked.

"Now they've been sent even farther from court—to Pavia."

"You have a ruthless patron, Leonardo," Lorenzo said. "It is a good thing *Il Moro* loves you so well."

A row of small chambers were revealed as *studioli* of Leonardo's various specialties. There were rooms for grinding colors and glazes. In another, circles of glass were being ground and polished into lenses. Another housed every sort of mechanism, from pulleys and ropes to screws and bolts and winches.

As we passed another chamber that was, quite openly, an alchemical laboratory, Zoroastre caught sight of a young apprentice inside, rather lazily fanning its furnace with a bellows.

"Put some elbow into it, Marco!" he cried, and strode over to the boy, who cowered under the reprimand.

"There's more to see," Leonardo said. "So much more."

As we continued down the hallway he opened the door to what

appeared as a great wardrobe stuffed with colorful, fanciful costumes—men's and women's and animals', and masks beaked and feathered, both grotesque and beautiful.

I was drawn inside this last room, and Leonardo followed.

"You know I am *Il Moro*'s revels master," he said.

"Ah, for the court pageants."

"And weddings. All we seem to have these days are weddings. Ludovico to Beatrice d'Este, Gian to Isabella. We are already planning Bianca Sforza's marriage festivities."

"I imagine they will be rather spectacular." Lorenzo had joined us in the costumery. "It is not every day the Holy Roman Emperor marries. Do you see much of Maximilian?"

"Only the payments that come for my work on Bianca's wedding portrait."

Leonardo led us out and across the corridor through an archway into the largest chamber I had ever seen. Three hundred feet by fifty was my guess.

"The old ballroom," he said. Pillars ranged on all four walls, and a high arched ceiling towered overhead. But now there was nothing left of a royal playground. It was a workshop, a veritable cauldron of creation. I moved to one wall. Every inch of it was hung with sketches—of waterworks and hydraulic systems, cathedral domes and a city designed on two levels. Drawings of a crossbow the size of a house, and a terrifying war weapon on wheels with a revolving quartet of scythes.

On tables were wooden models of cranes and hoists and aqueducts. In one corner was a mysterious arrangement of eight large rectangular mirrors, all hinged together in a perfect octagon.

There were numerous apprentices. Boys from ten to eighteen working with great industry at their chores. The youngest swept the floor. Another, slightly older, stretched and nailed a canvas onto a willow panel. The oldest, clearly a journeyman, was laying down the first color on a cartoon of what would later become a painting.

More than half of the hall was filled with scaffolding that surrounded a massive sculpture, a great prancing horse. Leonardo had been granted the commission for a much-sought-after equestrian monument, one commemorating *Il Moro*'s father.

"Strange," Lorenzo said to him, speaking my mind out loud, "to see you working as a sculptor—though of all the subjects you might have chosen first, this does not surprise me."

It was, indeed, magnificent—the great horse. Even enveloped in scaffolding with apprentices balanced on the wood, working on its various details, I could see the strength and beauty of the beast's musculature, even an expression of the animal's pride in its long face and soulful eyes.

"When the clay sculpture is finished, I shall cast it in bronze," Leonardo told us. "It gives me much grief, the planning for this casting." He kicked his heel into the floor. "I mean to cast it in one piece. It is so large I must dig a great pit to put the mold in the ground, here, upside down. Four furnaces shall have to be built around it, and the molten metal will flow, through pipes, into the horse's belly, air escaping through its feet."

I could see sketches on the walls of an iron framework for the mold of the head. Another of a great wooden contraption that would, by the look of it, move the finished horse from the bottega.

"And the problem?" Lorenzo asked.

"Groundwater," Leonardo answered. "The top of the head will come dangerously close to Milan's shallow water table. If moisture intrudes, the whole thing could collapse." He smiled. "But it will not. It *cannot*. I cannot have done all this work for *Il Moro*'s horse to have it collapse."

A high-pitched screech echoed through the cavernous hall and we all turned to find its source—a beautiful boy of about ten. He had an extravagant headful of soft blond curls, and was dressed not as the other apprentices but in scarlet silks. Just now he was jumping down from the horse's scaffolding, being chased by an older boy. The younger one made for the archway followed in close pursuit by the older, who shouted, "Give it back, you little demon!" A moment later both were gone.

We turned back to Leonardo. "Who is that?" I asked.

When he answered I saw on his face the oddest expression—one I had never seen before—a confusing welter of amusement, irritation, and love.

He shook his head. "That is Salai."

"Salai?" Lorenzo said. "In Arabic, does that not mean Limb of Satan?"

"He is very aptly named," Leonardo said simply.

I waited for a bit more of an explanation.

"I've recently taken him in as an apprentice."

"Awfully well dressed for an apprentice," I observed.

"Let us talk about Salai later. There's so much I still want you to see."

"And what is this?" Lorenzo asked, moving to the other side of the hall. A huge linen sheet covered a tall, square structure.

Leonardo strode over and, without hesitating, pulled it off. What was revealed was the most remarkable contraption imaginable. I observed Lorenzo's wide-eyed expression.

What had made it so wide, we now saw, were two pairs of thin "wings" that crossed like a dragonfly's appendages. The height was made up of a ten-foot-tall open wood-frame gondola, with pedals near the bottom, and large rollers at the top. All the mechanisms were attached in a web of ropes and pulleys.

Without a word to us Leonardo inserted himself into the center of the device, put his feet in the pedals and his arms into straps that attached to the wings. He fitted his head into a cloth sling, then began pumping hard with his feet, raising and lowering his arms. The wings began to move slowly at first, then picked up speed.

"He is determined to fly," I whispered to Lorenzo.

"And this is a flying *machine*?" he asked me quietly.

The rollers above Leonardo's head were now turning at a furious rate and the wings creating a breeze all around us.

"Look, Lorenzo!" I said, pointing to the base of the contraption.

The thing was quite miraculously lifting off the floor, if only a fraction of an inch. It hovered there for several moments, but Leonardo's exertions were taking their toll. The wings' motion slowed, and with a loud creaking sound the gondola settled back down onto the floor. He disentangled himself from the device, red-faced and perspiring.

I went to his side. "You never fail to amaze me."

Lorenzo joined us. "It came off the ground," he said, unable to hide his incredulity.

"It does come off the ground," Leonardo said, "though I'm quite sure now it will never fly. Too heavy. But I've other designs. Ones that are more birdlike. This is just the first I have *built*."

"Are you painting?" Lorenzo asked as Leonardo gestured for two apprentices to re-cover the flying machine with its sheet.

"Oh, yes. Mostly portraits. I've done one of Beatrice, and a lovely one of *Il Moro*'s mistress, Cecilia. She's pregnant with his child." Leonardo indicated we should follow him out the ballroom archway toward a grand staircase. Lorenzo took the steps slowly. Leonardo grasped Lorenzo's arm. "Only a few more steps," he said.

We were shown to our rooms, what had surely been Duke Galeazzo and Bona's apartments in the glory days of the ducal palace. Even in their downtrodden condition these apartments nearly rivaled our chambers in the Vatican.

Leonardo smiled. "I've a wonderful cook who indulges all my perverse demands—Julia makes a divine minestrone. We'll dine together tonight . . . if you're well enough." He looked with concern at Lorenzo.

"As long as I can rest awhile"—Lorenzo gazed at me with affection—"and your mother can lay her hands on my gouty old knees."

I folded myself into Leonardo's arms again.

He kissed the top of my head. "I cannot believe you're here. The two of you. I am complete."

Then he left us, shutting the door behind him. I turned to Lorenzo. "Thank you, my love," I said. "Thank you for bringing me."

That night we came down from our rooms to find a table long enough to seat Leonardo and all of the apprentices, though there were only four places set at its head. It had been tastefully arranged with a fine white linen cloth, modest plate and utensils, and vases of fresh-cut flowers in every color.

My son offered the seat at the head of the table to Lorenzo, who declined.

"This is your home, Leonardo, and you are the man of the house." He looked around, smiling. "The king of your own palazzo. You must sit at the head of your table."

I could see how proud Leonardo was. He had come so far.

"Who is joining us?" I asked.

"Salai."

"The Limb of Satan?"

The confused expression reasserted itself on Leonardo's face. "I must tell you about him before he comes to the table." He went silent for a long moment. Then he said, "Salai is my natural son."

I sat stunned, speechless, though not unhappily so. It was quite a large matter to comprehend. *Leonardo has a child. I am a grandmother.*

"How did it happen, Leonardo?" Lorenzo asked. "You've never spoken of him before."

"I only learned about his existence this year." Leonardo took some time before he went on. "When I first came to Milan, *Il Moro* was very kind to me." He turned to Lorenzo. "I have you to thank for that. One of the duke's 'kindnesses' was a visit to one of his courtesans." Leonardo rarely looked embarrassed, but now he did. "I had not been with anyone, man or woman, for a long time. This girl—her name was Celeste—was very beautiful. She had a temperament much like yours, Mama." He smiled, remembering. "I began to use her as a model for one of my Madonnas." Now Leonardo looked down at his plate. "She fell in love with me, and for a time, while I painted her, she refused all her other customers. Even *Il Moro*." Now my son smiled. "I think I might have risen somewhat faster in the duke's favor if Celeste had not ceased giving him her favors. But finally the Madonna was finished. In truth, I was not in love with her and"—the shy revelatory look reappeared—"Zoroastre was insanely jealous. Celeste left Milan shortly after, and my life went on."

Leonardo sat back in his chair and sighed a long sigh. "Last year a short, squat man I had never met came here and asked to see me. I thought he had come to give me a commission." Leonardo smiled ruefully. "In fact, this man brought me one I never expected. He said his wife, Celeste, had recently died. She had been a great beauty in her day. So great, that despite her having once been a courtesan, and despite her having a young child—she called him Giacomo—he felt lucky that she would accept his proposal of marriage. They had lived quite happily at first, he said, and he'd refrained from asking who the boy's father was. She never offered to say, and he thought perhaps, because of her previous trade, she did not know his paternity."

Now Leonardo turned his eyes to the ceiling and a bemused expression crossed his face. "The peace in their marriage began to shatter as soon as little Giacomo began to walk. He was a terror—as beautiful as his mother, but wholly unmanageable. Celeste indulged him and refused to let her husband punish him. He grew more and more willful. Spoiled. Husband and wife fought constantly over him. Much as the man tried, he could not bring himself to love the boy. Then Celeste grew ill. A cancer in her breast. On her deathbed she revealed *me* as the father. Of course, by that time I was a well-known figure in Milan. So her husband came to me. Told me the story. I knew it was true."

Leonardo looked at me then with the warmest of smiles. "He was my *son*." His eyes filled with tears and he shook his head. "I adopted him. Paid the man for him." Now Leonardo barked a laugh. "Giacomo was even worse than he'd been described. I've never known a child like him. He is so beautiful to look at. In that way there's much of his mother in him. But he lies. He steals. So far he seems to have neither interest nor talent for the arts. He is very loud . . . and exceedingly rude."

"What are his good qualities?" Lorenzo asked gently. "Even the vilest of children have one or two."

"Besides his physical beauty . . . ?" Leonardo thought a moment. "He is loyal to a fault. Keeps a secret well. And in his way"—he pressed his lips together as though to hold back emotion—"he loves me. Recognizes me as his father."

I put my hand over his and smiled. "When can I meet my grandson?"

Leonardo wiped at his eyes. "For now, of course, he will be your 'grandnephew.'" He sniffed sharply, and picking up a bell, jingled it.

A door opened and a plump, rosy-cheeked woman peeked her head around it. "Julia, meet my Uncle Cato and Lorenzo de' Medici."

"I'm honored to meet you both," she said, quite matter-of-factly. "Are you ready for your supper, Maestro?"

"Will you call Salai first?"

Julia rolled her eyes heavenward. "The last I looked he was out in the yard up to his elbows in muck."

"Please tell him to clean himself and come in," Leonardo told her with a pleasant resignedness I would come to recognize in all of his dealings with his son. "But I think we three can begin with the soup."

By the time Salai arrived at the table we were halfway through our antipasto. He fairly ran into the dining room, and with an odd combination of boredom and affection planted a kiss on Leonardo's cheek before taking the empty place next to Lorenzo. I was seated across from him, so I could easily look at the boy's face. Though his clothes had been changed, his forehead retained a smudge of dirt. While he had lips more full and pouty than Leonardo's, the long, straight nose and the pretty hazel wide-set eyes were clearly his father's. The mop of light curls was reminiscent of Leonardo's, too, though by the standard of the day for a young boy was now cut short.

The child was staring hard at me.

"That is your great-uncle, Cato," Leonardo told Salai. "And beside you sits a very important man from Florence, Lorenzo de' Medici."

He gave me a brief, insolent look and then turned to Lorenzo. "Are you very rich?" he asked.

Lorenzo controlled his smile. "Perhaps the richest man in Italy."

"They say *Il Moro*'s treasury is filled with chests of gold and diamonds and pearls and rubies, and a pile of silver coin so high a stag could not leap over it!"

"Salai . . . ," Leonardo began.

"But I wish to know who is richer!" the boy cried.

"Why does it matter?" I asked him.

"Because," he said, turning to me, "I must know to which man I should go for patronage when I am grown."

"But the maestro tells us you have no interest in the arts," I persisted.

"No matter," Salai replied chirpily, "I'll seek patronage for some *other* talent."

"Court jester perhaps?" Lorenzo suggested.

Salai looked at his father with open-mouthed wonder. "I could be a jester!"

"You would make a marvelous fool, Salai," Leonardo said, straight-faced.

"Did you know," Lorenzo continued to the boy, "that fools are the only people at the courts of kings who can say exactly what they want on any subject whatsoever—as long as it is humorously put—and not be punished?"

With a loud whoop Salai was suddenly out of his chair and dancing around the table in a wild *tarantella*, accompanying himself with a song far too ribald for one his age. He was making such a racket that Julia pushed her head through the door and watched as he danced. Salai ended with a set of whirls and a quite spectacular somersault, landing at Lorenzo's feet, grinning up at him.

"You're hired!" Lorenzo cried.

Everyone roared at that, all but Julia, who shook her head, muttering, "A mistake to encourage him," before disappearing back in the kitchen.

"Sit down and eat your supper," Leonardo instructed Salai.

The boy took a few bites of his *insalata*, then looked at me long and hard. I held his gaze very frankly. He tried to outstare me. Made a few faces. Crossed his eyes. Pulled his cheeks into a fish mouth. I refused to smile. Finally he gave up, but not before announcing, "He's a sour one."

I turned to Leonardo. "You're right. He is rude."

Salai made a farting sound through his lips.

Leonardo closed his eyes. "Take the rest of your supper in your room," he told his son.

"I'm finished anyway," Salai said, jumping out of his chair. He grabbed a heel of bread from the table, and with an exaggerated bow to Lorenzo, a fish face in my direction, and a peck on Leonardo's forehead, he darted from the room.

We all sat there a bit stunned.

"Remember the dragon on my pillow?" I finally said. "Perhaps he takes after you more than you'd like to admit."

"Was I that bad?"

"There were times . . ."

Then Julia came in with a steaming plate of savory mushroom ravioli. As we tucked into it with gusto, I regaled Lorenzo, to Leonardo's sundry amusement and mortification, with stories of his youthful escapades. By the end of the evening he had concluded that, after all, fruit did not fall so very far from the tree.

Next morning I explored the east wing of Corte Vecchio. It was a warren of small, interconnecting chambers, each possessing one or two overlarge windows, and each a feast for the senses. Embroidered tapestries that must once have hung on royal walls now hung here. Paintings and sculptures—gifts from his friends, the Florentine masters—were everywhere present, though some of the works were Leonardo's own. A series of four of his sketches stretched the length of one room, all depicting a catastrophic deluge—like the one Giuliano de' Medici had described as a dream that day in the country so many years before, with hurricane winds and monstrous curling waves that were washing away a mountaintop castle and the whole city beneath. On a chalk wall were scribbled mathematical diagrams and equations that I found completely baffling.

Underfoot, where there might have been one Turkey carpet, Leonardo had laid *three*, artfully, so that a piece of each showed through. Every possible surface was piled with treasures: a necklace of cinnabar hanging from the dismembered marble hand of a classical Greek statue; a wood carving of the goddess Isis displayed prominently in a niche, a garland of tiny living orchids encircling her neck.

In a music room were myriad stringed instruments and horns. There was a violin I recognized, one he'd designed with a fabulous silver sounding box molded into the shape of a horse's head. On his arrival at the Milanese court he and his unique instrument had been thrust headlong into a musical competition and won! After that, for some time, Leonardo had been strangely cast in the role of a talented musician and not a painter. Here, too, were piles of written music and charts that, to an untrained eye, would make no sense. There were sketches tacked on the wall of "musical waves" traveling through the air toward a perfectly rendered human ear and the inside of the listener's head.

I finally arrived in the main corridor and stepped into the ballroom studio. Leonardo saw me at once and strode toward me.

"Good morning, Uncle Cato!" he called out cheerfully. "Look, don't come any closer. Let me show you something." He came over and guided me back toward the workshop archway.

I saw four apprentices move to four points of a square around where Leonardo's flying contraption stood. They began working, hand over hand, tugging on an intricate system of pulleys, weights, ropes, and heavy chains. Suddenly, with a loud grinding and creaking of gears, the square of wood upon which the flying machine stood began to rise! As it ascended on the ropes and chains, another floor was rising from the story below to take its place. Then with the sound of heavy clanking, the new floor locked perfectly into the place of that which was now suspended high overhead. On this newly risen platform were five sheet-draped easels.

The operation complete, the apprentices returned to their various tasks, as though nothing out of the ordinary had occurred.

"What on earth have I just seen?" I inquired of the massive machinery.

"I think it should be the *work*, not the master, that moves up and down. Every night now I am able to put my paintings away and close them up, safely."

I moved amidst the easels, nosily lifting the sheet corners to peek at the subjects. Each one was more astonishing than the last. A profile portrait of a woman Leonardo identified as Beatrice d'Este. A wildly costumed Ludovico, who appeared as an overweight wood nymph. There was a somberly dressed physician, and a Madonna holding a vase, the Christ child clutching a delicate flower. In each and every one shone Leonardo's unique genius.

"I wish you would sit for me one day," he said quietly. "As the person you are under those men's robes and bindings."

"Why would you want to paint an old woman?" I said, amused.

"When I look at you," he replied, "I see you as you were when I was a boy his age." He gazed across the room at Salai, who was pounding with mortar and pestle at chunks of blue stone with so much ferocity that bits of its powder were flying up and spraying his face and doublet. He looked fondly at me. *"Madonna Mia,"* he said.

"Perhaps one day," I said, strangely embarrassed and shy. "But we've so much to accomplish here and now."

"Lorenzo is very ill, is he not?"

"He is. But there's a strength in him. Fathomless strength. As long as there is a Florence to save, that man will live forever."

In the next moment Salai, all gangly legs and blue-flecked cheeks, approached us. "I'm going out with my friends," he announced.

"You haven't finished grinding the cerulean," Leonardo said. He was met with an insolent pout.

"Alessio can do it."

Maestro and apprentice locked eyes. Salai's sparkled with mischief, past and future.

"Then you must finish when you return," Leonardo instructed,

trying for sternness in his voice. But this was a clearly outrageous in-
dulgence.

With a nod the master gave the boy leave to withdraw. He swiveled on his heels to go.

"Salai!" Now there was steel in Leonardo's voice. He motioned
toward me with his eyes. The boy turned back and deposited a per-
functory kiss on my cheek. Then, grabbing a feathered cap and tying
closed the front of his doublet, he was gone.

"He's a little monster," Leonardo said, removing the cloth from the
still unfinished Madonna and child.

"Because you allow it," I said, but there was no scolding in my
voice.

"Reds!" he called, and within moments the apprentice, Alessio, had
come to his side with a palette arrayed in every shade of that color.
Leonardo took it and praised the young man before dismissing him.

"Is it wrong, Mama," he whispered, "to want to give your child
everything?"

I smiled. "Of all people, how can you ask me that question? I've
always believed every child deserves one shamelessly indulgent parent."

Leonardo laughed a dark laugh. "The Limb of Satan. Let us hope
he is not the death of me."

Lorenzo, Leonardo, and I had visited with Ludovico and Beatrice.
Though we had little time to waste, we knew it was necessary to
oblige. It would have seemed odd for the Medici to travel to Milan
without a visit to his important ally, *Il Moro*. The Castella Sforza, an
utterly impregnable fortress of bricks the color of dried blood, was
impossibly luxurious within.

The welcome by *Il Moro* and his lovely young bride could not have
been warmer. Ludovico, in the years since I had last seen him in
Rome, had matured into a thick-bodied man with a broad, fleshy
face and a heavy, drooping chin. Beatrice, the youngest daughter of
Ferrante—that dangerous Neapolitan friend of Lorenzo's since his

youth—had been a sheer delight, happy and exuberant and spectacularly attired in a pearl-encrusted gown.

The couple had seemed quite at home in their role as "First Lord and Lady of Milan," while in fact Ludovico's nephew, Gian, was the true ducal heir. Gian and his wife, Isabella, were nowhere to be found at court, and Beatrice had whispered to me that Isabella was furious at this state of affairs. Furious to have a weak, effeminate husband who trembled under the gaze of *Il Moro*, whom Gian allowed to rule unchallenged, who beat her in private, and openly flaunted his affair with a country boy.

At Lorenzo's urgings we had had a quiet, intimate evening at the castella, treated to exquisite food, while beautiful music played quietly in the corner. Much praise was heaped on Leonardo for his talents, and assurances were made that he was accepted within the court's innermost circle.

While Lorenzo and Ludovico spoke privately, Beatrice had chattered about an endless list of projects for the court artist—a summer house for her garden and decoration of her already opulent private apartments. She wished him to design a *rappresentazione* for an upcoming festival. "Something celestial," she'd insisted enthusiastically, "with spinning planets, and the zodiac, and stars lit up like those in the sky!"

I'd come away feeling warmed by the sincere and openly appreciative patronage, though Leonardo did complain that for someone as wealthy as *Il Moro*, he was awfully slow to pay.

Within the week we were riding out into the countryside. Lorenzo revealed that his private conversation with *Il Moro* had been quite fruitful for our purposes, though Ludovico was unaware of the help he had given. I could see that the intelligence Lorenzo had gleaned troubled him deeply, for the duke's plans for his governance of Milan and its alliances would reach far beyond its borders. There would be time for us to discuss the details, but this day's mission was first in all our minds.

Our carriage deposited us at a lovely country villa surrounded by ancient olive groves. A horse-faced servant opened the door.

"Come this way," he said, leading us into a formal salon, where we were seated. We said very little as we waited for the person upon whose shoulders rested the substantial weight of our conspiracy.

"Bianca Maria de Galeazza Sforza, Duchess of Savoy," the servant announced in a funereal tone. The sixteen-year-old noblewoman entered the room with quiet dignity that matched her somber attire. She could not have been more different from her uncle's wife, Beatrice. I was momentarily startled to see she wore a crucifix at the high neck of her steel-gray gown.

She was similarly reserved in her greetings to us all, accepting kisses to her hand from Leonardo and myself, and one on the cheek from Lorenzo. She was especially deferential to him.

"I am deeply honored by your visit, my lord. My uncle has told me of your loyal friendship over the years." She nodded to my son. "Leonardo tells me you were a kind patron to him." She smiled with almost insipid mildness at me. "And you must be very proud of your nephew."

"I am," I said, beginning to feel uneasy, as though we had perhaps come to the wrong home.

"Bernardo," she said, turning to the servant who was standing at attention at the door. "I am going to take my visitors for a walk around the grounds."

"I will be glad to accompany you," he said with a clear note of disapproval born, I suspected, of severe protectiveness.

"That will not be necessary. These are all good friends of mine."

The servant withdrew, closing the door behind him. The moment we were alone an amazing transformation overtook our hostess. Her face softened into a smile. She embraced Leonardo and knelt, taking Lorenzo's hand to her lips, fervently kissing his swollen knuckles.

"Follow me," she said as she rose, then led us out a door into a flower garden. As long as we were close to the villa she kept her voice low, but once away she spoke normally, and with great enthusiasm. "I am so glad you've come," she told us. "The news from Florence is awful."

"So you understood the full meaning of my letter," Lorenzo said, more a statement than a question.

"Oh, yes. What secrets not buried in your code were in Greek, and the only one in this household who reads the language besides myself is my tutor. And for *him*, I must also thank you." She turned to Leonardo and me. "Had it not been for the Medici influence on the Sforzas—their love of the classic cultures—I would never have had a Greek tutor at all. . . ."

Her words hung unfinished as we arrived at a small building ringed by ancient trees. With a key she produced from a chain hidden in the folds of her skirt, Bianca unlocked the heavy door. She led us inside the gloomy chamber and closed the door behind us with a resounding crash. "And I never would have become a student of Plato," she finished, her voice echoing eerily.

With practiced ease, the duchess took from the wall a torch and went to a stone bowl in which flickered a single candlewick afloat in oil. Touching torch to flame she illuminated the room enough to see it was empty of all decoration save a Turkey carpet on the floor.

"Maestro," she said, "would you push aside the rug, just there?"

He did what had been asked of him, revealing the fine outline of a trapdoor in the stone floor and a metal ring that needed tugging on top to open it.

Holding her skirts high, Bianca led the way down some moldering steps, lighting numerous torches as she went, so that the vault that emerged from the dark was hardly ominous.

"Soon I will marry Maximilian," she said, lighting more torches. "I'll be the Holy Roman Empress." We had arrived at the bottom of the stairs. She turned to us with an earnest expression. "Had you not written to me when you did, come now to Milan, I would surely have been unable to help you. I have no idea where my future husband stands in all this."

"It's hard to say," Lorenzo told her. "He is a celebrated intellectual, a friend and patron of scholars, but his ties to Rome cannot be overestimated. And alliances are shifting as quickly as the Alpine weather. As for the rulers themselves—who takes a crown, a pope's throne, who dies and when, who wars with whom—all will determine the outcome of our endeavor. But if the Fates are with us—for we surely know that *right* is on our side—we will see success."

Bianca nodded hopefully, and in the warm glow of the torchlight she seemed pretty to me. I wondered what kind of life she would lead in the northern climes of Austria and Burgundy. Whether she would miss the soft Italian springs, the gray green of olive groves, her family and her countrymen.

Her Greek tutor.

This had been the key to her involvement with us, Bianca Sforza's knowledge and love for the Platonists . . . and Hermes Trismegistus. That, and the symbol of her learning, which she'd cleverly embroidered onto her sleeve in the portrait Lorenzo and I had seen in the Vatican—the Egyptian cross. The *ankh*. Symbol of Isis. A brave, shining beacon for all who had eyes to see that, even as a girl, here was a kindred spirit and philosopher.

The basement vault was stacked with sturdy chests. I imagined that some, like *Il Moro's* treasure chests, were piled with jewels and gold and silver coin. But now Bianca was kneeling before one that itself needed unlocking—another key emerged from the folds of her gown, this one made of gold. She spoke with her back to us. "I always wished that I could have been born a man, but not just any man, anywhere. I wished I could have been born a man who grew up in Florence in the golden years of the Medici—the years of Cosimo, Piero . . ." She turned and looked back over her shoulder with a tear in the corner of her eye. ". . . *Il Magnifico*. To have studied with Ficino, Alberti, Mirandola."

Lorenzo placed a hand on her shoulder. "Bianca, sweet girl. Know that we will be forever in your debt. That by your actions here today you become *one* with us."

The look on her face was one of transported joy. A few of her tears fell before she turned back to the chest. We watched as she reached in and withdrew its contents.

Her arms full, Leonardo and I helped her to her feet, and we all followed as she moved beneath a wall torch, where her treasure was revealed. From a crimson velvet bag she took a wooden case decorated with silver gilt nails. This was unlocked with her golden key. She brought out of the box a bundle draped in red silk. When this was laid open we saw a many-times-folded piece of yellowed linen. It did not look like much. But now she carefully instructed us in the way to unfurl the thing—one on each side, one on each end.

It was many times longer than it was wide, its width two feet across. Along its length was the image in dark red of a man's body, front and back—Christ's body, as though this had been his winding sheet, the blood of his wounds having stained the linen—limbs, torso, and head.

It was, to even an untrained eye, a painting. A forgery, and a poor one at that. This was the Savoy family's precious holy relic—the Lirey Shroud.

"Your uncle Jacque told us in Rome it had not been displayed in public for many years," Lorenzo said.

"I can see why," Leonardo said, unable to hide his disdain.

"Can it be done?" I asked him.

He was silent as he stared hard at the long, thin length of linen. I saw that look on his face, the changing tilt of the head. I was reminded of the day he had, as an eight-year-old, observed a flower's stem and stamen on my red rug in a sunny meadow outside of Vinci.

"Yes," he said, his lips tilting into a smile. "It will be my finest work. And if not my finest, the one I will most enjoy creating."

It was night before we returned to Corte Vecchio, and as we pulled into the courtyard I saw a carriage I recognized, though it was not one that made sense being there. A Medici carriage, the family's finest, one that took Lucrezia or the girls on the longest trips, to Rome or Naples, in grand style.

Its appearance here confused me. Who had traveled from Florence to Milan?

Zoroastre had come to greet us and opened our door. When I stepped out I saw in the shadow of the palazzo door the figure of a tall man stooped down and speaking to Salai. They both turned to face the new arrivals.

"Papa?" I whispered, and looked to see Lorenzo smiling broadly. "You did this?" I said, my whole body trembling.

"When he returned from India, he came to Florence," Lorenzo said. "Went to Verrocchio's when he found us gone. My mother wrote and told me. I had him brought here."

Now Leonardo recognized Ernesto. "Grandfather!" He strode quickly to the door and took the old man in his arms with a fierce embrace. Then he came back and likewise embraced Lorenzo.

I was finding it hard not to weep with joy and gratitude as my father and I closed the distance between us. I'd worried that all the years of traveling would have aged him, weakened him, but it was quite the reverse. When he took me in his arms and embraced me, his grasp had never felt so strong, nor when he pushed me back to regard my face did his countenance appear so vital. He was riven through and through with a great force of life.

We never slept that night. Leonardo, Papa and Salai, Lorenzo and I gathered in the ducal bedchamber, each of us taking turns feeding the fire in the hearth. We sat or lay sprawled across the great bed, nibbling on cheese and bread, and the grape and olive compote I had taught Julia to make.

For the most part my father regaled us with tales of his many adventures in the East. The barefoot and painted holy men who wandered the countryside wearing nothing but loincloths and twisted themselves into fabulous shapes. The almond-eyed, dark-skinned women in silken veils wearing gold bracelets and nose rings, their hands and feet decorated with intricate inked designs. Ancient temples carved with men and women in the most immoderate postures of love. Elephants with immense snakelike noses upon whose backs my father had ridden on a wooden saddle.

While on his travels he'd heard next to nothing of the Christian world. The Indians, he said, were so steeped in their own culture—more ancient by thousands of years than the Western world—that Europe barely existed for them. He did hear many stories about the Judean saint the people called "Issa," who had spent many years wandering India as a teacher, only to return to his home to be persecuted and crucified. Finally, so the legend went, Issa came back to India to live out his long life, and died there.

Lorenzo listened wide-eyed to this story. Like so many of his brother Platonists, he tried to reconcile the old religion with the new, and though he did not say so, I thought it disturbed him to think that Christ had never died on the cross but traveled back to India to die there.

Once Salai had fallen asleep in his great-grandfather's arms, Ernesto spoke of the wise men he had met. Of an Indian saint he had traveled for months into the high mountains to find. In a cave little larger than the apothecary storeroom, the man had lived for thirty years in a near constant state of bliss. We heard Papa's stories of Eastern gods, philosophies and ecstatic potions. Lorenzo and I talked of our "journey into wonder" at the Vatican.

Papa himself had eaten *hashish* in a flower-filled garden of a pasha's palace. He believed in his ecstasy that he'd died and gone to a heavenly paradise. When a peacock had come and fanned its huge blue-green tail with its dozens of "eyes" before him, he was sure the bird was a great and all-seeing god, and collapsed into tears when the fan retracted and the peacock strutted away.

"Once," Leonardo said in that tone he reserved for his most outrageous storytelling, "I greedily devoured too many of Mama's cakes. I flew up through the sky, past the blue into the blackness with the stars and planets. I landed on one. It was both heaven and hell. The whole place was a great machine with wheels and cogs and gears and ladders and giant screws. Monsters and demons roamed about. Winged creatures flew at will. *I* flew. Suns exploded." He paused, remembering. "When I came back to this world I found I'd pissed myself. I hadn't moved from the spot I'd laid down in almost a whole day before. I was worried at first. Had I damaged my brain? But I hadn't. So many of the images I had seen in here"—he tapped his forehead—"I could still recall. I began to draw them. Odd contraptions. Devices for walking beneath the water. Terrible weapons of war. And faces. Oh, so many faces! Hideous grotesques. Fearsome dragons. Men and women alike. Humans with animal features. Dragons with human faces. Remind me to show you sometime."

"All that from a little brown resin?" Papa said, amused. "I wish I had brought more home with me."

We all groaned loudly and abused him for his oversight, and he laughed, as I'd never seen him do before.

"Tell us about your wife, Papa," I said.

His face seemed suddenly to collapse in on itself. His closed lips trembled and his eyes filled with tears. "Perhaps another time," he whispered. Then, sniffing sharply, he looked directly at Lorenzo. "What I would like to tell since I have you all here is a little story of my youth. Of a journey that I took on behalf of your grandfather, with his friend, Poggio Bracciolini, to a monastery in Switzerland."

Lorenzo beamed with pleasure. "Would this be a tale of ancient manuscripts discovered in moldering basements and translated by the light of a single candle? Books that ended up in Cosimo's library?"

"It might be," Ernesto said with a sly smile.

"Leonardo," I said to my son. "Perhaps you should put another log on the fire. I think it is going to be a long night."

*W*e were all aware of how time was racing by, mostly visible in the progress of Lorenzo's disease. Less and less could he hide the pain. The dampness and cooler temperatures of Milan worsened his symptoms and now all of his joints had stiffened, making it difficult for him to walk or climb the stairs, to sit or rise from a chair or bed. But rise he did, every day, determined to see through to the end this vast complexity of intrigue against the demon Savonarola.

It was late afternoon in the great ballroom.

"This is a great and solemn occasion."

Lorenzo, Zoroastre, my father, and I stood very still listening to Leonardo's words. It seemed a mystical moment, with motes of dust suspended in the air so like the day thirty years before in the Vinci meadow.

"We have joined in conspiracy to defeat a self-proclaimed Lord of Destruction who will, if unchecked, obliterate all that we love in Florence. Much of what we do may seem profane"—he could not help smiling—"even to the most profane among us. But this cannot be helped. The cost of inaction is far too great. I, for one, must help in any way I can, so that this course should not be sped in vain."

"We are indebted to you, Leonardo," Lorenzo said. "With your dreams and your visions, you make our hopes possible."

The failed flying machine had been carted away. Now Leonardo drew our attention to a small rectangular box on a table. Within a foot away, at the same level, sat a plaster bust of a woman, the full light of the sun shining on her face from a window. The sculpture had been painted in bright colors—the hair yellow, the skin of her face and neck red, the shoulders of her gown cerulean blue.

Leonardo, hovering nearby, beckoned Lorenzo and Papa and me closer, gesturing that we should not step between the window and the box contraption. He wore a mysterious smile, and I was suddenly sure that we were about to be shown another wonder, perhaps greater than any before.

"While I understand the principles, I have not yet put this into words," he began, "so you must forgive me if I stumble while I explain." Without touching it, he pointed to the top of the box. "This is a *camera obscura*. Not my invention. Something Alberti used to watch the sun as it eclipsed. Come carefully around," he instructed us, then pointed to a small hole in the side of the box facing the bust. That side appeared to be made of metal.

"See the aperture here," he said, pointing at the hole drilled through a very thin sheet of iron.

Leonardo stepped back for a moment. "I have been studying the eye very deeply, and this *camera obscura* mimics how *we* see things. There is a hole in the center of our eye very much like that aperture." He pointed back at the pinhole in iron. He had to stop and think, creating the words as thoughts formed in his head. "When an object is illuminated"—he indicated the sunlit bust—"and its image penetrates through a small round hole into a very dark habitation"—he pointed to the box, which clearly was the "habitation"—"you will then receive these images on a sheet of white paper or cloth placed inside it somewhat near the hole."

It was difficult to grasp what Leonardo was saying, and he saw the questions in our eyes.

"Bear with me," he pleaded, grappling for his next words. "When I say the images will be 'received,' I mean that you will *see* the illuminated object on the paper or cloth with their true shapes and colors . . . but they will be less . . . and they will be upside down."

We were all quite speechless, unable to form the simplest question. A moment later he took us out of our misery into a state of magical illumination.

He pulled the top off the box and pointed into it to the side opposite the pinhole aperture. There, on a small expanse of white linen, was the distinct image of the painted bust! The hair was yellow, the skin red and the gown blue, though all of it was, as Leonardo had said, top at the bottom, bottom at the top.

Now Zoroastre appeared, and at Leonardo's nodded assent he carefully pulled the linen-covered back panel out of the box and raced away with it.

"What is he doing!" I cried.

Leonardo smiled. "Taking Alberti's *camera obscura* to a further level. Come." We followed him out of the studio and arrived at the door of Zoroastre's alchemical laboratory, where the young man was bent over several candles in a row, holding in front of it the square of cloth from inside the *camera obscura*.

"Before sliding the linen into the box we coated it with egg white," Leonardo said. "The sun's rays shining in through the aperture, hitting the cloth and making the image created a reaction with the egg."

I moved up close to Zoroastre and the candles. "The cloth is being scorched," I observed.

"But only in the places where egg white and sunlight did not react. The egg made the cloth *insoluble* in those places."

I could see the beginnings of the bust's image take form on the cloth in the form of a scorch mark. Lorenzo remained silent, though I heard Papa muttering, "Yes, yes, I see."

A moment later, Zoroastre rushed the cloth to a basin of water and pushed it in, scrubbing it together like a piece of laundry. This I found alarming—so delicate and precious a thing to be handling so roughly.

I fixed my son with a look of amazement.

"Just wait," he said.

Then Zoroastre turned to us triumphantly, holding up the linen square. There was the image of the woman's bust. Though there were no colors other than the reddish scorch, her features were clearly apparent, an outline of hair, her shoulders. . . .

We were dumbstruck.

"*Pittura de sole,*" Leonardo announced with pride.

"A painting made from the sun," Lorenzo murmured, altogether awestruck.

"We are still experimenting," Leonardo said, excitement in his voice. "I believe that by using mirrors to increase the light shone on the subject, and a lens inside the *camera obscura* to focus the image, it will be sharper, more lifelike."

"And I believe there are better fixatives than egg white," Zoroastre added. "I have tried gum Arabic, and gelatin, but there is something that I am missing." He cast his eyes to his feet. "I am, after all, just an apprentice alchemist."

I found Leonardo gazing at Papa and me. "Here are two of Italy's finest."

"What are you suggesting?" Lorenzo asked him. "That you not *paint* a forgery of the Lirey Shroud? Rather, create it as a *pittura de sole*?"

"I believe it can be done," Leonardo said. "But Zoroastre will need the help of experts. And of course the work must be accomplished in the greatest secrecy. Certainly not here."

"Do you know somewhere?" Lorenzo asked.

"The perfect place. Pavia. Twenty miles south of here. *Il Moro* has sent me there on several occasions to work on the horse. There is a villa. Empty now. Very private, with many small rooms, and one very large. A perfect studio."

"The owner?" Lorenzo pressed.

"A young nobleman with serious gambling debts."

"Get me his particulars," Lorenzo told him. "I will make him an offer he cannot refuse." Then he turned to me and smiled. "Ah, Cato, what a miracle of a man your sister has created!"

The Pavia house was purchased, and Zoroastre was dispatched to make it ready for use as a bottega and alchemical laboratory. Lorenzo's generosity made everything possible in the shortest amount of time. Meanwhile, Leonardo—even in secret from the rest of us—made his "unholy" plans, which, he did explain, were vital to the shroud forgery's success.

At dawn on the day we were meant to leave for Pavia I was stirred from sleep by Lorenzo's cry. I bolted awake to find him sitting in his nightshirt, his legs hanging over the side of the bed. He was frantically pounding his thighs with his fists. He turned and looked at me with desperation.

"I cannot feel my legs. I cannot move them."

I went round and knelt before him and took one bare foot in my hand and rubbed it briskly, then up and down the calf. I did the other, noting how alarming was the color of his skin—bruised and purple brown in places, deathly white in others. His knees were so swollen I dared not touch them.

I willed myself not to weep, to stay strong and calm, while inside I was wild with terror. I managed a smile up at Lorenzo. He had a strange look on his face, as though he were listening for a sound from a long distance away.

"Continue, Caterina. What you are doing . . . I feel something, just a little, in my right foot." I rubbed it more vigorously. He nodded, then smiled weakly. "Yes. It's pain." There was a choked laugh. "I have never been happier to feel pain."

I worked in this way until all sensation had returned. In no time he could move his toes, his ankles, his knees. Nothing was said of the sickly colored skin that remained.

"I think you should rest, Lorenzo. Get back in bed."

"No, I must walk."

"Please, my darling."

"I need to know if I can *walk*, Caterina."

With his arm around my shoulder I pulled him up, and quite miraculously he could walk with help, albeit slowly at first. Then he bade me step back. I was loath to let go of him. Wished in that moment I could cling to him forever.

But I released my grip. He straightened his back and with great effort took a step on his own. Then another, and another.

"Lorenzo," I said quietly. He turned. "Will you sit down now? You've proven you can walk. Do not tire yourself."

He shuffled to the morning table and with great agony of his bending knees, sat down. He was quiet for a long while, thinking, making plans. I knew that look so well.

"Caterina," he said finally. "Send for my chests."

"What do you mean? Lorenzo, you cannot mean to travel to Pavia today. Not in your condition."

"I'm not going to Pavia. I'm going home, my love. To Florence."

"Florence!"

He was silent again, collecting his thoughts while mine were racing, pounding inside my head.

"I must be back in Florence so that I am able to complete my part of our plan. You know what that part is."

I was shaking my head no. I did not wish to hear it. But he was determined that I would.

"My part is to die, Caterina."

"No," I said and began to weep where I sat, unable to go to him, paralyzed as he had been before.

"If I cannot say what must be said to Savonarola on my deathbed, our conspiracy will come to nothing. I thought you understood this."

"But you're not dying!" I cried. "You cannot be dying!"

"Come here," he said in his gentlest voice.

I went and sat at his feet. He pushed the damp hair back from my brow and stroked my head. I was grateful he could not see my face.

"My body is failing," he said. "My joints and limbs are the least of it. Inside I can feel the collapse. You know this is true."

"Why has nothing I've done helped?" I wailed.

"It is in my blood. My father and grandfather were not the only Medici men with the affliction. Their brothers died of it. If Giuliano had lived long enough, he would have succumbed as well." I heard a crack in his voice. "I can only pray for my sons."

"Must you go today? Surely you can stay . . ." I looked up at him to find his face as wet with tears as my own.

"I cannot stay. God knows I do not wish to leave you. You are my *heart*, Caterina. I share my soul with you. But if I do not go . . . Florence is lost." He stroked my cheek with the back of his hand. "I will make you a promise, and you know very well that I keep my promises."

"I do."

"We will see one another again, *in this life*. When the time comes I'll send for you. And you will ride as quickly as you can. No carriages. They're too slow." He looked away. "I will need you at the end."

"Will you leave me enough time?"

"That is my promise."

I wiped my eyes with the palm of my hand. "Lorenzo, oh, love . . . how will I live without you?"

"With memory, Caterina," he whispered. "Twenty years of riches. It is more than most lovers have." A smile split his face then, sincere, as though he were remembering.

"Tell me," I demanded.

"Your first weekend at Careggi. The Academy."

I nodded. "You opened a door for me . . . to the whole of the universe."

"And you?" he asked.

I knew the answer at once. "The expression on your face when Cato's breast bindings first fell away."

He laughed then, and I could see real joy in his eyes.

"You will survive, Caterina. I'm depending on you to survive. You and Leonardo and your father. This must be done. How long it will take is yet unclear. The prior is clever, but he deludes himself as to how clever he really is. As Roderigo said, the chink in his armor."

The time for indulging our pain and sadness had passed. I stood. "I'll tell Leonardo." When I turned to go Lorenzo grasped my hand and held it to his cheek.

"An embarrassment of riches," he said, then let my hand slip from his.

I closed the door behind me, and the sound it made, so strong and final, became a memory itself. *Lorenzo.* How the Fates had blessed us. Now memory would have to suffice.

*I*n the coming months Lorenzo's fortitude inspired me to perform no less nobly than he had done. The soul of Florence was at stake, and I steadfastly held to that thought, for it was imperative to be strong. There was no place for sentimentality in our task, nor the luxury of squeamishness.

A week after our small band of conspirators had moved into the Pavian villa, Leonardo arrived in the night with the corpse of a young man in the back of his cart. He was very tall with oddly long arms, legs, and fingers. He was deeply packed in Alpine ice—paid for handsomely by Lorenzo.

No one had the heart to ask who the poor fellow was, but we knew Leonardo's dissection privileges at Milan's hospital were making such a sacrilege possible at all. Zoroastre, Leonardo, Papa, and I were all needed to carry the body into the studio. We laid it out on the long table we had prepared beside the huge *camera obscura* box that had been erected under the large south-facing windows, stuffing as much of the remaining ice around the man as we could to see him through the night.

The fixing agent for the cloth was yet in question. By the light of the alchemical furnace, Papa, Zoroastre, and I had, for weeks, experimented with every substance from bitumen to chromium salts. The salts seemed most promising. When ferrochromite ore was roasted with soda and lime, a chromite salt was produced. The same ore heated with potash and lime gave us potassium salt. The residue, when mixed with acid, allowed for differing brightness and clarity of image on the cloth. It was a heated argument about which would be the best acid to use, and the precise proportion of either substance for mixing with egg whites.

Every few hours that first evening Leonardo would come to the laboratory and interrogate us of our progress or lack of it. In one of his notebooks he recorded everything.

During a late evening meal it began to rain and Leonardo grew more worried with every passing hour. Fully eight hours of bright sunlight were needed for exposure, he told us, staring straight ahead and not touching a morsel of food.

That night as I lay in bed I staved off my thoughts of dread with what sweet memories I could cull from the past. In the end, so that I would be strong and well rested for the day ahead, I mixed myself a potion of poppy and valerian and slept like the dead till Papa woke me at dawn. We were thrilled to see the rain had abated and the sun had blessedly complied.

Together we descended into Leonardo's studio and found the tall corpse facedown on the table, his arms tucked beneath him. Somehow— and I did not wish to know the method—his back had been horribly torn in a hundred places, as though by a whip used by flagellants. The wounds were dark red but bloodless. I silently blessed the herbs that had helped me sleep so peacefully during whatever the night's mayhem must have been.

"Uncle Cato, come help me here," Leonardo said when he saw me at the studio door.

I steeled myself and went to him. He handed me a large cotton puff like one he was holding.

"We'll make half the length of the shroud today—only the back view. We must dust the body with this," he told me, holding out a bowl of bright white powder. "The subject needs to be white for the image to fix dark on the linen."

He smiled at me. A hopeful smile. We were partners in this. A Great Work shared with my son. We had to succeed. So much was at risk.

As I powdered the man's flayed back Leonardo began arranging eight tall mirrors attached by hinges to each other. I thought to ask the reason for this, but then he gave a signal to his apprentice, who beckoned Papa and me into the alchemical laboratory.

"We need to work quickly," Zoroastre told us.

With great efficiency we mixed up a large enough batch of the egg and fixing solution we'd finally agreed would be the best—ferrochromite—to soak one end of the linen. Then we fixed it to a frame, where it dried. Urine, we had discovered just before we'd gone to bed, was the best of all substances for a scorching agent.

It took the four of us to carefully slide the framed linen into the *camera obscura*.

Leonardo and Zoroastre now positioned the octagonal mirror between the windows and the corpse. Finally Leonardo stood at the aperture, adjusting over it a finely crafted lens he had ground especially for the device.

In the last moments before the sun shone in through the windows, Leonardo's concentration reached such a furious pitch that, blazing with a bright terrible fervor, he seemed hardly present in the room with us.

At last the light came streaming in and struck the mirrors. With a few final adjustments to them—perceptible only to Leonardo—the exposure began. I could see instantly how the mirrors intensified the sun's rays, but it was clear, too, that such strong light and heat might accelerate the corpse's decomposition.

With a great heaving sigh, Leonardo herded us from the studio.

"All we can do is wait," he said. "Best we can do is take ourselves away. Eight hours will seem like a lifetime if we stay."

We did go, taking food for a lunch *al fresco*, blankets and pillows. We found a lovely spot on a hilltop with full sun and the shade of a tree. Leonardo had brought his notebook and scribbled furiously, sketching from memory the *camera*, the corpse, and the octagonal mirrors.

Zoroastre wandered about aimlessly, unused to being away from the constant work of the bottega, and nearly driving Leonardo mad. "Can you not sit still?" he asked his assistant.

Finally, Papa intervened. "Let me show you some autumnal plants," he said to Zoroastre, "whose properties will help you speed the process of putrefaction."

By late afternoon the wait had become intolerable for us all, and we barely spoke as we walked the distance home.

There was hardly a breath among us as we examined our handiwork. But there, to our relief and amazement, was a dark, ghostly image on the shroud. The back of the head and neck could be seen, the shoulders and shape of the back, the marks of the whip darker than the rest. The buttocks, thighs, and calves were there as well, the left more faint than the right.

Leonardo was ecstatic. It was more than he had dreamed possible. He hugged us each with joy, and once we'd laid the shroud out to dry, he pushed us into the kitchen, where he served us a cold supper, calling out to Zoroastre to open a new flask of wine for the celebration.

We had, he told us, accomplished a miracle that day. A feat of wonder. Alberti, if he could see us now, would be toasting us, and Nature herself blessing her divine children.

The next morning when I came into the studio I found the corpse lying faceup. It had been positioned with his hands crossed over his genitals. Again wounds had been made in the body. His wrists and feet looked as though they'd been impaled with spikes, and a gash in his side approximated the Roman centurion's lance wound. His thumbnails had been tied together with thread to keep the arms from flopping to his sides, and his legs were set parallel to one another. His legs were so long it was decided they must be bent slightly, so to fit on the table. Leonardo rigged them from below to prevent slippage, the last gruesome task I hoped my tenderhearted son would be forced to do.

But in fact the sun shone *too* strongly for that days-old body. By the time the mirrors were set in place, a stink was already rising from our poor Jesus. Zoroastre wondered if we could do without the mirrors, but Leonardo worried that the front image would then not match the back.

This time we stayed on vigil at the villa. Each hour one or the other of us would leave the dining table where we sat making nervous conversation to see how the body was holding up. At dinner hour we all barely picked at our food, and once Leonardo had returned with the news that all was still well, Papa—knowing how bad was our desperation—began to talk.

"I married the most beautiful Indian woman." His features softened and his lips tilted into a smile. "She was a widow of some age, not as old as I, but neither was she a girl. I had already traveled for several years before I came to the village where she lived. Mina was her name." He stared down at his hand as though it were one side of a locket and he could see her face there.

"She was already an outcast when we met. Not one of the 'untouchables,' as some are. She had been born high into the Brahmin caste and as an eleven-year-old girl had married a man of her own station. But he had been a cruel husband, beating her unmercifully, abusing her in every way, and threatening that if she did not obey his commands he would have his mother set her on fire."

My eyes went wide. Papa noticed. "It is custom there—wife burning. Mothers-in-law who disapprove of their sons' wives will oftentimes throw oil on an unfortunate girl and set her alight."

My father's story had the hoped-for effect. So riveted were we to the horrors he was describing in India, there was no thought for our conspiracy or the dead body lying in the studio before a *camera obscura*.

"Does the mother-in-law pay for her crime?" I asked.

"No. It is forgiven. You see, women are quite disposable in India. Another more docile wife can be found for the widowed son."

"A known murderer goes unpunished!" I cried.

"Only the murderers of *women*," he corrected me. "The Hindus believe that females are born without souls and only acquire them after marriage."

"That is preposterous," Leonardo said. "I thought the Indian pantheon included several *goddesses*."

"It does." Papa shook his head. "There is much complexity on the Indian continent. So much I was never able to comprehend."

"Why was your wife an outcast?" I asked him.

"I'm afraid you will not like my answer." He smiled, and I thought I saw a hint of pride in it. "Mina's husband died of a fever that, after having nursed him and contracting it herself, nearly killed her. She barely survived, but when it came time for his body to be cremated—the mode of dealing with remains in India—his family insisted she commit *suti*."

None of us asked the obvious, knowing that Ernesto was eager to shock us further.

"During cremation, good wives there throw themselves onto the funeral pyres." Now he smiled broadly. "Mina was not against the custom itself. She would have gladly gone on to her next incarnation, she told me, if her husband had not in this lifetime been such an ass."

We found ourselves laughing at the macabre tale.

"In refusing to die in the flames she acquired the scorn of her husband's family as well as her own. She had disgraced them all. When I met her, Mina was living alone on the outskirts of town, barely surviving by selling goat's milk to women who were secretly sympathetic to her plight."

"Did she let you take her away from that terrible place?" Zoroastre said.

Papa nodded. "She became my traveling companion, my guide, and after I taught her Italian—and with my smattering of Hindi—my translator as well. She was very bright, and as you must now realize, quite spirited and willful." He smiled at Zoroastre. "She reminded me of my dear daughter—Leonardo's mother. My wife and I traveled the length and breadth of India," Papa continued. "I have never had such a friend as she."

I saw his chin quiver. "Mina was younger than I. It never crossed my mind . . ." He paused and looked down at his hands again. ". . . that she would go before me."

Papa did not look in my direction, but I knew that his strength and love, like two swift arrows, were aimed directly at my own breaking heart.

He smiled at Leonardo. "I wish you could have done her portrait. In the East they do not often paint pictures of mortal men and women. Only their gods—with eight arms, or elephant trunks, or feet stomping upon human skulls." He chuckled. "I think you would like India very much, Leonardo."

I found I was suddenly near tears, so I offered to take my turn next in the studio. What I saw depressed me further. While the body was whole, the face had begun decomposing. The man's lips were shriveling back in a grim rictus of a smile, and the skin around the bony part of the nose was falling away. I was no expert, but even I could see that too many hours were yet left of exposure in the bright sunlight for success.

I returned to the dining room and made my report.

Zoroastre stood. "I'll pull the linen out."

"No," Leonardo said in a decisive tone. That mind of his was churning.

He rushed from the dining room and we all followed him into the studio. He had climbed to the top of the *camera obscura* and was very carefully peering inside.

"I don't believe any chemical change has occurred on the linen yet. Zoroastre, bring me a piece of cloth two feet by two feet. Quickly."

"What are you doing?" I asked him.

"We will use the front of this body, but not the front of the head."

Horrible visions swam before my eyes. Puncturing and flaying a corpse was one thing. Beheading it was something else again.

"Son," I whispered to him urgently as he descended the ladder. "You cannot . . ."

"Don't worry, Mama. I may be a ghoul, but I am not a monster." He set the square cloth atop the linen where the face would appear.

As we had been the night before, we were rewarded by a perfect image of the corpse's front, the chest and arms dark with laceration marks, the torso, rounded thighs, and calves ghostly shadows on the light linen. Where the face should have been was blank. Leonardo had been correct. The solution had not yet reacted to light, and washed out completely in the boiling water.

But everyone was more than curious to hear how Leonardo planned to add the face to the nearly completed shroud image.

"I will use myself as the model," he said.

We all stared at him in uncomprehending silence.

"A place on the shroud is waiting for Jesus's face. Whose better than *mine*?"

"Could anything be more sacrilegious?" I said.

"A perfect blasphemy," Papa added.

"A better practical joke than a stinkball," said Zoroastre.

"You could be caught, Leonardo," I said, bringing an end to the levity. "They would burn you at the stake."

"I will not be recognized," he assured me. "Look at what we have so far." He led me to the wall where the shroud was tacked up to dry. "The high places that appear to touch the winding sheet appear the darkest. The image of my face that will be seen by the pilgrims as they pass will be the line of my nose, my forehead with its bloody thorn holes, my mustache, beard, and cheekbones. I believe the entire area of my eye sockets will be light. Without sight of that part of my face, I will not be recognizable. But of course we must do several trials first. We cannot afford to ruin the work we've already done."

I was unconvinced, too worried as a mother to listen to sense, but there was nothing to do but try.

The next day we positioned a powdered Leonardo on the table, placing the square of treated cloth in the *camera* where it would fit on the shroud. Before Zoroastre fixed the mirrors on him, Leonardo told us, "The most difficult part of this is lying still for eight hours. Not moving a muscle."

He was right. Two hours into the first trial some of the powder strayed into a nostril. He sneezed so violently he nearly came off the table.

The next sunny day we were more careful with the powder. Papa spoke to Leonardo quietly, telling him how the great mystics of India were able to slow their breathing so extremely that they appeared, for all intents and purposes, dead to the world. For hours he sat as close as he was able, guiding Leonardo through breath after shallow breath. We had made it through six hours when a stray cat who'd found its way into the villa, slipping past everyone's notice, leapt onto Leonardo's stomach.

Such a rude awakening from a near trance caused a terrible shriek, which made us all scream and then fall about in gales of laughter . . . and no little frustration.

This was, in fact, the first time I had seen Leonardo give in to despair. For the days were getting shorter, the hours of full light less and less, and fewer without gray skies and rain.

I watched him as he stood over a bowl of water to wash the powder off his face and hair. He stared at his reflection and sighed deeply. The consternation was palpable in his expression. He was altogether unused to failure. There was always a solution to be had. Always another experiment.

Finally he leaned down and splashed his face with water. But as I watched, I saw him freeze in that position, stay still as a statue for the longest moment. Then he straightened slowly and stared at his own image in the looking glass. His face was still white with powder, but rivulets of water dripped down his cheeks and through his beard.

"Bring me the powder," he whispered. Only I had heard him.

"Zoroastre," I said, "will you bring Leonardo the bowl of powder?"

He rushed away and was back moments later with the bowl, which he set before my son.

Leonardo looked down and, splashing his cheeks and nose and forehead once more with water, thrust his hands into the powder bowl, then brought them to his face. He pressed them into the wetness till it caked there, thick—like plaster.

I gasped quietly, for I knew his thinking.

That divine mind, I thought.

"Death mask," he said quietly. "A living man's death mask."

He turned and smiled at me, the thick wet powder cracking his face.

"A white plaster cast of my face!" he fairly shouted at Papa and Zoroastre. "It cannot move. It will not need to breathe. And we shall lock all the doors against cats!" He laughed joyously. "How did I not think of this before?"

He hugged Papa, then Zoroastre, then me.

"We must work quickly. We cannot be sure of the sun much longer." To Zoroastre he said, "Drive into Pavia now. To Bellmonte's bottega. Get us a barrel of plaster.

The boy was gone in an instant.

"If this works, we shall have our forgery. The perfect holy relic. The Lirey Shroud with the face of Our Lord . . ." He grinned at Papa and me. ". . . Leonardo da Vinci."

Of course it worked perfectly. On the last full day of sun in November 1491 the *camera obscura*, using our refined fixative, captured the image of my son's face from the plaster death mask, perfectly aligned with the body of the Milanese corpse. A straight dark slash at the neck separated the two parts, though otherwise it appeared a flawless match.

There were several anomalies—a foreshortened forehead, and eyes a bit too high on the face. With more of the fixative on a paintbrush and another full day of exposure, Leonardo added the long hair, and dabbing a mixture of his own blood and reddish pigment at the line of the crown of thorns, the centurion's spear wound, the wrist and foot holes, he added droplets and rivulets where, with his precise knowledge of anatomy, he knew blood would likely have appeared.

The new Lirey Shroud was perfect.

*W*e'd barely had time for celebration when a letter arrived from Lorenzo asking me to come home. The messenger he'd sent was, in fact, one of his fiercest *conditores*, so that my journey to Florence would not be without protection.

I remember very little of that hard ride, except gratitude for my male disguise. I had become a proficient "horseman" over the years, and had I been a lady in a carriage, the week traveling would have stretched into two.

This time the sight of beloved Florence filled me as much with dread as with joy. Once within the city walls I could feel a kind of foreboding in the streets, for it was well known that Lorenzo was dying. Most Florentines now outwardly cleaved to Savonarola's austere principles and practices, but still wondered if it was enough to protect them from an eternity of fire and brimstone.

I overheard two men whispering that two of the lions at the Via de Leone, always quite peaceable, had the night before fought so violently they had mauled each other to death. A woman went mad during mass at Santa Maria Novella the day before and began shrieking about a raging bull with flaming horns that was pulling down the church. She-wolves were said to be howling at night. All these were ominous portents.

I found streets teeming with sinister activity. A steady stream of monks scurried from the San Marco Monastery in through the front door of Palazzo Medici with no guards in sight. My heart sank to see more of them exiting, their arms piled high with books. One carried Lorenzo's much-prized ninth-century *Tragedies of Sophocles*, that ancient volume he had proudly shown me on my first visit to his home.

I entered unmolested to find a small contingent of guards at the stairs to the upper floors and at the door to the garden; the colonnaded courtyard had been invaded by brown-robed clergy. Someone had thrown sheeting over Donatello's *David*. Surely Savonarola's work. Had he desired to spare his minions so disgusting a display of sensuality, I wondered, or was he afraid it might arouse them? Doors to the *banco* were shut tight, and I could see that Lorenzo's magnificent library had been all but emptied.

I approached a stony-faced guard at the stairs, a man that I recognized. "Where is the family?" I said.

"They have gone to Careggi." His voice was as lifeless as his eyes.

"Who is in charge?" I asked.

"Piero." His face suddenly twisted in agony. "*Il Magnifico* . . . I pray for him, but these maggots," he whispered, sneering at the San Marco monks, "they desecrate the man's home before he is even dead."

I knew I must leave at once.

The whole perimeter of the country estate was heavily guarded, though I had no difficulty reaching the villa. The ground floor was a hive of activity—the salon Piero's makeshift command center. As I climbed the staircase I heard loud arguing and caught sight of Lorenzo's heir surrounded by *conditores*, a new circle of young *consiglieres*, and several elder members of the Signoria, shouting and waving their hands, all demanding attention. Utter chaos reigned where perfect order had once prevailed. *Day and night, it is. Heaven and hell.*

I forced my thoughts from Careggi's back garden—the Temple of Truth, the ancient tree under whose bowers the Academy had searched and debated the far limits of understanding.

Our Great Conspiracy is Savonarola's own Pandora's Box, I mused as I climbed to the first floor, *but the key that unlocked it was the death of the man I loved.*

Here, above, was chaos of a different nature. I saw physicians streaming in and out of Lorenzo's bedroom. There was the family's foremost doctor, who had stalwartly refused to believe Lorenzo's illness was fatal, instructing him that all would be well if he refrained from eating grape pits and pears, and made sure to keep his feet warm and dry. Lucrezia the Elder sat weeping on a hall bench with her namesake daughter trying to console her. Pico Mirandola, himself distraught, was beleaguering a hapless page trying to explain how Savonarola's monks had gained entrance into the palazzo.

"Then the library is lost!" I heard Pico cry.

"It is," I said, rescuing the poor boy, giving him leave to go and turning to Pico. "We can only hope the Prior of San Marco has enough sanity left not to burn the books."

He and I embraced. "Silio is barricaded in his rooms claiming that ghostly giants are fighting and screeching in his garden. Angelo is in there," he said, looking at the bedroom door, "arguing with a specialist from Pavia, who is insisting that Lorenzo drink a concoction made of ground-up diamonds and pearls." He shook his head in disbelief. My heart went out to Angelo Poliziano, who, of all the men who had surrounded Lorenzo, loved him most deeply.

"Is he in terrible pain?" I asked Pico.

"It is unimaginable. For no reason he bleeds through the skin of his hands and arms. He aches in the very marrow of his bones. He is so tormented he gets no rest whatsoever, and yet . . ." Pico laughed ruefully. ". . . Lorenzo seems more concerned to soothe his physicians' feelings than to alleviate his own suffering."

"I would like to see him," I told my friend.

"Go in," Pico said. "Perhaps you can save him from that mad Pavian and his crushed pearls."

I steeled myself as best as I could, attempting if not a smile, then a pleasant expression, when all I could feel was crushing grief.

The sight of Lorenzo, close as he was to the end, was so joyous a vision that I had to restrain myself rushing into his arms. Angelo Poliziano stood in one corner haranguing a haughty-looking man in dark robes I assumed was the physician.

Lorenzo saw me at once, and his face, though racked with pain, lit like the sun moving out from behind a storm cloud.

"Angelo," he said with the greatest affection, "would you show the good doctor out for now?"

"*Gladly,*" Poliziano replied and, nodding a respectful greeting to me, steered the man to the door, closing it behind them.

"Lock the door, Caterina," he told me, and as I approached the bed he whispered, "Lie down here next to me."

I did, and marveled at how safe I felt in the arms of a man so close to dying.

"Tell me of our *pittura del sole,*" he said.

I hardly knew how to begin. "I have never believed in magic, Lorenzo. Like my son, I adhere to the infinite possibilities of Nature. But what Leonardo created out of natural substances and alchemical processes is something *magical,* even to these skeptical eyes of mine."

"And will it serve our purposes in all the necessary ways?"

"Perfectly."

Lorenzo exhaled a long satisfied sigh. "Then I will leave this world content," he said. "How wonderful it would be if all people knew that by their death something great would be gained."

It was inconceivable how sanguine he was at the thought of dying.

"Piero . . . ," I began.

"Piero will prove a disastrous leader," Lorenzo said. "He hasn't a prayer of overcoming the prior's influence. Things in Florence will grow far worse before they can improve. I want you to go back to live with Leonardo in Milan."

I nodded my assent. It was, with every moment, growing more difficult to speak, with no sorrow, no regret.

"Can you move closer?" he whispered hoarsely, unable to keep the pain from his voice. "Your heat is soothing."

I pushed as close as I could to him and laid one arm over his chest. I felt his lips on the crown of my head.

"There is something I must tell you now—what I learned from *Il Moro* when we last visited him. What he and Roderigo are planning. Roderigo," he murmured with no little awe, "the first Borgia pope. When he takes the tall hat you must go to Rome and see him. He holds the final intelligence that will secure our conspiracy's success."

When he groaned I released my hold on him, knowing the touch of my body, while perhaps warming him, must also be causing him pain. We lay side by side staring up at the underside of the bed's carven canopy.

"If Innocent is that close to dying," I said, "do you realize that Savonarola correctly prophesied the year of your death *and* the pope's?"

"I do. In its own perverse way, that is what will make what I tell our friend so perfectly believable. Caterina, I need you to bring me a pen and paper."

I rose reluctantly and went to the desk.

Leaning on one elbow, Lorenzo struggled with his gnarled fingers to do the necessary writing.

"Let me do it," I said.

"No. The invitation must come from my own hand."

When it was done I poured red wax over the folded letter and closed it with the Medici seal.

He lay back, exhausted with that small exertion.

"How long do you think the pulverized gems will take to kill me?" he asked unexpectedly.

I turned and strode back to his bedside.

"Lorenzo, no! I cannot even imagine the pain it will cause."

"It can be no worse than what I'm already suffering. Caterina," he said, grabbing my hand, "I must know when to take it. I want to *die in his presence*. Think what he will make of that!"

I lay down again to embrace him, finally unable to hide my desperation or contain my tears. His arms went around me and he kissed my face a hundred times.

"Go now, love," he finally said.

I rose, and hardly knowing how to put one foot in front of the other, went to the door.

"You must thank Leonardo for me," I heard him say. "And all the world will thank you, sweetest of all women . . . for Leonardo."

I turned back for my final sight of the man whom I had been so blessed to love.

"One last smile, Lorenzo," I said. "I wish to remember you smiling."

I rode into Florence and again to Via Larga.

It took all my courage to walk into the Monastery of San Marco. I spoke quietly to a fresh-faced young monk, saying I held a correspondence from Lorenzo de' Medici that must be delivered to his prior in person.

He scurried away, no doubt puffed with importance that he should be the one who would bring this momentous news to Savonarola.

A different Dominican returned, this one older and more severe. He looked as though he might never have smiled in his whole life, and eyed the sealed letter in my hand, as though it had been written by Satan himself.

"You will follow me," he instructed, and turned away.

Up we went to the first-floor hallway. The place stank of urine, as though the monks rarely bothered to piss out of doors, and each tonsured man that saw me glared, as though he believed his evil eye might frighten me.

The door to a small, plain cell was opened. The Prior Savonarola, sitting at a spare desk on a backless bench, was gazing out an arched window, the one I knew to overlook the Medici sculpture garden. Without looking up he gestured for the severe-looking monk to leave us.

Then we were alone.

He turned, and I was struck once again by the man's hideousness—lips, nose, close-set eyes ringed with brown shadows, and suffused with a sick, simmering rage.

"Why should I believe this comes from the Medici tyrant?" Savonarola said, skewering me with the beady green eyes.

"Because, Father," I said in my humblest tone, "here is the Medici seal." I handed him the folded letter. "I know how severely I would be punished for bringing you a forgery."

He plucked the missive from my hand and brought it to the window, peering closely at the seal before opening it. He stood with his back to me as he read Lorenzo's words, and I could see the slightly hunched back straighten.

"You realize I have already rejected a dozen of his invitations to visit with him," he said.

I shook my head stupidly.

"Do you know what is in this letter?" Savonarola asked me, turning back to watch my face as I answered.

"I do, Father. Lorenzo—"

"The Medici tyrant," he corrected me.

"The Medici tyrant," I continued obediently, "is in full cognizance of his sins as he lies dying, and wishes to confess them to you."

"He is at Careggi?"

"Yes."

"And he has no trap laid for me along the way?"

"No, Father! He has simply seen, as the end draws near, the shrieking abyss of his sinful life, and wishes for redemption." I fell to my knees before him. "Please be merciful."

He stared at me suspiciously. "Do I know you?"

"Yes, Father." I looked down at the floor. "Some years ago your angels brought me to the Office of Night for an infringement of God's law. I quickly saw the error of my ways and was fortunate to have received personal instruction from your fair, correcting hand."

"And you are yet an intimate of the Medici," he accused.

"Only *recently*, Father. Only since I have helped guide him to God. Please . . ." I grabbed the prior's hand, forcing myself to kiss it. "Please hear his confession. Do not let him die unshriven!"

"How close is he to death?"

"Hours. The doctors say he will be gone by morning."

"Leave me," he said dismissively.

"But will you see him, Father?" I pressed. "His is a soul worth saving. Imagine how many would benefit from knowing Lorenzo de' Medici has, with your help, stepped from the shadows into the light."

I dared look up only enough to see Savonarola nodding in silent agreement. I lowered my eyes quickly.

"Rise," he said. "I will see this wretched devil. It will take a merciful God indeed to bring him from the edge of the great abyss to salvation."

"Thank you, thank you!" I cried, kissing his hand again and again. Then I rose, revulsion in my throat, and quite unable to look into that face again, I left his cell and walked swiftly from the monastery.

Outside on Via Larga, sure no one was watching, I spat the filth of his person from my mouth onto the ground. I walked the short block to the Palazzo Medici and stood in the front doorway peering back at San Marco. It was not long before a band of angels began pouring forth into the street. Now a carriage appeared, and the prior emerged, a phalanx of Dominicans surrounding him. They helped him inside and the carriage drove away.

Soon enough, Via Largo began to fill with Florentines. Word had gone out. Angels were spreading the news. *Il Magnifico* had called for Savonarola to hear his confession!

With that knowledge, and realizing some hours must pass till the next measure of success, I disappeared into the palazzo.

The courtyard was deserted but for a few guards. Lorenzo's library door was wide open, the shelves obscenely empty. I pulled the door shut and went to the man guarding the grand stairway.

"Did you see him?" he asked me.

I nodded. "He is very brave," I told him. "He means to die a good death."

The man began to cry. He moved aside and let me pass. I took the steps for what I knew to be the last time, to the first floor, now all but deserted.

There was glory here, I thought, *glory of a kind perhaps never seen before and once disappeared, never to return.* Beauty reigned without question—towering colonnades, statuary, paintings and gardens. But something greater lived in the House of Medici.

Love of family. Care and passion and pride. Reverence for ancestry. Hope for the young. Loyalty. Goodness. Grace.

It would die with Lorenzo. *The time of greatness has passed.* I knew this as I walked the echoing hallway. Stepped into the great salon. Stood gazing at Gozzoli's frescoed chapel.

I went to the east wall where Lorenzo had shown me the artist's two renditions of the one-day Medici ruler—the idealized, handsome young man with fair curls riding a proud horse, and the red-hatted scholar pressed amidst a gaggle of boys, his squashed nose and swarthy complexion easy to miss in a crowd.

Lorenzo had been both of these, I thought. Friend to princes and philosophers alike. Bawdy. Reserved. Playful. Fearless. Common. Kingly. Humble. Generous. Kind.

Il Magnifico. He had earned his title.

It had been my honor to have loved him.

Even now he lay dying, pearls and diamonds coursing through his veins. With his last breath he would whisper secrets into a devil's ear, the slender dagger blade of lies that would pierce the fine chinks in that glittering armor of false righteousness.

Lorenzo. Florence.

They would live as one until the end of time.

Sitting alone in the great salon I heard the noise of the crowd below on Via Larga as it grew in size in anticipation of Savonarola's return. I had willed myself to be numb, without feeling of any kind. I thought that if I allowed myself even a dram of emotion to seep to the surface I might lose my grasp of this world. Like Silio Ficino see ghostly battles in the sky, or that poor woman with her visions of a raging bull pulling down the church. I must, for all our sakes, for the sake of the city, for the memory of Lorenzo, hold tight to my own sanity. Save my grief for later.

There'd be time enough for that.

A great cry rose up from the crowd and I knew the prior had returned. I took myself down the staircase and out the door of the palazzo to find the length of the street overflowing, all the people pressing in the direction of the chapel's front door. My body became the sharp prow of a ship slicing through waves as I pushed through the mass of humanity to the base of the church steps.

There he stood in his glory, burning with obscene religious passion.

"My children!" he shouted, quieting every voice, "I come with great tidings! The Medici tyrant is dead! Remember my sermons! Remember that I foretold of his death *in this year!*"

Now there was murmuring in the crowd. I felt my knees go weak, but I forced myself to straighten, knowing worse was to come.

"As I arrived at the Devil's lair of Careggi, fiery lights blazed in the sky above! I trembled at the sight, for I knew it was God's beacon leading me to help in that sinner's salvation! In his luxurious bed he writhed and suffered in great agony, but less of the body than the spirit, for he knew how atrociously he had lived! He begged me to absolve him of his sins, desperately afraid of dying unshriven, screaming at the prospect of Hell for all Eternity!"

I turned myself into stone to endure the words, hoping for some sign that Lorenzo had managed to accomplish his part.

Savonarola raised his arms to the heavens. "The fiery star above Careggi began to dim as the life did from the sinner's body. In that moment he pulled me close and whispered in my ear a confession that I believed sincere!" He closed his eyes as though in ecstasy. "And then a miracle happened! Another voice spoke to me through the lips of this sinner . . ." The crowd was still and the silence fearful. "And it was the voice of God!"

There were shouts of surprise. A woman began to weep in terror. I heard Lorenzo's name called, and "God save us!" all around me.

"What did the Lord say!?" someone called from the street.

"This prophecy is one that shall be revealed in the fullness of time!" Savonarola cried with grave portentousness.

I felt my body sag with relief. Like carefully aimed arrows, Lorenzo's words whispered to this unholy monster in his final moments of life had found their intended mark. As Savonarola had done in the past—culling his parishioners' most secret confessions to create his corrupt predictions of the future—he had greedily pulled the loosened threads of our shroud conspiracy to use for his own self-exalting purposes, never realizing that *we* were the weavers, and that the completed fabric would become his very own winding cloth.

In the fullness of time, indeed.

The wait would seem interminable, but the reward would be savory.

*I*t was a year of death and of new beginnings, 1492.

Pope Innocent, upon hearing of Lorenzo's passing, proclaimed, "The peace of Italy is at an end!" then promptly succumbed to a final convulsion and died.

Roderigo Borgia, to great acclaim, ascended the papal throne, assuming the pagan name of Alexander—after the Greek sodomite general who had conquered the world. His first act as pontiff was to write Pico della Mirandola a personal letter of support, absolving him of his heretical crimes of Cabalist scholarship.

What Jews Queen Isabella had not murdered in her brutal Inquisition she expelled *en masse* from Spain, while her navigator Christoforo Columbus, sailing west across the Ocean Sea, found a new world, claiming all the gold and heathen souls there for Christendom.

King Louis of France went to his grave, leaving his throne and the first standing army in Europe's history to an ambitious twenty-two-year-old named Charles, who, with his huge flaring birthmark near one eye, a fearsome facial twitch, and six toes on each foot, was most sympathetically described as appallingly educated, most disparagingly as "an abortion."

I remained in Florence alone in my little house living half a life, for though Lorenzo had left me well provided for, I had no work to do. Without my apothecary I had no means to heal my neighbors, even if they had dared seek help from one of the "sorcerers" the Prior of San Marco decried from his pulpit. Books were too dangerous to own except for Scripture. If one was found it was burned along with its owner.

There was no one left in the Palazzo Medici who knew me, Lucrezia having followed her beloved son to the grave within months. After Lorenzo's death at Careggi, Piero and his family had slinked back to Florence like dogs who cower at the sound of thunder. And though he ostensibly ruled in his father's place, he was granted neither credence nor respect.

My friends of the Academy were taking shelter in Rome or Venice, or keeping their heads down in the sad city of Florence. No festivals, horse races, gambling, no dancing, no Sunday *calcio* matches. All that was left were solemn masses and sermons that grew blacker and blacker, and a populace beaten by their fears of eternal damnation into dull submission.

I had begun attending Savonarola's church services, knowing it was there at the Duomo that I would receive the first signal that our conspiracy had sprung to life.

"Oh, my sinning children," he sang out to an overflowing crowd at the cathedral one Sunday in early 1493. "I must speak to you of prophecy today. Of a holy relic that will shortly be revealed to us."

The audience pressed forward, straining to hear, for there was nothing more dear to the hearts of Christians than their relics.

I covered my smile with my hand, remembering all that had transpired at the Corte Vecchia and in the Pavia house. In the last moments of his life Lorenzo had whispered word of the shroud not as a message from God—the prior would never have believed such a sinner. But we knew the man was a cheat. He called intelligence gleaned from confessions made to his priests "the word of an all-knowing God." We'd gambled that the self-proclaimed "Prophet of Florence" would be unable to resist so exciting a prediction, as a *bribe* from Lorenzo to save his soul.

The Prior of San Marco.

I wondered what thoughts must be crashing round in his head. His prophecy of Lorenzo's and Innocent's deaths in 1492 was surely no more than educated calculations. All knew how ill the two men had been. But this, *this* revelation would be proof of his infallibility. And news of it had come from Lorenzo, his greatest enemy.

After that day, the people of Florence, already aquake at the prior's words, grew excited, and impatient for further news of the relic's public showing. But now, finally, it was my time to leave the city.

There was so much more work left to be done.

I left for Rome immediately, this time allowing myself the comfort of a coach.

Two cardinals came out to greet me—Ascanio Sforza, now the right hand of the pope, and Lorenzo's son Giovanni, whom I'd known since birth. He was only sixteen but looked as serious as could be in his red cassock and cap. Ascanio asked after my nephew, Leonardo, and we shared condolences on our loss of Lorenzo. Just before his death, Lorenzo had written Giovanni a long letter, the boy told me, knowing that his son was about to take up his cardinal's position in Rome and wishing to impart to him the best of his knowledge and wisdom as he took his place in the world of powerful men. Knowing what dear friends we had been, Giovanni offered that before I left the city he would allow me, if I wished, to read Lorenzo's last letter.

Then he slipped away and Ascanio escorted me through the Vatican with no further delay and into the Holy Father's private apartments. I found it a scene of great artistic industry, the scaffolding just then being removed from newly painted frescoes in the four rooms of his personal sanctuary.

Roderigo Borgia had, as did so many Italian men, thickened with age. There were remnants of his handsomeness, but the nose had sharpened into a beak, and a bloated wattle of skin extended from chin to collarbone.

I began to make the appropriate kneeling obeisance to the most Christian man in the world, but he pulled me upright, dispelling all formality. In the Room of Saints he, Ascanio, and I sat in three chairs in front of the grandest hearth I had ever seen—solid gold pillars upholding a green marble mantel over which was painted a fresco from which I could not take my eyes.

"Pinturicchio has done a marvelous thing with my apartment, do you not agree, Cato?" said the pope, aware of my steady gaze on the fresco.

"He is the painter of all these new works?" I asked.

"The man has been decorating the Vatican for twenty-five years." Roderigo smiled and cocked his head. "He is no Leonardo, but perhaps we shall yet have your nephew in Rome."

"Forgive me, Your Grace," I said, tilting my chin at the painting above the fireplace, "but is not the lady on the throne *Isis*?"

"She is."

"And if I might presume," I went on, "that the man sitting to the right of her is Moses, then may I assume the man on her left is Hermes Trismegistus?"

"You have a good eye for the heretical, my friend."

I was startled. Though I knew where Roderigo Borgia's sympathies lay, it had never occurred to me that as the pope he would so blatantly flaunt his own Hermetic bent. *Thus is the nature of absolute power,* I thought. *In such a position a man believes himself unassailable, infallible. Godlike.* I thanked the Fates that at this crucial juncture, the most powerful man in Christendom was a like-minded soul, and dedicated to the same mission I was.

"Yes," he said lightly, calling for more wine with a mere twitch of his finger at a silk-clad page. "Later I will show you the other frescoes. I've got Hermes again in the Room of Sibyls, and behind you, it's yet to be uncovered"—he pointed to a canvas-draped wall—"is a wonderful scene indeed. The bull is the Borgia family emblem, as is the Egyptian bull, Apis."

"Apis is worshipped as Osiris, the sun god, if I am not mistaken," I said.

Roderigo nodded. "In the frescoes I have Egyptians worshipping the holy cross as well as the pyramid, as well as the bull."

"In the end, they are all worshipping *you*, Roderigo," Ascanio Sforza quipped.

"As it should be," the Holy Father said with a wicked grin. "Now, Cato, you must tell us the news of Florence and the Prior of San Marco."

With some relish I described Leonardo's shroud hoax. Both pope and cardinal might have been bolted to their chairs for all they moved during my telling of our failures with the decomposing corpse, al-chemical adventures, and the magic of the *camera obscura*.

"And when will this masterpiece be shown?" Roderigo asked me.

"On Easter Sunday in Vercelli, the most Christian Holy Roman Empress, Bianca Sforza, will for the first time in forty-five years display for all pilgrims the Savoy family's Lirey Shroud."

"Though much improved," Roderigo added with a sardonic smile.

"Beyond all imagining," I said. "I believe that our work, together with Savonarola's obsession for sainthood, will coalesce into our conspiracy's first triumph."

"Well," said the pontiff, sitting forward, "I can now enlighten you as to the second chapter of our conspiracy. While the first was of a scientific nature, this one, I'm afraid, is of a most political and strategic complexion."

Political? I thought. Of all the civilized arts, and though Lorenzo's forte, politics was the one of which I understood the least.

"My brother Ludovico *Il Moro*," Ascanio began, "has for reasons of greed and revenge set into motion a most disturbing chain of events that will affect all of Italy. As it cannot be undone, we have happily conceived of a way to use it to our advantage. Once more, we will need Leonardo's artistic skills."

"And Savonarola's appetite for self-aggrandizement," Roderigo added.

"Both of which are already in great supply," I said.

Roderigo sat back and began to drum his fingers on the gilt claw arm of his chair. "What do you know of the French king, Charles?"

"Nothing but the greedy and lecherous reputation that precedes him," I replied.

Roderigo and Ascanio exchanged a mysterious look.

"Think a hundred times worse," the cardinal said to me, eliciting a smile, then continued. "Now consider a scenario in which *Il Moro*, the King of France, and Savonarola himself all become unwitting players in the tragic downfall of our favorite prior."

"I do not believe I can imagine a more pleasurable pastime," Roderigo said.

"Then all I will need to set things in motion," I said, "are the details for my nephew."

"Bring me *Il Moro*'s letter," Roderigo said to Ascanio, "and let Cato see the means to our end."

I was needed in Milan for help with the showing of the Lirey Shroud. I looked forward to traveling north again. Florence now held more evil memories for me than happy ones. Indeed, there was no place on earth that I would rather have been than Milan, for there lived my father, my son, and my grandson.

The day I arrived a small army of workmen was installing four large furnaces at the corners of the great pit that had been dug for the bronze horse casting. The clay model itself was nowhere to be seen.

Leonardo was beside himself with excitement, though in perfect control of his senses, directing the burly iron smiths as to the specific placement of the smelters. Stacked in a corner nearby was a huge pile of scrap metal.

"He's gone mad collecting metal," Zoroastre told me, coming to my side.

"I've only begun," Leonardo said. "It's frightening to think how much I shall need for the statue. But *Il Moro* has promised me a great load of it."

"Like he promised to pay you for decorating Beatrice's rooms?" Zoroastre sniped.

"Ludovico withholds your fees?" I asked Leonardo.

"Let us say he is slow to pay. But he did unveil the equestrian monument—the clay statue—at the Castella, in honor of Bianca's marriage to Maximilian."

"Everyone loved it," Zoroastre added, then said to me, "It's a disgrace that Leonardo is reduced to sending letters begging for money owed him."

"I would stifle my complaining about Ludovico until we are thrown out of the palace he has given us to live in," Leonardo said.

"What is that?" I said to change the course of conversation, pointing to an enormous sheet-draped object on the far side of the ballroom.

It was all points and angles beneath the cover. I walked across to the sheeted mountain. On the wall behind it were endless, obsessive sketches of bird wings, bat wings, insect wings, angel wings. Wings from every angle, paying most attention to their articulated joints. Leonardo came up behind me and stood silently for a moment, appraising the drawings almost as though they were new to him.

"I don't suppose I need to ask what is under the sheet," I said.

"Would you like to see it?" His eyes were suddenly alight.

I nodded, and in the next instant the cloth had been pulled away.

Despite having seen Leonardo's first attempt at a flying machine, and now the sketches on the wall, the massive contraption was still a shock to my eye. The two long bat wings fashioned from oiled leather and stretched over struts of pine were clearly constructed to move with their mechanisms of springs, wires, and pulleys. The wings attached to a slender, almost delicate gondola with stirruped pedals sticking out the bottom, and an intricate canvas harness was designed to hold a man inside the machine—and the wings to the man.

"Isn't she beautiful?" Leonardo said.

"I find 'her' rather alarming."

"This one will fly," he said, ignoring my worry. "I'm sure of it. It's light. Perfectly proportioned. With the right wind . . ."

"Leonardo . . ." Zoroastre had come up behind us. "Why don't you show Cato to his room. He must be exhausted from his journey."

"Thank you, my friend," he said to Zoroastre, then to me, "I do get caught up with myself and need reminding."

Leonardo and I went up the great staircase together, passing by the old ducal apartments where I had spent my last nights alone with Lorenzo.

"I've brought all your notebooks and folios that I've been keeping for you," I told him.

"Why now?" he asked.

"Because I feel you are safe now. In your own home. And they belong to you."

"And this," he said, ushering me through another doorway and into a single bedchamber, "belongs to you."

I might have been stepping into a sultan's harem, what with lengths of vermilion silk draped and woven above, altogether tenting the ceiling. Brilliant-hued brocade cushions were piled around the room's perimeter on the intricately patterned Turkey rug. Crossed scimitars hung on one wall, an exotic stringed instrument inlaid with tortoise-shell on another. The latticed window threw patterns on the low, satin-draped bed, and a hookah to one side, its long tube mouthpiece hanging down, seemed to await languid partaking.

"It's lovely, Leonardo."

"I decorated it for you myself, though many of the artifacts are Grandfather's."

I turned and went into his arms. "No one has ever had a sweeter child than you."

"Come look," he said, taking me by the hand to a prettily painted Chinese wardrobe. "I've bought you a few things." He threw open the doors. Nothing could have startled me more than what I saw inside.

It was filled with women's clothing. Simple dresses, festive gowns, skirts and bodices and sleeves. The floor of the cabinet was lined with pairs of silk slippers.

"Mama," he said gently. "There's no longer a need for your disguise. You put it on to protect me. Finally I am in a position to protect you." He kissed me on both cheeks that were suddenly wet with tears.

Then he turned and left, shutting the door behind him.

I was quite unprepared for the flood of emotions that rolled over me like waves. Relief. Gratitude. Love. Loss. The masculinity I had assumed for these twenty-five years had been my soldier's armor. My hide cloak. While my nearest and dearest had known what lay beneath the men's smocks and scholars' robes, only had Lorenzo in stolen moments beheld my femininity. On his death that tie to my sex had been severed.

Is Leonardo right? Have I no use for the male gender now? Can I relinquish all deception and walk in the world as a woman?

Suddenly I felt warm, too warm in my clothing. Kicking off my leather traveling shoes, I unbuttoned the sleeves of my doublet, then untied my hose from eyelets at the garment's hem and stripped them off. Undoing several laces and freed from the doublet I felt a breeze through the open window ruffle my thin shirt. With my roll-brimmed hat removed, my long graying hair fell loose to my shoulders.

I pulled the shirt over my head and let it drop to the floor. Then, as I had done many thousands of times, I began unwinding the long linen strip that encased my chest, round and round till I'd loosed my breasts from their bindings. I stood naked, letting the breeze cool me.

My nipples hardened and I smiled at that, strangely pleased. Then I reached into the Chinese cabinet and pulled out a dress in my favorite colors.

It was more than odd walking through the halls of the ducal palace in a gown, a deep olive, its low rounded bodice finely pleated and trimmed in gold ribbon. Its separate sleeves were soft and tawny as a doe, and I'd found a lighter olive cape that I'd thrown over one shoulder.

When I arrived at the dining room door I heard familiar voices from within and stopped outside it, unsure how to arrange my features for what would surely be a memorable entrance. I settled on a dignified half smile and went in.

Everyone at the table came to their feet at once, Papa with tears in his eyes, Leonardo beaming with pleasure. Julia stood in the doorway clapping her hands above her head. Zoroastre pushed back his chair and came to me, pulling me into a sweet embrace.

"I was completely fooled by you, signora. All these years. Come, sit down."

He pulled out a chair for me and I took my place at Leonardo's right hand. Across the table sat Salai, staring at me with a beady eye.

"You look wonderful in that dress. I'd like to paint your portrait in it," Leonardo said. He regarded me with his artist's eye. "You are a handsome woman."

"An old woman," I corrected him.

"That's right," Salai said. "She *is* old. I liked her better as a man."

"And I'd like you better with a rag stuffed in your mouth," I said, tossing my napkin across the table at him.

Everyone laughed. Then Leonardo lifted his wineglass, and the men in my little family did likewise . . . even my pesky grandson.

"La Caterina," Leonardo said.

The toast was repeated by all, and my name, together with the sound of Venetian glasses clinking merrily together, rang like music in my ears.

The narrow road west to Vercelli from Milan was nearly impassable, thronged as it was with pilgrims—thousands of them from all parts of Italy and some, I could tell from the language they spoke, from over the Alps in France. No matter their rank or status, the pilgrims wore white robes and cowry shell necklaces, and each carried a cross and a begging bowl. Most walked, some barefoot, though the infirm were carried lying down on biers or in pole chairs. It was a solemn procession, all marching with downcast eyes and muttering heartfelt prayers. Here and there were groups of flagellants, their robes pulled down to their waists, whipping themselves bloody.

Several days before, we had stationed Zoroastre on the road leading north from Florence, and his report was heartening. There had been an endless parade of citizens from there. Zoroastre, himself disguised as a pilgrim, had fallen into step beside many of the faithful and engaged them in quiet conversation.

Yes, they were coming to view the holy relic, the shroud in which Jesus had been wrapped as he lay in his tomb. Yes, they had heard of this wondrous gift from God from the Prior of San Marco. He had revealed from his pulpit that the shroud, owned for *two hundred years* by the great family of Savoy, though not on display for the last *forty-five*, would, for a small price, finally be shown to pilgrims by a Savoy descendant, Bianca, now the wife of Maximilian, the Holy Roman Emperor himself.

And yes, their beloved Savonarola was said even now to be walking behind them on the road to Vercelli to view the holiest of all Christian relics. Zoroastre pressed farther south until he found the Dominican envoy from San Marco and spotted the gnome himself, his dark hair and complexion set off starkly against his white pilgrim's robe. The penitent martyr that he was, he at times carried on his shoulder a large wooden cross, affecting great suffering under its weight. Zoroastre reported that he'd watched one evening as the cross was taken from the prior's shoulder and laid on the ground near where the monks slept. Our conspirator had crept in the dark to the cross and, upon lifting it, found it light as a feather—made cleverly of cork.

Then, renting a horse, he had ridden hell-bent to Vercelli.

Our little troop was gathered at the church in that tiny village, making preparations for the showing. It had been wonderful to again see Bianca, whom we told of my identity at once. No one could have been more delighted than she at my male disguise, for it was this ruse, she rightly observed, that had allowed me entry into the Platonic Academy and the inner circle of Hermeticism.

"How I envy you," she said on the evening before Savonarola was due to arrive. We were sitting by the fire in the villa she had rented for us all in Vercelli. "How did you have the courage?"

I looked in the direction of Papa, who, with Leonardo, was bent over a map of Milan that Leonardo had drawn. It was rendered, quite strangely, as though seen from above—what my son called "a bird's-eye view." "There," I said to Bianca, pointing at my father and son. "There sits my courage. It is born of many causes. Fear is oftentimes the greatest spur. Terror of losing Leonardo from my life was the prime mover for me. But Papa provided two others without which all the fear in the world could not have taken me down this long road.

Belief in me was one. Education was the other." I took Bianca's hand. "But look at *you*."

"Me? I was born into a life of privilege, untold wealth," she said, sitting back in her chair. "I had everything handed to me on golden platters. Even a classical education. Where is the courage in that?"

I stared into the fire as I spoke. "Every female who is born into this life, no matter her station, can be called courageous as long as she keeps a part of her soul private and intact. Outwardly she may be a downtrodden daughter or wife, scolded or beaten by father or husband, suffer the agonies of childbirth. She can be preached to of hellfire and damnation by her priest, her body abused by ignorant women-loathing physicians. But as long as a tiny seed of self-consciousness lives within her . . ."

"The divine spark," Bianca said, grasping my other hand, tears welling in her eyes.

"Yes, child, the divine spark. As long as it is never allowed to wither and die, anything is possible. I can live the better part of my life as a man. You can quietly defy your powerful family and become the linchpin of history's most outrageous hoax!"

Bianca hugged me to her. "Bless you," she whispered.

"Surely I am blessed," I said and, fixing her with the warmest smile, added, "by the pope, the Holy Roman Empress, Isis, and Mother Nature. For what more could a person ask?"

All was ready the next day. We conspirators, dressed in white as pilgrims, were stationed round the dimly lit Vercelli chapel, Zoroastre and I on either side of the front door, accepting payment for the viewing of the holy relic. Already, after two days, thousands had filed past the shroud, gazing at the vague spindly image in the shape of a man. Many would drop to their knees, the most devout prostrating themselves on the cold stone floor. Some, braver than most, would move closer and stare at the linen, with some innate sense that they were seeing something unusual. Perhaps some of the older ones among them had viewed the Lirey Shroud before and saw it was different.

Most, however, were little more than pious cattle, heeding the admonitions of the church that to call themselves good Christians they must trudge many miles as penitents and pay their money for the privilege of viewing a piece of religious history. Being in the very presence of "Saint Peter's shriveled finger," or "a sliver from Barabbas's cross," would infuse the pilgrims with God's grace and bring them a step closer to salvation. That people would believe anything made our task so much easier.

Out the door I could see in the orderly line waiting for entrance a wider clumping of pilgrims, as though they surrounded someone of importance. Then I saw the tip of the balsa wood cross perched on the shoulder of a bent-over dark-haired man.

Savonarola had arrived.

With a nod to Zoroastre I moved to the front of the church. We had, until that moment, allowed but a single file of pilgrims to move along the right-hand wall of the chapel. Before the stained-glass window and behind the long, cloth-draped altar table, we had mounted the shroud on a horizontal plane, at eye level. Above the stained glass was another window of clear Venetian glass that Bianca had recently donated to the church and had had installed, which threw clear light on the shroud. When the pilgrims, one by one, had seen and prayed before the image, they'd been steered out a side door behind the altar.

Now, with Savonarola approaching, the side door was closed and all the faithful, after their viewing, were steered back into the chapel, so that they filled the church to overflowing. It was whispered to them by Leonardo and Papa that they had been chosen to be present when the famous preacher, Savonarola, laid eyes on the holy relic. They were agog at the honor.

When the prior, shorn of his cross, came through the door, he made his way up the line. I watched from the front as he gazed approvingly at the huge crowd that now stood on the floor of the church—his audience.

Indeed. The show was about to begin.

The prior, having been personally welcomed to the viewing by the

Holy Roman Empress, passed by me, looking me right in the face without recognition. I was, after all, a mere woman now.

Then he went and stood squarely in front of the shroud. He moved back, nearly as far as the altar table, then moved closer—closer than anyone else had dared. Starting at the right he moved along the length of its back view from foot to head, then from the head to the foot of the front view. The pilgrims were quiet as he observed the darker puddles of shadow where spikes had been driven through the corpse's feet. He saw the shadowy calves and thighs, the high, dark forehead, the long skeletal arm bones and fingers crossed over the genitals.

I saw his nose wrinkle in disgust and remembered Lorenzo saying Savonarola was repulsed by sex, that he secretly harbored a distaste for even the thought that God had lowered himself by placing a part of himself in a filthy human body. By my own memory Jesus was, in fact, rarely mentioned in the prior's sermons. It was the Lord God alone who inspired his devotion.

He viewed the shroud so long and so silently that tension grew among the faithful. Something was stirring in Savonarola's mind, they were thinking. He must be hearing the words of the Almighty. If only he would speak and share the words of God!

Finally, with slow deliberation, he turned and faced the audience.

"My children," he said, his voice reverberating effortlessly through the chapel. "We have before us an ancient relic belonging to the illustrious House of Savoy."

My heart was beating so hard I could feel it thumping in my throat. His next words would determine the success or failure of our entire conspiracy.

"Despite what you may perceive as the bloody stains made by Christ's body on his winding sheet, I will tell you now that God has spoken in my ear and told me the truth about the Lirey Shroud. The thing is a hoax!"

A great commotion rose in the church. Savonarola allowed it to rumble and grow for a time, then silenced it with his next shouted words. "It is an abomination! I know how deeply you sinners long to see the true face of the Christ. How easy it is to see the outlines of a flayed back, a dark shadow at the place the centurion's spear entered the body. But where are his eyes?" He flung his arm backward toward the shroud. "All I see are pale sockets. I say not only is this a forgery, but it is a pitiful one at that!"

He turned and glared at Bianca, who was playing the part of a terrified woman who had offended God. "Fie on you and your House of Savoy!" Savonarola fairly spat the name. "Your husband, the Holy Roman Emperor, should punish you for your stupidity and greed. For accepting money from poor, unsuspecting pilgrims traveling hundreds of miles for some hope of salvation." To the pilgrims he continued, "It is this kind of corruption to which we have been subjected time and time again by Rome, that unholy pit of iniquity!"

"Good people," came a kindly and humble voice from the front door of the church. Everyone turned in surprise to see a cardinal in his scarlet robe and skullcap. "I am Ascanio Sforza and I come from Rome," he continued, making his way up the center of the church, allowing pilgrims to kiss his hands. "I will not say that place has not seen its fill of corruption, but since the recent ascension of Pope Alexander, Rome has become a place of dignity and tolerance. The Holy Father abhors persecution of any kind, and gives much credence to a person's freedom of action and speech. He is much loved in that place." Ascanio placed his hand over his heart. "And much loved by me."

He had reached the front of the church and, moving around the altar table, came and stood beside Savonarola, over whom he towered. "Now let us have a look at this 'forgery.'"

The cardinal steered Savonarola with him to the right. At that moment, Leonardo, hidden beneath the skirted altar table, dropped the cloth that had hidden his eight-part mirror leaning against the table. It was spread out to its full length and faced the shroud. At the same moment, Papa pulled away a second linen cloth that had backed the shroud, making it opaque.

The sun, through the clear Venetian glass window, struck the carefully angled mirrors with its full force. With light illuminating the linen from front and back, a stunning vision suddenly appeared. Miracles of alchemy, art, and nature coalesced to present a perfect portrait of "Jesus." That which without light had been dark, now with light flooding through it came fully into sight. The face, while long and narrow, was plumped with recent life. The eyes closed in peaceful death, were in clear focus. The beard and mustache and hair were real and human, and the bloodstains dripping from Christ's wounds were painfully visible.

People pressed forward for better sight of it, but everyone could see it was a true image of a crucified man, as though he were lying there before them.

"It is He!" someone cried, and all the congregation fell to their knees, crossing themselves and whispering desperate prayers.

Savonarola's flabby brown lip hung open in disbelief. I could see he was quite speechless. But Ascanio Sforza was not.

"Good people," he called out soothingly, "faithful children of a merciful God, can you not see with your own eyes what I see? This is no forgery. This is the greatest miracle I have ever in my life witnessed. I will return to Rome and tell the Holy Father that I have lived to see the face of Jesus Christ!"

Pilgrims were weeping and moaning in joy.

Ascanio held his hands out in front of him in a benedictory gesture. *"Ecce, imago nostae salvator. In nomine Patris, et Filius, et Spiritu Sancte."* Everyone murmured "Amen." Ascanio turned and glared at the Prior of San Marco. "As for you, Girolamo Savonarola, you are a *false prophet!*"

He tried to speak, but the cardinal silenced him with a finger pointed at his face. "Do you have no recollection from your ecclesiastical studies that the church forbids false prophets?!"

The prior spluttered stupidly for only a moment before Ascanio went on. "You are hereby proscribed by the Church of Rome and in the name of the Holy Father Alexander to cease all your preaching in the city of Florence until no more prophecies are uttered from your pulpit!"

"I object!" Savonarola cried.

"You may not object!" the cardinal shouted back, leaning into the prior's face. "You are an obedient priest of the Church of Saint Peter and subject to all its laws. Now stand down and allow these blessed pilgrims sight of our Lord Jesus Christ."

Savonarola and his Dominican retinue stalked past the shroud and disappeared out the side door. Zoroastre, Papa, and I moved among the pilgrims, restoring the single-file line so they could view the new Lirey Shroud in all its glory.

Blessings of every sort abounded that day. But none so great as for the members of our little coterie and in the memory of Lorenzo *Il Magnifico* de' Medici.

or the first time when I returned to the city of Florence it was as a *woman*, she with her elderly father in tow. We moved into the house Lorenzo had bought me, keeping our heads low. I had always kept to myself in that place, so no one questioned the identities of their new neighbors.

The next part of our conspiracy was about to begin. If it failed, the rest of it would have been for naught, so Papa and I worked quietly and feverishly to see it through to the end.

After Savonarola's humiliation at Vercelli we kept our ears open for word of the shroud spreading through Florence. Certainly some of the crowd in the chapel that day had been Florentines. And like all people, pilgrims or not, they were gossips.

I would go to the Mercato Vecchio every market day and chatter like a housewife to the merchants and other women filling their baskets with fish and eggs and tomatoes. *Had anyone been to view the Holy Shroud at Vercelli?* I asked as a faithful Christian desiring to make the pilgrimage myself. I knew that our beloved Prior of San Marco had been to see it. *What was his opinion of it? Was it worth the month's walk?*

Some recalled Savonarola preaching about some holy relic's reappearance. Others vaguely remembered that he had traveled north to view it for himself, and some were planning a pilgrimage there. But all in all there was little talk about the Lirey Shroud.

Papa was making the rounds of tavernas, themselves the somberest of establishments where—since drinking, gambling, gaming, and whoring had all but ceased—there was little to be enjoyed but rumor-mongering and watered-down wine. There, too, he heard nothing even *whispered* of Cardinal Sforza's dressing-down of the prior before a churchful of devotees. And even more peculiarly, there was no word of the spectacular nature of the shroud itself.

One hot summer evening as Papa and I took the air on the banks of the Arno we heard a small commotion—the drunken shouts of a man and some others trying desperately to quiet and subdue him. We moved closer to see that the old drunk was sitting on the muddy bank with his feet in the water, clutching a wine flask to his chest as two men attempted to take it from him and pull him back from the riverbank.

"I tell you it was *real*, as if the Lord had been just laid to rest in his tomb!"

"Come away, Grandfather," the younger of the two men said.

"I won't come away," the old man slurred. "I wish to be baptized in the water as Christ was by John."

"You've already been baptized," said the other in a gentle tone, tugging the sodden man's arms to no avail.

"But I saw the face of Jesus, I tell you! And that godforsaken preacher with one eyebrow saw it, too!" the old man shouted. "Saw it and called it a forgery, a work of the Devil! How could anyone have doubted it?!"

"Father, please, you'll be arrested. You'll get us all arrested."

Finally the old man allowed himself to be dragged to his feet.

Papa and I, arm in arm, kept our heads together as we passed by, as if uninterested in the scene.

"Well, the pope's man had no doubt," the drunk muttered. "The cardinal from Rome saw what I saw. Told that filthy priest to keep his mouth shut. I don't see how that cardinal was any more corrupt than the prior from San Marco!"

We were forced to move on and heard nothing more. But more was unnecessary. Some Florentines *had* been at Vercelli, *had* seen Ascanio Sforza berate Savonarola. *Had* seen the Lirey Shroud in its full illuminated state.

But the prior was a careful man. He and his retinue must have stood at the side door of the church and questioned all who followed him out. Found the Florentines among them and threatened them with all manner of monstrous and eternal damnations if they whispered a word of "the Devil's Work" and the "corrupt cardinal from Rome."

But the public's knowledge of the shroud or Savonarola's reprimand did not matter in the larger scheme of things. That he'd been warned by Rome to cease his false prophesying did. And continuing to do so most certainly would.

But he would need another message, the news of which he could speak "in God's voice" from his pulpit. A message so terrifying and unexpected that he would be forever glorified as a modern Moses. Prophet of Prophets. A very saint.

We had just the one. It would, we were sure, prove irresistible.

Leonardo's forged letter—except for the hand in which it had been written—was nothing but the truth. Such a document had certainly been penned by *Il Moro* and delivered to the new French king. In his hubris and desire for revenge against his Neapolitan rivals, Ludovico Sforza had, unbelievably, *invited* Charles of France to swarm across the Alps and invade Italy.

His people, *Il Moro* promised, would give no resistance to the occupying army as long as it left Milan in peace and moved swiftly down the length of the peninsula to crush Naples. He had assurance from the Borgia pope that his Papal States would remain neutral, and that Florence, under Piero de' Medici's weak rule, would likewise pose no threat to his designs.

Charles could thereafter claim Don Ferrante's duchy—long believed by the French to belong, by the claims of heredity, to them—and leave Italy a happy man . . . one with a most powerful Italian ally—Ludovico *Il Moro* Sforza himself.

All of this intelligence had been relayed from Roderigo to me and on to my son. Leonardo, using his skills and many handwritten notes from *Il Moro* at his disposal—endless instructions on the equestrian statue—had no trouble duplicating Ludovico's script.

On a visit to Castello Sforza while decorating the ceiling of a chamber with a thicket of knotted tree limbs, the trusted court artist had slipped into the Milanese Secretary's office and made a cast of the ducal seal.

The forgery itself was perfection. The clever "interception" of the document by someone loyal to Savonarola, on the other hand, was something of a stumbling block. It was imperative that suspicion be avoided at all costs.

Leonardo and Zoroastre quietly hunted for anyone in Milan with connections to and sympathy for Savonarola.

Strange how things happen.

Salai, at fourteen, had taken up with a pretty young choirboy at the pink cathedral across the piazza. They'd done some of their dallying in the Duomo itself and had, quite by accident, overheard two of the priests discussing the moral turpitude of Milan. The choirboy had found it hilarious that, kneeling behind a cupboard of ecclesiastical garments a dozen feet from the priests scandalized by the impure Milanese, two boys were merrily sodomizing one another. But Salai shushed his friend so he could hear more.

One of the friars, Odotto, was a devotee of Savonarola's and had already successfully petitioned his superiors for a transfer to the Florentine monastery of San Marco. Salai made his report to us with much glee and as many salacious details as he could manage, but for once he was celebrated for his devious behavior and rewarded with a fat purse.

The rest was nothing more than an elaborate masque written and conducted by the court Revels Master for the benefit of Fra Odotto.

A few ducats in the pocket of Salai's friend had my grandson in choirboy garb, wandering into the friar's path with Leonardo's forged document. Salai was "confused and distressed," he admitted to Odotto. Coming to the Duomo that morning he had found near the entrance of the Castello Sforza a letter lying on the ground—something that might have fallen from the saddle pack of a messenger. He was not sure but it looked to him like an official seal.

Where was the document? Odotto wanted to know. Salai pretended to blanch with embarrassment. He had it with him, under his tunic, but, he admitted, he had been unable to resist and had steamed open the seal and read the thing.

The friar had been instantly aghast, but when Salai turned to go saying he must return it and take his punishment like a man, Odotto had grabbed the boy by the collar and dragged him into the privacy of his cell.

The letter was already opened, Odotto reasoned. Perhaps he should read it, too. Unable to resist an opportunity for reward, Salai extracted a bribe from the cleric. All Odotto had was a small jeweled cross given to him by his father when he'd entered the church, but such a luxury would be unnecessary and quite frowned upon at San Marco, where he was headed.

With trinket in hand, Salai left and came across the piazza to Corte Vecchia to give his report. There was no doubt that "*Il Moro*'s letter to the King of France" would reach its intended destination, as Leonardo had included in it a small but vital reference to Savonarola himself.

"Lorenzo's son is no *Il Magnifico*, Your Majesty," Leonardo had written as Ludovico. "Piero de' Medici has not the strength to withstand your occupation, and I do believe you will find a friend in the Prior of San Marco." Then Leonardo had added drawings of some hideous war machines he had designed during his first years in Milan—particularly that giant, four-bladed scythe.

He was always one for a bit more drama, my Leonardo.

From the time we learned that Fra Odotto had left Milan for Florence, Papa and I attended every one of Savonarola's masses and sermons. After Vercelli, though he had continued preaching, the prior had shown a modicum of restraint with his prophesying, referring to nothing other than predictions he had made in the past.

He did escalate his attacks on Piero de' Medici, attacks that found many listeners. The man, so unlike his father, was weak and irresponsible. Though wishing desperately for the success of our plans, I trembled when I thought of the family's fate. True, Giovanni was safely away in Rome living under Roderigo's protection. Lorenzo's daughters were married. But what of Giuliano's son? Where would he find safety when the great calamity came?

Finally one Sunday as Savonarola strode to his pulpit in the great cathedral, Papa and I could see his green eyes flashing. He sped through the Latin mass as a man rushing to a house afire. Then it was time for his sermon. He began it with a long silence, staring down at his congregation, fiercely eyeing every part of the crowded floor.

"Now it is coming," he began in a low, tremulous voice. "It is come! The sword has descended! The scourge has fallen! Repent, O Florence, while there is still time," his rant continued. "Clothe thyself in the white garments of purification. Wait no longer, for there may be no further time for repentance!"

The congregation, even much used to Savonarola's dire words, sensed some new horror to be predicted.

"I have had a vision," he cried. "A vision placed before my eyes by God Himself! Unless you turn to the Golden Cross, disaster will befall you. But this is no mere pestilence, my children," he raged, reaching his arms high above his head. "This is the apocalypse of *war*!"

Above the frightened murmuring and shouts of fear from a people who had not in their lifetimes known war, the prior went on.

"The Lord has placed me here as a watchman in the center of Italy that you may hear my words and know them for the truth." He paused again, so that the petrified listeners had quieted completely. "A foreign enemy will soon be pouring down across the Alps. You had perhaps feared invasion from the East—the Turks. But no, it will be a great king from the *north*, bringing with him hordes of soldiers like barbers, armed with gigantic razors!"

A woman near me fainted into her husband's arms.

I squeezed Papa's hand. *The prior had read the forged letter and fallen into our trap.* The "king from the north" crossing over the Alps with his hordes was certainly Charles, and his "gigantic razors" could be nothing other than Leonardo's scythe weapon. As we made for the door I nearly collided with a tall, elegantly dressed man. It was Piero da Vinci, his face looking like one of Leonardo's carnival masks—the face of fear. Piero was old to my eyes. There was no remnant of that beauty of his youth, not that at our age anyone was beautiful, or much cared about such things. But all I could see was the toll that a lifetime of greed and stinginess with love had carved into his features. Now in addition there was the ugliness of terror. Like so many other Florentines, he had fallen victim to Savonarola's threats of fiery damnation.

And now war.

*K*ing Charles and thirty thousand soldiers climbed over the Alps and invaded Milan. In a turn of events that took *Il Moro*'s subjects—if not we conspirators—by surprise, he welcomed the army with open arms and an open purse. Even though the French hordes did not come brandishing Leonardo's "gigantic razors," they caused much death and destruction with their fearsome "cannon"—large guns that propelled not the stone projectiles that had always been used, but iron "cannonballs." By the banks of the river Taro more than two thousand Venetians were killed in one battle alone.

Of course Prior Savonarola was positively exuberant. "My prophecy has proven true!" he cried from his pulpit from the moment word came that a "king from the north" had crossed the Alps. As glad as I was that the Dominican had fallen into our trap, it was horrible to watch the final downfall of Florence and the pathetic flailings of Piero de' Medici.

Lorenzo's arrogant son decided he would face his enemy and negotiate a settlement. But once shat upon by the King of France, and after acceding to every one of Charles's outrageous demands, he slunk back into Florence to report his defeat. The gates of the Signoria were literally slammed in his face, and the disgusted citizens threw stones at him and his family. Stones! Then the city fathers banished the Medici forever from Florence. They fled, every one, like thieves in the middle of the night.

But there was worse to come.

Florentine mobs broke into the deserted Palazzo Medici and looted it. I forced myself to bear witness as they desecrated that place of beauty, comfort, and learning. I was glad my love had not lived to see this day.

Two days later, Charles and his enormous army marched into a panic-stricken Florence.

With everything here destroyed and Lorenzo gone, I took some solace as I began my prearranged correspondence with Roderigo, dispatching the messenger with plenty of gold to hurry him on his way.

> *Holy Father,*
>
> *I write to report that Savonarola—puffed with self-righteousness and vindication—bowed before the French invader, welcoming him as the Instrument of Divine Will. "And so at last, O King, thou has come!" he cried on his knees before Charles. "You are sent by God!"*
>
> *The French king showed great leniency to the Florentine citizens. But this was expected. We all knew Naples, not Florence, had been the prize Charles sought. Only a handful of people died in the weeks of the occupation, no more than did without a foreign army on its streets.*
>
> *The true casualty was Florence's soul.*
>
> *It has been flogged and battered unmercifully, its pride in tatters, its status as a republic dismantled. It is into your hands that we must now lay all our hopes of salvation for this city.*
>
> *Rebirth. Rinascimento. What the Medici so brilliantly began, we will once more see reborn.*
>
>
>
> *Your devoted servant,*
> *Cato*
>
>

* * *

> *Holy Father,*
>
> *In the months since the French invasion, the Prior of San Marco— having declared Florence a Holy City, a "New Jerusalem," with Christ*

its king—has, with the consent of the Signoria, created it a theocracy. Savonarola has proclaimed that all Medici supporters must be put to death immediately. His bonfires glow weekly from the main piazza.

He demands continual fasting from the people, most of whom comply, grateful that their "Great Prophet," Savonarola, first warned them of the French king's invading army, then spared the populace from his fury.

There is, however, some resistance to report. A faction calling themselves "Mad Dogs" have quite boldly begun deriding the prior's most ardent followers, calling them "prayer mumblers" and "snivelers," and even banging drums in church trying to drown out Savonarola's sermons. Of these men there are few, but it is said their numbers are growing.

I will keep you informed of all progress.

> I remain your devoted servant,
> Cato

✳ ✳ ✳

Cato,

As you must know by now, Charles's army moved through Rome without a struggle. Once he had left to successfully capture his main objective—Naples—I took the action you and I discussed on your last visit here; and believe me, we will, though not without bloodshed, see a happy outcome to the problems that now plague Italy.

> Yours in Christ,
> Roderigo

✳ ✳ ✳

Holy Father,

I am thrilled that all is going according to plan. The "Holy League" you created to drive the French from Italy was a stroke of pure genius. Of course every Italian leader in his right mind became a member. How well you knew that Savonarola was not in his right mind and would refuse to join.

Now that you have summoned the prior to Rome to explain his support of the invaders, do you think he will come?

Your faithful servant,
Cato

✱ ✱ ✱

Cato,
It does not surprise me that our friend has refused my summons into Rome to answer charges of consorting with Italy's enemy, calling King Charles "The Chosen of God," and continuing to make his false prophecies. Savonarola's excuse for not coming was that Florence could not spare him, and that "God did not wish for him to come." To my amusement, he warned me that I should make immediate provisions for my own salvation, and has taken to writing letters to the French king suggesting that I be deposed from the papacy, though when he calls me an "infidel and heretic" he may not be far from wrong.

When I wrote him back I forbade him to deliver any more sermons, but by your letter I see he has been conducting them daily.

I have no further choice. The courier that brings you this correspondence has also delivered to the prior his Writ of Excommunication. The Florentine Signoria has also been admonished to keep this son of iniquity out of any pulpit, or else to dispatch him to Rome. I believe they understand my displeasure. If the church is disobeyed in this most serious matter, all of Florence will find itself under a papal interdict.

Yours in Christ,
Roderigo

✱ ✱ ✱

Holy Father,
Though Savonarola silenced himself for half the year—a period during which I worried that our entire enterprise might fall to ruin—the Prior of San Marco has finally shown his true colors. On Christmas

Day he openly defied you, celebrating High Mass in the Duomo to a congregation in the thousands. From his pulpit he denounced the Church of Rome as a Satanic Institution, one that promoted whoredom and vice.

I cannot imagine there is much more to say.

Your faithful servant, Cato

*　*　*

Dearest Leonardo,
You must come to Florence at once. Savonarola has been arrested.

Your loving mother

I knew that when I opened my front door Leonardo would be standing there, yet the sight of him thrilled me as deeply as had seeing him at sixteen, posing as the biblical David in Verrocchio's bottega garden. Ours had been a lifetime of separations and homecomings, none of them ever the same, except for the solace we always found in each other's arms.

Papa had come down to greet him and I watched them embrace, my son in the full bloom of manly vigor, my father on the cusp of frailty.

"I worried I would be recognized in the city," Leonardo said, pulling off his hooded cloak, "but it is more that I do not recognize Florence. What a sad, gloomy place it's become." He looked around him at the sparsely furnished ground floor—a few benches and a storeroom. "Not to see an apothecary where you two are . . ."

"We haven't even a garden," Papa said, climbing the stairs to the first floor.

Leonardo and I followed him into the salon. This was comfortable enough, with some cushioned chairs and a table. But the books that had always been so evident in all our homes were strangely absent. Of this there was no need to comment.

We sat at the table. The simple dinner I'd prepared awaited. Papa poured wine.

"I'm glad you and Grandfather were together in such terrible times," Leonardo said.

I reached for Papa's hand and closed my fingers around his. "We were very blessed. Poor Pico. He died on the morning the French marched in and occupied the city. I'm sure that one tragedy caused the other."

"Thankfully there were no casualties from the invasion in my household but one," Leonardo said. "My bronze horse. All that metal I'd collected for it was melted down to make shot for the French military. Certainly I was bereft for a time. I'd worked so long on the thing. Then to see it used that way . . ." He allowed himself a wry smile. "But Ludovico took pity on me."

"*The Last Supper* fresco on the refectory wall?" I asked, remembering mention of it in a letter from him.

Leonardo sighed. "I am mightily tired of all these Christian subjects demanded of me, but that is where my living is made, I suppose." He turned to Papa. "I'm sorry to say I had to kill your daughter. Neighbors and vendors kept asking me why they had not seen Caterina, so I told them she was ill. Signora Ricci insisted she must come see her friend and bring some remedies." He looked at me with a long face. "Sadly, you died. I tearfully bought three pounds of wax for your funeral candles and paid eight soldis for your bier. I applied for the license for burial, but the ceremony took place so quickly—and I was so distraught—that you were dead and buried before anyone knew it. When you return to Milan I'm afraid you'll have to assume another woman's disguise. Perhaps you could be my housekeeper," he joked.

"What of your flying machine?" I asked.

"My first attempt to soar was off the roof of Corte Vecchio. It was a failure, though it could have been a bit less humiliating. I came close to murdering Salai. After I'd crashed to a landing in the center of the Cathedral Piazza . . ."

I gasped aloud at that. I could tell Leonardo was enjoying his storytelling.

". . . my darling son came running over at the head of a concerned crowd of Milanese, and once finding me alive and in one piece, began to laugh so hard that he bent over double and fell to the ground. Of course his merriment was contagious to everyone . . . but me."

"I know you take it lightly," Papa said, "this obsession of yours to fly. But if something should happen to you, Leonardo, think of your mother. . . ."

My child was suddenly contrite, but when he turned to look at me he found me trying to suppress my amusement. "Are you smiling, Mama?"

I put my fist to my lips. "Sorry. I was just remembering . . ." I gazed at my father. "When I was a girl . . ."

"A wild creature," he said.

". . . all I wanted to do was run in the hills and the meadows. Throw my arms wide and pretend I was a hawk, gliding in the clouds, graceful and free." I fixed my eyes on Leonardo, understanding. "It is the *freedom*, is it not?"

He nodded once, overcome, his eyes suddenly glittering with tears. But when we looked to my father we found him gazing blankly at his plate.

"No shop, no garden, no customers," he said with an air of self-indulgence I had never in all my life heard from him. "Not so long ago I was traveling the Silk Road on the back of a camel. Now I can feel the fingers of decrepitude clutching at me."

"Well, you just slap them away, Papa," I said. "A new day is dawning in Florence. And you've no excuse for getting old."

He seemed to collect himself, sitting up straighter in his chair.

"To Pico. To Lorenzo. To Florence," Leonardo intoned. "And to the return of Reason."

We three clinked our glasses in a solemn, triumphant pyramid and drank in grateful silence. I was afraid to believe it possible. But that day was coming, and we at this table had helped to make it so.

The sweet, sickening stench of roasting human flesh assaulted my nostrils, yet I could not bring myself to turn away from the sight atop a single platform in the center of the Piazza della Signoria—two burning figures, now unrecognizable save for bits of heavy brown cloth still clinging to their charred bodies. As I clutched Papa's and Leonardo's hands for strength, I prayed that the men had died a quick death by hanging before their incineration.

I could see some onlookers in the crowded square, "Mad Dogs" more than likely, who seemed to derive satisfaction from these deaths. But many more Florentines were watching with grim, fearful expressions.

Now from the Signoria came a flurry of motion. A handful of city fathers, somber in their long tunics, were followed out by two Signoria guards, dragging by the armpits a man in the coarse brown robe of a Dominican monk toward a second larger and yet-unlit pyre, piled thickly with pitch-covered logs and branches.

Though his black hair was matted with sweat and blood, and his face covered with purple bruised swellings no doubt inflicted during torture in the previous weeks, the man was clearly recognizable. While conscious, Savonarola appeared almost boneless, his arms hanging limp from the shoulders, the tops of his bare feet dragging across the stone piazza.

"Leonardo?" I heard whispered behind us by a familiar voice, but I hesitated turning.

Leonardo did. "Sandro?" he said quietly.

"Is that you?" Botticelli whispered back, incredulous.

"It is."

They were keeping their voices very low. Leonardo grasped Papa's and my elbows and turned us. "This is my mother, Caterina—Cato's sister—and my grandfather, Ernesto. They've moved from Vinci. They're living here now."

"As I understand it," Botticelli said to Papa, "Cato's father was also his tutor."

"Correct," Papa modestly said.

"Cato is a brilliantly trained scholar. Even Ficino was impressed with your son's learning."

Papa beamed with pleasure.

Botticelli then turned to me, taking up my hand to kiss it. He stared up at me. "Cato never told me his sister was a twin. The resemblance is uncanny."

"My brother has probably told me more about you," I said, working hard at elevating my voice to a womanly timbre, "than he told you about me."

We all heard a low groan from the prisoner.

"*Strappado,*" Botticelli muttered. "It's said that when they drop a man from a height—his arms bound above his head—the bones and sinews of his shoulders break and snap." He could not hide a hint of a smile. "And how is Cato?" Botticelli asked. "We haven't seen him since Lorenzo . . ." His voice trailed off.

"He's well," Leonardo answered. "Traveling in the East."

"We've missed his company."

"*We?*" Leonardo said.

Botticelli moved even closer. "Some of us have recently begun to gather again. Very quietly." He turned to Papa. "Perhaps you would like to join our little circle, Ernesto."

I saw a light come into Papa's eyes. "Nothing would give me more pleasure."

Savonarola moaned loudly and called out the name of his savior.

My eyes were drawn back to the platform as the man was hoisted, his broken legs bumping up the platform steps, and tied to the hardwood stake. Conspicuous in his absence was a priest to give the convicted man his final blessing. The hooded executioner, allowing his charge no time for last words, unceremoniously wrapped a knotted rope around the Prior of San Marco's neck.

"Is it not fitting that he should die in this way?" said Botticelli.

"He will no doubt burn in the Hell of which he so eloquently spoke," Leonardo answered with more than a little bitterness.

As the garrote tightened and the beady eyes began to bulge, I turned away. Leonardo and Papa did the same. None of us enjoyed the suffering of our fellow humans.

"Are you leaving now?" Botticelli asked. "Before he burns?"

"Knowing he burns is enough," Leonardo said, clapping a hand on Botticelli's shoulder.

"It's good to see you, my friend," Sandro said. He nodded to Papa. "Ernesto." Then he bowed to me. "Signora da Vinci."

The three of us made our way against the crush of Florentines, who, whether ghoulishly pleased or mournfully beating their breasts, were now surging forward to witness the final moments of the monk's agony.

A pair of boys who still had the short-cut hair of Savonarola's angels, but now dressed as other lads of their own age, stood on a cart on tiptoe, straining over the crowd to view the spectacle.

"They're hoisting his body to the top of the pole!" one cried.

"They'll soon light the fire!"

"Come on," said the other. "I don't want to miss it."

They jumped down from their perch and plowed into the seething mass. The boys would no doubt be at the front when the torch touched the tar-soaked pyre of the one they had not so long ago called "the Mouthpiece of God."

Just as we reached the edge of the piazza a great cry went up from the assembled, and a blast of heat at our backs signaled Savonarola's destruction into ashes.

My stomach turned at the thought of what must now be occurring, but as I felt arms on either side of me sliding round the crooks of my elbows and guiding me away, I heaved a long-awaited sigh of relief.

With every step we took farther from the square our spirits grew lighter. I noticed people coming out from the houses and standing in the streets, silently gazing in the direction of the pillar of smoke rising from the piazza. It was hard to know what they felt—free-falling terror that the man to whom they had entrusted their immortal souls was no more, or the sweetness of waking from a long bad dream.

With a glance at one another, Leonardo and I stopped in our tracks, pulling Papa to a rather sudden halt.

"What is it?" he said. "Is something wrong?"

"No, Papa."

"Why have we stopped?"

"We are on Via Riccardi."

He turned and looked at the boarded-up shop in front of which we now stood.

"Is this the house I own?"

Without another word Leonardo and I steered him to the end of the block and back into the alley. When I pushed open the gate we were greeted by the sight of a riotously overgrown garden and two carts piled high under their canvas covers.

Leonardo was pulling vines away from the green and gold apothecary sign, which was propped up against the back wall. While faded, it was still as pretty as the day he had painted it.

"What have you done, Caterina?" Papa said, never taking his eyes from the wagons.

"You might ask your grandson. He was the one who stopped in Vinci before coming here."

"I saw my uncle Francesco while I was there," Leonardo said. "He helped me pack your things up." He turned to Papa. "He sent you his fondest regards."

I had unlocked the door and stepped inside. My father and son came in after me.

The look on Papa's face was one of childlike wonder, and I admit I was not unaffected myself. The years had gone easier on the house this time. Some rodents had had their way with the bins, and some spiders with the ceiling corners, but when I opened the door to the shop I was shocked that aside from a mild mustiness, the ghosts of herbal fragrances still lingered in the air.

Papa walked through but it was too dark to see. Leonardo went to the front door and pulled it open. He was confronted by nailed boards, which he commenced to kick out with his booted heel. He was making a terrible racket, but I found myself transfixed.

All I could hear was the tinkling of the bell on the lintel above the door, and I saw again the moment I had first laid eyes on Lorenzo standing there, taking in the sights and smells of my brand-new apothecary. I smiled recalling how we had laughed, nailing the bell in place, the first of our many adventures together.

Suddenly the room was filled with light, Leonardo having also pulled away the boards from the large window.

I heard my father's exclamation of delight, and watched him turn round and round, taking in the lofty ceiling and soft green walls and shelves, the dusty but still bright white marble countertops.

"What's all the noise?" I heard a man cry, and looked through the front glass to see Benito, a grown man, now carrying a small child in his arms, a young woman and a twelve-year-old boy beside him. Leonardo and Benito were embracing.

Papa looked at me questioningly.

"Our neighbors. Lovely neighbors. We should go out and let Leonardo introduce us."

Benito had helped us empty the carts, moving our belongings into the house. His sweet wife, Elena, had rushed next door for a pail and rags, and had gone to work scrubbing the shelves and counters, so that by the time the light started to fail us, Papa and I and Marcello—a jolly boy with a thousand questions—had already begun returning a few of the pots and jars to their proper places.

Leonardo himself carried our boxes of precious books to the first-floor sitting room, and our neighbors promised to come back for all the help they could possibly give.

Earlier, outside the shop, when Leonardo had introduced me to Benito as his mother, I'd seen a look in my old friend's eyes that told me he knew the truth. Perhaps that he, of all the men and women I had met in my male disguise, had known it all along. But nothing was said. There were no sly smiles of collusion. Just a quiet and graceful acceptance that Cato would not be returning and that Caterina, Leonardo da Vinci's mama, had suddenly come to live with her father above the apothecary next door. There was also a suggestion made that Marcello had not been promised into any apprenticeship yet, and perhaps if Ernesto had need of a helper . . .

When our neighbors had gone we lit three torches, and with silent purpose climbed the stairs. We rose past the sitting room, and then my bedroom, and up a final flight to the third floor. We stood, the family trio, staring at the laboratory door.

"It is safe, Mama," Leonardo said. "We have made it safe to think again. Inquire. Experiment."

I inhaled deeply and pushed it open.

Before us was a scene that reeked of fear and hurried leavings. An overturned bench. A glass beaker broken on the floor. The alchemical furnace dusty and stone-cold.

A fierce upwelling of visions assaulted me—*opening this door thirty years before, the four walls that had admitted me into a brotherhood of brave and venerable minds; the elderly man standing behind me who had dared school a daughter in the secrets of enlightenment, making possible that admittance; the son without whose close presence I refused to live, he whose love had drawn me to this city, this house, this room; and back further still to the night in Vinci that, in my agony of lost love and Papa's fear of losing me, we had together allowed his alchemical fire to die. I saw Vespasiano Bisticci squinting over a thousand-year-old manuscript and calling out its mysteries as Ficino, Landino, and Pulci debated the properties of quicksilver. I saw dark Lorenzo in his loose white shirt propped lazily on the stool, knees wide, arms open and inviting me into his embrace. And of course that smile.*

"Help me with this," I heard Leonardo say. He had dragged several rotted boards from the shop up the stairs. He told Papa and me to break them into small pieces, then began stacking them in the furnace. I saw him pull from his satchel his folio, ripping out several sheets of paper, crumpling and stuffing them beneath the wood.

My heart began to race at the thought of the sudden industry and the purpose of what we were doing. I glanced at Papa. His eyes were aglow.

We gathered round the furnace, and in the moment before Leonardo struck the flint, we each whispered our own blessing.

"To the great teachers . . ."

"The Eternal Wisdom . . ."

"The heart that loves . . ."

A tiny flame was held to a corner of crumpled paper. I watched breathless as it caught and burned blue for an endless moment, then spluttered merrily to yellow white, setting the tinder-dry wood alight. The heat was sudden, warming our faces and chests.

My father's hand on my shoulder drew me to him. Leonardo he had embraced with his other arm. Papa was strong again, as he had been on returning from his travels. Even now he grew younger, not older, with every pop and crackle in the furnace.

"Is there thanks enough to offer?" I heard him say.

"Between the three of us," I replied, "there is more than enough."

A knot in a burning board exploded noisily, causing us to startle, then laugh at our fright.

Leonardo, as though roused from a reverie, sprang to the woodpile and threw more fuel on the blaze. And it *was* a blaze, burning with an almost conscious force. Dead for so long. Given new life. Our promise of eternity.

Leonardo would surely be seeing the Phoenix rising from the cold ashes, taking to the air as he dreamed himself doing. *Would* succeed in doing one day. *Leonardo in flight.* The thought made my own heart soar. *The oiled canvas wings in graceful curves, his long hair whipping behind him, the wind lifting him higher and higher into the clouds. . . .*

"So many books to unpack," I heard Papa mutter with delight.

"You'll show me which ones you want brought up here, Grandfather," Leonardo told him, "and which ones should be left in the sitting room."

"There are some he likes to keep at his bedside," I told my son, "to read by candlelight."

"Come, tell me now." Leonardo took the lead, and Papa followed him down the stairs.

I added one more large wood fragment to the furnace, thinking ahead to the future source of its fuel. There was enough from the boarding-up of the shop, I thought, surely enough for this night. Tomorrow we would put in a large supply. Young Marcello would have his first job helping Papa.

I pushed the furnace door closed very slowly, loath to lose sight of what we had begun today, but as it clanged shut, despite the lost sight of the alchemical fire, I knew how it would burn—unstoppable, warming and fomenting the minds of all who lay themselves open before it.

I sighed with the deepest pleasure, remembering the Medici—Lorenzo, his father, and his father's father, wondering now if, from where they stood, they saw that the Light of Reason had been lit once again in Florence.

Somehow I believed they did.

*P*apa had insisted on staying the night at his new home, but Leonardo and I had come back to Castella Lucrezia and both of us, exhausted from the day's events, slept well into the next morning.

When I came down the stairs into the sitting room I saw he'd set up an easel near the street window, a thin wood board standing up in it. He was laying out his brushes and some colors he had just ground up himself.

He smiled when he saw me. "Will you indulge me with a sitting today?"

"How can I say no to you? And what a day of celebration it is, Leonardo. I believe I will be able to breathe more easily than I have in a very long while."

As he arranged several down pillows on the chair he had set in place, I thought, *For better or worse I am with this man, have been with him as a barnacle holds fast to the hull of a ship, and that after all the years grow together—wood, shell, muscle—into one impossible amalgam.*

I went to stand before the undraped work. It was one I recognized. I'd begun sitting for it after my second arrival in Milan. It was quite small, bordered on either side by a painted pillar. The background, exceedingly dark, even foreboding, featured a winding road that led to a rocky inlet below, confined on all sides by jagged, fearsome-looking peaks and precipices. That background had always seemed a strange compliment to the woman of the portrait, who sat so softly and perfectly composed in the foreground.

I found her somehow familiar, somehow unrecognizable. Surely she was me. But how would I know? I had spent so little time over the years appraising myself in a mirror. This woman was dressed in the low-bodiced olive gown that Leonardo had gifted me when I'd taken back my womanhood, its pale green cape slung over her left shoulder. The long tawny sleeves had been pushed up her arms in many soft folds, allowing the gently crossed hands to be seen clear above the wrists. The woman in the painting was younger than me by some thirty years, and was strikingly beautiful. If there was something slightly masculine about the broadness of her face and the defiant glint in the eyes, it was balanced, if not overridden, by the feminine quality of the features and an overwhelming sense that this creature was, if not the Madonna herself, a mother who had known every pleasure and every pain of womanhood.

Leonardo's artistry had rendered more than the details of her features—the black hair parted in the center curling prettily on the softly rounded breasts, a delicate fringe of dark eyelashes, rosy pink nostrils, and pulsing blue veins in the hollow of her neck. He had imbued in the woman's expression an air of all-knowingness and deep compassion.

"Tell me honestly"—Leonardo had come to stand by my side—"did I ever look this way?"

He regarded his work for some time.

"You were far more lovely. Your chin was more oval than square. But the eyes are yours, and the lovely high bones of your cheeks."

"Will you *ever* finish it?" I said, teasing him.

"I think it will take a lifetime to satisfy me."

He led me to a chair, tucking some cushions into the small of my back and under my arms for comfort, arranging my hair around my shoulders and covering it with a fine black gossamer veil. He arranged my hands right over left, as the woman in the painting, and gently pushed my sleeves away from my wrists.

"I so wish Lorenzo could have lived to see this day," I said.

"He knew it would come," Leonardo replied, moving to one side to observe the canvas in a different light. "There was so much *Il Magnifico* had already accomplished before he died. The Academy. The library. His part in the conspiracy." Leonardo's expression grew suddenly shy. "The two of you together. . . ."

I looked down at my hands as I added, "The Great Work."

"Have I not captured it in your portrait? All of it? The dark. The light. The female. The male. Your magic. Your memories."

I sighed. Aristotle had rightly said that memory was the "scribe of the soul," and Aeschylus believed it "the mother of all wisdom." But the great sage Pericles spoke most truly for my life, I thought then, saying that what you left behind was not what was engraved in stone monuments, but what was woven into the lives of others.

"So many memories," I murmured, my eyes softly tilting upward, beginning to see it all again.

"Come, Mama," said Leonardo in the gentlest voice, "before I lose you entirely to the past . . . won't you give me a smile?"

EPILOGUE

Dearest Leonardo,

I would say I hope this letter finds you well, but I am not at all certain that this letter will find you at all. I write from the deck of the Portuguese galleon Isabel, *flagship of Captain Fernão Cabral's fleet, finally within sight of our destination. It is hard to breathe, though whether this stems from the excitement of our imminent landfall or the air so hot and humid it feels thick as soup, I cannot say.*

I am no stranger to excitement after this voyage of six months' time, having sailed west all the way to the New World to avoid unfavorable winds at the Gulf of Guinea, and being scared out of my wits during a violent storm at the Cape of Africa when four of the fleet's twelve ships, with all their crews, were lost.

It may be my imagination, because we can barely see the little town we are headed toward nestled low on the western coast, the one renowned for its spice trade, but I swear I've had whiffs of coriander and cumin wafting in my nose.

Some rowboats have apparently come out to meet us. I can see the dark-skinned, close-bearded fishermen in their long gauze shirts and white head-wraps waving, as though they expect us.

The question is, what shall I expect from my travels? Nothing? Everything? Perhaps, like Papa, I will fall in love again. Climb into the Northern Mountains that he said dwarfed the Alps. Visit erotic temples. The tomb of Jesus. I will open my heart and my mind to all of it.

I do hope to find India a friendly, peaceful place where somewhere, someday, under the spreading boughs of an ancient tree sits a cadre of philosophers—wise men from the East—who might enjoy a long afternoon of conversation with a hoary old gentleman from Florence.

On the 16th day of September in the year 1500
from Calicut,

Your loving mother,
Caterina

* * *

She sat on the thronelike chair in her sleeping chamber and sighed deeply. Her eyes were closed, not out of weariness but of boredom. Bianca, the Holy Roman Empress, felt this day, as she did every other day, neither holy, nor Roman, nor imperial. She had just sent away her ladies and that insufferable religious tutor Maximilian had imposed upon her—he and his droning scriptural lessons every day but the Sabbath.

Her husband had let go the one intellectual companion she most valued—her old and beloved Greek master—replacing him with the hated Catholic cleric. She was, Maximilian commanded her, to dedicate herself to embroidery and lute playing, though she was forbidden to sing as her voice, in his estimation, was as screechy as a cat in heat.

This treatment, she knew, had been punishment for failing to provide Maximilian with children. Heirs—male or female. "What earthly good is a barren wife?" he said with repetitive cruelty. "More particularly a barren archduchess?" She was beginning to believe such sentiments were true. *Why did I have to be a wife at all?*

Bianca rose, cursing the jewel-encrusted gown she was forced by her high and mighty station to wear every waking hour of the day. She moved to the window and looked out at a bleak wintertime Vienna. Court was here now, and not Innsbruck. She wondered which palace she hated more.

Not the palace, she corrected herself. *The people who live in it.* All of Maximilian's time and thoughts were spent on armies and weaponry, allies and enemies. Italy, the Swiss, Turkish pirates, the blasted French. Whenever she'd tried to engage him in conversation on any other topic he'd snapped at her. "Politics, not philosophy, rules the world," he liked to say. "War, not words, forms the future." His heart was as cold as the frozen ground in the courtyard.

At least to her. He doted on the children from his first marriage—Phillip, who had been blessed with so much unnatural beauty for a Hapsburg man he was called "the Handsome," and Margaret, who, to everyone's chagrin, had been uglier than sin but imbued with a mind like a steel trap.

Maximilian did spare Bianca the humiliation of a string of mistresses, though sometimes she wondered if the endless flowery poems he wrote about the wooing of and marriage to his first wife, Mary, were not somehow more insulting.

The knock on her door was startling, lost as she'd been in the self-pity that had in the last months settled over her thoughts like a heavy blanket. "What is it, Marta?" she called out to her lady. The door opened and the woman entered wearing an expression Bianca had never seen on her maid's face in all the years she'd attended her.

"There is a . . . crate for you, madam. A rather heavy one."

"For me? From whom?"

"I don't know," Marta said, her eyes wide with excitement. "It has an odd smell about it. Something like spice."

Bianca gestured to have the thing brought in and four footmen—one on each corner of the red-painted wooden crate, thickly banded by iron—set it down heavily in the center of the empress's Turkey carpet.

"Shall I open it for you?" said one of the servants.

Bianca eyed the box warily, but excitement was beginning to rise in her. "Cut the bands and loosen the lid," she ordered. "Then leave me."

"My lady," Marta pleaded, "at least let *me* stay with you when you open it. There's no telling . . ."

"It's too small to be hiding an assassin," Bianca said. "I'll take my chances alone."

When they had all gone she circled the red crate and one by one discarded the iron bands. With some effort she wrenched off the top, and with a crash the sides collapsed outward, leaving in the center of her floor what looked to be an ordinary Italian marriage chest. Whomever the bride had been, she'd clearly not been a noblewoman. The birds and flowers were painted with only moderate skill, and no gold or precious gems had been used in its decoration.

Why would someone send me a marriage chest? she wondered. She sat back on her throne chair to gaze at the thing. She was not afraid of what she would find inside. And she was exceedingly curious. She just wished to prolong the mystery of it. Mystery had become so rare in her life of late. She would savor the moment. Think of every possibility of the treasure within it, and from whom it had come. She began this exercise, but found her mind blank. She could not, after all, conceive of anyone who would care to send her anything.

Bianca jumped up and strode to the marriage chest. The lid came up easily, and a strong whiff of pungent spices wafted up in a fragrant, invisible cloud. Her jaw dropped at the sight of the contents.

Books. Many books.

Some were bound in leather and looked to have come from Guttenberg's revolutionary press. Some were rolled parchments. Others were ancient manuscripts decorated in gold leaf. Now her pulse pounded in her neck. She lifted one vellum volume and opened the cover. *The Sonnets of Lorenzo de' Medici.* She placed it aside, then took up another. It was in Greek—Plato's *Timaeus.* Her heart soared at the sight of that beloved language.

Beneath was a huge tome. She went to the lectern on which her Bible lay open and put it on the floor. She carried over the heavy book and laid it open to a random and well-thumbed page. It was in Latin, but the contents were certainly Hermetic in nature. *Are these recipes,* she wondered, *for alchemical processes?*

Now she removed a muslin bag that reeked of an exquisite and exotic fragrance. She loosened the string and peered inside. Smaller muslin bags! Each must hold a different spice. They smelled, unquestionably, of the East.

Then there were more books. Some in Hebrew, a language she had never learned. Here was a scroll in a leather pouch. It was incomprehensibly old. With all the delicacy she could manage she unrolled it. *Antigone!* Bianca could not be sure, but it occurred to her this might be—no, could it possibly be a copy from the time of the great playwright himself?

She slowed her plundering of the chest as she could not bear the thought of coming to the end of her gifts. But here was something different. A large, flat notebook. Nothing on the cover revealed its contents. This she took to her bed and laid out carefully upon her ermine coverlet.

She opened it to the first page and was baffled. There were sketches of a boxlike device with lines emanating from it. The rest of the page was filled with handwriting that was quite unreadable. When she looked more closely she saw that the script was written backward, from right to left.

Bianca turned the page. Here was an array of eight connected rectangles with the sun's rays from a nearby window bouncing off them. And another page with the box device again, but this time she could see quite clearly a brilliantly rendered sketch of a naked man lying on a table nearby, his arms crossed over his groin.

Sweet Jesus, she thought. *Blessed Isis!*

Despite her desperation to view the rest of the notebook, she found herself unerringly gentle. But within a few pages she was sure—here was Leonardo's shroud! The fruit of the great conspiracy of which she had been a part. Had the maestro sent her this box full of treasures?

She rushed back to the marriage chest. There on top of the remaining books was a parchment letter folded and sealed with red wax. Bianca took it up and held it to her heart, then walked as slowly to the window as a bride to the altar. She broke the seal and by the cold winter light began to read.

Bianca, dear girl,

How do you like your treasure chest? Which is your favorite book? There are so many I love. This copy of the Timaeus was my favorite as a young girl. I hope the contents will provide you with many months, perhaps years, of reading and translation. If I'm not mistaken you are not schooled in Hebrew, so that language you will be compelled to learn.

I have placed in your keeping Leonardo's notebook documenting our labors with the unholy shroud that now, I understand, is displayed and venerated in Turin. If you wish to read the notebook's writing you must employ a mirror. But my purpose for sending you this folio is twofold. Of course I know it will be in the best of hands, our secret perfectly safe.

But more important it is a reminder to you, Bianca, of all that you are—truth-seeking, warmhearted, and courageous. I understand that the Fates have blessed you with neither a loving husband nor any children of your own. I imagine that you—tender soul that you are and bereft of friends—might sometimes get sick with loneliness. At times like these it is easy to forget your true worth and to belittle yourself.

I remember so well that day you led us down the moldering stairs to the place that hid your family's treasure, unlocking the crypt with a golden key in an act so dangerous that if discovered could have been the end of you. Remember it was a relic that, in its natural state, was no more than a worthless rag but one that, by your will and wisdom, became the weapon that slayed the unholy beast of Florence.

Take comfort in such memories, Bianca. Lorenzo taught me that before he died, and I have lived by it. You are a champion. As brave as any knight riding into battle.

There is one final gift to be found in a small metal box at the bottom of my mother's marriage chest—the recipe for a sweet confection and its vital ingredient, tiny balls of bitter resin. Eat the cake and your chilly chamber will dissolve into celestial light and sound and the wonder of fantastical worlds without and within.

I will write of my travels till these old fingers of mine can no longer hold a quill.

I remain your friend and fellow seeker,
Caterina

ACKNOWLEDGMENTS

While I dove into dozens of books about the Italian Renaissance and their brightest stars to research *Signora da Vinci*, there were two that served as my impetus and inspiration for the direction I took, and provided priceless insights into that period—what I came to call "The Shadow Renaissance."

Lynn Picknett's and Clive Prince's two brilliantly researched and utterly compelling books—*The Templar Revelation* and *Turin Shroud*—opened a little-known world-beneath-a-world to me. Reading about the all but ignored philosophical and esoteric underpinnings of the movers and shakers of the Renaissance—particularly Leonardo and his ties to the Lirey Shroud (later known as the Shroud of Turin)—exploded in my mind and literally set me and my characters on the path to my plot.

Picknett and Prince did not stop with compiling and comparing the best theories and solutions to the greatest mysteries of the times. When it came to proving their own theory that Leonardo da Vinci perpetrated the shroud hoax using his own face for Jesus's, they did months of scientific experiments in their garage with a homemade *camera obscura*, plaster models, and several types of chemicals and salts known to be available in fifteenth-century Europe. They were relentless with their trials and errors until they had convinced themselves—and me—that not only was it possible for Leonardo to have orchestrated this masterpiece of deception, but quite probable indeed. I cannot recommend the Picknett/Prince books more highly.

I was fortunate to have as inspiration for my characterization of Leonardo one of my oldest and dearest friends—Los Angeles artist and philosopher Tom Ellis. He is the one true genius I know, who has generously decorated my life with his masterful and wildly eclectic works of art. Outrageous, flamboyant, intellectual, and eccentric beyond measure, he shares with da Vinci a sweet temperament, worship of nature, and an obsessive desire to explore the deepest wells of religion, sexuality, psychedelics, and the human condition. I couldn't have had a more perfect template to reference the maestro than Tom.

I owe a special debt to my mom, Skippy Ruter-Sitomer, who, in 2006, left us for that great South Florida Retirement Community in the Sky. Had it not been for her, I would never have had firsthand knowledge of a mother like Caterina—one who unfailingly believed in her children and wholly accepted them, warts and all. Skippy was kind, and unfailingly generous with her love. She knew how to sacrifice without martyrdom. She was a woman who rolled with the punches, continued to evolve, and surprisingly became more mentally and philosophically flexible with age . . . not less. Nothing shocked her, she was always good for a laugh, and by the age of eighty-nine had learned to swear like a sailor. Skippy enjoyed every one of my heroines, but I think she would have loved Caterina the best, identified with a woman whose proudest achievement in life was being the very best of mothers.

This is the third of my books to benefit from my good neighbor James "The Padre" Arimond, who is always ready with Latin benedictions and religious expertise. Kathleen Chambers braved my scribbled, scratched-out, arrow-ridden yellow pads to type the first draft of this novel, and lent her knowledge about herbal medicine.

My mentor, Betty Hammett, gave me the first read and a thumbs-up. Old friends and fellow authors Billie Morton and Gregory Michaels offered insightful notes and myriad helpful suggestions.

My trusted agents of many years, David Forrer and Kimberly

Witherspoon, believed in *Signora da Vinci* from the get-go. David, especially, has been like a dog with a tasty bone, something any author in her right mind dreams about in a representative. Wonderful, too, when your agents are creative and can be counted on to give you worthy story input. Many, many thanks, you two. And a special acknowledgment to Susan Hobson, my foreign agent—a broad who works tirelessly abroad.

What can I say about the perfect editor? Kara Cesare loves her work and is dedicated to that old and most honorable profession. She has proven herself to be a wellspring of brilliant ideas and clever solutions to the stickiest of my stumbling blocks. Moreover she has helped me understand the fine balance of art and commerce in the publishing world. Kara is young enough to be my daughter but wise enough to be my mother. I am so grateful to have her as a working partner.

How do I thank the person without whom my life would not be worth living? A melodramatic description of Max Thomas, my husband of twenty-five years? Perhaps. But he's also the silliest man I know. There are no depths to which he will not stoop to make me laugh—a lifesaving talent so necessary in these whacked-out times. All my love to you, Barney.

Signora da Vinci

ROBIN MAXWELL

A CONVERSATION
WITH ROBIN MAXWELL

Q. You've written six novels about fifteenth- and sixteenth-century England and Ireland. What possessed you to abandon the Tudors and head south to Renaissance Italy?

A. I feel that, for now, I've "written myself out" with the most fascinating individuals of that most fabulous and colorful place and time. I always insist on being, if not the first to write about a given character (nearly impossible with such well-known figures), then having a strong and wholly original "angle" or "hook" for my story: Elizabeth I and Robin Dudley's illegitimate son in *The Queen's Bastard*; the intimate mother/daughter connection from beyond the grave in *Secret Diary of Anne Boleyn*; and the early lives of Anne and Mary Boleyn at the erotic French court in *Mademoiselle Boleyn*.

For some time I'd been intrigued by the ridiculously fertile mind and staggering accomplishments of Leonardo da Vinci. Long before *The da Vinci Code*, he was a firmly entrenched icon in human culture and consciousness, but my research piled mystery upon mystery about this polymath genius. However, Leonardo was so obsessively secretive about his personal life, and was such a success in that regard, that with all his thousands of pages of notebooks and various works of art, invention, science, architecture and philosophy, very little was revealed about Leonardo the *person*.

And while we do know something about da Vinci's father, Piero—his social climbing and business successes, his almost inhuman coldness to his bastard son, and his struggle to sire legitimate children—we know next to nothing about da Vinci's mother. By my own simple logic I deduced that Piero, while an intelligent and resourceful man, never displayed an ounce of creativity, that divine spark that utterly defined Leonardo.

That would, of course, leave his mother as the donor of the "genius genes." But of the woman who gave birth to one of the world's most remarkable minds, we possess exactly two facts: 1. Her name was Caterina. 2. Leonardo was taken from her the day after his birth to be brought up, as a bastard, in the Vinci home of Piero's father, Antonio.

Virtually everything else is conjecture. We don't know Caterina's age when she gave birth to Leonardo—fifteen or twenty-five; whether she was a mideastern slave girl or "a girl of good blood"; if Piero loved Caterina, or simply used her; whether she was a Vinci native or an out-of-towner. What I can (and did) imagine is how any woman would feel having her child ripped from her arms one day after he was born, knowing that the household he was going to be raised in would be an unloving one.

Clearly, Piero's grandfather, who recorded Leonardo's exact date and time of birth and baptism, believed that Leonardo's mother had married Antonio "Accattabriga" Buti several years after his illegitimate grandson's birth, but in those days all sorts of additions and subtractions were made to family rolls for purposes of tax breaks and evasions and business scams, and the da Vincis and Butis did, according to records, do business together.

Q. Why did you choose to have Caterina come to live with Leonardo at the old ducal palace in Milan?

A. In 1493, according to notations in Leonardo's writings, an old woman named Caterina came to live with him for a little more than a year before he paid for her funeral. It's not clear whether it was his mother or a servant. Another phrase written on a notebook page asks, "What does La Caterina want?" Some historians believe the maestro would never have mused about the thoughts and desires of a mere serving woman nor made detailed lists about the costs of her funeral arrangements. Others say that calling her "La Caterina" gives her a certain stature. Still others insist that the "La" is used in a cynical way—that she was a nobody.

Whoever this Caterina might have been, she was the only female member of his household that Leonardo ever mentions in his voluminous notebooks, and she was old enough to be his mother.

Q. Isn't it a stretch to create an entire novel around a woman with so little history?

A. All of my research added up to an enormous hole in a most fascinating period, within the life of its most compelling personage. Because I'm a writer of historical fiction, these gaping chasms are what I live for. They provide a rare opportunity to create something from little or nothing. I am happily forced to take the tiniest cluster of cells, no larger than a fetal blastula, examine the medium in which it develops, the world into which it is born and grows, its ancestors and associates, until it blossoms into a living, breathing, thinking, feeling human being. With so little known about Caterina, the sky was the limit.

Because I had chosen that she was the parent responsible for not only Leonardo da Vinci's brilliance, but his sweet temperament and supreme open-mindedness, I was free to give her the best qualities a woman could possibly have. I made her the mother that every child deserves to have—one who, without becoming a martyr, would do anything and everything to protect that child, shower him with love and tenderness, and provide him with every possible opportunity.

Happily for me, what began as sacrifices Caterina made for Leonardo, turned into the greatest adventure a woman in fifteenth-century Italy could imagine in her wildest dreams. Disguising herself as a man, being accepted into the Platonic Academy, becoming the lover of Lorenzo the Magnificent, meeting and conspiring with the greatest minds of the times, were not only boons to Caterina's character arc, but they were doorways into the topics that I was keen to explore in a book about the period.

Q. *Signora da Vinci* was a highly unusual take on the Renaissance. Was it really the way you wrote it?

A. For me, the Italian Renaissance was not simply an explosion of the art and architecture that most people think of when they hear the words. What my research uncovered was a "Shadow Renaissance" steeped in Platonic and Hermetic philosophy and Egyptian magic. Almost every ruler, writer, scientist or thinker in those years at least toyed with alchemy and the occult. Despite the church's prohibitions, most of these great men (and a few women) took these views very seriously indeed. Few admitted to being outright atheists like Leonardo, but attempting to meld Christian Scripture with the pagan mysteries was extremely common, especially in educated and highly cultured circles . . . even in Rome.

Despite its importance, one finds little if anything written about the Platonic Academy and its impact on the early Italian Renaissance—as though it was a men's social club and not an overarching philosophy that informed the lives of its members, making them especially vulnerable when Savonarola came to power. Authors—of both fiction and nonfiction—tend to ignore the implications of such towering figures as Lorenzo de Medici—one of the greatest patrons of the Academy—adhering to such heretical beliefs.

Q. You rarely see Lorenzo's name tied with da Vinci's. Yet in *Signora da Vinci*, Lorenzo acts as Leonardo's "godfather."

A. Lorenzo's tie with Leonardo is pondered in some detail by historians. Some say the maestro was ignored by *Il Magnifico*, who felt the lowborn artist was "below him socially." Others go so far as to suggest that Leonardo—like Michelangelo after him—was actually housed for a time in the Palazzo Medici and treated as a son.

While there's little evidence that the artist lived in the Florence palace, I find it hard to believe that Lorenzo would not have held the insanely talented young man, apprentice to the family's own court art-ist, Andrea Verrocchio, in very high regard.

And I believe that in 1484 Leonardo's leave-taking from Florence for Milan, to the court of Lorenzo's friend, Ludovico *Il Moro*, was a well-planned move, probably to protect the well-known heretic and necromancer (scandalized by his sodomy trial) from the worsening religious persecutions he would certainly have suffered had he stayed. Too, Lorenzo was such a man-of-the-people that I cannot imagine him snubbing Leonardo simply because he hadn't been born noble.

Q. Don't most people believe Leonardo da Vinci was a homosexual?
A. As for the maestro's sexuality, that subject, too, has mystified his biographers. When people learn I've written about da Vinci's life, it's usually the first question asked about him. Once more, his secretive na-ture serves him very well, for while everyone seems to have extremely strong opinions about the man, no one—biographer or historian—has conclusive evidence about whether Leonardo was straight, gay, bisexual, or asexual.

My best guess is that his sexual preferences changed according to his age, his social setting, and the emotional and political pressures brought to bear upon him. You can't forget that sodomy was considered a burn-able offense by the church in Florence, even before Savonarola arrived on the scene. As a young apprentice in Verrocchio's bottega (Verrocchio was himself openly homosexual), Leonardo was surrounded by lots of "pretty boys," who had little or no money to spend on whores, so homo-sexual behavior was perhaps more of a necessity than a choice.

The famous sodomy trial (that most people cite as proof of Leo-nardo's proclivities) in which two of the others arrested were related to the Medici (and probably a means to embarrass them) proved nothing whatsoever about Leonardo, except that he caroused (or hobnobbed) with the boys of "good families." Once he was a bit older, there was every reason to think he visited female as well as male prostitutes.

I do think the sodomy trial had an effect on Leonardo's sexuality—

putting him off it for a time. Despite charges being dropped for lack of evidence, the scandal seemed to traumatize the young, exquisitely sensitive young man. Once an outgoing, fancily clad man-about-town, he became quite reclusive and dove into his human dissections in the nether regions of Santa Maria Novella Hospital. That his professional relationship and friendship (perhaps love) with the alchemically inclined Zoroastre began to grow during this period and last through many, many years, was perhaps a result of sharing that terrible experience.

Later in life, Leonardo appeared asexual to me. While he adored having beautiful young men surrounding him as apprentices, he was so caught up in the "life of the mind" that sex may have become quite unimportant to him. Some of his writings suggest that he thought the sex act silly, the sex organs repulsive, and the only redeeming qualities the attractive faces of the participants—all that kept the human race from dying out. Even later in Leonardo's life he carried on close friendships with several women, and it's been suggested that any one of them might have been his lover.

Many people believe that Salai was Leonardo's young lover. I thought a better explanation of why he might have taken in the lying, cheating ten-year-old thief, spoiled him excessively, and kept him at his side till two weeks before the maestro died was that Salai was a son he would never have considered abandoning like his own father did to him.

Q. How plausible is it that a woman could successfully live as a man, as Caterina does in *Signora da Vinci*?

A. Cross-dressing in history has always interested me, especially women who have taken on the guise of men. The nearly unbelievable examples are females who have put on soldiers' garb and gone to war for extensive periods, serving on the battlefield with male comrades, only being found out after their deaths.

Caterina, living alone as she does in my story, had it easier. It was my creative choice to have her menstrual cycle disrupted when, through misery, she lost a great deal of weight after Leonardo departed for his apprenticeship in Florence. This simplified certain parts of her existence. My favorite tidbit of historical research on the subject was the "horn" that cross-dressing women used to have a normal-looking male piss in public.

Certainly one needs readers who enjoy a "suspension of disbelief" in this regard, but not only was Caterina's disguise possible—such behavior was commonplace enough to have several books written about it (see my bibliography).

Q. Is it remotely believable that Lorenzo de Medici could have taken Leonardo da Vinci's mother as a lover?

A. It is. Lorenzo was a famous poet in his time. His love sonnets were most highly regarded. While the objects of his adoration in his earlier poetry were the Florentine beauties Lucrezia Donati and, platonically, his brother Giuliano's mistress, Simonetta Cattaneo, in his last thirty-seven sonnets Lorenzo fixates on anther woman—never named—but definitely not his wife, Clarice.

His lover, "my lady," as he refers to her, provided "a beneficial touch that ennobled his life." Under her influence he transcended suffering and achieved intense pleasure and happiness in his otherwise difficult, pain-ridden existence. We may never learn who Lorenzo's lover was, but I like to think it was Caterina.

QUESTIONS
FOR DISCUSSION

1. Caterina's life seems, from the beginning of the story to the last page, to be based on deceit. Did this bother you at all? Do you think she should have regretted it more, or do you think the ends justified the means?

2. Did you find it believable that Caterina fooled as many people as she did with her disguise?

3. What did you feel were Caterina's strengths? Her weaknesses? How did you feel about her relationship with Lorenzo? Her father? Leonardo?

4. Did you ever feel that Caterina was an overbearing mother, or became too involved in her son's life?

5. What surprised you the most about Caterina's character as you went through this journey with her?

6. As portrayed in this novel, was Leonardo da Vinci a sympathetic character? If you had lived at the end of the fifteenth century in Italy, would you like to have known him?

7. Did knowing that the heroes and heroine of *Signora da Vinci* believed in pagan and Hermetic principles rather than Christianity make

you like them any less? Any more? Have you explored any religions outside the Judeo/Christian/Islamic tradition?

8. Did the practice of alchemy by the members of the Platonic Academy strike you as a plausible pastime? Do you feel, after reading this book, you have a better understanding of medieval alchemy?

9. What aspects of Leonardo's life and career were most interesting to you: his art, inventions, dissections and anatomical drawings, or philosophies and notebooks? If you had had a chance, what questions would you have asked the maestro?

10. All the Medici men suffered from severe gout and many of them died of its complications. Does this surprise you? When you think about the Middle Ages, what other diseases do you associate with the times?

11. Does reading this book make you want to further explore any aspects of the Italian Renaissance, the characters or plotlines Robin Maxwell has written about?

12. Some historians see the Dominican friar Savonarola as a church reformer and martyr. Do you feel that the citizens of Florence deserved his extreme "reining in" of their luxurious lifestyle, his "bonfires of the vanities"? Do you think he deserved burning at the stake?

13. Before reading *Signora da Vinci*, did you believe the Shroud of Turin was authentic or a hoax? After reading this book, have your feelings shifted? Is a *camera obscura* photograph of a corpse's body and Leonardo's face a reasonable explanation in your mind?

14. The author portrays Roderigo Borgia quite sympathetically. From what you know, or have read about the Borgia family in general, was

his positive characterization plausible? Did you find it hard to believe that even a pope might have Hermetic and pagan leanings?

15. Did Lorenzo *Il Magnifico* Medici seem too good to be true as a medieval ruler? As a human being? Do you think he should have been written with more foibles, or did you enjoy falling in love with him as Caterina and the author, Robin Maxwell, did?

16. Superstition, with its omens, heavenly signs, talismans and worshipping of holy relics, played a huge role in medieval life. What are the modern equivalents of these beliefs?

GRAPE AND OLIVE COMPOTE

Friend and extraordinary epicurean Susan Jeter created this simple but spectacular recipe. It has always made for compulsive consumption and, with its ingredients as common to Italy now as they were five hundred years ago, cried out to be included in *Signora da Vinci*.

> *1 bunch seedless red grapes*
> *1 jar (or equivalent) Kalamata olives, pits removed*
> *3 tablespoons balsamic vinegar*
> *3 tablespoons extra virgin olive oil*
> *1 tablespoon fresh chopped thyme (optional)*

Mix all ingredients in an ovenproof dish and bake uncovered for one hour at 350 degrees Fahrenheit, turning the fruit every twenty minutes with a spoon to recoat them with the oil and vinegar. Serve warm or cold with soft goat cheese on crusty bread or with crackers, or use as a side dish with fish or poultry.

BIBLIOGRAPHY

Hermeticism, Alchemy, Philosophy, the Occult, Apothecary

Frank L. Bochard, "The Magus as Renaissance Man," *Sixteenth Century Journal*

Robin DiPasquale, "The Aboca Museum: Displaying the History of Herbal Medicine in Italy and Europe," on the Web

David Melling, *Understanding Plato*

E. J. Holmyard, *Alchemy*

Jonathan Hughes, "Base Matter into Gold," *History Today*, August 2005

Art Kunkin, "Practical Alchemy and Physical Mortality," *Gnosis, A Journal of the Western Inner Traditions* #8, Summer 1988, and conversations with Art Kunkin

Francis Yates, *Renaissance and Reform; The Italian Contribution: Giordano Bruno and the Hermetic Tradition; The Rosicrucian Enlightenment; The Occult Philosophy in the Elizabethan Age*

Leonardo da Vinci

Serge Bramly, *Leonardo, The Artist and the Man*

The Notebooks of Leonardo da Vinci, arranged, translated, and with an introduction by Edward MacCurdy

Leonardo da Vinci—The Complete Paintings and Drawings, Frank Zöllner

Charles Nicholl, *Leonardo da Vinci—Flights of the Mind*

Giorgio Vasari, *Vasari's Lives of the Artists*

Michael White, *Leonardo, The First Scientist*

Lorenzo de' Medici

James Wyatt Cook, *The Autobiography of Lorenzo de' Medici the Magnificent*

Christopher Hibbert, *The House of Medici: Its Rise and Fall*

Nicholas Saladino, *Lorenzo the Magnificent and the Florentine Renaissance*

Hugh Ross Williamson, *Lorenzo the Magnificent*

Florence

Michal Levey, *Florence*

Palazzo Medici, "In the time of Lorenzo the Magnificent," *www.palazzo-medici.it/eng/ museo.htm*

A. Richard Turner, *Renaissance Florence*

Gender, Cross-dressing, Female Studies, Society

Philippe Aries and George Duby, *A History of Private Life—Revelations of the Medieval World*

Rudolph M. Dekker and Lotte C. Van de Pol, *The Tradition of Female Transvestism in Early Modern Europe*

John M. Riddle, *Contraception and Abortion from the Ancient World to the Renaissance*

Valerie R. Hotchiss, *Clothes Make the Man: Female Cross-Dressing in Medieval Europe*

Renaissance Art

The Age of the Renaissance, edited by Denys Hay

Barron's Renaissance Painting, text by Stefano Zuffi

Rome and the Papacy

Will Durant, *The Story of Civilization V, The Renaissance*

William Manchester, *A World Lit Only by Fire*

R. A. Scotti, *Basilica, The Splendor and the Scandal*

Jesus in India

Elizabeth Clare Prophet, *The Lost Years of Jesus*

*R*omeo moved closer to me. Without invitation he threaded his fingers through my hair. "Is that what you wish for yourself?"

Something melted inside me. "I have no wish to be a man," I said. "Honorary or otherwise. I only wish to write."

"Do you wish to love?" he whispered.

He was so audacious. Yet I nodded.

"Close your eyes, Juliet."

Without thought or fear I did as he asked. I believed I would soon feel his lips on mine. But instead he lifted my hand and, with infinite delicacy, pushed back the sleeve of my gown. Then I felt warm breath on the tenderest inside of my forearm.

"I believe in the senses," he murmured, sending tiny waves of air across my skin.

I shivered with delight. "Give me another," I demanded.

"This is mine," he said, releasing my hand and moving away, but in the next moment his face was buried in my hair. He inhaled deeply. "Aaahh," he sighed. "The natural perfume of Juliet."

I tilted back my head to lean upon his and there we remained, still and breathing. Did he know that I wished his hands to circle my waist, slide across the naked skin of my breasts?

"Listen," he said softly in the shell of my ear.

This I did, allowing Romeo to teach me. "It is the nightingale," I said. Its trilling notes in the darkness had never sounded so sweet to me. How was it that suddenly I heard magic in that song?

I felt his arms on my shoulders, turning me a half turn. Then, with both hands enclosing my head, tilted it skyward. "Open your eyes."

They fluttered open. There before me at what seemed as close as arm's length was the full moon, a dark brace of clouds skittering across its bright and shadowed surface.

"Touch. Smell. Sound. Sight," he uttered. "All so easily gratified."

"What of taste?" I said, pressing him.

"Ah, now you become greedy."

I turned to face him. "It *is* one of the senses."

"True."

Again, I thought that he would kiss me, to this way prove the fifth sensation. Instead he turned, and searching the fruit-heavy branch snapped from it a fat ripe fig. When he faced me again he held in his hands its two halves.

"Were there more light," he said, "we would see the luscious . . . pink . . . flesh." His voice caressed the words. Then holding my eyes with his, he took a half in his palm and brought it to his mouth. I grew suddenly alarmed as he buried his lips in the soft fig's center and closed his eyes, ecstatic.

"My lord!" I cried, breaking the spell.

His eyes sprang open and he gazed without apology into mine. "I think I should go. I've overstayed my welcome."

"No, no . . ."

But he had leapt to the balcony wall and swung his body up into the tree. Hanging loose from the branch by one arm he leaned down and held out his hand to me. The fig's other half was cupped in his palm.

"For you, my lady—the final sense."

I took it, words failing me once again.

"When you taste it," he said, "think of me."

Then he was gone, all rustling leaves and shadows.

I stood stupidly, staring at the half fruit and, smiling, brought it to my lips.

ABOUT THE AUTHOR

Robin Maxwell lives in the high desert of California with her husband, Max, and her avian muses, Mr. Grey and Cookie.